Praise for Martin Walker

'A potent read. Walker wacy, luscious meals and ple   the result is as warm as th

'This series of novels m   *Literary Review*

'A winning combination . . . Walker's relaxed style and good humour help to bring to life his engaging hero and his delightful home and make this one of the most enjoyable books I've read in a long time' *Sunday Telegraph*

'A satisfyingly intriguing, wish-you-were-there read with lashings of gastroporn' *Guardian*

'A gripping read . . . descriptions of the French countryside and food make you wish you were in Saint Denis, despite its crime rate' *Destination France*

'Martin Walker has carved out a niche with his Bruno, Chief of Police novels. They are well written and evoke a strong sense of the French countryside' Crime Squad

'Traditions and cuisine, countryside and characters . . . are the real heroes of the Bruno novels' *TLS*

Martin Walker is a prize-winning journalist and the author of several acclaimed works of non-fiction, including *The Cold War: A History*. He lives in Washington and spends his summers in his house in the Dordogne.

Also by Martin Walker

Bruno, Chief of Police
Dark Vineyard
Black Diamond
The Crowded Grave

THE
DEVIL'S
CAVE

MARTIN WALKER

(5)

Quercus

First published in Great Britain 2012 by Quercus
The paperback edition published in 2013 by

Quercus
55 Baker Street
7th Floor, South Block
London W1U 8EW

A CIP catalogue record for this book is available
from the British Library

ISBN 978 1 78206 392 6
EBOOK ISBN 978 1 78087 069 4

10 9 8 7 6 5 4 3 2 1

Printed and bound in Great Britain by Clays Ltd, St Ives plc

Typeset by Ellipsis Digital Limited, Glasgow

for Gabrielle and Michael

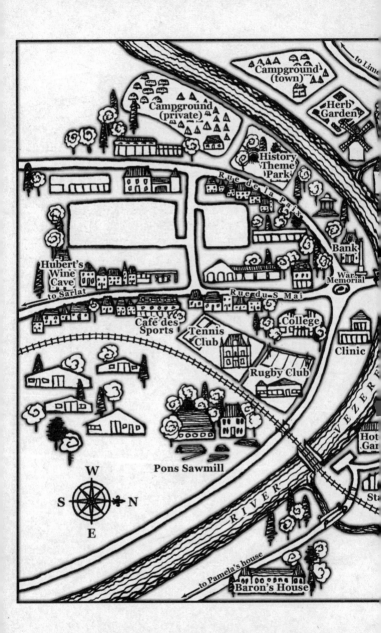

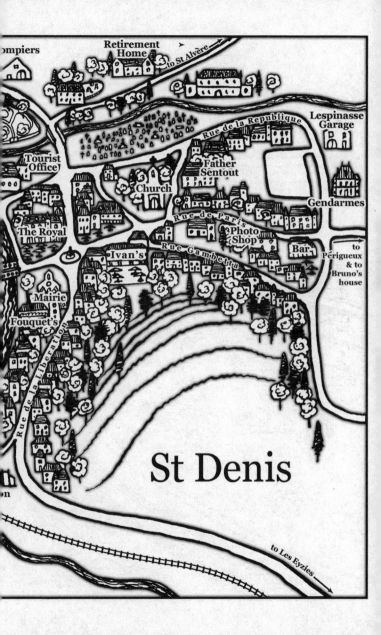

1

Bruno Courrèges seldom felt happier about the community he served as Chief of Police than when standing at the rear of the ancient stone church of St Denis, listening to rehearsals of the town choir. Unlike the formal ceremonies at Mass when they dressed in neat white surplices, the choir practised in their normal dress, usually gathering directly after work. But Father Sentout's daring decision that the choir should reach beyond its usual repertoire to attempt Bach's *St Matthew Passion* had required some additional rehearsals early in the morning. Farmers stood alongside schoolteachers and accountants, waitresses and shopkeepers. These were people Bruno knew, wearing clothes he recognized, and usually singing hymns that were familiar; perhaps the only memory of his church orphanage that still gave him pleasure.

On this Saturday morning two weeks before Easter, the twenty-four choristers were mostly in casual clothes and the front pews of the church were filled with coats and shopping baskets they would take to the town's market, about to get under way in the street outside. As he entered the twelfth-century church, Bruno heard the first notes that led into the chorus of 'Behold Him as a Lamb'. The noises of the street seemed to ebb away behind him as Florence's pure soprano voice filled the nave. He knew there should be two choirs and two orchestras, but St Denis made do with its trusty organ and the enthusiasm of its singers plus, of course, the determination of Father Sentout, whose love of choral music was matched only by his devotion to the pleasures of the table and the fortunes of the local rugby team. It made him, Bruno thought, an entirely suitable pastor for this small town in the gastronomic and sporting heartland of France.

The early morning sun lifted above the ridge to the east of St Denis and flooded the top of the stained-glass window. Shafts of blue, gold and red lanced into the body of the church. Father Sentout's black soutane stood out against the roseate glow that now suffused the choir. Bruno's eye was drawn irresistibly to Florence, dressed in white with a bright red scarf at her throat. Her head was raised as she sang alone, knowing the music too well to need to look at her score. Her fair hair was lit by the sunlight into something almost like a halo.

It had been one of his better moves, Bruno thought, to have found Florence the job of science teacher at the local *collège*. The post brought with it a subsidized apartment in the *collège* grounds, more than big enough for a divorced young woman and her infant twins. She was a fine addition to the life of the town and particularly to the choir. Father Sentout might not have dared attempt the *St Matthew Passion* without her. For the first time, she seemed to notice Bruno standing in the nave. Her face softened into a smile and she nodded to acknowledge his presence. Other choristers raised their hands in greeting. Bruno felt the familiar trembling at his waist as his mobile phone began to vibrate. Reluctantly, he slipped outside to take the call.

'Bruno, it's Marie,' he heard. She ran the Hôtel de la Gare beside the railway station, now unmanned to cut costs on rural lines in order to finance the massive investment in high-speed trains. 'I've been asked to pass on a message. Julien Devenon says there's a naked woman in a boat drifting down the river. He says he saw her from the railway bridge as he walked along the line.'

Her voice sounded strained. Bruno thought of Julien, just entering puberty, transfixed by the sight of a naked woman. But this was troubling. Despite the spring sunshine, this was no time for sunbathing; not even for the Dutch, German and Scandinavian tourists who seemed to discard their clothes at the slightest opportunity.

'He gets the train to his *lycée* in Périgueux,' Marie added. She paused and her voice took on a deeper note. 'He thought she was dead.'

'Is Julien still there?' Bruno pictured the boy's eager face as he trotted out for rugby practice.

'No, he had to catch his train. He would have called himself but his dad had confiscated his phone.'

There would be a story behind that, Bruno thought.

'So when did he see this boat? Was it just in the last few minutes?' Bruno tried to calculate how long a boat drifting downstream might take to reach the great stone bridge at St Denis, probably the nearest place he'd be able to intercept it and bring it ashore.

'He said he ran to tell me and the train was just leaving

3

with him as I called you. So maybe three minutes ago, not much more.'

Bruno ended the conversation and darted up the Rue de Paris, dodging between the market stalls and unloading trucks. He brushed aside the outstretched hands and proffered cheeks of the men and women he usually greeted twice each week on market days. He ducked under bales of cloth, dodged trolleys laden with fresh vegetables and skirted men carrying giant wheels of cheese on their heads as he made for the town square and the bridge. Just as he reached it his phone vibrated again and this time it was Pierrot, the town's most dedicated fisherman.

'You're not going to believe what I've just seen in the river,' he began.

'A naked woman in a boat. I heard already. Where are you exactly?'

'By the campsite, where the bank is high. There's a bend in the river there and the trout—'

'How fast is the river moving this boat?' Bruno interrupted.

'Five minutes and it will be at the bridge, maybe a bit more,' Pierrot said. 'It's pretty waterlogged. One of those old flat-bottomed boats, haven't seen one for years. Thing is, Bruno, she's lying on her back, naked as a worm, arms outstretched. I think she's dead.'

'We'll find out. Thanks, Pierrot,' said Bruno, closing his phone as he reached the stone bridge. He looked upstream, blinking against the dazzle of the sun on water. There was no sign of a boat so he had a little time. He punched the autodial for the medical centre into his phone and asked for Fabiola.

4

'She's not on today,' said Juliette at the reception desk. 'Something about a private patient, which I never heard of before. I'll put you through to Dr Gelletreau. He's on call today.'

'Don't bother,' said Bruno, talking as he walked briskly back to the church, ducking and weaving through the obstacle course of market stalls. 'I don't have time to talk. Just tell the doctor to get to the stone bridge where it looks like we might have a dead body floating downstream. I'll meet him there.'

He needed Antoine, with a canoe, and Antoine was in the choir. He slipped in through the small portal that was cut into the huge wooden doors, and was rocked by the sheer volume the choir was now generating, one half singing 'See him!' and the other half replying 'Whom?'

Just before Florence could soar into the solo, 'O Lamb of God Most Holy', Bruno strode forward to tap Father Sentout on the shoulder. The choir stopped raggedly, uncertain, but the organ notes swept on and Father Sentout opened his eyes, blinking in surprise at the sight of Bruno.

'I'm sorry, Father, it's an emergency,' said Bruno, his voice loud to carry over the organ. 'There could be a life at stake. I need Antoine most urgently.'

The organ music stopped with a dying wheeze from the pipes.

'You want my Jesus?' the priest asked, uncertainly.

Bruno swallowed hard, trying to comprehend the meaning of the question. Then he remembered that Antoine was singing the role of Jesus.

'He's a waterman and there's a body floating down the river,' Bruno said, speaking to the choir as much as to Father Sentout. 'A woman, in a boat.'

'I don't have a canoe here,' Antoine said, striding down from the apse and picking up a jacket from the front pew. A burly man, he had wide and powerful shoulders from a lifetime of paddling and manhandling canoes. 'My canoes are all back at the campsite today.'

'I'll need you anyway,' said Bruno. He led the way through the thickening market crowd and back to the river, suddenly aware that most of the choir seemed to be following, along with Father Sentout.

Passers-by and some of the stallholders looked up at the swelling line behind Bruno and with the automatic curiosity that draws a crowd when they sense a drama unfolding they joined behind. Soon they were clustering at the side of the bridge as Bruno and Antoine spotted the half-sunken vessel tracing lazy circles as it drifted with the current.

'It might get caught up on the sandbank,' said Antoine. 'Otherwise we'd best get down to my campsite and take out a canoe, tow it ashore.'

'Could I wade into the river and catch it here?' Bruno asked.

'Better not,' said Antoine, demonstrating why Bruno had been right to interrupt the choir and summon the boatman. 'See that current where it comes through the first arch of the bridge? That's the deep channel. You'd be up to your neck or even deeper. You wouldn't have the footing to drag it ashore.'

More and more of the townsfolk were gathering on the

6

bridge, craning their necks to watch the boat draw steadily nearer. Among them, camera at the ready, was Philippe Delaron from the photography shop, who doubled as the local correspondent for *Sud-Ouest*. Bruno groaned inwardly. A ghoulish newspaper photo of a corpse in a boat was not the image of St Denis that he or his Mayor would seek to portray.

'It's a punt,' said Antoine, surprise in his voice. 'I haven't seen one of those in a long time. They used them for hunting wildfowl in the old days before they built the dams upriver, when we still had wetlands with the flooding every spring.'

'Should we head for your campsite and get the canoe?' Bruno was eager to do something.

'Better wait and see if it gets through the current around the bridge,' said Antoine, lighting a yellow cigarette, a Gitane *maïs*. Bruno had forgotten they still made them. 'If it founders, there's no point. And it might still get stuck on the sand-bank. If it doesn't, I've got an idea. Follow me.'

Antoine thrust his way back through the crowd and down the steep and narrow stone steps that led from the bridge to the quay where the annual fishing contests were held. Three fishermen sat on their folding stools, each watching his own float and casting the occasional sidelong glance to see if his neighbours were having better luck. None of them seemed to pay much attention to the crowd on the bridge.

'Patrice, can you cast a line into that drifting boat and see if you can pull it into the bank?' Antoine asked the first of the anglers.

Patrice half-turned and eyed them sourly. He mumbled something through closed lips.

'What was that?' Bruno asked.

Patrice opened his mouth and took out three wriggling maggots from where he'd kept them under his tongue. It was something Bruno had seen the Baron do when they went fishing. Maggots were sluggish in the chill of the morning and a devoted fisherman would put some in his mouth to get them warm and energetic enough to attract fish once they were on the hook. It was one of the reasons Bruno knew he'd never be a real angler.

'I'll lose my bait, could lose a hook and line,' Patrice said, putting his maggots back into the old tobacco can where he kept his bait. He paused, squinting against the sun. 'Is this your business, Bruno?'

Bruno outlined the discovery to Patrice, a small, hunched man, married for forty years to a woman twice his size with a loud and penetrating voice to match. That probably explained the amount of time he spent fishing, Bruno thought.

'I'd try it myself but you're the best man with a rod and line,' Bruno said. He had learned back in the army days that a little flattery was the easiest way to turn a reluctant conscript into an enthusiastic volunteer.

Across the river, a white open-topped sports car with sweeping lines came fast around the corner of the medical centre to the bank where the caravans parked. It braked hard and stopped, wheels spitting up gravel. A fair-haired young man climbed out dressed as if for tennis in the 1930s. He wore a white sports shirt and cream trousers with a colourful belt, and ran towards the river bank shedding his shirt. He paused on the bank to remove his white tennis shoes.

8

'The bugger's mad,' said Antoine, spitting out his cigarette. 'He's going to dive in.'

Behind him another figure stepped gracefully from the car, a woman with remarkably long legs, dressed in black tights and what looked like a man's white shirt, tightly belted with a black sash. Her face was pale and her hair covered in a black turban. The way she moved made Bruno think of a ballerina. She advanced to the bank beside the fair-haired man and they looked upriver as if trying to assess when the punt might be in reach. The man began wading into the shallows as Bruno called out to him to stop.

Patrice had his line out of the water. He had removed his bait and float and was fixing his heaviest hook, looking up every few seconds to watch the speed of the punt's approach.

'I'm ready,' he said. 'Stand aside and don't get behind me. This will be a hell of a cast.'

Standing at the river bank, Bruno could see nothing of the dead woman. But something close to a metre tall and black was standing up in the punt, almost like a very short mast. Antoine shrugged when Bruno asked him what it might be.

The punt's corner seemed to catch on the edge of the sandbank and it slowed and turned as if heading for the far bank. Bruno heard cheers and whistles coming from the crowd on the bridge as the young man plunged deeper, assuming that the shallows ran all the way to the sandbank. They didn't, and he sank beneath the surface, then rose, shaking his head and striking out for the punt in a powerful crawl.

But some eddy or wayward current caught the vessel and pushed it free of the sandbank and into the deeper, faster

9

current where it begin drifting toward Bruno's side of the bank. Patrice tensed, lifted his rod over his head and cast high and far. Bruno watched as the line snaked out and the hook and sinker landed just on the far side of the punt, and held.

'Got it,' breathed Patrice.

The man in the water suddenly stopped. He must have reached the sandbank. He stood and staggered across it to where the punt was fast moving out of his reach and launched himself into a desperate, flailing dive almost as if he wanted to land inside the punt itself. One hand landed hard on the flat rear corner and the punt rocked, shipping water.

'The stupid bastard's gong to sink it,' said Antoine.

As the punt tipped towards him, Bruno caught a glimpse of the woman, her fair hair glinting gold in the sun, her arms outstretched and her head lolling as the vessel rolled. Something else inside the boat flashed a bright reflection, possibly a bottle. There seemed to be some marking, perhaps a large tattoo, on the woman's torso. Whatever stumpy mast had been rising from the boat had now fallen.

The swimmer sank beneath the water, his hand slipping from the wood. Patrice gently began to apply pressure to guide the punt towards him. But like some whale leaping from the sea the swimmer launched himself up again for a final, despairing effort. Again his hand just touched the side but once more his grip failed and the punt rocked even more as he plunged back down into the river.

The woman on the far bank strode back to the car, started the engine and swiftly turned the car so it was heading out again. She left the motor running as she climbed out, taking a towel from the back seat, and hurried down to the bank to help the swimmer.

'The damn fool broke my line,' said Patrice, spitting in disgust. The punt gathered speed as it moved into the deeper current and headed for the bridge. 'That's my best hook gone and no time to tie another. There's no more I can do for you, Bruno.'

2

Bruno asked Dr Gelletreau to follow them as he and Antoine drove separately to Antoine's campground with its small beach on the river. Bruno passed through the ornate gateway where two stone lions guarded the portal. He crossed the field where the gaily coloured jumps for the gymkhana had already been put in place. Four tents showed the campground's season had begun. He parked and headed across the open terrace to the wooden chalet where Antoine kept his canoe paddles and life jackets, and where he cooked omelettes and sausages for his guests. Bruno collected a couple of paddles and handed Antoine a life jacket as soon as the boatman joined him. But Antoine was heading for the bar. A fresh Gitane smouldered on his lower lip and he scratched his head through thick grey hair as he pushed aside the pile of paper that comprised his accounts and reached for a bottle of Ricard.

'We've got some time,' Antoine said. 'Another ten, fifteen minutes before it drifts down here. Want a drink?' He pointed to the bottle and opened his fridge to pull out a wine bottle filled with chilled water. His eyes squinted against the smoke. He looked an unlikely candidate to sing the role of Jesus, but nobody in St Denis could match his powerful voice.

'Too early for me, thanks,' said Bruno. 'But maybe I'll take an orange juice.'

'Suit yourself,' said Antoine, adding water to his *anis* and savouring his first drink of the day. Just as well there were no breathalysers on the river, Bruno thought.

'Did you see that tattoo?' he asked.

'Is that what it was?' Antoine shrugged. 'I couldn't rightly make it out. Looked like something mathematical, triangles maybe. I only caught a glimpse when that fool sent the punt rocking. I thought for a minute he might have been trying to sink it.'

'I suppose he was just trying to help,' Bruno said. 'He looked a bit familiar but I can't recall where I've seen him before.'

'I'd have remembered that girl,' Antoine said with a wink. 'Legs all the way up to her shoulders. Nice car, too.' He finished his drink and led the way to the small beach, past the trailer whose racks were already filled with canoes. He would pile his clients into his battered Renault Espace and then attach the trailer to tow the canoes to Les Eyzies or St Léon or even as far as Montignac, where they could paddle downstream with the current. A row of red canoes had been turned upside down and placed just above the beach. A hose and brush suggested Antoine had been washing away the dust of storage to prepare them for the new season.

'Get that one launched,' he said, pointing to the largest canoe, one that could easily fit half a dozen people. It was made of a tough and rubberized red plastic that could survive repeated scrapings over the pebbles of the shallows. It looked almost unsinkable, with big flotation chambers at bow and stern and others serving as seats in the middle. 'I'll get some rope and a hook to tow the thing in.'

Bruno took off his boots and socks, his uniform tunic and trousers, put on a life jacket and hauled the canoe down from the beach to the shallows. Motorboats were forbidden on the river and it was too narrow for sailboats, so canoes were the only option. Some fishermen carried battery-driven electric motors for small outboards that could just about take them upstream when the currents weren't too strong. The sand that Antoine shipped in every spring to cover the mud of his beach was still fresh and felt pleasantly cool under Bruno's feet, but the river itself was cold. It could not have been a pleasant dip for the young man with the sports car.

Antoine fixed one end of his rope to a bracket on the bow and Bruno took the rear of the canoe so Antoine could handle the hook. They pushed the canoe knee-deep before clambering in. The current here was quite strong and they had to paddle steadily just to stay near the beach. Antoine dug his paddle deep and set a brisk rhythm to take the canoe upstream, explaining that he'd need some time to fix the tow and didn't want to drift back. The punt had looked close to sinking anyway. It must have been forty years since anybody had punts on this river, so it would be old wood. Already waterlogged, it could slip beneath the surface at any time.

As the crow flies, they were no more than a few hundred yards from St Denis. But from Montignac upstream down to Limeuil below them, where their river flowed into the bigger Dordogne, the Vézère took a series of long oxbow bends as it meandered across the fertile valley. These were the water meadows that used to flood each springtime and autumn when the river rose, creating the vast wetlands that had attracted the ducks and geese that had made this region a paradise for hunters and for the foie gras they produced. Now the river had been largely tamed but the waterfowl had stayed. And with each springtime flood, the river carved more deeply into the banks on the outside of each bend so the loops became larger ever year.

'There they are again,' said Antoine, pointing at the entrance to his campsite where the white sports car was turning in from the road, Dr Gelletreau's big old Citroën lumbering along behind. The girl waved. 'Determined bugger, ain't he? And with that car, I don't think he's coming here looking for a place to pitch a tent.'

Bruno briefly lifted a paddle in acknowledgement of the girl's wave as the car disappeared behind the hedge and headed for the parking area. He tried to match Antoine's experienced strokes as they drove the canoe forward against the river's flow. On any other occasion, it would have been a pleasant excursion, the sun dappling the water as it filtered through the budding leaves of the trees along each bank. To their left loomed the high white limestone cliffs that dotted the valley with caves. Many were filled with paintings, testaments to the artistic skills of the people who had lived here tens of thousands of years ago. Others still showed traces of the medieval fortifications where men and women had taken refuge against the marauding English.

'There it is,' called Antoine, not turning round, but kneeling up in the bow and picking up the coil of rope he had prepared.

'Just keep us going straight and try to bring her alongside.'

There was little of the punt to be seen as it drifted slug-gishly towards them, maybe an inch or two of freeboard above the water. Antoine stretched out an arm as the punt approached, caught hold of the side and muttered, 'The good Lord preserve us,' as he looked at the woman within. A bird that had been perched, pecking, inside the punt flew away. When he caught the rusty iron ring at the stern of the punt, he deftly threaded his rope through it and tied a quick knot.

'That'll do,' he said. 'She's too sodden for a tow, we might drag her under. We'll just drift down to the beach and guide her in.'

The woman was almost awash, the water in the punt lapping over her legs, pubis and ears so that only her breasts, face and feet were visible. Her fair hair floated behind her head and her hands trembled in the water, the fingers seeming to move in the eddies of water almost as if she were waving. The bird had been at her left eye. The other stared sightlessly at the sky, but it was evident she had been an attractive woman, with good skin and fine features. Her nose and chin were well shaped and her cheekbones prominent. Bruno caught a whiff of something burned and also something oily, it might have been paraffin. An empty bottle of vodka stirred at her side.

As they neared the landing beach, Antoine skilfully steered them across the current and climbed out of the canoe when the bank shelved to guide the punt up onto the sand. The young man in white, his trousers still wet, came down to help him haul it up, but Antoine waved him away. Bruno beached the canoe, climbed out to haul it higher and shook Dr Gelletreau's hand before the doctor moved across to look into the punt. Antoine had tipped it slightly onto its side to let some of the water out, but small streams were dribbling from cracks in the hull. One large black candle, nearly a metre in length, toppled out of the punt and a second one rolled against the gunwale. Bruno had only ever seen candles that size in church, but never in black. At least he now knew what the stumpy mast had been.

'How is she? Is she dead?' the young man from the sports car asked. Bruno recognized him now from the previous year's tennis tournament when the girls had flocked around him. He had the arrogant good looks of a model in a glossy magazine. He'd played with someone in the men's doubles, reaching the semi-finals with an aggressive game of serve-and-volley.

'We'll wait for the doctor's verdict,' Bruno said. 'Didn't you hear us yelling at you not to dive in back at the bridge? You must have seen I was a policeman. You might have sunk the boat.'

'I was only trying to help,' he said pleasantly, with a slightly mocking tilt to his eyebrow. He had an educated voice, an accent that sounded Parisian and a manner that suggested he was used to getting his way. 'I thought I could stop it crashing into the bridge.'

'What brings you to St Denis?' Bruno asked.

'We have a business meeting at the *Mairie*,' he said. 'We were crossing the bridge when the crowd turned up, climbed out and saw her drifting down and I thought I might be able to reach the boat from the other bank. Sorry, I'm Lionel Foucher.'

He put out a hand, and Bruno shook it, turning to look at the young woman sitting in the driving seat of what Bruno now saw was a new-looking Jaguar. She was wearing sunglasses and raised her hand in languid greeting. Bruno suddenly remembered he was wearing only his underpants, shirt and a life jacket. He grinned at her and waved back.

'That's Eugénie, my partner,' said Foucher. 'Well, you've got her safely ashore. We'll leave you to it.'

'I'm sure the Mayor won't mind your wet trousers, not in the circumstances,' Bruno replied, and turned back to the punt as Foucher climbed into the car and was driven off.

'No name or markings on the punt,' said Antoine.

'I can't give you much of a time of death,' said Gelletreau, rising from beside the punt. He had a pair of tweezers in his hand, holding something that looked like a small circle of wet cardboard. He took a plastic bag from his medical case and put the object inside.

'Water plays the very devil with body temperature and lividity, all the usual signs. No obvious cause of death so we'll probably need an autopsy. No jewellery and no sign of any belongings so there's no indication of identity. Some bruising around the vulva and the anus. I'd say she had indulged in some pretty energetic sexual activity before she died, but there are no bruises on the wrists and shoulders so I doubt it was coerced.'

'So you don't see it as a suspicious death?' Bruno asked. The woman's pubis had been carefully trimmed into the neatest of triangles.

'Obviously it's mysterious, but suspicious . . . I don't know. That item I put away for the pathologists, I found it inside her vagina. I've no idea what it is,' said Gelletreau. 'Frankly, looking at the vodka bottle my best guess would be suicide, a very demonstrative way to go for a probably disturbed woman. That in itself would not be unusual. People quite often dress up in strange ways or strip naked to commit suicide. We'll have to see what the toxicology says but I'd be surprised if they don't find a lot of alcohol and barbiturates . . .' He broke off, muttering 'That reminds me.' He bent down to rummage in his medical bag and came out with a shiny metal tool that Bruno recognized from ear examinations.

'No needle tracks so I rather discounted drugs,' the doctor said, bending down over the body. But instead of inserting the device into her ear, he poked it up a nostril and squinted inside.

'Aha,' he said. He tried but failed to lever his heavy form up again. Bruno gave him a hand and hauled Gelletreau to his feet.

'Signs of very heavy cocaine use. The septum is almost destroyed,' he said. 'A pity. She must have been a good-looking woman. I'd put her age at no more than forty.'

Bruno nodded. There was little sign of wrinkles nor of ageing at her neck. Her legs were long and shapely, with no sag to her thighs or buttocks. Her waist was well defined and the breasts generous.

'Are those stretch marks signs that she had given birth?' Bruno asked.

'I'd say so, but we'll need the autopsy to be sure.'

United in an unspoken sense of sadness and of waste, the three men fell silent as they gazed down at the body, robbed in death of any sexual allure. But the painted shape on her trunk disturbed Bruno.

'What about that marking?' he asked. He could see now that it was no tattoo, more something that had been daubed on her belly, a vaguely familiar shape.

'It's a pentagram, some kind of mystic symbol,' said Gelletreau. 'And it's no tattoo, it was drawn with something like a magic marker. It's waterproof, whatever it was. I don't know what those two black candles are doing in there. Nor that.' He pointed to a sodden and shapeless mass in the bottom of the punt.

'It's a cockerel,' said Antoine, poking at it with a stick. 'And there's its head, over there at the far end of the punt. Somebody must have cut it off.'

Bruno bent down to look at some charred sticks floating on what little water was left in the boat and sniffed, catching that whiff of paraffin again.

'Do you think somebody tried to light a fire here?' he asked. 'And what's that dark patch down where the water's almost gone?'

All three men knelt to peer at the bottom of the punt, just in front of the dead woman's feet. As the water drained, they saw that the dark patch was simply charred wood and the burning had gone quite deep. There were some more sticks scattered around the bottom of the punt, some of them so thick they were almost logs. Right in the middle of the burnt

20

patch was a long crack where the last of the water was now draining away.

'Somebody tried to light a fire, but the wood was so old it cracked and water came in and put the fire out,' Bruno said, thinking aloud. 'That's why I smelt paraffin.'

'Bloody stupid, setting a fire in a wooden boat and not putting a stone or something underneath,' said Antoine. 'It was bound to burn through.'

'Like a Viking funeral that went wrong, only with black candles and a dead cockerel,' said Gelletreau. 'Funny stuff, this. I don't like it at all. The sooner we get a proper autopsy the better.'

Bruno nodded, went back to where he had left his trousers and used his mobile phone to call J-J, the chief of detectives at national police headquarters in Périgueux. He was told to leave a message and then went through to the switchboard to report a mysterious death, adding that the doctor had requested an autopsy. That would mean taking the dead woman to the pathology lab in Bergerac.

'I'd better wait here,' he said. 'You two can go about your business, but thanks to both of you. I'll come to the medical centre later to pick up a copy of the death certificate if you could leave it at the desk.'

Antoine headed back to his bar and his accounts. Dr Gelletreau turned to his car.

'By the way, Doc,' Bruno said. 'I thought Fabiola was on duty today.'

'She said she had something to attend to. I got the impression it was some private patient.'

'That's not like her,' Bruno said. 'She's always been critical of private practice. Medicine for the people, you know Fabiola.'

'I know, that's why she likes working at the clinic,' said Gelletreau. 'Odd, isn't it? Maybe she needs the money. She was saying she needed a new car.'

He stood, looking at Bruno, as if there was more to be said but he didn't know how to say it. Bruno felt the same way but decided to take the plunge.

'This funny stuff as you call it, the pentagram and black candles,' Bruno said, still not quite sure how to voice the suspicion in his mind. 'Does it look like she was dabbling in black magic, some kind of Satanism?'

'Exactly that,' said Gelletreau, nodding. 'It's been on my mind. When I get home I've got an old book somewhere on historic legends that refers to it. Maybe you might want to ask Father Sentout about it; Satanism has been an interest of his for years. It makes me wonder whether I ought to join Antoine in a quick Ricard and one of those disgusting cigarettes of his. In fact, as your doctor I'm tempted to prescribe a stiff drink for you as well. If this death has something to do with black magic then I suspect you're going to need it.'

3

Back in his office at the *Mairie*, Bruno settled down at his desk to study the handwritten letter that had arrived in his mail. All in capitals, it was one of the anonymous denunciations that regularly came to him and many other policemen in France. He'd always blamed the war years of the Vichy regime for encouraging the practice, until he read a book on the history of the French Revolution which quoted extensively from the anonymous letters sent to the Committee of Public Safety in the 1790s that had condemned thousands of people to the guillotine. Most of the ones Bruno received denounced people for sexual immorality, which he ignored, or for tax evasion or working on the black market, which he was obliged to investigate. This one at least was written in black ink, rather than the green or violet that usually recounted sins of adultery. But its tenor was disturbing, denouncing a farmer whom Bruno knew only slightly for beating his wife.

It was a crime he detested, but one that frequently complicated his life. Most magistrates were reluctant to press charges, even when the medical evidence was clear, because the wives so often refused to testify against their husbands.

The old ways were strong in St Denis, particularly on the more remote farms, and Bruno had more than once heard mutterings in the bars and cafés about a nagging wife deserving a clip around the ear. And there'd always be some old codger ready to spout the doggerel:

'*A dog, a wife, a walnut tree,*
The more you beat them, the better they'll be.'

Bruno's predecessor, Joe, had a rough and ready way with domestic violence. He'd ignore the occasional slap or punch on a Saturday night after drink had been taken. But if he knew that the beating was a regular occurrence, or above all if the children were also beaten, then Joe would go to the court of public opinion, letting it be known in the bars that a situation was getting out of hand. When a consensus developed, Joe and a couple of his chums from the rugby team would go out to the farm, take the offending husband behind the barn and treat him to some of his own medicine. Bruno gave a wry smile at the recollection that Joe had called it his own version of community policing. He claimed it was very effective. Maybe it was, but it was not the kind of rough justice that policemen could apply these days, and it was not Bruno's way.

He turned back to the letter. The farmer, a taciturn and hard-faced man who scraped some kind of living from the poor tract of upland and hillside that he had inherited from his father, was named Louis Junot. His wife came from somewhere in the north, where Junot had met her while doing his military service. They had a daughter, Francette, whom Bruno remembered from his tennis classes. She had been a promising player, fast around the court and with a good eye for the ball, but not a girl to spend much time at practice. Once she entered her teens Francette had spent more time eyeing the boys than working at her tennis. She had begun wearing make-up at an early age, but Bruno remembered seeing her scrub it off when she boarded the bus that took her up the hill towards home. She had left school early and worked at the checkout of the local supermarket and as far as Bruno knew she still lived at home. Perhaps he should start with her.

On his desk phone was a recorded message from Delaron, who knew that a formal query on Bruno's phone at the *Mairie* would have to be answered.

Bruno listened to Delaron's chirpy voice telling him that the newspaper was very interested in his photos of the dead woman in the boat, but they would make sure it was decent enough for a family newspaper. Could Bruno confirm in time for his deadline that the woman was dead, that she had been murdered and that it was looking like a case of ritual Satanist killing?

'*Merde*,' Bruno muttered to himself, as Delaron went on to say that Father Sentout had already said that the corpse 'carried all the hallmarks of a Satanist outrage'.

'*Putain de merde*,' Bruno muttered. The Mayor was not going to like this and Father Sentout should have known better. Bruno picked up the phone and rang Delaron to tell him that all inquiries should go to the official police spokesman in Périgueux. Bruno could confirm only that the woman was dead, but there was no visible cause of death and it was not

25

even yet decided that the death was suspicious. Off the record, the doctor reckoned it was suicide. What about the Satanism? Delaron demanded. Any reference to Satanism was pure speculation, Bruno told him. He put the phone down and went to warn the Mayor.

Gérard Mangin had been the Mayor of St Denis for over twenty years. He had hired Bruno as town policeman and educated him, a former soldier still battered in mind and body from his time in the Balkans, in the traditional and peaceful ways of St Denis. Bruno revered him as a Mayor, loved him as a father, but had few illusions about the Mayor's ruthless pursuit of what he saw as the interests of St Denis. The most important, of course, was that Gérard Mangin should remain as Mayor.

'Ah, Bruno, I have excellent news,' the Mayor said, as Bruno knocked and entered the light-filled room with its view over the Vézère. The Mayor laid down the fountain pen that he still used for all his business, refusing any suggestion that he adopt a computer. He closed the large notebook in which he was writing the history of the town and opened a manila file with a green ribbon attached to its corner. Green meant a project that the Mayor supported.

'I think I mentioned this proposal for a holiday village, very exclusive, golf course attached, up the river toward Montignac. A big investment group based in Paris, impeccable credentials,' the Mayor said, looking pleased with himself. 'It's at the very edge of our commune and some of the land will be in two other communes, but it looks like we'll get the bulk of the taxes. Of course, we'll have to put sewers in and widen the river road, but we'll get our money back in a few years and then it's all income. And our people will get the building and landscape work, and the maintenance and cleaning jobs, and a couple of hundred wealthy new customers for our restaurants.'

Much of the Mayor's time was spent finding jobs for St Denis, or trying to save jobs that were threatened, or securing grants from Brussels and Paris for training and retraining schemes. He had always been obsessed with finding jobs for the young people who left for the universities of Bordeaux and Toulouse and never came back, but the global recession had made it more urgent. That St Denis flourished, when so many other French country towns were shrinking and dying as the populations aged, was testimony to his efforts and to his political connections. Bruno supported the Mayor's plans in general, but tended to express only polite interest in the particular projects. He was thinking that an affluent holiday village with many of the homes empty throughout the year would be a magnet for burglars, which would be his problem, even though the village was at the far end of the commune, ten kilometres from St Denis. But he thought he'd better sound supportive.

'Very good news, particularly if they agree to open the golf course to local people as well,' Bruno said.

'Good idea, I'll raise it with young Foucher when he calls again.'

'Would that be a young man with fair hair, dressed in white, accompanied by a dark-haired young woman?'

The Mayor looked surprised by Bruno's knowledge. 'That's

the man himself and the girl, a damn handsome couple. I didn't know you were paying attention to these planning matters, Bruno.'

'It wasn't the planning aspect that struck me,' Bruno replied drily. He knew the conversation would take a less agreeable turn as he recounted the story of the punt, the dead woman and Philippe Delaron's inquiries about Satanism.

'Why the devil can't he just run the camera shop rather than dash around filling the newspaper with dirty laundry we don't want washed in public?'

Bruno refrained from replying that as often as not the Mayor found ways to turn Delaron's reporting to his own advantage. This was the moment for one of the Mayor's occasional rants, and as long as Bruno was not the target he rather enjoyed them.

'Satanism is the very last thing I want associated with this town. It's quite the wrong image. Delaron must be made to see that. Tourists will stay away in their droves, and that will hurt his business as well as everyone else.'

Bruno wasn't so sure. The more he thought about it the more he suspected that tourists might flock to a town associated with such sensational events. In any event the story was now out of their control. He told the Mayor of Father Sentout's statement to Delaron.

'Interfering old busybody,' the Mayor snapped. 'That priest should stick to his choir practice. Would it help if I rang the editor?'

'Knowing journalists, it would probably make it worse. But I'll go and have a word with the priest. Once they read the story in *Sud-Ouest* all the other reporters will be calling him. The suggestion of suicide might help.'

'I'm not sure that will work,' the Mayor said, shaking his head. 'Exorcism has always been one of Father Sentout's interests. He even did a couple of them around here, driving out devils from some poor mad soul. He told me he'd taught exorcism when he was a tutor in the seminary up in Dinan. I suspect he's been aching for another chance to try it. No, you won't find it easy to talk our priest out of his latest brush with the devil.'

Before he left, Bruno mentioned the anonymous letter and said he'd drive out to Junot's farm.

'Junot's a drunk, just like his father,' the Mayor said, looking at his watch. He rose from his desk and put on his jacket. 'Excuse me, but I have to pick my wife up from the hospital at Sarlat.'

'Nothing serious, I trust?' Bruno liked the motherly woman who spent much of the year knitting socks and scarves to hand out to the *Mairie* staff at Christmas.

'No, Fabiola said it was just some routine tests.' The Mayor held the door to let Bruno out. 'Good luck with Junot. He'll never make that farm work now they've cut the subsidy for sheep. Do what you can, Bruno. But keep it discreet.'

Bruno started at the supermarket, but learned that Francette no longer worked there. She'd left a couple of weeks earlier, claiming to have a new job. That was all the manager knew. Bruno asked Michèle, the veteran cashier, but neither she nor anyone else seemed to know what the new job might be nor where. But apparently she had looked a different girl when she handed in her notice, with new clothes, new hairstyle and make-up and a more cheerful manner.

'One of her friends said she was in love,' Michèle told him. Bruno was directed to the staff room where two of Francette's friends were enjoying coffee and a cigarette. Neither one knew anything about the boyfriend, except that he was not from St Denis, and they confirmed that Francette hated her father and had complained regularly about him.

Before he left, Bruno asked if the supermarket sold black candles, big ones. The manager said he'd never heard of them, nor did he know anywhere that sold them, but he gave Bruno the number of the main distributor for candles in the region, based in Sarlat. Bruno sat to take a coffee at the small restaurant beside the supermarket and dialled. He learned that large black candles were speciality items and always imported. He was given the Paris number of the main importer, and from them got the names of four stores, two in Paris, one in Lyon and another in Marseille.

'Apart from the theatricals, that is,' the voice from Paris went on. 'We have a regular order from Gallotin, the big theatre supplier. They supply the film industry and the Opéra and the Avignon festival, all the main events. That's the biggest market for things like that.'

Bruno made a note, finished his coffee and checked his watch, thinking he'd have time to visit the Junot farm before lunch, when his phone vibrated. It was J-J, chief of detectives for the *Département* and a good friend, asking for a briefing on the dead woman.

'Sorry I didn't call back earlier,' J-J said. 'I was with the new *Procureur de la République*, seems a real live wire. He's from Lyon but keen on rugby so you'll get on fine with him.' With wide powers to define the scope of criminal inquiries and to appoint *juges d'instruction* to lead investigations, the new Public Prosecutor could make J-J's life a misery. The last *Procureur* had been close to retirement and content to let J-J run his own show.

Bruno strolled back to the *Mairie* to pick up his official van, and was surprised to see a small procession of a dozen or so townsfolk crossing the bridge ahead of him. They were in single file except for two of them at the front who carried poles bearing hand-made posters. One read, 'Homes for Locals, Not Tourists'. Catching them up, Bruno saw a number of familiar faces, some of them regulars from other demonstrations over the years. But he was surprised to see Gaston Lemontin carrying the other poster, which read 'The People Say No'.

Lemontin had for years been the quiet deputy manager of the local bank. Married, with grown children who had moved away, he lived with his wife in a remote but pleasant home overlooking the river at the far end of the commune. As he recalled this, Bruno began to guess the nature of the demonstration. He also recognized two of the people filing along behind as neighbours who lived down the same side road as Lemontin.

'What's this about, Gaston?' he asked, in a friendly tone. 'It would have been a courtesy to let me know, in case I have to do something about the traffic.'

'There aren't that many of us, Bruno, more's the pity. We're just here to deliver a petition to the Mayor,' the banker replied. 'We've got over a hundred signatures. The *Mairie* will have to listen to us now. Here, why don't you sign it?'

With what was now a practised gesture, Lemontin whipped out a petition form and pen from his shoulder bag. Bruno took the form, but ignored the pen and began to read. As he'd suspected, the petition was against the plans for the holiday village that the Mayor had mentioned earlier that morning. According to the petition, the golf course would waste water, the need to provide roads and sewers would raise the town's taxes and no environmental assessment had been done. The banks of the river would be at risk, and it would make it even harder for local youngsters to afford homes of their own. There were far too many holiday homes in the region anyway, without adding more places that would be empty most of the year.

Bruno agreed with a lot of that. But he also agreed with the Mayor's focus on the jobs, taxes and tourist trade the development would bring to St Denis.

'All very public-spirited,' said Bruno, as he handed back the petition and fell into step beside Lemontin. 'But you didn't put in the bit about it spoiling your view and maybe shaving a bit off the profit you've already made on that house of yours. Isn't that what this is about? I've never known you to attend any other demonstration in these parts.'

'Well, what if I do have a personal interest?' Lemontin replied, a faint blush spreading on his cheeks. 'I'm entitled to make my point, just like any other citizen. And those arguments are real – there hasn't been an environmental assessment but the Mayor is hell-bent on pushing this through. I'm told that he's already granted preliminary approval without any public discussion and without the council even seeing the plans. And the more I look into it, the more I smell something fishy in this investment house that's behind it.'

'I thought it was some big reputable firm in Paris,' Bruno said. Now they were almost at the *Mairie*.

'That's what they say, but when you look into the real owners you get into a maze of finance companies in Luxembourg and investment trusts in Switzerland and offshore places like the Cayman Islands. There's even a Lebanese connection.'

It all sounded a bit too sophisticated for St Denis, Bruno thought. 'Well, all this can be sorted out at the next council hearing. Have you got any councillors on your side?'

'Only Alphonse,' Lemontin said glumly. Alphonse was the local Green, an elderly hippy who had come to establish a commune in the hills above the town at the end of the Sixties. 'I know, he'll support anything. Or oppose anything, more likely. I can't say I've ever voted for him and I'm not sure I would even now.'

'He'll still be listened to,' Bruno replied, noting that Alphonse hadn't bothered to turn up for the demonstration. 'Besides, a lot of people think highly of Alphonse, and I'm one of them. Do you want me to take that petition inside for you?'

'No, I want to put it into the Mayor's hands, but then I have to get back to the bank. I'm on an early lunch break.'

4

The Junot farmhouse had one of the best views in the valley, a privilege it paid for with thin, infertile soil and by suffering the chill winds that swept the high plateau in winter. Built in the boom time of the 1880s when the new wonder crop of tobacco had brought prosperity to the Périgord and a sharp rise in the population, it had seldom prospered since. Sheep and goats were the only livestock that could thrive on the tussocks, thorns and bracken. Generations of Junots had hauled up topsoil from the valley to build a sheltered vegetable garden to feed the family on turnips, beans and potatoes. A very modest living could be scratched from the place with hard work and determination. Louis Junot seemed capable of neither.

Bruno paused at the crest of the hill, looking at the tiles that had fallen from the farmhouse roof and not been replaced, at the broken fencing and the weeds in the garden. More weeds choked the half-dozen rows of spindly vines, and Bruno winced at the thought of the sour wine that Junot would be making. It was probably all he could afford. There was hardly any chopped wood left on the terrace. Any decent farmer up in these hills would have at least another winter's worth of firewood in hand. The ducks and chickens looked healthy enough, but they were traditionally the responsibility of the farmer's wife and the source of her pin money.

His problem, however, was the husband. Louis Junot was known to drink, and was no doubt capable of violence, but so far the only justification for his arrest was an anonymous letter, which was not enough. Without a complaint from his wife, Bruno had few options. Before coming he had checked the list he kept in the office of those who'd paid for that year's hunting permit. Junot's name was not on it, so any evidence of hunting – even for rabbits – would justify Bruno in making an arrest. That would be a last resort and the Mayor had asked him to be discreet. His first task was to assess whether the beating was happening; the second to see if the wife would testify; the third to issue a warning. It was one of those tricky moments of policing when Bruno had few cards to play.

Bruno heard the sound of hammering and a curse from the barn below the house. He saw a curtain twitch at the window by the door to the house. Junot's wife had seen him coming, but she took her time answering the door and opened it just a crack. She knew him from open days at the tennis club, watching her young daughter play and mixing with the rest of the mothers as their children attacked the refreshments afterwards. But still she eyed him with suspicion as he removed his hat, smiled and asked if he could come in.

'What for?'

'I have some questions I have to ask you.'

'What do you mean, questions?' She had opened the door

a fraction wider and he saw a bruised cheek and a black eye.

'Questions about a written complaint we've received,' Bruno said. 'Either I come in and ask you about them or we'll have to take you and your husband to the Gendarmerie.'

It was not a threat he liked to make, but he had to. All anonymous letters were supposed to be filed, and the Inspectorate of Police had the right to read them and demand why a case had not been pursued. Wife-beating had become a prominent issue and Bruno could be in trouble if the Inspectors thought he were ignoring complaints.

'I'll get Louis,' she said, opening the door with reluctance.

'It's you I need to speak to first,' he said, stepping briskly inside in a way that made Madame Junot step back. As she moved, she lifted her hand to her side, as if her ribs hurt.

'You've been hurt, Madame. What happened?' He cast an eye around the big kitchen with its stone floor that would be bitterly cold in winter and an original stone sink. There were no taps. Water would have to be pumped up daily from the well outside. The only modern amenities were an electric light bulb hanging from the ceiling and an elderly cooking stove fuelled by bottles of gas.

'I fell down the stairs.'

'The stairs did not blacken your eye. What caused that?'

She did not answer, but turned back to the stove where a large pot was simmering. She lifted the lid, releasing a scent of duck stock and of garlic, broke two small eggs into the soup and began to stir with an age-blackened wooden spoon.

'Making *tourain*?' Bruno asked, noticing the bowl filled with evidently stale bread she had placed beside the stove. A classic

36

dish of the Périgord, it was the traditional cheap but filling lunch of the farmers, and simple to make. Based on the stock from the carcass of a duck, some garlic and salt, stale bread and an egg or two, it could be thinned out with water or milk or thickened with more bread or vermicelli. And when the bowl of soup was almost finished, any true Périgourdin would make *chabrol*, pouring in half a glass of red wine to swirl it around the plate, and then lift the bowl to his lips.

She shrugged, keeping her back to him. She was wearing a wrap-around apron, washed so often that the floral print had faded almost beyond recognition. Underneath she wore sagging woollen stockings and a long pullover that she had knitted herself with wool from their own sheep. There was no sign of a TV, far less a computer. A shelf on the wall opposite the window carried an elderly radio, what looked like a bible, a farmer's almanac and a battered cookbook. There were no other books in sight, no newspapers or magazines. What a strange childhood Francette must have known, Bruno thought. How could she hope to fit in with school classmates who'd talk of the latest TV shows and pop songs?

'Where's Francette?' he asked. 'I hear she's left the supermarket, got a new job.'

Her mother's back stiffened. 'Is this what you came to ask?'

'No, I came to ask about your being beaten. We had a complaint, an allegation. Domestic violence is a crime and Louis could go to prison.' Out of the window, he could see her husband working on an old tractor at the entrance to the barn. 'I can see from the way you wince that it's true.'

'No, I fell. I told you.' Her head down, it was as if she were talking to the soup she was stirring. Bruno wondered why the house had been built uphill, just above the barn, open to the winter winds, when the barn could have provided shelter. The answer came almost as soon as his mind formed the question: the animals' waste would have seeped downhill into the home. There were still a couple of farms up in these hills, older than the Junot place, where the animals still lived on the ground floor with the humans above, taking advantage of the warmth from the bodies of the livestock below.

'He used to beat Francette, too, didn't he?' Bruno asked. 'Is that why she left home?'

Silence from the stove, but her shoulders seemed to sag a little more. Then he saw that the shoulders were shaking and she was trying to damp down some huge, racking sobs. He moved across to stand beside her and looked at her face, tears spilling down her cheeks.

'You don't understand,' she whispered. 'Francette could get away. She has her life ahead of her. I have nowhere to go, even if I wanted to.'

'There are places you can go, shelters in Bergerac and Sarlat,' he said. 'I can drive you there now.'

'I don't want to,' she said firmly, stooping to wipe her eyes on her apron. 'He isn't always like this. It's just that everything has gone wrong, the subsidies and then the sheep dying and the bill from the vet that we can't pay and now the tractor . . .'

'This beating has to stop,' Bruno said. He didn't know what else he could say and he had the feeling that there was something she wasn't telling him. Not for the first time, he thought how useful it would be to have a policewoman working alongside him.

'Louis is not a bad man,' she said, standing straight now and more sure of herself. 'I know him better than anyone.'

'Is he drunk when he beats you?'

She shrugged, and then winced again, her hand going to her ribs. Whatever the outcome of his confrontation with her husband, Bruno resolved that he'd take her down to the clinic.

'His own wine is all he can afford to drink and there's little enough of that,' she said, turning off the gas beneath the soup. 'Nobody would drink it but him.'

She turned to the rear wall where Bruno saw a haybox, something he used for long, slow cooking. But he remembered from his childhood, when he was taken in by cousins, that poor families used them because they could not afford the gas.

'I'll get it,' he said. He put it on the counter alongside the stove, lifted the soup pan inside and then packed the extra hay on top and sealed the box. It would keep on cooking all day.

'After I've spoken to Louis, I'm taking you down to the clinic,' he said.

'I'll be all right.'

'It doesn't matter. Either you come with me, or I'll have to arrest you for obstruction of justice and get a doctor to see you in the cells.' Bruno was bluffing, but he was determined that she see a doctor, preferably Fabiola. She should be back by now from whatever private patient she was seeing.

He lifted Louis's shotgun down from the hooks that held it to the wall, opened the breech, held the barrel to the window and squinted. Never much of a gun, it had been badly cared for. The barrels were pitted and it had barely been cleaned since it was last used. There was no sheen of gun oil around the breech and trigger and the wood of the stock was dry. Bruno sighed and took it outside to lock it inside his van before heading down to see the owner.

Outside, the sky had clouded over and the breeze that never really died up here on the high plateau had turned chill with a hint of rain in the air. A pair of goats gazed up at him before lowering their heads once more to the rough grass. He could see Louis bent over the front of the old Somua tractor, trying to get the engine to turn over with a starting handle. As he approached, Bruno could hear curses interspersed between the dry wheezing of the cylinders. He noticed a jug of wine on the floor beside the vehicle. The wood of the barn needed a coat of creosote and one of the hinges on the doors was hanging loose.

'What in hell do you want?' came the surly inquiry. Junot barely looked up from the tractor and his voice was slurred with drink.

'I want to talk to you. We've had a formal complaint that you're beating your wife, and it's clear that she's been hurt. Was it you?'

'None of your business.'

'I'm afraid it is. It's against the law. And where's your daughter gone?'

Junot stood up, throwing down the starting handle. He was a stocky figure of about Bruno's height, heavy in the shoulders and with thick, well-muscled forearms. He glared at Bruno, his eyes red and his jaw clenching as if he was ready to fight.

'Why don't you leave us alone?'

Bruno shook his head, keeping his eyes on Junot. 'This is my job, Louis. I have to find out what's going on. Where's Francette? Or did you beat her up as well? Did you hurt her so badly that she left? Is that what happened?'

Junot's eyes narrowed and Bruno saw him shift his weight to his front foot and his left shoulder moved a fraction forward. Bruno knew the signs: Junot was going to throw a punch with his right fist.

It came, slightly faster than Bruno had expected. As he ducked beneath the swing he saw Junot's left coming from the other direction and his leg lifting for a kick. Bruno moved forward inside the left, caught the rising leg and jerked it upwards, sending Junot crashing onto his back. Junot rolled, clambered to his feet and was coming back at Bruno with the starting handle.

'Don't be a fool, Louis. Put it down and there's no harm done,' Bruno said. 'Otherwise you're facing a prison term.'

With a cry that began as a curse and became a desperate wail, Junot attacked, swinging the handle like a cutlass. Bruno stepped back out of range and then slammed a punch into Junot's kidney as the momentum took the man around. Junot came full circle, the handle still in his hand, but Bruno was expecting him, stepped inside the swing and hit him hard just under the breastbone. It was a short punch but all of Bruno's weight was behind the blow.

Junot stopped as if he'd run into a wall. The handle dropped from his hand and he sank heavily to his knees, bending his head down and making retching sounds as he tried to suck air into his lungs.

Bruno went across to the well, where a full bucket stood beside the stone rim. He carried it back to Junot and emptied the contents over the man's head. He looked up and saw Junot's wife standing at the door of her kitchen, a dishcloth twisting in her hands but her face impassive. At least, Bruno thought, she had not rushed to her husband's defence. He'd taken a bruise or two from battered wives in the past. She turned and went back into the kitchen, closing the door behind her.

Junot was half panting, half sobbing, but he seemed to be getting some air. He raised his head and a long trail of drool fell from his mouth. His eyes began to focus and he looked up at his house with its closed door and then at Bruno.

'Bastard,' he said, and vomited.

Bruno picked up the jug of wine and emptied it onto the ground. He could smell its sourness, as bitter as the sense of defeat that seemed almost to ooze from Junot. His farm and family falling apart around him, and now he gets knocked down on his own land and his wife doesn't want to back him up. Bruno went back to the well and loosened the ratchet to send the bucket down to fill it again.

'It's not so easy when someone fights back,' he said, coming back with the bucket and putting it down by Junot's knees. 'Least of all when you've been drinking all day.'

Junot put his hands in the bucket and lapped from them, and then splashed water over his face.

'What's wrong with the tractor?' Bruno asked.

'Bugger won't start.'

'You checked the plugs?'

Junot shrugged. Some rusty tools were piled into a plastic box that had once held ice cream. Bruno pulled out the only spanner but it didn't fit. He went back to his van and came back with his own tool box, took out a can of lubricating oil and poured it onto the rust around the sparking plugs. He checked the wiring and then fitted his own ratchet wrench to remove the plugs. The first one took a couple of taps with the hammer but the others came out easily enough. They looked as if they hadn't been cleaned for years, the gaps clogged with old carbon. He used his wire brush to clean them, put them back and then handed the starting handle to Junot, still kneeling by the bucket as he watched Bruno work.

'Give her a try,' Bruno said. Maybe Junot would open up enough to talk if something went right for him today. He lumbered to his feet, looking first at Bruno and then at the starting handle, squared his shoulders and inserted it into the hole at the base of the engine. He braced himself and turned it, getting a reluctant mechanical cough for his effort. He turned it again, the handle kicked in his hands and the engine roared into uneven life.

'It must recognize your touch,' Bruno said, speaking loudly over the sound of the engine.

'I've known it since I were a lad, when my dad first got it,'

Junot said, climbing into the seat and driving it from the barn into the yard.

'Can you give me a hand with the harrow?' he asked as he jumped down. 'I want to get the potatoes in today.'

Bruno helped him push out the broad harrow with its eight discs, and they fixed it to the tow bar. Then Junot turned off the motor, leaned against the big side wheel and began to roll himself a thin cigarette.

'You going to arrest me?'

'You tell me. Are you beating her?'

'It wasn't like that.' Junot lit his cigarette and squinted at Bruno through the smoke. 'It was Francette. She disappeared one weekend, came back two days later with some fancy new clothes, new hairstyle, perfume. I never saw her look so good.'

Junot shook his head, half-smiling at the memory, but then his face darkened. Bruno could almost see the frustration in the man, his pride in his daughter battling against his fears for her and his own shame at not being able to provide her with the clothes and life she craved.

'She looked like a different girl, but it was more than that,' Junot said, a harder note back in his voice. 'She acted different, like she had stars in her eyes. But she wouldn't say where she'd been or who paid for it all.'

He fell silent. Bruno waited a long moment and asked, 'What then?'

'She went away for a whole week, not telling us. I was frantic, wanted to call you or the Gendarmes. But the wife said, no, we had to let her go, have a bit of fun. Brigitte and I had a row after that, and then Francette came back, more

44

new clothes and one of those fancy bracelets and a little gold chain round her ankle. And then she said she'd be leaving home, and leaving her job at the supermarket. That rocked me. It's the only money we've got coming in. I mean, we always knew she'd leave one day, but it's been a bad couple of years and I didn't know how we'd be able to cope. So then there was a row, a bloody big one, shouting across the table. She called me a useless old drunk.'

'What did you call her?'

'What do you think? She comes back after a weekend away, new clothes, new hairdo, jewellery. If it had been a regular boyfriend, someone we could meet, well that would be all right. But she wouldn't say anything about him. I was frightened for her, Bruno. You hear things these days, about pimps and that. I was worried sick and I was drinking, so I said she was bloody well staying at home instead of going off like some cheap tart, and that's when it all went wrong.'

Bruno nodded encouragement, not wanting to break into Junot's recollection.

'I told her to go upstairs to her room, like I had when she was younger. She just laughed at me. So I went to give her a push up the stairs but she wouldn't go and we were shouting and then she slapped me. So I clipped her round the ear, but it was worse than I'd meant and she went down and then Brigitte was pulling at me so I backhanded her and she went down as well, and banged her side against the table and her face on the chair.'

He fell silent, looking at the ground by his feet. 'Twenty years married and that was the first time I ever laid a hand on her, and I wish to God I hadn't.' He drew on his cigarette but it had gone out and was too short to relight. He tossed it away and looked up. 'You going to arrest me?' he repeated.

'Just tell me what happened next.'

'It was a proper mess, nosebleed and everything. I stopped the nosebleed, cleaned her up and carried her upstairs. When I came down, Francette was gone. I don't know how but I thought I heard a car. That was the last we've heard of her. But if it was her fancy man, he must be local because I wasn't that long upstairs.'

'And that was the only time you hit Brigitte?'

Junot nodded. 'I wanted to take her down to the clinic to be looked at because there's a hell of a bruise on her side and I know she's in pain. But she wouldn't go. She said if she went there'd be an inquiry and I'd go to prison.'

'Let's take this one step at a time, Louis. Brigitte is hurt and I'm going to take her down to the *toubib*,' Bruno said, using the slang term for a doctor. 'But in the meantime, you better get that tractor started again and get those potatoes in.'

5

As a child in the church orphanage, Bruno's best friend had
been the little terrier that belonged to the cook. So he had
been distressed to hear in one of the sermons that he attended
as part of each day's Mass that animals had no souls. In his
memory, he had been six, perhaps seven. Not long after that
he had been released from the orphanage and dispatched to
the noisy, undisciplined home of the woman he was told was
his aunt. On his first night there he had cried, not for the
orphanage nor for the chaos of the six other children he was
told were his cousins, but for the loss of the little terrier. He
couldn't believe that it had no soul and that he would never
see it again in this life or the next. His refusal to accept that
sentence and the priestly authority from which it came was
the first moment he had known that he was Bruno, a person
who thought for himself and questioned whatever he was
told.

Now, as he greeted Hector and fed him his daily treat, he
relished the horsy, oily smell of the saddle that he placed on
Hector's back. He listened to Hector crunching the carrot and
rested his head against the welcoming warmth of the great
neck. Since the shooting of his dog Gigi by Basque terrorists,

Hector had become an emotional anchor for Bruno. As if by instinct at Bruno's loss, Hector after Gigi's death had drawn closer. He could never feel comfortable without an animal close to the centre of his life, a creature with intelligence and warmth in its eyes, with affection and trust in its greeting.

Bruno felt an understanding with his horse and a sympathy that confirmed his childhood conviction that the priest and the Church were wrong. He seldom thought much about faith and he liked his religion to be traditional and simple. But of one thing he was convinced; if *le Bon Dieu* was half as wise and merciful as they said, then he would want dogs and horses in heaven.

He led Hector from the stable with Bess and Victoria ambling behind on the leading rein. It was rare for him to ride alone. Usually he rode with Pamela, who owned the house and stable and had taught him to ride. Still known to most of the town by her first nickname as the Mad Englishwoman, she had become a popular figure in St Denis, where people thought of her as Bruno's girlfriend. Bruno would not have put it like that. He thought himself fortunate to be invited on occasion to share Pamela's bed. But she had made it clear that after a failed marriage back in Britain, she had no desire for any permanent relationship. And now she was back in Scotland caring for her mother after two devastating strokes, and Bruno had no idea if or when she planned to return.

Fabiola the doctor, Pamela's tenant in one of the gîtes that she normally rented to tourists in the summer, usually accompanied the morning and evening rides. But when Bruno had taken Brigitte Junot to the clinic Fabiola had explained that she'd have to be on duty this evening since she'd missed the morning surgery.

Bruno swung himself into the saddle and up the familiar lane from Pamela's house toward the bridle path up to the ridge. Pamela's two horses were a little older and slower, so Bruno guided Hector up the slope to the ridge at a gentle walk. Only once did his horse toss his head in a moment of impatience. Hector was accustomed to his evening gallop.

At the town clinic, Fabiola had simply ignored Bruno's inquiry about her absence in the morning, and steered Brigitte straight into the consulting room while Bruno was told to wait outside. After twenty minutes, Bruno had been summoned inside to be told that Junot's wife had two cracked ribs, suffered in a fall she insisted was an accident, and in no circumstances would she testify against her husband. Fabiola had been cool and businesslike with Bruno, warm and sympathetic with Brigitte. But she had asked Bruno to make regular visits to the Junot farm to ensure that no such 'accident' took place in the future.

Bruno had driven Brigitte home, where Junot was waiting at the farmhouse door. He came down to help his wife out of the passenger seat and lead her inside. A long stretch of land alongside the vegetable garden had been ploughed and tilled. The potatoes had been planted. Bruno followed them inside, and saw that Junot had cleaned the kitchen and set the dinner table for two without wine glasses. A jug of water stood on the table, alongside a small jam jar containing some freshly picked wildflowers. Bruno went to his van, took Junot's shotgun from the back, and hung it again on the pegs on the wall. 'You'd better have a hunting licence for my next visit,' he said. Then he left them alone.

He thought he had done the right thing in taking Brigitte back and Fabiola had seemed to agree, but Bruno wished he could have talked to her at greater length. He trusted his own instincts but he had come to rely on Fabiola's professional judgement when it came to medical and family matters. Her disappearing with some vague reference to a private patient was quite out of character, so Bruno sought another explanation. He wondered if some mutual friend had developed an illness too grave to be made public. It couldn't be the Mayor; he had seen him that morning. What of those tests on the Mayor's wife? Or Sergeant Jules at the Gendarmerie, whose rubicund face always seemed just a few more *p'tit apéros* away from a coronary. He grimaced; this was foolishness. Fabiola would tell him when she was ready.

Where the trees began to thicken into a forest, Bruno slowed the horses and dismounted. A wide firebreak was cut into the trees. Its smooth turf reminded Bruno of the fairways he'd encountered on those days when the Baron had tried to teach him to play golf. It had become a favourite spot for a brisk gallop. Today he could see a solitary rider standing silhouetted in the notch the firebreak made on the horizon, perhaps a kilometre away. He undid the leading reins from Bess and Victoria before climbing back into the saddle. Now the horses could go at their own speed, and Hector lengthened his stride into the run along the ridge that he enjoyed so much. The solitary rider had gone. It was at this time of evening, even more than when night fell and Bruno retired to his solitary bed, that he most missed Pamela.

She had taught him to ride, organized the birthday gift of Hector and become a trusted friend as well as a lover. For almost all of his life, in the orphanage and then in the military, he had been in masculine surroundings. Women were placed in convenient categories: wife and mother, nun and teacher, colleague and sister, lover. But women had never been friends before. Indeed, he remembered nodding in agreement when some rugby club sage had suggested that friendship between the sexes was impossible: the sexual current would always flow. So it did, he thought, and so it must. But just because he found Fabiola attractive, or because he was privileged to spend some of his nights with Pamela, that didn't mean that there was no friendship. He liked them, enjoyed spending time with them and their shared responsibility for the horses. Above all, he trusted them, in the way that he trusted the Mayor and the Baron, some old army friends and a handful of men in the town.

Now the gathering speed of Hector's run through the firebreak blew from his mind all thoughts of anything save the gallop and the sense of Hector's power beneath him. With the drumming of the hoofs and the wind in his face, Bruno felt wonderfully alive and knew that he was laughing aloud as he passed a small clearing and caught, from the corner of his eye, a glimpse of another rider on a white horse.

It took something from his pleasure, his assumption that he was alone with a horse he adored in woods that he knew. He was being foolish; his communion with nature did not require solitude and the woods were big enough for everyone. Still, slowing Hector to a canter and then to a trot as the end of the turf approached, he felt the real world start to intrude once more. Once stopped, he checked his phone and saw that he'd missed a call from Pamela. As he waited for Bess and Victoria to amble up the ride towards them, Bruno returned her call.

'How is your mother?' he began, after they exchanged greetings.

'Not much change. My aunt insists that she recognizes us, but I doubt it. She seems to react the same way whoever comes into her room, the doctor or a nurse or even the cleaner. Anyway, I'm going to have to make a decision, because the doctor says she's stabilized now and she'll have to leave the hospital.'

Her mother would need full-time care. Pamela had looked at various homes in Britain but the only ones that she deemed tolerable were alarmingly expensive, so costly that they would devour the value of her mother's house and her savings within a few years. Bringing her to France might be an option, but Pamela had no illusions about the emotional drain it would be to keep a comatose mother at home. They had talked it through on the phone before; there were no good options.

Bruno told Pamela of the ride, of the horses, and of the strange appearance of the dead woman in the punt, the pentagram and the candles and the bottle.

'What was the brand?' Pamela asked at once. 'The vodka.'

'I didn't notice and it's gone to the lab now to be tested for prints and probably contents. Why?'

'If it's a rare brand, it might give you a lead. I don't know, it just struck me as possibly important.' She broke off. 'Listen, Bruno, I'm going to have to come back, maybe next week, for a few days to do some admin and find out if it's going to be possible to cope with my mother at home. Maybe I can find a young school-leaver who can combine some cleaning with keeping an eye on Mother, like babysitting, to give me a break.'

'You know what the minimum wage is here, and then you can almost double it for the social charges,' Bruno said. 'But I'll ask around.'

Pamela rang off, and Bruno saw that Bess and Victoria, who had done this ride with Pamela a thousand times, had reached the end of the firebreak and had now turned round and begun to trot back. He put the phone into its holster and urged Hector into a trot, pondering the impact the arrival of Pamela's mother might have on their affair. At that moment he spotted a white horse being led by a tall woman emerging from the small clearing. It was presumably the same horse he had seen from the corner of his eye.

'Can you hear me this time?' came a woman's voice. She was standing at the far side of the horse, and as she spoke she removed her black riding cap and pulled something at the back of her neck to release a great rush of dark, glossy hair that fell over her shoulders. She stepped forward, and he heard the clicking of spurs on her riding boots. Pamela had taught him never to wear them; his horse should work with him through trust rather than fear. It took him a moment to recognize the woman from the white sports car. Her name came to him: Eugénie.

'Yes, I hear you,' he said, stopping. 'But I didn't know you'd spoken before. Can I help?'

'My horse started limping. I think maybe he has something caught in his shoe.' She spoke like a Parisian but there was some regional accent underneath it that he couldn't identify, perhaps Alsace or somewhere near the Swiss border. Without the sunglasses, her eyes were dark brown. With her raven-black hair he'd have expected an olive complexion, something of the south. Instead she had the light skin of a blonde.

Bruno dismounted, tying Hector's reins loosely around the nearest tree, and fixing the leading rein to Victoria and Bess. The two mares ambled across to Eugénie's horse, which whinnied in greeting. She looked lame, favouring a foreleg.

'Do you know your horse well?' he asked her when his horses were secure. 'Have you looked at her foot?'

'It's only the second time I've ridden her and she won't let me look at it.'

The horse didn't look temperamental. A mare, she was smaller and looked a lot older than Hector. She seemed calm in the company of Bess and Victoria. Bruno approached her through them, trailing his hand across Bess's flanks. The white mare let him stroke her nose and he began whispering to her as he'd seen Pamela do to a strange horse. Finally he knelt and felt the foreleg. There was no swelling so he picked up the foot to examine the shoe and found that it was hanging slightly loose, two of the nails gone and others on their way. He didn't see how Eugénie could have ridden it without noticing it, or hearing it. He took a small all-purpose tool from the pouch on his belt and unfolded the pliers, pulled out the remaining nails and handed the woman the horse-shoe.

'I'd walk her home if I were you,' he said. Some might have called Eugénie beautiful, her complexion a perfect ivory and her features classic. But there was a lack of animation or perhaps too much self-control in her face. He would like to see her laugh, or be excited by something. 'And she'll need to see a *maréchal* before you ride her again.'

'You know your horses, *Monsieur le chef de police*,' she said, making no move to leave nor to comfort her horse. 'You must be an expert, from the speed you were going when you raced past me.'

'I'm a beginner,' he laughed. 'I only started riding last year, but I've had a great teacher and a wonderful horse. This is Hector. He's the expert, not me.'

He expected her to say, 'Hello, Hector,' or to make some friendly overture or even to thank him. Instead, after a brief pause to consider what he had said and while keeping her features immobile, she asked, 'Where do I find this *maréchal*?'

He raised his eyebrows. Any horsewoman should know that. 'In the phone book, under c for *chevaux*. There's one in Sarlat and another in Bergerac, or try the stables at Meyrals. There's an old stable hand called Victor who knows a lot more about horses and horseshoes than most blacksmiths.'

She gave neither acknowledgement nor thanks, and her face remained impassive. And again there was the pause before she spoke.

'Is there any news about the woman in the boat? Has she been identified yet?' she asked.

Bruno shrugged. 'Not that I've heard. We're waiting for the pathologist's report. But she's not on any of the lists of missing persons in this *Département*.'

'I thought you could identify everybody these days, with teeth and fingerprints and DNA.'

'Sure, if you simply want to confirm someone's identity and you have their dental records and the DNA of a relative. But if you have no reference to go on, as in this case, then it's very slow and uncertain. If we're lucky, her fingerprints may be on file somewhere. Otherwise, we may never identify her.'

'So what you need would be a national data base of DNA and dentistry, then you could identify anyone.'

'In theory, yes, if the computer program worked and if the dentists never misfiled their records and the courts didn't condemn it as a breach of human rights.' He spoke lightly, trying to be jocular, conscious of a slight sense of challenge in trying to provoke some life into her face. He did not succeed.

'What about those markings on the body?' she asked. 'Perhaps they could help identify her.'

'If they had been tattoos, you could be right. But they were temporary markings.'

She raised an eyebrow. 'You must have heard the radio, that business about Satanism.'

'No, I didn't hear the radio. But I talked to the reporter and said it seemed far-fetched. It doesn't seem to have stopped him.'

'You don't take it seriously?'

'Death is always serious, but I don't know what the devil has to do with it.'

'Your local priest sounded rather alarmed, according to what I heard on the radio. And he seemed to know what he was talking about.'

'So he should. He's a priest,' Bruno said. 'Getting alarmed about the devil is part of his job description.'

She considered this. 'You mean like that line from Voltaire – "God will pardon me; it's his profession."'

Bruno smiled. 'That sounds about right, but I didn't know it came from Voltaire.'

'These clever sayings usually do,' she said with a sudden and unexpected smile. It felt to Bruno like a reward. 'That's why I always say Voltaire when I don't really know.' She fell silent, but the smile lingered on her lips and she waited, as if expecting him to say something.

'Are you living down here or just visiting?' he asked. He remembered that Foucher had called her his partner. She wore no wedding ring, just a curiously shaped black band in some dull metal that seemed to curl sinuously up her index finger like a tiny snake. Her eyes followed his glance and she shifted her grip on her horse's bridle.

'Visiting, but I might end up staying some time,' she said. Again there was that short pause, as if waiting for a translation, before her reply.

'The Mayor told me about the plans for a holiday village,' he said, aware that his probing was clumsy and that she'd realize he was simply trying to prolong the conversation. 'That's a big piece of land to put together.'

She said nothing, didn't even shrug. 'I must be getting back. Among other things, there's an old lady I have to look after.'

Bruno's thoughts went back to his phone conversation with Pamela. Perhaps this woman would know something useful about caring for the elderly.

'Do you do it yourself or do you hire specialists?' he asked.

'I do it. I had a very wise . . .' She paused, as if choosing the next word with care. 'A very wise guardian who said I would grow too tall to be a dancer, so he made sure I trained as a nurse.'

This time there was a hint of another expression on her face; the faintest tightening of the mouth and a lowering of eyebrows. It passed as quickly as the dappling of sunlight through the hesitant leaves of springtime. She turned, leading the horse back through the clearing to the bridle path that led down to the river. '*Au revoir.*'

He wanted to ask her if she still danced and how far she had pursued it, but instead he watched her go, hearing her spurs catch and click, thinking he should have advised her to remove them while she walked through the wood.

6

Bruno had risen early, fed his chickens and been for a run through the woods behind his home, knowing the paths too well to be distracted by the mists that rose from the river at this time of year. It was at times like this that he most missed Gigi, the way the dog had trotted beside him and then darted away to follow some new scent, before finding his way back to rejoin Bruno for the final sprint along the ridge back to the house. He would have to find another dog. But Gigi had come from a litter of the Mayor's hunting hound, and she was now too old for breeding. He would wait until he found a puppy from a strain he knew that he could raise and train himself.

He stopped at the newest of the town's five *boulangeries*, a place with an artificial windmill that had become popular partly because it was the only bakery with its own car park. The other reason was Louise, the baker's attractive wife, who pursed her lips to blow Bruno a kiss as she staggered back into the shop carrying a tray filled with fresh loaves. He waved back and stood in line, greeting the others who were waiting, and bought three croissants and a baguette. They were still warm when he parked at Antoine's camping site where he could smell fresh coffee.

'Thanks for doing this,' Bruno said as Antoine pushed a cup of coffee across the bar towards him followed by a jar of apricot jam made by his wife, Josette.

'He's looking forward to it,' Josette said, coming in from the kitchen with butter and hot milk. 'He always likes doing a trip down the river at the start of the season, to see how the banks and currents have shifted.'

'And I'm just as curious as you about where our mystery woman could have gone into the river,' Antoine said, tearing his croissant in half to dip it in his coffee. 'Any news about her, who she might have been?'

His mouth full of croissant, Bruno shook his head. 'Still waiting for the autopsy,' he said, swallowing. 'By the way, do you remember anything about that bottle in the punt?'

'Vodka, some Russian writing, can't say I remember.' He turned and looked at the bottles lined up on the shelves above his bar. 'It looked like the Smirnoff I sell.' Bruno made a mental note to check if the forensic team had followed up.

They loaded a canoe onto the trailer and climbed into the van for the drive upriver to Montignac, nearly thirty kilometres away and the farthest point from which the punt could have drifted in the time the woman had been dead. Antoine reckoned it had been put into the water much closer to St Denis, but it was best to be sure. Bruno assumed that the woman had been alive when she got into the punt and took her lethal cocktail of pills and vodka, so time of death might not be the most reliable guide to her embarkation point.

The morning was still fresh when they donned life jackets

60

and put the canoe into the water, while Josette drove the van back to the campsite. Antoine settled at the stern, sending Bruno to the bow, and baited the row of hooks before fixing his fishing line to a bracket beside him. Then he put an unopened bottle of Bergerac Sec into a string bag, tied the bag to the boat and lowered the wine into the water to keep cool. There was no one else on the river as they paddled downstream, pausing to look at each boathouse and landing stage. Most of them were still padlocked from the winter, and they saw no signs of recent footprints or launchings.

Bruno thought he knew his river reasonably well, but it was the road and pathways he knew far better than this special viewpoint from the water. The trailing fronds of the willows cast a dappled light before being overtaken by the sudden darkness cast from the majestic oaks and chestnut trees. The river could seem black and still as night one moment and as clear as glass the next before frothing into ripples over the sudden shallows. The current was steady, a little slower than walking pace, speeding as the river turned into a curve before slowing into a deceptive stillness that seemed so perfect Bruno hardly wanted to disturb the surface with his paddle. The rhythm of his paddling was almost soporific, and even as he tried to focus on each possible landing, his thoughts kept drifting.

Helping Eugénie and her horse the previous evening had made him late for dinner. He'd been looking forward to it, an invitation to Florence's apartment beside the college where she now worked. They had been six at table: the headmaster

61

Rollo and his wife Mathilde, Serge the sports teacher and one of the stars of the town's rugby team, and an unusually subdued Fabiola.

It had been a simple meal. Smoked salmon to begin, roast chicken, a salad with an array of local cheeses followed by an apple tart bought from Fauquet's. Sensibly, Florence had bought local wines. With the bottle of Pomerol that was Bruno's contribution and Rollo's bottle of Chablis, and the table made colourful by the bouquet of daffodils that Fabiola had brought, the evening had been a success.

Bruno had been pleased for Florence. Not only was it her first dinner party in St Denis but in Rollo she was also hosting her boss. Bruno had known Rollo so long it was a mild shock to think of him that way, but Florence had ever so slightly deferred to him and gone out of her way to include his wife, Mathilde, in the conversation. Inevitably, some of the talk had turned to questions of the college: the shortage of teachers prepared to work in rural areas, the lack of jobs for school-leavers, the curriculum changes. Bruno had taken advantage of the theme to ask if Rollo or Serge remembered Francette Junot.

'She could have been a good athlete, but like a lot of girls she lost interest after reaching puberty,' Serge had said. Rollo recalled that she'd had a gift for maths, but had never applied herself to schoolwork, as if determined to leave school and start working as soon as she could. The conversation had been about to take another turn when Mathilde said, 'I didn't know her well, but she was a deeply unhappy girl.'

Everyone sat up at that point. Mathilde, who worked part-time in a local accountant's office, was not known for involving herself much in school affairs.

'A man probably wouldn't notice, but she never had the right kind of clothes, and the other girls made fun of her. Once I heard them sneer at her for wearing clothes from the *Action Catholique*, one of the other girls' cast-offs. Kids can be so cruel at that age. That's probably why she couldn't wait to leave school.'

A silence had fallen until Florence said brightly that with her new job, her own days of getting clothes from the charity shop were now in the past. Bruno was relieved that he had remarked on entering how attractive Florence was looking, and had noticed that her blonde hair had been cut and shaped so that it softened her rather long face.

A grunt from Antoine and a sudden flurry of movement at the back of the canoe brought Bruno back to the present. Antoine had a bite. The green hills that rose on each side of the river had begun to give way to cliffs of white chalk and grey stone and the bridge at Thonac was just coming into view. Antoine put down his paddle and pulled in his line. Two small trout were wriggling on his hooks.

'That'll do,' he said, and pulled a small wooden board and some limes from his bag and took his Laguiole knife from his belt. 'You keep paddling, Bruno, and we'll have our *casse-croûte* before you know it.'

Bruno kept glancing back to watch Antoine gut the fish and put the slim fillets he had carved into a plastic bag. Then he halved the limes and squeezed their juice into the bag until there was enough to cover the white flesh. He re-baited his hooks and continued to paddle.

By the time they reached the church of St Léon-sur-Vézère after the first of the long bends, the sun was climbing steadily and Bruno had taken off his shirt. They had looked at three more locked boathouses and some rickety landing-stages with so much moss on them it was plain they had not been used since the previous year. There were two possible sites where the punt could have gone into the river, and Bruno had marked them on his map. Each was a place where canoes were rented out in the summer, and Antoine knew the boatmen and promised to call them and check.

Just after St Léon the river divided into different channels as it ran between sandbanks covered with pebbles. Antoine beached the canoe on one of these and opened the wine. Bruno halved the baguette as Antoine opened the plastic bag and shared out the strips of fish soaked in lime juice. Bruno relished the sensation, tart but fresh, tasting a thousand times better here on the river with the sounds of water lapping over the shallows.

'My favourite *casse-croûte*,' said Antoine. 'And with any luck we'll fry up fresh trout for lunch. There's a place I know just downstream by the old monastery that teems with fish. My dad used to tell me it was centuries of the monks' latrines seeping into the river.'

'Now you tell me,' Bruno replied, grinning.

They pushed off and paddled further into the familiar landscape of limestone cliffs and caves. The cliffs towered above them and the erosion of the river over centuries had carved

64

deep overhangs so that the stone loomed overhead as if ready to topple down upon them. The trees were thick on the inner bank, and without the heat of the sun Bruno shivered in the sudden chill, made all the more eerie by the way the skirls of mist rose from the water.

Up to his right Bruno now saw emerging high on a cliff a regular formation of stone that looked like the battlements of some giant's castle. Beneath them ranged a series of cave entrances and then what looked like a gallery carved deep into the rock, the interior lost in shadows.

'This is where they always bite,' Antoine's voice broke in. 'That's the old monastery up there and the hermits' cells. Over on the other side you can just see the towers of Château Marzac above the lower ridge . . .' He paused. 'Got one.'

He pulled in his line to reveal two wriggling trout, each about twenty centimetres long. He detached the hooks and put them in his catch net and dropped it back over the side of the canoe. No sooner had he re-baited his hooks and put the line back into the water than he caught another, and a fourth bit as he began to haul the line back in.

'Told you this was a good spot,' he said.

They came to a stretch where the river widened and the sun shone down over a low pebbled island in the middle of the stream. Antoine steered the canoe under some low-hanging boughs that made Bruno duck. Then they were in a small and hidden lagoon with a tiny pebble beach and beside it a tumbledown wooden boathouse.

'*Tiens*,' said Antoine. 'The river's broken through.' He pointed with his paddle to a spot beneath overhanging trees where Bruno could see the flow of the main river coming into the lagoon. He took them close to the point where the river gushed in, less than a metre wide, but he and Bruno had to paddle to hold the canoe steady against the strong current.

'How would the river have done that?' Bruno asked.

'*Ecrevisses*,' said Antoine. Crayfish, small freshwater crustaceans that looked like miniature lobsters and tasted even better, had probably nibbled and nibbled away at some long-sunken log that held the dam together even as the river scoured and eroded it from the other side. Then came a strong rain, a flood surge in the river and the dam gave way.

'So if she committed suicide here, she could have expected that her boat would remain inside the lagoon,' Bruno suggested. 'She wasn't to know it was no longer a lagoon, and the new current carried her out to the main stream. Could it have happened like that?'

'Maybe,' Antoine replied, 'but only if she wanted to keep her death secret. Remember the *toubib*'s theory? Gelletreau said she might have wanted the world to see her body, to make a big display.'

Antoine let the current take them back into the middle of the tree-fringed lagoon and steered them to the small beach where they landed and walked up to the old boathouse. There was no padlock on the door, just a simple wooden latch. Inside was the wreck of an old sailboat, big enough for an adult and a child, its mast worm-eaten. To one side was a space with smears in the dust. Old clothes hung on hooks on the wall alongside loops of ropes of different sizes. He

66

touched some of the hanging clothes and dust rose, except for one dark garment. He took it from the hook and held it up. It was a robe of some kind with a hood, of coarse wool. It carried a faint scent of something, possibly perfume, possibly the merest hint of woodsmoke. The aroma was elusive, disappearing before Bruno could begin to identify it. But at least it had been used fairly recently.

'I'd say that it was a punt that lay here,' said Antoine, gesturing at the gap beside the crumbling sailboat. He pointed up to the sagging rafters where two long poles lay across the beams. 'Those are punt poles.'

They went outside and looked at the scrape marks from the doors to the water. The earth around them was scuffed, but that could have been the usual markings of ducks, voles and water rats that used the riverbanks.

'A punt could have been launched here, and one was certainly kept there,' said Antoine. 'You may have found your spot.'

The boathouse was part of the land that belonged to the Red Château, Antoine explained, so named because of the owner, the Red Countess. The name rang a very distant bell with Bruno.

'You're too young to remember,' Antoine said. 'But she was famous in her day, an aristocrat in the Communist Party. She was always in the papers, leading demonstrations, making speeches. But the Red Countess was also a celebrity, Cannes film festival and the races at Longchamps, all that sort of thing. Yves Montand was a boyfriend, and Camus before he killed himself. And Malraux, of course.'

The Red Countess, thought Bruno. It was one of those names you knew you ought to know, from an era just before his own. Somehow it sparked memories of newsreels he'd seen of another, much older France in the 1950s: Jean-Paul Sartre and a huge Communist Party, Piaf at the Olympia and Jacques Brel and smoky nightclubs on the Left Bank. But the name triggered other associations: the *Chant des Partisans* and the parade of the heroes of the Resistance at the Arc de Triomphe each year on 18 June, the anniversary of the day de Gaulle had launched the Resistance over the radio from London. He asked if there was a connection, and Antoine nodded.

'She was a courier for the Resistance round here when she was a kid, an upper-class teenage girl on a bike. She always got through the roadblocks. She got medals for it, after the war.'

'She was born here?' Bruno asked. He'd been in St Denis for more than ten years but there was still a lot of the local history that he didn't know.

'It's the family estate and it's where she grew up. She used to come from time to time but I haven't heard anything about her for years. My uncle worked for her as a gardener, worshipped her. I even met her once when she came to see my uncle in his shed, sometime in the late Fifties. I'd have been eight, maybe nine. She was a stunner. I've still got the book she gave me, about King Arthur and his knights of the round table.' He paused and laughed. 'I kept imagining her in it, you know how kids do.'

Bruno nodded. 'How far is the château?' he asked.

'A few hundred metres, but it's up the slope above the

flood level and behind that cliff, in a kind of fold in the hill.'
Antoine looked at his watch. 'If you want to make some
inquiries, you'd better come back another time. We've got a
lot of river to cover.'

As they returned to the main stream and rounded the bend
that led to the bridge before the Grand Roc, they saw on the
far bank a handsome new dock and terrace. Steps of bright
new stone and a gravel pathway led upwards to a fold in the
hills, with a large terrace and restored building of the local
honey-coloured stone just visible. A woman was standing on
the dock, shading her eyes. Bruno raised his paddle in salute
and she waved back.

'I haven't seen that dock before, but they were working on
this place last year. It's just down the hill from the old village
of St Philippon, the one that was abandoned. You can just
see the top of the chapel up on the ridge,' said Antoine. 'Better
take a look.'

'Welcome to the Auberge St Philippon,' the woman said
once they crossed the river to greet her and introduced themselves. She had the long-limbed look of a tennis player and
beautifully cut fair hair. Bruno felt sure her hairdresser was
based a long way from St Denis. She told them to call her
Béatrice and that she was the manager of the newly restored
inn. Bruno guessed she was in her early forties and spending
time and effort to look younger. Dressed in a blue and white
striped shirt-waist dress, she had a twinkle in her eye, as if
to say she found life endlessly delightful. Bruno explained
his mission and her face turned grave.

'I've seen no dead women floating past here, but you're

welcome to come and ask the staff and guests. And perhaps you'd like a drink. That paddling must be warm work,' she said. 'As you can see, we've no boathouse yet and no boats for my new dock. You'll be christening it for me, the first guests to arrive by water.'

The dock stood a good metre and more above the level of the river. There was as yet no ramp to haul boats ashore and not even the foundations of a boathouse. Bruno had heard of plans for the new hotel but was surprised to learn it was already open. Antoine tied the canoe to the dock and they took off their life jackets and donned their shirts, Bruno conscious of Béatrice casting an eye over his naked torso, and clambered up a wooden ladder. Once on the dock, Bruno realized that looking upward from the canoe he'd misjudged Béatrice's height. She barely came up to his nose, but somehow her clothes made her look taller. Her watch was a Cartier Tank, a model he recognized because a previous girlfriend had brought a counterfeit back from a trip to China, and worn it even after it stopped working. Bruno felt certain Béatrice was wearing the real thing.

As the path curved uphill, a windsock on a large and flat stretch of grass signalled a helicopter pad and beyond it the auberge began to emerge. Inn seemed too modest a term for the building. He guessed it was eighteenth-century, and expensively restored. It had two main storeys of tall windows with open grey shutters, and smaller semicircular windows in a mansard roof of dark slate. Wide steps led up to a handsome pillared porch with double doors flanked by two weathered stone cupids holding vases filled with daffodils. There was no hotel name that Bruno could see, no brass plate and no porter at the entrance.

'It's quite a place, Madame,' said Bruno. 'You must have earned a great reputation in the hotel business to be appointed manager here. Where did you work before?'

'In Paris, mainly corporate hospitality and private dining,' she replied smoothly. 'We expect that to be the main focus here.'

Béatrice led them to the side of the auberge where tables under umbrellas half-filled the wide stone terrace. Part of it was shaded by a trellis of vines. Some of the tables were set for lunch, and at one Bruno saw two Arabs, who looked like military men in civilian clothes, eating fish while an elegant businessman spoke to them in French. At another table three men were speaking Russian. The table nearest a modern sculpture that was also a fountain was filled with three men enjoying their apéritifs. As they turned to look at the new arrivals, Bruno saw one tall and handsome stranger in middle age and two men he knew. The first was Foucher, the young man in the white Jaguar who had plunged into the river the previous day. The second was Bruno's friend and tennis partner the Baron, the retired industrialist who was the main landowner of St Denis.

'My dear Bruno, what a pleasure,' said the Baron, rising and stepping forward to embrace him and then to shake Antoine's hand. 'I see you've already met the entrancing Béatrice and I gather you've met young Foucher here, but let me introduce my new friend César de Vexin, who unlike me is a real aristo with a name that goes far back. He's a Count as well as being the man behind this new holiday village project, and we're just talking a little business.'

'Don't let me interrupt,' said Bruno, amused to see the appreciative sideways glances the Baron kept casting at Béatrice. 'Antoine and I have been searching the river, looking for the place where that dead woman could have entered the water. You probably heard of it.'

'Heard of it,' said Vexin, raising a thick eyebrow and smoothing his rather long and glossy black hair back with a hand that wore a gold signet ring. 'It's all over the paper.'

From a vacant chair he lifted a copy of *Sud-Ouest* and held up the front page. The main photo had been taken from the bridge at St Denis and showed the woman lying on her back, arms outstretched. Conscious of their family readership, the editors had put black bars over her breasts and pubis, but there was a close-up of the pentagram on her belly and the large headline read: 'Satanism in St Denis?'

7

'This is monstrous. Not at all the image of St Denis that we want to present,' said the Mayor, flinging the copy of *Sud-Ouest* onto the council table with disdain.

'I'm not sure about that,' said Jérôme, who ran a small history theme park where Joan of Arc was burned at the stake twice a day. 'This kind of thing makes us stand out from the crowd; it could be just the kind of publicity we need.'

'We've had a rush of bookings this morning,' added Philippe, who ran the Hôtel St Denis. On the council he usually acted as the spokesman for the town's businessmen. He pointed down to the town square. 'The bars and cafés are full already. It may not be the image you want, but it's certainly attracting visitors.'

'The devil moves in mysterious ways,' said Father Sentout. No great friend of the Mayor, his presence at this meeting of the town's elders testified to the Mayor's unease.

Bruno leafed through the paper, to a photo of Foucher in mid-air, diving towards the punt and another of Bruno and Antoine standing beside Maurice as he cast his fishing line in vain. The paper seemed to have missed the significance of the black candles and there was no reference to the decapitated cockerel. Bruno would try to keep that to himself.

'The immediate reaction was bound to include some ghoulish interest. But think about the longer term. I really don't think we want to be known as a town of devil-worshippers,' the Mayor said. He turned to Bruno. 'Perhaps you could give us an interim report on the investigation. Do we yet know who this unfortunate woman was?'

Bruno told them no. She did not appear to be on any lists of missing persons. With no obvious cause of death and no sign on the body of foul play but evidence of heavy cocaine use, the most likely explanation was a suicide.

'I have some leads and I'll be following those up with the *Police Nationale*.'

'Maybe we can turn this talk of Satanism to our advantage,' suggested Jérôme. 'We could get some good publicity from that.' He turned to Father Sentout. 'I'm thinking of an exorcism ceremony at the bridge.'

'Ridiculous, we'd be a laughing stock,' snapped the Mayor. Bruno looked up in surprise. That wasn't like him. The Mayor was a wily old politician who usually waited to gauge the mood of any meeting before he committed himself. A silence fell.

'It might be a little premature,' the priest said, smoothing over the sudden tension. 'There's no sign that anyone has been possessed. But there is one thing that disturbs me . . .'

He paused for effect, and everyone at the council table leaned forward. Bruno smiled to himself. Father Sentout was just as skilled a player as the Mayor.

'It's the nature of the ritual that intrigues me. Features of this death remind me of one of the classic examples of Satanism. The naked woman with arms outstretched in the rough form of a cross, the pentagram scrawled on the body, the black candles . . .'

'Go on,' said the Mayor, as fascinated as the rest of them.

'It has most of the trappings of a classic Black Mass, but not all. In the classic form of this abomination there would be a mockery of Holy Communion. The Host, which in a real Mass becomes the body of Christ, becomes a tool of the devil's depravity in the Black Mass. It is usually placed in the private parts of the naked woman on whom the Mass is performed.'

Bruno remembered the item that Dr Gelletreau had taken with his tweezers from the dead woman's vagina. He'd have to call the pathologist and get him to check.

'There would also be some form of sacrifice,' the priest went on. 'A black cockerel was the usual victim, its head cut off and its blood smeared on the naked woman, another mockery of the way that Holy Communion transforms the wine into the blood of Christ.'

'When you say the classic form of the Black Mass, Father, what's the basis of that?' Bruno asked. He was curious, and unlike the Mayor he had a soft spot for the plump little priest. He'd enjoyed some magnificent meals at Father Sentout's home, but also the priest was devoted to the fortunes of the town's rugby team and to supporting the *minimes*, the kids' team that Bruno coached. The priest held a special service for them each year, with the proceeds from the collection box going to the purchase of rugby shirts and the travel budget for away games.

'Most of what we know of the Black Mass comes from the reign of *le roi soleil*, the Sun King Louis XIV, and the incident known to history as the Affair of the Poisons,' the priest began, visibly preening at this chance to display his knowledge. 'It was the great scandal of the age, the seventeenth-century equivalent of the Kennedy assassination. There were pamphlets about it published all over Europe.'

He reminded them that the king had a famous mistress, the celebrated Madame de Montespan, who came from one of the oldest and noblest families of France. Thanks to her noble blood and her mother's connections at court, she had been appointed a lady-in-waiting to the King's wife, Queen Marie-Thérèse of Austria.

'*Putain de merde*,' muttered Montsouris, the town's only Communist councillor. 'I knew the bloody aristos would be behind all this.'

At the time, the priest continued, the King already had a mistress, Louise de la Vallière, and Madame de Montespan resolved to replace her. To do so, she resorted to witchcraft. Her first ally was a wise woman or witch, used by several women at the court to abort unwanted pregnancies, named Catherine Monvoisin. She then recruited a renegade priest, Etienne Guibourg, to perform a Black Mass that would produce a love potion to win the King's heart. The potion was concocted from the desecrated Host that had been placed in Madame de Montespan's vagina during the Black Mass. The result was a scandal and a trial in which the witch was executed and the priest imprisoned, but with Madame de Montespan securely ensconced in the royal bed.

'How did she get away with it?' asked the Mayor. Bruno smiled to himself. Father Sentout had seldom had such an avid audience.

'Some say her sensual charms won the king's devotion and thus her immunity, but I prefer to think it all the work of Satan,' said the priest. 'And what we know of the dead woman who floated through our town yesterday replicates very closely the Black Mass performed on the naked body of Madame de Montespan over three centuries ago.'

Jérôme suddenly spoke, a curious, almost greedy light in his eyes. 'You know, this gives me an idea. We've been thinking of expanding the theme park, and this might be just the thing for a new exhibit. Louis XIV, a royal mistress, a Black Mass – it would certainly bring in the punters.'

The Mayor quelled Jérôme with a glance. 'Any such proposal for an expansion would not be welcomed by the *Mairie*,' he said, and glared around the table. 'Now you know why I'm so cross at all this talk of Satanism. You, Father, should have known better.'

'I'm aware that some of you may wish to criticize me for the remarks quoted in the newspaper this morning, but the history cannot be gainsaid,' the priest replied equably. 'And it is my duty, when I see Satan's works unfolding, to take up arms in the name of *le bon Dieu*.'

The priest looked around the table, seeing scepticism replace fascination on several faces. Bruno saw him weighing each one, dismissing those who were known to be devout Catholics since their support was to be expected, and looking for those who occupied that middle ground between mild agnosticism and a vague, traditional loyalty to the teachings of the Church. The priest's eyes finally alighted on Bruno.

'You may never have come to confession, Bruno,' he said. 'But I know that some of the things that you saw in Bosnia showed you that evil still stalks the world.'

'The evil was done by men, Father, not by any supernatural being,' Bruno replied.

'How are you so sure? You of all people, my dear Bruno, must know that there can be love and kindness in the midst of such horrors. Is that not a proof of the presence of God?'

Bruno wondered how much Father Sentout knew of his time in Bosnia and his tragic, aborted love affair with Katarina, the Bosnian schoolteacher whom his unit had rescued, along with some other women, from the Serbian military brothel where they had been imprisoned and forced into prostitution. It was a deeply private memory, of which he very seldom spoke. But each year when the dampness of autumn came, the ache in his hip where the Serb bullet had knocked him spinning into the snow took him back to that nightmare time in the hills around Sarajevo. He sighed inwardly, thinking how few secrets anyone could keep in a small town.

'Love is what happens between people, Father,' he said. 'I don't know that we need God to explain it.'

'It is because, my dear Bruno, some of those same people who committed the greatest evils are also capable of great acts of mercy and gentleness,' the priest said. 'They are forever at war within us, God and Satan, and our souls are never in greater danger than when we forget that. Whatever the motives of those who dabble in Satanism, real evil is at work here. We ignore that at our peril, and while my fear is for your immortal souls, you must think of the danger to our town if this wickedness thrives unchecked.'

The priest sat back, slumping as though suddenly exhausted, and then spoke from deep within his chest. 'This is not the end of it, you mark my words,' he intoned.

The Mayor cleared his throat. 'Thank you, Father, for that very interesting historical perspective, but I'm not sure the intrigues of the court of Louis XIV are our particular concern. I think it's clear that we're probably dealing with the suicide of an unbalanced woman, and that is the line we should all take, including you, Father, in the event of further inquiries from the media.'

'Just one more thing, *Monsieur le Maire*,' said Bruno, and went on to explain the results of his search of the river. 'We have three likely spots for the launch of the boat and a couple of possibles. I'll be visiting each of them from the land side with a detective from the staff of Commissaire Jalipeau of the *Police Nationale*.'

Bruno described the lagoon by the Red Château, a busy boathouse and landing dock near Les Eyzies and a small creek with a crumbling landing stage below the Maison-Forte of Reignac.

'The Red Countess,' said the Mayor, sitting back with a wistful smile on his face. 'I haven't heard that name in years. Whatever became of her? She must be well into her eighties.'

'Not dead, that's for sure,' said Montsouris. 'She'd have had a hell of a funeral and I'd have heard about it. The Party loved her. *Merde*, I'd have gone up to Paris for that and we'd have had mourning on all the trains.'

'De Gaulle called her a heroine of France, you remember?' said the Mayor. 'It was after she had that illegitimate child by some dead Resistance hero. Didn't they make a film about her?'

'It was called *The Red Countess*,' said Louis Fouton, a retired schoolteacher who was the oldest man at the table. 'I saw it when I was a boy and I remember a lot of misty close-ups and German soldiers shouting "*Achtung*" and "*Donner und Blitzen*" as we clever French ran rings round them. An escaped Russian prisoner-of-war played the hero. I remember the photos of the Red Countess in the Kremlin when she went for the Moscow premiere.'

'She used to lead those demonstrations against our war in Indo-China back in the Fifties, and then she supported the Algerian independence movement,' said the Mayor.

'She never saw a national liberation movement she didn't like,' said Fouton, filling his old pipe. In respect for his age, he was the last person allowed to smoke inside the council chamber. 'And she never saw a handsome man she didn't appreciate.'

'She's a descendant, you know, of Madame de Montespan,' Father Sentout said into the silence as the men around the table searched their memories for half-remembered stories that explained the Countess's fame.

'The Red Countess?' scoffed Montsouris. '*Va t'en foutre.*'

'No, she's descended from Montespan and one of the illegitimate children of Louis XIV,' the priest insisted. 'I remember looking into it. The château was one of the gifts from the king after he took her back in defiance of the Church.'

'If she's still alive, where is she?' the Mayor asked. 'If she were living down here, I imagine we'd know about it.'

'She's mainly lived in Paris. There's a younger sister who's here from time to time,' said Father Sentout. 'I was called once to say Mass in the private family chapel. It's an impressive place, a bit run down.'

'I presume there's a housekeeper, someone to answer the door when I make inquiries,' Bruno said.

'It's not in our commune so I don't know if they pay the *taxe d'habitation* but we can find out,' said the Mayor. He stood up, signalling that the meeting was over. 'And remember, gentlemen, this is a tragic suicide by a disturbed woman, probably under the influence of drugs, and we'll have no more speculation about devil worship or long-dead royal mistresses, if you please.'

8

Bruno usually took Hector on a different route for his evening ride. Today, almost without thinking, he found himself once again cantering into the long straight track through the heart of the forest in the hope of another encounter with the mysterious Eugénie. Even as the thought took shape, a familiar figure on a white horse emerged, silhouetted against the evening light, into the gap between the trees at the far end of the trail. He felt a boyish urge to impress, to gallop towards her and then haul Hector to a magnificent halt, up on his hind legs and neighing like a warhorse, front hoofs pawing at the air. Bruno repressed the temptation, reminding himself that he was not that good a horseman and he'd look ridiculous if he fell off. Instead, he kept the eager Hector to a stately trot, which gave him plenty of time to consider this meeting and his own motives.

He found Eugénie to be a strikingly attractive woman. He was lonely, he told himself, and feeling bruised. Pamela had been away in Scotland this past month. Isabelle, the fiery police inspector, had such a grip upon him that she could entice him into her arms almost at whim. But she was back in Paris, on her fast-track career on the staff of the Minister of the Interior. A wonderful summer and a love affair that seemed to consume them both had been followed by one truncated weekend together and then one solitary but passionate night.

Why do I always fall for women who would never be satisfied with the simple life I offer? he asked himself. But Bruno knew his own nature well enough to supply the answer. The problem was not the women; it was him. The women who appealed to him were independent, ambitious and determined to build a life on their own terms. Family life and children were not high on their priorities, although Bruno felt them becoming steadily more important to him.

'Do you always ride this way?' Eugénie asked when he drew rein. Hector ambled slowly towards the white mare and the two horses nuzzled one another with politeness. She was dressed, he saw with surprise, rather like him, in jeans and a blue denim shirt. He was wearing his police uniform sweater over the shirt against the expected evening chill; she had a dark blue sweater tied around her waist.

'Not always,' he replied. 'But Hector tends to turn this way if I let him.' He had been aware of her eyes on him as he had trotted up the forest ride.

'I see you got your horse shoed,' he went on.

'I came back this way in the hope that I'd see you. I wanted to thank you. I called the stables at Meyrals and Victor took care of it, the man you recommended. He's a sweet old man and he gave me a map of the bridle trails.' She tapped her pocket.

A small alarm bell tinkled somewhere at the back of Bruno's

head. If she was staying at a place where horses were already installed, they would have their own arrangements for a farrier. If she had hired a horse herself for the duration of her stay, it would have come from a stables that could take care of matters like shoeing. She should have had no need of his advice.

'Which way are you heading?' he asked. She paused before replying, much as she had the previous evening, in a calculated way that put him on edge, awaiting her response.

'I was going to ask you for suggestions back to the ford at Mauzac or the bridge above Les Eyzies. I know my way from there.'

'And where have you ridden from today?' he asked. He found the stillness in her face strangely fascinating.

'From the stables at Meyrals. A friend dropped me off there when Victor called to say my horse was ready.'

'From here there's a bridle path through the woods to the big cave where all the tourist coaches go, you know the one?'

'You mean the one they call the Devil's Cave, with the stalagmites and the jazz concerts?'

He nodded. 'That's the old name. We usually call it the Gouffre de Colombac, which the management thought was better for the tourists. After the cave there's a hunting trail where you can canter that takes you to the quarry at Campagne and to the right of the entrance there's a bridle path signposted to Les Eyzies. Do you have far to go from there?'

'Not far,' she said vaguely. She dug her heels into her horse's sides and set off down the bridle path at a pace slightly too fast for the track and the overhanging branches. He held Hector on a tight rein as he followed, knowing his horse always preferred to take the lead but this trail was too narrow for him to overtake.

At the cave, not yet open for the tourist season, her pale face was flushed and her eyes shining from the speed of her ride. He pointed across the car park to the path that led to the hunting trail and she took off once more, bending over her horse's mane to avoid low branches. He followed at a slightly slower pace, aware of Hector's impatience beneath him. He murmured reassurance to his horse, telling Hector he'd have his chance on the wide hunters' trail. Bruno assumed Eugénie would stop at the bottom of the trail, uncertain which path to take. But she turned the correct way without hesitation and was twenty metres ahead by the time Bruno emerged from the trees.

For Hector, the sight of the other horse in front on the wide track was a challenge and Bruno felt the kick that signalled the animal's lengthening stride. Hector's neck stretched out and Bruno felt the landscape flash by as he began to gain steadily on Eugénie. Bruno hadn't noticed the riding crop until she suddenly began to use it to drive her horse on, determined to turn the ride into a race. If that was what she wanted, thought Bruno, she hadn't reckoned with Hector's strength and eagerness to lead. Bruno knew Hector was still running well within himself, easily able to step up into a higher gear if need be.

Eugénie's mare was beginning to labour as the track climbed. Specks of foam were flying back behind as Eugénie rose in the saddle to work her crop. His respect for her horsemanship went down a notch. He'd been taught never to treat a horse in such a way.

The brown gash in the green hillside that was the quarry still lay five hundred metres ahead as Hector drew level and then almost effortlessly stepped up his pace to ease into the lead. With a rhythm so smooth Bruno felt he could carry a full wine glass without spilling a drop, Hector galloped on, his breathing easy and not a fleck of foam at his muzzle. The trees on his right gave way to wooden fences and parkland. A car park and the road loomed ahead. Hector slowed his pace, knowing that his run was ending, and Bruno sat back in the saddle and turned to see Eugénie lumbering up at a heavy canter, at least fifty metres behind. Bruno was patting Hector and telling him what a fine horse he was when she finally drew rein alongside.

'Is that horse of yours for sale?' she asked.

'Never.' He shook his head in emphasis.

'Well, thanks for the run anyway, and guiding us up that track.' She dismounted, took a silk scarf from around her neck and used it to wipe her mare's muzzle, murmuring to her and stroking her neck to thank her for the ride. She turned and looked up at Bruno. 'I can find my way back from here.'

'Very well,' he said, not moving. 'The track to Les Eyzies is marked but I'd take it easy if I were you. Your horse is blown.'

Again came that pause before she replied. 'Yes, I know, and she'll need a good rubdown when I get her back. But it was worth it for that gallop.'

Bruno turned Hector's head to take the high road back to the stables at Pamela's house.

'I was told that you're an important man in these parts,' she called as he faced away from her. 'You could help our project or hinder it. Is that true?'

He turned in the saddle and looked down at her, disconcerted by her remark. 'I'm not sure what you're asking. I'm just a village policeman. I'm not influential, and even if I were, your project is not my business. It's for the council to approve or not.'

'That's not quite what I heard,' she insisted. 'I ought to be lobbying you for our project, but I think I'd rather just get to know you.'

'Where do you live?' he asked, wondering what she meant by that.

'Where I can, while making the money to live where I wish,' she said. There was neither humour nor coquetry in her voice, simply a statement of fact.

'When you say *our* project,' he asked, 'do you mean you and Foucher, or you and the Count?'

He felt her scrutinize him coolly before she turned and swung back into the saddle.

'The Count has the money and Foucher does the paperwork but the idea for the holiday village was mine,' she said. 'I have a share of the project, probably less than I deserve. But I'm still determined to make it work.'

Her horse plodded wearily away, and as he watched her leave Bruno pondered what business his friend the Baron might have in this project. He was the main landowner in the commune, so it would probably be some land that they needed, and once he realized they needed it he'd charge them a pretty price. It could even be the Baron's old dream of having a golf course nearby, rather than having to drive to Siorac or Périgueux whenever he wanted a round. Bruno resolved that he'd simply ask his friend over a quiet drink; the Baron was not much of a man for secrets.

It was the darker end of twilight by the time he got back to the stables at Pamela's house. It was becoming tiresome, this daily commute between his own place and hers. When she'd first flown off to Edinburgh to take care of her mother, they had both assumed she'd be away for only a few days and he'd been happy to agree to move into her place to take care of the horses, her Bess and Victoria as well as his own Hector. But the moving back and forth was becoming a logistical nightmare as he ran short of clean shirts and underwear and made late-night runs to look after his chickens.

A light flared in the stable yard as the door to Fabiola's gîte opened and the young doctor stood silhouetted in its frame.

'*Bonsoir*, Bruno. Have you eaten?' she called.

He walked across, kissed her in greeting and confessed that he was starving and had been thinking about getting a pizza or a *croque-monsieur* from Ivan's bistro in town.

'I'm cooking and I made enough for two,' she said. 'Come in.'

'Your mother's risotto again?' he asked, teasing. Fabiola was perversely proud of her limited cooking skills, and boasted that she had learned only one dish from her mother.

'No, my father's fondue, it's the best comfort food I know,' she said. Fabiola had a complicated family. Her mother was half Italian and half French, and her father was half French and half Italian-Swiss. Hence the fondue.

'It's good to see you,' he said, beaming at her. 'I thought you'd been avoiding me for some reason.'

'No, I'm not avoiding you,' she said, leading the way into the kitchen. Other than her books, her open laptop and a large framed photograph of a village in a valley overwhelmed by mountains, the house looked exactly as it had when Pamela was renting it out in the summer. 'I'm avoiding a question you want to ask me about private patients and I don't intend to answer. So having got that out of the way, how are you?'

'Fine,' he said. 'A bit worried about Madame Junot and trying to trace the identity of this dead woman we fished out of the river. And I spoke to Pamela. She's planning on coming back, but not for long, just to see whether she can find some care for her mother here in St Denis.'

Fabiola nodded, some of her dark hair falling from the loose bun in which she usually kept it. She pushed the lock behind her ear and began to open a bottle of white wine. Seeing Bruno trying to look at the label, she grinned at him and held up the bottle; one of his favourites, a Bergerac Sec from Clos d'Yvigne.

'I know. Pamela rang me and asked what I thought and I told her it wasn't a good idea. I've seen good people turn into depressives when they start taking care of a parent who's become a vegetable. From what the doctor says, her mother can only get worse.'

'You spoke to the doctor in Scotland?' he asked, sitting at the kitchen table, already set for two, the frame and tiny candle holder for the fondue already in place. As well as the wine glass, there was a small liqueur glass at each setting and a bottle of some clear liquid. He turned it to read the label: Willisauer Kirsch. She must have planned to ask him in.

'Sure, why not? The prognosis is not good. And the retirement home here isn't equipped for patients in that condition. Her mother would be better off in a specialized home, if she can afford it,' Fabiola said, pouring out the wine. She took a sip, put down the glass, yawned and stretched. There were black circles under her eyes, as if she had not been sleeping well. She reached for the pack of Gitanes on the table and lit one.

'Are you OK?' He'd only rarely seen her smoke before. 'You seem a bit down.'

'Are you surprised? Telling cancer patients they don't have long to live. Abused wives who won't make a formal complaint. Old people who are dead in everything except that they still breathe and eat and shit. And lots of hypochondriacs who want me to give them antibiotics for everything. If it wasn't for the horses and my friends I'd go mad.'

Bruno had never seen Fabiola in this mood before. He didn't know what to say. She turned aside to the kitchen counter where Emmenthal and Gruyère had already been grated and a baguette of bread chopped into bite-sized chunks. She peeled some heads of garlic, chopped an onion very finely and put them all into the fondue pot.

'I'm hungry, so I'm going to cheat,' she said. 'I should do this at table but it takes for ever.' Instead, she put the pot on her kitchen stove, splashed in some of the white wine and a dash of the kirsch, added some pepper and mixed spice and began to stir.

'All those depressing things you mentioned, is that all that's getting you down?'

'No,' she said and paused. Then the words came out in a rush. 'We had an incident at the shelter this afternoon, just before I got there, and the Gendarmes took ages to respond.'

Bruno knew that Fabiola volunteered at a hostel in Bergerac for battered wives who had taken their children and left their husbands. She treated their cuts and bruises, checked on the health of the children and used her medical title to write letters to recommend that the mother be given social housing in a new town where the husbands would not easily find them.

'What happened?'

'One of the husbands found out where his wife was, burst in, smashed the place up, beat her senseless and took his kid. The usual story. Thing is, we're supposed to have this panic button for the Gendarmes. They took twenty minutes to turn up and I could have walked to the Gendarmerie faster than that. I had to take the woman to hospital, but he'd really done a lot of damage to the shelter. And he'd belted the two volunteers who were there.'

'Have they arrested him yet?'

'By the time they got to his home, he'd gone, with the car and the kid. It's not the first time, Bruno.'

She brought the bubbling fondue pot to the table, lit the candle beneath it and then brought the basket of bread and two side salads she'd prepared.

'Not very authentic, the salads, but good for us,' she said. She pushed a long, barbed fork toward him.

'I put the bread on this, then dip it in the melted cheese, is that right?' he asked. Cheese fondue was a first for him.

'Try dipping the bread in the kirsch first, and then in the cheese,' she said.

He followed her instructions, and chewed with pleasure. It was spicy, tasty and nourishing all at once. She grinned at his grunt of pleasure and then fed herself, each of them taking turns.

'What did the Gendarmes say when you complained about how long they took to get to the hostel?'

'That they were busy on another call. It's what they always say, and we can't disprove it.'

'Is there a sympathetic woman on the town council?'

'Two or three, the ones who finally got us the panic button. They'll write to the head of the Gendarmes and to the Prefecture.'

'Get them to write to all the local papers,' he said. 'And get Périgord-Bleu to come in and do a story and run one of their talk-shows on the issue. The Gendarmes hate that kind of publicity. And we've got a woman Minister of Justice now; your councillors should write to her, too. There's nothing like a query from Paris to get the Gendarmes jumping.'

'I wish we had you there in Bergerac.' Like his own face, hers was flushed from the fondue. The scar on her cheek, the result of a mountaineering accident, stood out as a jagged red line against her pale skin. As if she sensed the direction of his eyes, she pulled something at the back of her bun, shook her head and her hair tumbled down, hiding her cheeks.

Bruno addressed himself to the kirsch glass and the fondue, then deliberately allowed his piece of bread to fall from the fork.

'Sorry, clumsy, not used to this,' he said, using his salad fork to fish into the fondue for his sunken bread. She watched him coolly as he ate it.

'You can be a very transparent man,' she said, turning her attention back to her fondue. 'By the way, I rang my friend at pathology. Your mystery woman had been involved in an orgy, sperm front and rear from different men. They weren't sure about the mouth because of the alcohol.'

He put down his fork, swallowing. 'You certainly picked your time to impart that news,' he said.

'Yes, we *toubibs* can be famous for our lack of sensitivity. She'd also given birth at some point in the past. Keep on stirring your fondue, we don't want it to set. And eat up, the crust at the bottom is the best bit.'

Bruno woke early the next morning in Pamela's spare room, some delicacy restraining him from using her bed in her absence. He took the horses for a quick trot around the paddock, made sure there was hay in their stalls and then drove home in search of a clean shirt and underwear. There was one of each left. He fed his chickens and watered his vegetable garden and then bundled his laundry into a big plastic bag before driving into town. He left his dirty washing at the cleaners, paying the extra for Georgette to iron his shirts, before joining the usual customers at the counter in Fauquet's café. He skimmed through *Sud-Ouest* while eating a croissant and enjoying the first coffee of the day.

'Nothing new in the paper,' said Roberte, a cheerful woman who ran the social security office at the *Mairie* and was his tennis partner in mixed doubles. 'Just the interview with Antoine about how you and he picked her out of the river and then went searching the banks yesterday, but I'm sure you'll have seen that.'

He hadn't, and read the piece with rising irritation when he saw that Antoine had mentioned the Red Château as one of the possible launch sites for the punt. He couldn't blame

Antoine; it was a full page of free publicity for his canoe business and a good photograph of him standing by the big sign for his campsite. But Philippe Delaron was getting inventive in order to keep the story going. It was the headline that jarred – *River Search for Devil Woman*. The Mayor was not going to like that.

In his office, Bruno skimmed through his predictable post while waiting for the computer to fire up. Most of the envelopes contained brochures for the coming summer's local music festivals, the usual string quartets playing in ancient churches or jazz ensembles in town squares. He typed in his password and opened his email, to find an announcement of new speed limits from the Prefecture and a characteristically curt message from Isabelle.

'Have two days off. Arrive tomorrow with special gift from me and Brigadier. *Bisous*, Isabelle. xx'

Remembering that emails from Isabelle were like a crossword puzzle with emotions attached, he leaned towards the screen intent on deciphering her meaning. *Bisous* was at the lowest rung of affection, the literary equivalent of an air kiss. The extra xx gave it a slightly warmer tone, but not enough to persuade him that any advance would be met with Isabelle's open arms. Tomorrow was tricky, since it had been sent at two minutes after midnight. Did that make it this day or the next? There was no request for him to book a hotel, but that was not necessarily a signal that she'd want to stay with him. There was nothing about trains to be met, nor any time or place for a rendezvous. And what might the special gift be? Since it also came from the Brigadier, her boss, it was hardly personal. It also gave her trip a slightly official flavour. The next test was to draft his reply.

After some moments of slightly edgy reflection, he typed: 'Wonderful news. Intrigued by gift. Do you arrive 18th or 19th and will you be here in time for dinner? Where shall we meet? *Bisous* and hugs, Bruno.'

He read it again, pondered the 'Where shall we meet?' but decided a little precision was justified after Isabelle's vagueness, crossed his fingers and hit the Send button just as his desk phone rang and another email pinged into his inbox.

'Tomorrow being today. On morning train from Austerlitz and on usual mobile number. Warning: a new man in my bedroom but he sleeps on floor. Will msg ETA. Ixx'

She must have sent that before getting his reply. At least he had the right date, and there were no more than four trains from the Gare d'Austerlitz in Paris, each arriving in St Denis at very different times. He decided that while he knew he was being teased he couldn't bear to interpret the phrase about the new sleeping partner. He answered the phone to hear a friend's excited voice.

'Bruno, it's the Baron. Something very urgent has come up, not for the phone. Can you come out to my place? And be discreet, park at the back and bring a civilian jacket.'

The Baron was convinced that Claire at the *Mairie*'s reception desk eavesdropped on phone calls, fuelling her taste for town gossip. Bruno had too few secrets to care, and if discretion was required he had his new mobile phone, supplied by the Brigadier during a previous case, that was reputed to be secure against all invasion. He always kept an anonymous dark windcheater in his official van. Checking that he had his notebook, pen, phone and torch, and a set of latex evidence gloves and bags in his pocket, he told Claire he was going on patrol. He used his phone to text Isabelle with the message 'What time do you arrive?' and headed down the stairs.

The Baron lived in a *chartreuse*, the local name for a historic home just one room wide that was too small to be a château and too large to be a manor house. His family had owned it for centuries. The rear of the building, which faced away from both the hillside and the river, was an almost solid wall of stone, interspersed with arrow slits for windows and flanked by two formidable towers. Bruno turned into the courtyard to park before the much more welcoming façade. He sat for a moment, enjoying the way the Renaissance builders had softened the look of a fortress with large stone windows, a handsome staircase and a balustraded terrace. The main door, a massive structure of wood reinforced with iron studs and bars, still carried the scorch marks of the Revolution. Having failed to storm it, the local peasantry had vainly attempted to burn the home of the Baron's ancestor, their feudal oppressor. This same ancestor had gone on to become one of Napoleon's generals. As a result, the Baron liked to say, the peasants had been taking on rather more than they had bargained for.

The door opened and the Baron came out, car keys jingling in his hand. 'Got a call from Marcel at the Gouffre,' he said. 'There's been a break-in overnight and he said he wanted both of us there to see it. He sounded worried.'

'Any details?' Bruno asked.

The Baron shook his head. 'He just said he thought there might be a link to that dead woman you pulled out of the river.' He led the way across the courtyard and over a wide lawn to the barn where he kept his cars. He steered Bruno to the battered old Peugeot rather than his Mercedes, reversed out and set off through the archway into the tiny hamlet that surrounded his home and up the hill.

Part of the wide stretch of land that the Baron owned, the Gouffre de Colombac was one of the largest caves in the region. Unlike the more famous caves such as Lascaux with its prehistoric paintings, this was simply a vast space beneath the earth. Its main chamber was almost spherical, over a hundred metres wide and almost as high. The space was unevenly divided by an underground river that led to an ominously still lake. Bruno had been inside several times for concerts, the musicians performing from the far side of the river and the audience on chairs and benches or perched on the wide stone steps that nature had somehow carved into one wall. He had once paid the entrance fee just to see the place, one of the largest caves in France, and with a dark reputation.

For centuries, the locals had called it the Devil's Cave, for the puffs of smoke they saw sometimes gusting from a hole in the earth. This phenomenon was now known to be a form of condensation from the micro-climate inside the vast cave rather than smoke from the fires of Hell. The land around it, part of an old pilgrimage route from the shrine of Rocamadour and the Abbey of Cadouin that led to Compostela at the far north-western tip of Spain, had for centuries attracted bands of brigands. They lay in wait to rob ill-guarded pilgrims and tip their bodies down the smoking hole into the gulf below. When the cave had first been opened in the nineteenth century, an intrepid explorer had been winched down on a rope, trying vainly to pierce the darkness with a puny lantern. When he had finally touched bottom, he found he had landed on a great heap of bones, mainly human but also animal, from beasts that had stumbled into the hole.

Now, cleverly lit and with pedal-boats for hire to explore the sunken lake, it was a tourist attraction. As well as the entrance fee, the café and souvenir shop and the special concerts, the cave made a steady profit from the stoneware it produced. Rack upon rack of plates, jugs, glasses, vases and every other implement that the managers could think of were left under the places where the water, heavy with particles of limestone, dripped down and slowly calcified the objects beneath. After a year or so in the cave, the items looked as though they had been carved from solid stone, and they were so popular that Marcel could barely keep up with the demand.

Smaller chambers led off from the main space, and the eerie formations of stalagmites and stalactites had been carefully lit to justify the rather fanciful names they had been given, such as the Chapel of Our Lady, after a thick rock that looked like a praying woman in a hood and a long cloak; or Napoleon's Bedchamber, which resembled a massive four-poster bed with hangings swooping around it and a curious shape that could be interpreted as a giant letter N.

Marcel was the second generation of his family to lease

the cave from the Baron, paying him a modest rent and a healthy share of the annual profits. Marcel's wife and sisters, his sons and cousins all worked in the family business, investing cautiously in improvements. Bruno had heard they were working on a *son et lumière* show for summer evenings when no concert was booked.

Marcel greeted them at what he called the stage door, a secondary entrance high enough for the musicians' trailers and wide enough for the pedal-boats. The public entrance around the corner was deliberately low, narrow and dark, so that the visitor's eventual sight of the majestic scale of the cave would be all the more impressive. Marcel unlocked the double doors of green metal and pulled down the master switch for the lights. The three men walked down for perhaps fifty metres before reaching the cave itself. They were standing on a balcony carved into the side, with a metal railing to prevent them from falling and a long wide ramp leading down to the floor of the cave. Off to one side a storeroom had been found or perhaps carved from the rock. Bruno could see long rows of folding chairs stacked up inside.

'We haven't opened yet for the season, but we've been doing work all winter,' Marcel said. 'For the last few days, we've been working outside, so the cave has been locked and sealed.'

There was just one other way in, he explained: the route the first explorer had taken. Customers paid extra to be lowered in a small basket operated by a winch. All three entrances had been securely locked, and the only keys were held by Marcel and his family.

'And by me, one complete set,' the Baron added.

'I came in this morning to check the lighting, because the damp can be a problem with the junction boxes, and I knew something was wrong because one of the boats was missing,' Marcel continued. 'It must have been taken under that shelf of rock and through the tunnel that leads to Our Lady's Chapel. That's the only place where you could hide a boat in here. So I took another boat and went across and then saw what had been done in the chapel. That's when I called you,' he said, addressing the Baron.

'Have you touched anything in there?' Bruno asked.

Marcel shook his head. 'It's not exactly damage – I think it's worse.'

Down at the lake, Marcel directed them into another boat which he began to pedal across the still, dark waters. Occasional drops of water plopped from the roof above. When one landed on his hand, Bruno could see the tiny flecks of limestone that had come down with the water. Occasional stumps of stone rose from the surface of the lake where the drops had formed over centuries, perhaps over millennia. They ducked their heads as Marcel pedalled under the shelf of stone and they emerged into a long tunnel, lit with an eerie blue light.

He pulled alongside a low stone wharf, where they could climb out and keep their feet dry, and tied up to an iron ring set into the stone. He led the way from the water's edge into a wider passage where he opened a small plastic junction box and flicked some switches. At once, the sound of Gregorian chant echoed from the stone walls and a clear light gleamed from the end of the tunnel.

Bruno remembered the chapel and the religious music from his previous visit. It had been the largest of the smaller chambers and shaped liked a triangle, roughly ten metres deep and almost as wide at the entrance, narrowing to two metres wide at the far end where the stone Madonna stood. A large but low boulder with a flat top sat on the floor before her and had inevitably been dubbed the altar. Two church candles, an altar cloth and a small crucifix had been placed on it to complete the tableau. The rest of the chamber was empty except for the artful lights. The effect was of the interior of a church, dimly lit by natural sunlight. But on each of the side walls a projector cast an image of a stained-glass rose window which suffused the space with tones of gold, red and blue. Two small spotlights lit the Madonna, clear white from the left and blue from the right.

But now this Madonna was black. The whole stalagmite had been covered in black paint and the two church candles on the altar had been replaced with black ones. A severed goat's head stood between them, its horns almost touching the candles and its tongue lolling. A cheap metal cup lay on its side beside the goat's head, wine dregs drying inside, as if some perverted form of communion had taken place. There was a smell of stale tobacco smoke and something different, perhaps incense. An empty bottle of vodka had rolled to one side of the cave. This time Bruno noted that the brand was Smirnoff. And a large pentagram had been scrawled in black paint, the precise size of the projection of the rose window.

'That's the window at Chartres they defaced,' said Marcel. 'It's Rouen cathedral on the other side, but for some reason they left it alone. But you can see why I thought of that dead woman, Bruno. I don't know about Satanism but this is for sure the devil's work.'

'And you've touched nothing?' Bruno asked again. Marcel shook his head. Bruno looked at him closely, wondering if this was all some clumsy publicity stunt to take advantage of the media interest in the woman from the river.

Bruno walked across to the altar. It was smeared with dried blood from the goat. A long drop of blood hung from its tongue. It was still sticky, so the goat could not have been killed much before the previous evening. He'd check the local butchers and goat farmers. He turned his attention to the candles. These were different from those he had found in the punt. They were the original white church candles, smeared in black paint. The wax had not been a hospitable surface for the paint, which had run and pooled at the foot of each candle.

'How old were these candles?' he asked Marcel.

'New this year and never lit.'

'Well, they've been lit now. How long would you say they burned for?'

Marcel shrugged. 'Two or three hours, maybe a bit more.'

Bruno turned to the Madonna. Here the black paint seemed different. It hadn't run. He leaned forward and sniffed, then put the tip of his little finger against the paint. It was slightly sticky and smelt of turpentine, as if it were oil-based. The paint on the candles looked water-based.

There was a jumble of footprints in the dust before the Madonna and what could have been cigarette or cigar ash at her feet. In the passage outside he found one small cigarette stub, or perhaps the end of a cheroot. It was brown. As he lifted it to his nose in his gloved hand he scented that elusive incense again. He bagged it, and told Marcel to keep the place secure until he could persuade J-J, the chief of detectives for the *Département*, to assign his overworked forensic team to the inquiry. He'd have to stress the link to the dead woman, but since that appeared to be a suicide, it wouldn't be easy. His only other find was a screwed-up piece of coloured paper in the bottom of the beached pedal-boat, which turned out to be a bubblegum wrapping, most likely left by some tourist the previous year. He bagged it anyway, along with the empty vodka bottle.

'What do you think, Bruno?' the Baron asked.

'The most important thing is there's no dead body.' He didn't mention his suspicions about the publicity stunt. The Baron was his friend, but he was also a clever businessman with a financial interest in boosting visits to the cave.

'As for criminal damage, there's nothing that a few hours of cleaning can't fix, so there's not much of a crime here,' he continued, leading the way down the passage to the boat. 'It's curious and it's troubling, but it won't be easy to get the *Police National* to take much of an interest. Looking at that bubblegum wrapper, I'd have said it was most likely kids larking about, except for the goat's head and the break-in. Even so, I'd start by asking your own kids if they're behind this. Do they have access to the keys?'

Marcel looked disappointed, and a little angry. 'I already asked them before they went to school, and all the keys are accounted for. That's the first thing I checked.'

'When are you planning to open?' Bruno asked him.

'This weekend.'

'Well, leave the boat and chapel untouched until we can see if I can interest the forensics guys in this. It might be a day or two.'

When they crossed the lake to the inner shore, the Baron asked Marcel to carry on with his work on the café and asked Bruno to stay behind.

'There's something you may as well know,' he said when they were alone. 'There's another way in.'

'And Marcel doesn't know?'

The Baron shrugged. 'I never told him but he may have found it. My father showed it to me when I was sixteen. It was something they used in the Resistance, and maybe at other troubled times.'

He led the way past a rack of calcifying crockery and along the passage leading to Napoleon's Bedchamber to the far side of the cave where stood the display called The Organ, an array of stalagmites of steadily diminishing height and width. Off to one side was a triangle of three gigantic stalagmites known as the Dragon's Teeth, so close they were almost touching. Another few centuries and they would be. The Baron eased his way into the narrow space between them and the cave wall. There was no room for Bruno to join him, but he peered through a gap to watch the Baron bend down and began brushing thick layers of pebbles and rock dust to one side. A wooden trap-door with an iron ring appeared and with an effort the Baron levered it open, took a torch from his pocket and turned it on so that Bruno could see stone steps descending steeply.

'Follow me, and close the trapdoor behind you.' The Baron descended carefully, facing the steps that had so much space between them it was like descending a ladder rather than a staircase. As Bruno followed, his own torch held between his teeth, he noticed dust thick on the steps. It had been some time since anyone had come this way. The Baron waited for him at the bottom, a circular chamber large enough for both of them to stand, and shone his light into a low tunnel that led uphill into the distance.

'Nobody's used this for years,' the Baron said. 'The Resistance used to hide guns here in the war.'

'So anybody from a Resistance family could know about it?' Bruno asked.

'Not really. They weren't fools, they had a need-to-know system, and most of the old *Résistants* are dead.'

'Where does this come out?'

'St Philippon, in the ruined chapel by the old cemetery. There's another tunnel branching off that used to go down to the Grand Roc near Les Eyzies, but it was closed by a rock-fall decades ago. We'd better get back before Marcel wonders what the hell we're up to.'

'You mean we're not going to follow this tunnel all the way?'

'Not today. Any time you want you can borrow my keys and explore it at your leisure, or try it from the other end. See if you can find the entrance. The Germans never did, nor the *Milice*,' the Baron said, referring to the notorious police of the Vichy regime.

'Did they look for it?'

'Oh, yes. One of the prisoners they took knew about it and died under torture without saying a word.'

The Baron turned to climb back up the steps, but Bruno put a restraining hand on his arm. 'Tell me the truth, *mon vieux*, is this break-in genuine or is it some publicity stunt?'

'How do you mean?'

'You know what I'm asking,' Bruno said. 'The point is, if I'm to report this and ask for a forensics team, I'll have to give Périgueux a good reason to dig into their budget. If it all turns out to be some kids giving you a bit more publicity, we'll both be in trouble.'

The Baron, his face cast into ghoulish shadows by the upward glow from the torch at his waist, turned back from the steps and looked Bruno in the eye.

'You know me better than that, Bruno. If I were trying to fool you, I wouldn't have shown you the secret passage.' He turned back and began climbing the steps. He spoke, almost to himself. 'Anyway, that's my duty done.'

'You mean that you've convinced me nobody used this secret passage to get into the cave?'

'No.' The Baron stopped in his climb. 'It means that I've carried out my duty to my father. He made me promise to pass on the secret to somebody I trusted. As he said, you never know when the Germans will come again. Or the English.'

10

Back at the *Mairie*, Bruno headed for the Mayor's office to tell him of the break-in and found himself called in to attend a meeting with the regional bank manager from Périgueux. Bankers made courtesy calls every few months to discuss building projects and financing plans for each of the communes in the *Département*. In the more important towns like St Denis the banker would first visit his local branch and afterwards invite the Mayor to the best lunch in town. But today was not so agreeable. The Mayor had removed the chair from in front of his desk and the banker stood before him like a naughty schoolboy.

'Ah, Bruno, just the man I want to see,' said the Mayor. 'You know Monsieur Valentin from the bank, and you can tell him of the effort you have put into raising funds for a sports hall. Cake sales and *vide-greniers*, bingo evenings and collection tins, you name it and Bruno here has tried it. And now we're being offered on a plate the sports hall of Bruno's dreams.'

'Get yourself a chair, Bruno. Monsieur Valentin here can remain standing while I explain to him why the commune of St Denis will no longer do any business with his bank.'

'I beg your pardon?' The banker's voice almost choked.

'You heard me,' said the Mayor coldly. 'No loans and no bonds. We'll be closing the account we use to pay salaries and shifting the pension fund to the Banque Nationale de Paris. Along with my personal account and credit cards, and every other bank account in this town if I have anything to do with it.'

'I don't understand . . .' The banker looked stunned. He cast his eyes appealingly toward Bruno, seeking some explanation. The Mayor's voice ground on implacably.

'I do not deal with my enemies, Monsieur Valentin. Least of all do I let them have access to my money.'

'Enemies, *Monsieur le Maire*? We've worked together for years, been the banker for St Denis for over a hundred years . . .'

'And now you've turned against us, deliberately setting out to block one of the most important projects this *Département* has seen in years, maybe in decades. It's worth at least twenty-five million in the first phase and probably a hundred million by the time they're through. Why are you against it?'

'But I'm not, I haven't heard . . . I mean, it sounds like just the thing we'd want to support, since it's backed by you as one of our most valued clients. Please, I'd like to know more.'

'And they're going to throw in Bruno's sports hall for free, just like that. An asset for our youngsters that we've been sweating over for years. The bank, to whom we've been loyal for years, is trying to sabotage the whole deal. What can you possibly have to say for yourself?'

The banker swallowed, apparently speechless, and waved his hands uncertainly in the air in appeal to whatever gods bankers worshipped.

'Well, I suppose we'll get some sort of explanation from the chairman of the board in Paris to this letter of complaint I'm writing him. We were at ENA together, you know,' the Mayor went on, referring to the *Ecole Nationale d'Administration*, the elite graduate school founded by de Gaulle.

The banker's face was shiny with sweat and he seemed close to tears.

'I really don't understand. Please, tell me what's wrong.'

With narrowed eyes peering over his spectacles, the Mayor tossed a sheaf of paper onto the desk.

'Read that,' he snapped. 'Just the first page will do.'

Bruno recognized the petition that Gaston Lemontin had drawn up against the plans for the holiday village. He realized that the Mayor was out to make a very public and cruel example. Anyone who opposed one of his pet projects would regret it, a simple lesson in the iron laws of politics that the Mayor felt it necessary to teach every decade or so.

'What is the first name on that petition against a project that is so important for the future of St Denis?' the Mayor asked, in the tones of a schoolteacher with a particularly dense pupil.

'Gaston Lemontin, followed by his wife Madame Lemontin,' Valentin stammered. 'I'm terribly sorry, there must be some misunderstanding, I shall take care . . .'

'I didn't ask you for the second name,' the Mayor interrupted.

Bruno pursed his lips but kept silent at the sight of his mentor behaving so badly. He had understood by now that he had not been invited into this meeting by accident, but because the Mayor wanted him to witness the slow and careful humiliation of a proud man. He wondered whether the Mayor was enjoying this, as he seemed to be, or simply exercising a political muscle that needed to be flexed occasionally.

'And what can you tell me of this Gaston Lemontin?'

'He's the deputy manager of our branch in this town.'

The Mayor picked up the petition fastidiously between finger and thumb and dropped it into his waste-paper basket. 'Are you telling me he is *still* the deputy manager of your branch in my town?'

'If you will excuse me a moment, *Monsieur le Maire*, please allow me to address this matter immediately, and then to wait upon you later today, at your convenience.'

The Mayor nodded, and Valentin scurried out. Bruno leaned back in his chair and blew out a long breath, shaking his head at the same time.

'Is that admiration or condemnation?' the Mayor asked, with a twinkle in his eye and not a trace of the anger he had displayed to the banker.

'A bit of both; I'm not sure yet of the proportions. That will wait until I learn Lemontin's fate.'

'This is France; they can't sack him or demote him. I imagine he'll be transferred to another branch. And I also expect us to get extremely favourable terms for our next loan, and as a taxpayer you should be grateful for that.'

Bruno nodded. 'There is one other thing that troubles me, the thought that Lemontin might have been on to something. He told me there were some real questions about this Paris investment bank we're getting involved with.'

111

'The bank will presumably do its own due diligence. That's why we pay their fees,' the Mayor said.

'The economy of Europe is currently littered with the wreckage of banks and finance houses that we presumed to have done due diligence on American mortgages, Greek debt and Irish banks,' Bruno replied.

The Mayor nodded, looking thoughtful. 'Might you make a discreet inquiry into just what has got Lemontin so concerned?'

'I'm no financial expert,' Bruno replied.

'Go ahead with my blessing,' said the Mayor. 'I always suspected that any financial transaction that cannot be completely understood by an honest man is probably best avoided.'

Isabelle's text message had said simply '12.50', which gave Bruno a little time. He stopped at Ivan's Café de la Renaissance to check the *plat du jour. Soupe aux haricots* and Wiener Schnitzel, he was told, which meant that the buxom German tourist Ivan had brought back from his winter holiday in Morocco was still installed in his bed and his kitchen. The development of Ivan's menu was a reliable guide to his love affairs. She might depart next week, but the Schnitzel would remain for ever a part of Ivan's repertoire, at least until a Greek came to introduce him to the possibilities of moussaka or a Spaniard to lure him into deep bowls of paella. Bruno approved of the German girl. He'd never had veal quite like the Schnitzel she'd brought to St Denis. It was hammered out so thin that it almost hung over the edges of the plate and covered with a delicate coating of bread crumbs. It was served with a whole lemon cut into quarters, and a bowl of potato salad and another of coleslaw on the side. Bruno was thinking how a glass of Bergerac Sec would go perfectly with the veal when Ivan beckoned him inside, tamping down a new serving of coffee into the filter basket.

'Try this,' Ivan said. 'It's Griselda's latest idea. She said she had it in Italy, called an *affogato*, so I'm going to try it here.'

He took an espresso cup, spooned in a small helping of vanilla ice cream and put the cup beneath the coffee machine.

'What do you think?' Ivan asked, as Bruno tried to decide whether he should eat it with a spoon or try to drink it first. He compromised with a small sip of what seemed to him like a particularly good coffee ice cream.

'Be a good dessert for the *plat du jour*,' said Bruno.

Ivan shook his head. 'I want them to buy a coffee as well as the menu. This will be something different, mid-morning maybe.'

Bruno asked him to hold two places for about one o'clock and then headed to Karim's Café des Sports, also licensed to sell tobacco and close enough to the *collège* to stock a vast selection of confectionery. Beyond the sweets were racks of magazines and newspapers, and beyond the tobacco stretched the big coffee machine and the bar. Rashida was serving glasses of Ricard for the pre-lunch crowd, her baby asleep in a shawl-like pouch that kept him tucked against her breast. Her husband Karim, star of the town's rugby team, loomed over the till.

'*Un p'tit apéro*, Bruno?' he asked. Bruno shook his head and handed him the plastic bag containing the bubblegum wrapper he'd found in the cave. He asked if Karim recognized it.

'It's this one,' Karim said, reaching over the counter to pick out a small pack in garish colours. 'It has cards inside, all the footballers who've played for France, and the kids collect them. I must sell fifty a week, maybe more. It's a new line, running just this year.'

So it can't have been litter from last year's tourists, Bruno thought. Whoever had thrown away the wrapper had kept the card, which Bruno assumed meant it could have been a collector. That would suggest that the tableau in the cave had been the work of kids.

'Would you know the main collectors?' he asked.

It was a mixture, Karim explained, of the older kids in *collège* and the younger ones in primary school, all the football fans, and quite a few girls. He broke off to sell a copy of *Télé-Journal* and some lottery cards to Ahmed from the fire station.

'What about this cigarette end?' Bruno asked, handing over another plastic bag. 'It smells funny.'

Karim looked at the dark brown filter and sniffed at the bag, and grinned.

'It's a *kretek*, from Indonesia. I'm the only one round here who sells them. I keep them for my cousin Hassan, who won't smoke anything else. It's flavoured with cloves, supposed to have been invented by an asthmatic. It took me ages to find an importer.'

He pulled a pack from the rows of cigarettes behind him

and handed it to Bruno. The pack was dark brown, and marked Djarum Black. Bruno sniffed at it, and picked up the faint scent of cloves.

'Anybody else buy them?'

'Hardly anybody, these days. When I began stocking them, a lot of people bought a pack to try after they smelt Hassan smoking them. Smells like apple pie. But once the novelty wore off, it was just Hassan. I can't think when I last sold a pack to anyone else.'

Hassan lived in the nearby village of St Chamassy, where he worked for Electricité de France as a travelling maintenance man. His route would take him past the Café des Sports on most days.

'I'm trying to remember how old his kids are,' Bruno said.

'Just the little girls and the one boy at the *collège* here, Abdul,' Karim said, a touch of alarm in his voice. 'Is there a problem, Bruno?'

He shook his head. 'Just routine inquiries. I presume the boy is a football fan.'

'Mad about it, plays on the school team. Are you sure this isn't trouble?'

Karim was obviously worried, and something in his tone made Rashida turn to look at her husband.

'He could have been involved in some larking about, nothing that will need more than a good talking-to if it does turn out to involve him,' Bruno replied. 'Don't worry about it, and don't say a word to Hassan.'

Bruno took his plastic evidence bags and headed for the *collège*. It was almost noon, when classes ended for lunch. By the time he parked, the courtyard was thronged with adolescents jostling to get to the dining hall. Bruno turned left to a row of two-storey buildings in faded white stucco. These were the subsidized apartments for the teachers, one of which housed Florence and her twins. Rollo had excused her from the rota of supervising the school lunches so she could pick up her children from the *maternelle* and feed them before dropping them back at the crèche.

A flustered Florence answered the door holding a wooden spoon. She leaned forward so he could kiss her cheeks in greeting.

'Bruno, I'm afraid you've come when it's feeding time at the zoo,' she joked.

'I know, I'm sorry. I wouldn't have come if it wasn't urgent.'

With a glance at the mirror, hanging on a hook that Bruno had affixed when she was moving in, Florence invited him in to the kitchen. The twins broke off from squabbling over the flavours of their yogurts and shouted a welcome to Bruno.

'*Bonjour*, Dora, *bonjour* Daniel,' he said, bending to kiss each of them on their upturned brows.

'They've almost finished,' Florence said. 'Would you like something? A coffee, perhaps a sandwich? I was about to make myself a quick *tartine*.'

'I'm fine, thanks. I'll be lunching later but go ahead and eat. It's just that I need your help about one of the kids, the El Ghoumari boy from St Chamassy. Do you know him?'

'Nice youngster, he's in my junior science class. What's your interest?' Her tone was guarded and her face neutral. It reminded him of her closed and formal way when they'd

116

first met. He'd been investigating fraud at the Ste Alvère truffle market where she was working. He had no doubt that despite their friendship her first loyalty would be to her pupils.

'It's not official, otherwise I'd have gone to Rollo,' he said. 'I think the boy might have been larking about. I just want to know who his best friends are so I can clear something up. It's nothing serious, at least not for the boy.'

Florence looked at him dubiously.

'You'll have to tell me more than that,' she said. The children, aware of a sudden tension, kept their big eyes switching from Bruno to their mother as they spooned in their yogurts.

Bruno explained about the cave, and his suspicion that it had been kids playing at re-enacting what they had read in the papers, probably spurred on by a grown-up with an interest in keeping the Satanist story going.

'It's not something that can get them into trouble, it's just that I need to know what's going on,' he said. 'So if the best friend turns out to be Jean-Paul whose dad runs the cave, I'd like to go and talk to the father. If I go through Rollo, it starts to get official.'

'Your uniform makes it official, Bruno.'

'I don't like things being official, not when kids are involved,' he said. 'You know that.'

She turned from piling plates and yogurt pots to look him in the eye.

'Will you let me be there when you talk to them?' she asked. He nodded, and watched her as she considered what to do.

'Jean-Paul is a friend of his. And so is Luc Delaron, Philippe's nephew,' she said, standing to take a butter dish and a fat sausage from the refrigerator. The bread board was already on the table with most of a baguette. She sat and began to slice the sausage. 'The three of them are pretty much inseparable, and sometimes there's a fourth with Mathieu, the boy you pulled out of that manure pool last year. Do you want me to see if I can find them now? Or once I've eaten?'

Bruno checked his watch. He had to get to the station to meet Isabelle's train.

'I'd like to,' he said. 'But I'm expected somewhere so I'll have to talk to them later, maybe when school ends today.'

'I still want to be there when you talk to them,' she said. 'They're all in my last class today, so why not come by the science lab at four o'clock and I'll keep them there. And now I've got to get these kids to the crèche.'

She stood up, took a cloth from the kitchen sink, cleaned the faces and hands of her children, and then wiped the table.

'If this turns out badly for the boys, I'll be very disappointed in you,' she warned.

11

The only other person waiting on the station platform was Fat Jeanne from the market. A jolly and almost spherical woman, she had cheerfully embraced the nickname given her by the stallholders whose fees she collected. She was, she informed Bruno, heading to Agen to visit her sister for a few days. That meant that everyone in town would learn that he'd been meeting that police inspector from Paris that he'd been in love with. But they might not hear it for a day or two unless, Bruno reminded himself, Jeanne thought it an item of gossip so delicious that she'd pull out her mobile phone the moment the train got under way.

'Meeting someone?' Jeanne asked after they had touched cheeks. He could see her brain churning, wondering who might be coming to see him on a train from Périgueux, or Limoges or perhaps even Paris. 'Something official, is it? To do with this Satan business?'

'A police colleague from Paris. You'll remember her,' he said.

The train whistle blew from around the bend and at the end of the platform the automatic barrier dropped to close the road. 'Ah, that one,' she said, knowingly. She was probably thinking that these days he was supposed to be attached to the Mad Englishwoman whom everybody liked.

Bruno wondered what it would be like to live in Paris or some big city where he could go out anonymously to meet someone without word spreading to all his friends and neighbours within moments. The train slowed to a halt, and even though it stopped for less than a minute Jeanne delayed her boarding, eager for a sight of the policewoman from Paris and the confirmation of her suspicion that Bruno was reviving an old affair.

'Ça va, Bruno?' Isabelle asked with a smile as she stepped down from the train, and he felt his heart leap happily in his chest. The line of her jaw and cheekbones still had a sharp look; she had yet to replace the weight she had lost from her already slim body after being shot. She was dressed as always in black, an open raincoat that fell almost to her ankles and black slacks with a wide red leather belt whose colour matched her lipstick. Her hair was cut even closer than usual to her enchantingly shaped head. Another millimetre and Bruno would have called it a crewcut. She had a small overnight case in one hand, a laptop bag over one shoulder, a cane in the other hand, and by her feet was another square case in plastic.

Carefully avoiding any darting glance at the cane, which he'd hoped would no longer be needed, Bruno took the square case and her bag, and kissed her soundly on both cheeks. His hands encumbered with her luggage, he hugged her as best he could with his upper arms. The square case shifted and squirmed in his grip, as if it had a life of its own.

'Careful, Bruno, it's alive,' she said. Jeanne looked baffled as she pulled herself onto the train and the doors began to close. As the train started to move Isabelle fell into his arms, hugging him tightly. But it was more the embrace of a fond relative than an impatient lover, Bruno thought.

'What's alive?' he asked. He heard a tiny mewing as the case he was holding seemed to quiver of its own accord.

'It's the man who's been sharing my bedroom,' she said, leaning back to look at him but still holding his hand. 'It's your present from me and the Brigadier, and I want you to call him Balzac.'

Bruno went down on one knee and turned the case to see the small metal grille, and behind it the pink tongue and eager eyes of a puppy. Its feet were far too big for its small body and its ears were so long they trailed in the layers of newspapers that lined the travelling cage. One half of his heart lifted at the sight of a baby basset hound. The other half regretted that Isabelle had not understood his wish to choose his new dog himself. He opened the grille and the puppy bounded out and clambered up one thigh to perch on his other knee and then start squirming his way up Bruno's arm to lick his face.

'It looks like he's chosen you,' Isabelle said.

'Balzac,' Bruno said, holding the puppy in both hands and bringing it close to his face to study it with a hunter's eye.

The snow-white legs, pedalling merrily, were short and sturdy, the hips almost as broad as the shoulders. The puppy's chest and belly were the perfect pink of new flesh, the brown fur on its sides becoming black from the white collar along the spine to the rump. Balzac's tail had the characteristic white tip, so in the woods Bruno would be able to see it above undergrowth. The pads of Balzac's paws were still pink and soft, and his tiny teeth were like needles as Bruno looked inside his mouth. A white stripe from his scalp ran down between eyes that already carried the wisdom of generations of bassets. With the rational part of his mind, Bruno knew this was a hound of classic breeding, and all the rest of him was falling in love.

'I was worried at picking one out for you, rather than letting you choose,' Isabelle was saying, an unusual tone of nervousness in her voice. 'But the Brigadier insisted on this breed. He called the head of the hunting pack at Cheverny and asked where to find the best bassets in France and got him to pick this one out.'

She explained that Balzac came from the original kennels of the legendary French breeder Léon Verrier, and his grandmother had been crossed with the Stonewall Jackson line from America.

'You know that the Marquis de Lafayette took bassets to George Washington as a gift when we helped free the Americans from the British?' Bruno interrupted.

She shook her head. 'My briefing didn't go that far.'

She paused and put her hand on his shoulder, where Balzac quickly began to lick it. 'Now, pay attention, Bruno, because I learned this little speech off by heart just for you.'

She coughed to clear her throat and Bruno stood, his puppy nestling against his chest and licking the underside of his chin, as Isabelle closed her eyes and began to recite.

'We know that no dog could ever replace Gigi, but this comes with the personal thanks of the Minister of the Interior and his staff. We were going to pay for your new dog with Ministry funds, but when the kennel heard how Gigi was killed, they wanted you to have it as a gift. By special arrangement, Gigi's name has been inscribed on the roll of honour at the headquarters of the 132nd Bataillon Canine, at Suippes in the *Département* of the Marne.'

She stopped, opened her eyes, and smiled at him brilliantly. 'Oh yes, and they'll be in touch with you in a couple of years because they want to breed from him.'

Bruno's eyebrows lifted. 'Is this a joke?'

Isabelle shook her head. 'We in France deploy and train more military dogs than any other country on earth. I found out a lot about this when the Brigadier took me down to Suippes, seven hundred dogs in the biggest military kennel in Europe.'

With his spare arm, Bruno reached for her and drew her into a close embrace, little Balzac squirming to lick first Isabelle and then him and back again.

'The dog is wonderful, and I'm very happy. So thank you,' he said, trying to kiss a part of Isabelle's face that was not covered by a tiny head and enormous ears. 'I'll give you a letter to take back to the Brigadier to thank him and you'll let me have the address of the kennels. I hope this means you'll be making regular maternal visits.'

'Maternal?' she said in mock horror, moving Balzac's head to one side so that she could kiss him in return. 'You've got the wrong girl, Bruno. That's the last thing I have in mind.'

'What's on my mind right now is lunch,' Bruno replied.

'Ivan's doing his *soupe aux haricots*, the one where he makes his stock with a pig's tail.'

'And I'm justifying my little trip down here with a visit to the *Ecouteurs*' school, telling them our latest priorities,' she said. 'But that's not until later this afternoon. And since the school director is an old chum of the Brigadier, I'm under orders to stay on for a reception and dinner afterwards.'

'Am I supposed to know about that?' There was a teasing note in his voice, disguising the disappointment he felt at her disappearance for the evening. But he was surprised that Isabelle was so open about her plans.

The *Ecouteurs* were the listeners, a secret arm of the French state that monitors phone calls and emails plucked from the airwaves. Massive computers selected certain messages containing pre-programmed trigger words that were then checked by human ears. Naturally, they listened in languages other than French. The English-language school for the *Ecouteurs* was located in a hideous nineteenth-century château up the valley, taking advantage of the many native English-speakers in the area. For the same reason, the German-language school for the *Ecouteurs* was in Alsace, the Italian in Nice and the Arabic schools were in Marseille, Toulon, Paris and Lille.

'Since I'm hoping you'll give me a lift there, it wouldn't be much of a secret. Besides, the Brigadier has renewed your security clearance.'

'Does that mean he's planning to dragoon me into something again?'

She shrugged. 'Are we going to stand here on the station platform all day or are you taking me and Balzac to lunch?'

'Lunch,' he replied.

'Good, I'm dying for some good Périgord food again and I think we've given quite enough of a show to the lady behind the lace curtain.' She waved gaily at the window.

Bruno turned to look and saw the curtain twitch as someone pulled quickly back. Damn! He'd forgotten that after they left the ticket office unmanned, the cash-starved rail system had sold off the station as a residence. News of their embraces, and of Bruno's new dog, would be common knowledge by the time they finished lunch.

Isabelle plucked a thin black leather lead from her pocket, attached it to Balzac's collar and limped off with her cane towards Bruno's venerable Land-Rover, an inheritance from a dead hunting friend. Bruno picked up the dog case, Isabelle's case and her laptop bag and followed on somewhat clumsily behind.

'And over lunch, you can tell me about your local witches' coven or Satanist cult or whatever it is,' she said, settling herself in the passenger seat, the puppy in her lap, and turning to look at him with the gleam of mischief in her eye. Her voice sounded affectionate, Bruno thought, but suspected he was about to be teased.

'I did enjoy reading *Sud-Ouest* on the internet yesterday,' she said. 'At least you can be relieved the Brigadier's interest in your latest case is purely for his own amusement. However many enemies of the French state he tracks, he doesn't yet include the Evil One among their number.'

'Knowing your boss,' said Bruno, 'he could have Satan on the payroll already.'

125

12

As so often with Isabelle, Bruno felt he was swinging between elation and gloom as he turned off the main road to park outside the *collège*. He was despondent that Isabelle had said casually as he dropped her off that she would be spending the night at the hotel that had been booked for her by the *Ecouteurs*. On the other hand, she was staying for the weekend. Better still, she had jumped at the chance of accompanying him the next day on his visits to the possible launch sites for the punt. And her presence in St Denis had been sufficient to entice Commissaire Jean-Jacques Jalipeau, head of detectives for the region and known to all as J-J, to join them for the day. Isabelle had been J-J's star Inspector and his favourite colleague until she was tempted away to Paris to join the staff of the Minister of the Interior.

It was not just the renewed presence of Isabelle in his life that explained the lump in Bruno's throat. It was also the small bundle curled up asleep on the passenger seat beside him. Since Gigi's death, he'd wondered whether any dog could ever replace him, but Bruno had already been surprised by the delight he found himself taking in the new puppy, even after a few hours. He'd almost forgotten the endearing clumsiness of young bassets and the way they tripped over their own long ears. It was impossible to look at one without smiling, and Bruno heard himself chuckle as he gently picked up the dozing dog.

Balzac, he thought, was an inspired choice for a name, a constant reminder that he should start reading the classic novels of his new dog's namesake. He remembered the Mayor telling him soon after Bruno took office that all he would need to know about the politics and passions, the feuds and dynamics of St Denis, would be found in the pages of Balzac. He tucked his own warm and sleepy Balzac into the crook of his elbow as he went up the stairs to the science lab where Florence held her classes.

He had assumed there could be no better prop for a conversation with youngsters than the puppy, but the four boys had a guarded and almost shifty look as they lined up to greet him and shake his hand. Their defensiveness continued even when he put Balzac on the teacher's bench before them, taking worried glances at one another from under lowered brows. At least Florence was instantly charmed, smiling indulgently as she took a paper towel to wipe a little dribble the puppy left as he ambled towards her.

Bruno knew all four boys through his tennis and rugby lessons. They were normal, healthy youngsters, still a year or two short of puberty. They had grown up in the countryside where they could roam free all day and where there were few dangers. Other than the tourists, everyone knew everyone else in St Denis, a town where people seldom bothered to lock their doors at night. Raised in a community where their parents would swiftly be told of any bad behaviour, the boys were polite to their elders and almost always cheerful and noisy with one another. Their subdued and troubled manner itself was for Bruno a clear signal that something was wrong.

'I'm trying to find out who made a mess in Our Lady's Chapel in the Gouffre, and I found some clues that I think will tell me who was responsible,' Bruno told them.

He took out the evidence bags with the vodka bottle, the bubblegum wrapper and the strange cigarette end and laid them on the bench. He smoothed out the bag with the bubblegum so the trade mark could be clearly seen, and the boys began to fidget.

'You know what fingerprints are, don't you?' he asked, glancing from one to the other.

'It's what you look for to find out who did something, the lines on people's fingers that get left when they touch something,' said Luc, Delaron's nephew.

'That's right. Everybody on earth has different fingerprints, so if we find some on a clue, we know who it was.' He paused, and smoothed out the bubblegum again. 'The glass on that bottle or shiny paper like this is wonderful for showing fingerprints, so I'll soon know who touched this. People have been sent to prison on the evidence of their fingerprints.'

'I've seen it on TV,' said Jean-Paul. 'It was an American show. I'm not allowed to watch *Engrenages*, my mum says I'm too young.'

'Your mum is right, sometimes I wonder if I'm old enough to watch it,' Bruno said, thinking of the hit TV series that always seemed to start with a dead body in a rubbish dump or in the boot of a burned-out car. 'What about you, Abdul?' Bruno said, turning to Karim's cousin's son. The boy almost jumped out of his skin. 'Do you know what DNA is?'

Abdul looked across at his teacher, who smiled at him encouragingly.

'Genetics,' the boy said.

'That's right. Whoever smoked this cigarette in this bag left some saliva on the filter. The saliva contains DNA so we can identify who it was. Did you know that?'

Abdul shook his head. Luc was swallowing hard and Mathieu, the youngest, was looking on the verge of tears. Jean-Paul, son of the manager of the cave, had gone white. Bruno did not feel at all proud of himself but he couldn't see how else to go about his questioning. He looked up at Florence for reassurance and she nodded for him to continue.

'I'm pretty sure I know which boys were in that cave, and when I take fingerprints or DNA I'll be able to confirm it. But if I have to do that, I'll have to bring in your parents and a magistrate and it all becomes very serious. Do you all understand that?'

The boys nodded.

'Now, I'm just going to ask you, Jean-Paul, because you know where your family keeps all the keys, how did you get into the cave?'

Jean-Paul looked across at his friends, chewing his lip. At that moment, Balzac tottered across from sniffing Florence's sleeve to stand in front of the boys. He looked at their faces and then slumped down, paws and ears outstretched, in front of Jean-Paul and looked up at the boy with big, sad eyes, his tail thumping the bench. The boy stretched out a hand to stroke him and Balzac licked it.

'We keep a spare key under the stone by the stage door, just in case the musicians arrive early and we can't find my dad,' the boy said, his eyes on the puppy. 'I used that.'

'Did your dad know about this?'

'I asked him to open it,' said Luc, standing beside Jean-Paul. 'It was doing a favour for Uncle Philippe.'

'I was there, too,' said Mathieu, almost proudly. 'They said they didn't want to leave me out.'

Bruno grinned at them. 'At your age, I wouldn't have wanted to be left out either. What did Uncle Philippe want you to do? Did he give you the black paint?'

'He said it was washable and would soon clean off,' said Jean-Paul. 'It was just to make a story, to get more people coming to the cave.'

'And you were the one with your dad's cigarettes, Abdul,' Bruno said. 'You know you're too young to smoke. You'll never play good football if you start smoking.'

'Will you tell my dad?' Abdul asked, evidently far more worried about his father's reaction than about Bruno's questions.

'Why not tell me all of it, and you can start by telling me where you got the goat's head,' Bruno replied.

'But we didn't,' said Jean-Paul. 'It was there already when we arrived and so was that funny painting on the wall. We had the candles and we'd already painted them, but we didn't paint Our Lady. We went in with the candles and put them on the big stone and then we saw all the other stuff so we ran away.'

Bruno nodded, as if he understood, but this was suddenly becoming much more complicated. If the boys hadn't done this, who had?

'When did you have your cigarette, Abdul?' he asked.

The boy looked across at his friends. They were all leaning forward now almost eagerly, clustering around the puppy who rolled happily between them. The shamefaced look on the boys' faces when Bruno arrived had long since gone.

'We all had a puff, when we crossed the lake, before we went into the chapel,' said Luc. 'Even Mathieu took a puff, although it was his first time.'

'And what about the vodka bottle?'

'Uncle Philippe gave it to us, but it was already empty,' Luc answered.

'And did he give you the candles, as well?'

Luc nodded.

'So Uncle Philippe gave you the candles and the paint and the vodka bottle and asked you to put them in Our Lady's Chapel,' Bruno asked, keeping his voice as light and casual as he could. 'But when you got there, you saw that Our Lady had already been painted black and the goat's head was already there, and that funny painting on the wall. Is that how it happened?'

'Will you have to tell Uncle Philippe I told you?' Luc asked. 'I don't want to get him into trouble. It was just so he could do a story to get more tourists coming.'

'I understand,' Bruno said. He turned to Jean-Paul. 'Did your dad know you were borrowing the keys?'

Jean-Paul looked at Luc and then at Abdul and Mathieu, and then looked down and mumbled, 'I think so.'

'Uncle Philippe said it was all arranged,' Luc said.

'Did he give you anything for doing it?' Bruno asked, thinking that Delaron would have some explaining to do, to Bruno and to his editor back in Périgueux. A trick like this could probably put a very swift end to his embryonic career as a press photographer. 'Or did he just buy you an ice cream and some bubblegum?'

'He gave us five euros each.'

Usually Bruno had a soft spot for Delaron, a good-natured and cheeky young man who was evidently bored running the family's camera shop and taking wedding photos and studio portraits. From the snaps of rugby matches and school prize days in St Denis, he'd turned himself into an accomplished news photographer. But this manufacturing of reality was outrageous. And it smelt like a plot, with Marcel the cave manager behind it and quite probably Bruno's friend the Baron, in the interests of bringing more trade to the cave and to St Denis. Even as he felt his irritation build into anger, Bruno realized that exposing this little scheme would primarily hurt the four boys.

'So what happened when you saw the goat's head and that Our Lady was already painted?' Bruno asked.

'We didn't see it at first, we just had a torch,' said Jean-Paul. 'But I know where the switches are, so when Mathieu bumped into the goat's head I turned the light on, and then we saw everything else and that's when we ran.'

'You ran back to the boat? Then pedalled back to the other bank?'

'Yes, but I didn't tell you. There was already a boat on the shore by the chapel when we got there. We took our boat back but I'd put on the master switch by then so everything was lit. Then we left by the stage door and I turned off the master switch.'

'And did you tell your dad?'

'No, we were all too scared.'

Delaron was the one who should be in trouble, but the four boys would probably pay the worst price once their role was exposed. Had Delaron thought of that when he recruited his own nephew into the scheme? No doubt he assured the boy it was just a lark.

But if he couldn't expose Delaron without exposing the boys, could he stop the newspaper from printing the false story? He'd need some powerful evidence to convince them to drop it, and without the boys he had no evidence at all, except his and Florence's word. She was pensive as she glanced from one of her pupils to the next, all the time stroking Balzac and letting the puppy nibble at her fingers. Would she confirm to the newspaper that the story was false, if it meant bringing the boys' role into the open? He rather doubted it, which was one of the things he admired about her.

'I don't want their names connected with this,' Florence said once the boys had clattered their way downstairs.

'I was thinking the same thing, even though if we keep quiet about this, it lets Delaron publish a lie.'

'If you want me to swear to Delaron's editor that I know the story to be false, I'll explain why I know but I'm not prepared to reveal the boys' names.'

The thought struck Bruno that he now had Delaron's career in the palm of his hand. Even without the boys' evidence, he could ensure that the newspaper would never employ him again. As he dismissed the thought, a sneaky little voice at the back of his head was suggesting it might be quite useful to have a hold on Delaron in the future.

'After all, the story's not altogether false,' Florence said. 'I believe the boys when they said that somebody else had been there before them.'

'Delaron can't have been responsible for that, or he'd have had no need to send the boys in.'

'So there is truth in what Delaron is peddling,' Florence replied. 'Somebody is playing Satanist games in the cave, just as they did with that woman in the boat.'

13

Bruno, intent on a serious talk on the ethics of journalism with Philippe Delaron, had left Balzac with Florence. She wanted to show the puppy to her own children. But his visit to Delaron's camera shop was in vain. Delaron's mother explained that her son had gone to Périgueux. Bruno took the back road over the hill, cutting across one of the great bends of the river to the home of Gaston Lemontin, no longer the deputy bank manager after signing his petition. Bruno found him in his garden with his wife, planting vegetables in the *potager*.

'Time I did that myself,' Bruno said. 'I thought I might try some beetroot this year.' He gazed down beyond the garden to the edge of the cliff and the impressive view along a stretch of the river to the far side of the valley. There was no other building in sight. No wonder Lemontin was prepared to take some risks to protect it.

'You didn't come here to talk about beetroot,' said Lemontin. 'You heard what happened at the bank?'

'No, but I can guess. You've been transferred to Timbuktu.'

'Not quite that far. I'll be commuting up to Sarlat from Monday, and I get tomorrow off.'

Lemontin's wife turned from the beanpoles she was placing and said, 'I'll never vote for that damn Mayor again.'

'I thought this might happen,' Lemontin said. 'I know how these things work. It might even be a blessing in disguise. I'm going to be deputy manager to a man who's close to retirement, so I could get promoted.'

'I really came to pick your brains,' Bruno said. 'You said there was something fishy about this deal and I need to know if you're right.'

Lemontin looked at him sceptically. 'Is this you needing to know or the Mayor?'

'Both. But it's mainly local taxpayers like you who need to know whether this is a solid project or something that's going to land us in trouble.'

Lemontin led the way back up the gravel path that bisected his garden. His house was a modern copy of a traditional Périgord stone building. But it seemed somehow fake: the stones too regular, the tiles too new and the doors and windows were all too freshly painted, with no weathering by sun and rain. Leaving his gardening gloves and clogs at the door, Lemontin donned a pair of slippers awaiting him just inside the kitchen, washed his hands at the sink and turned on the kettle to make coffee.

'Have you heard of a place called Thivion?' he began. Bruno shook his head. 'It's in the next *Département*, the Corrèze. A small place, a bit like St Denis, with a river and some nice old buildings. They're trying to build up the tourist trade. Out of the blue, they got an offer from a property company to build a high-class holiday resort with golf course. They were promised individual swimming pools for each of the luxurious holiday villas, which were to be built in the classic local style. No expense spared, they were told.'

The kettle boiled and Lemontin made coffee and steered Bruno into a small room beside the kitchen, evidently his private study. It had the same spectacular view down the river, but no armchair from which to enjoy it, only Lemontin's office chair at the desk, and a straight-backed wooden chair beside the filing cabinet. On the desk lay a telephone, a laptop and a notepad, with a single newly sharpened pencil. A bookcase stood next to the desk, with the annual copies of the telephone directory neatly in order and going back at least ten years. Bruno had never seen anyone who stored such stuff before. There was no painting nor poster on the walls, only the cheap calendar issued each year by the bank. While it struck him as slightly odd, the extraordinary neatness of the study gave Bruno confidence in the rigour of Lemontin's files and researches.

'It sounds a bit like the deal we're being offered,' said Bruno, taking the wooden chair, but turning it so that he could enjoy the view. 'Is it the same company?'

'Hard to tell,' said Lemontin. 'The names are different. Our company is called Mortemart Investments and theirs was Gondrin Investments, but they have some of the same directors and use the same bank. You'll want to speak to the people in Thivion yourself, but here's what they were promised.'

He rose, opened the filing cabinet and withdrew a fat file. He handed Bruno an architect's drawing for what looked like a very handsome development indeed, in a style very similar to the one Bruno had seen in his Mayor's office.

'And here's the reality,' Lemontin said, handing him a large print of what looked like a barracks, undistinguished buildings of one and two storeys jammed closely together with a communal swimming pool and vast common car park. The walls had recently been repainted in a less than successful attempt to cover large displays of graffiti.

'The promised eighteen-hole golf course has turned into a small place for miniature golf,' Lemontin said. 'The buildings are not luxurious individual villas. The town ended up heavily in debt.'

Under the original deal, the town was required to arrange full planning and construction permission and to install the roads, water and sewerage systems, the electricity and gas and to pay for new telephone lines. The development company would do the rest. This meant that all the town's investment took place at the beginning of the project. Once the roads and sewers were built, Gondrin announced that it had been taken over by another company, which said the original plan was no longer viable and would have to be scaled back. Even to go ahead with a much cheaper project, the new company would require further investments and bank guarantees from the town. Having already invested nearly a million euros, the town council reluctantly went ahead.

'And this is what they got for their two millions in debt,' Lemontin said, pointing to the photograph of the barracks. 'It's leased out to one of the more notorious *banlieues* outside Paris as a holiday home for disadvantaged families. Not quite the upmarket clientele that Thivion was promised.'

'Where did the two million debt come from?'

Roads, sewers and legal fees, Lemontin explained, plus the town found itself responsible for architect's fees and some very stiff management and accounting fees to Gondrin Investments. That was the first million. A further million to start the building work and another mortgage to complete it; otherwise they threatened to walk away from the deal. Wanting to save something from the wreck, the council agreed.

'Oh yes, one more thing,' Lemontin added. 'The new company, Pardaillan Investments, had some of the same directors as Gondrin and our own Mortemart Investments. They made out like bandits, and they'll still own the land when the lease runs out. All they paid was the initial cost of the land, and the Mayor helped them get it for a song.'

'Have you shown these pictures and your file to our Mayor?'

'He refuses to see me, and when I got Antoine to show him the file as a councillor, he said it was all speculation and St Denis would make sure its own legal contract was watertight. That's what Thivion thought.'

'What are the names of the directors that they all have in common?' Bruno asked, reaching for Lemontin's notepad and pencil. Lemontin read the names out from a photocopy of a legal document.

'Lionel Joseph Foucher and Eugénie Marianne Ballotin and then a lawyer in Luxembourg.' Bruno had expected as much. 'But they're just fronting it. There's an investment trust behind it all called Antin, again based in Luxembourg and it uses a Swiss bank so I can't find out who owns Antin.'

Lemontin pushed the file across the desk to Bruno. 'Take it, I have copies.'

'Did you try and get any of the newspapers interested in this?'

'I spoke to Delaron, but he said he only did picture stories and I didn't know who else to ask.'

Bruno opened the file and leafed through to find a photo-copy of a letter from the *Mairie* of Thivion. He punched the number into his phone and rang, keeping his eyes on Lemontin. When the call was answered he asked for the office of the *police municipale*, was put through and introduced himself.

'Bruno Courrèges,' came a hearty voice down the line. 'I remember you from the rugby team at the police college. Bernard Laprade, I played fullback.'

Bruno vaguely remembered a beefy type with a vast reper-toire of bad jokes and rugby songs. They exchanged a few pleasantries and then Bruno explained the reason for his call.

'You want to know what happened?' His voice was so loud that Lemontin, who could not help but listen, began to smile sadly. 'We got screwed, taken for a bunch of bumpkins by these city slickers with fancy suits and a big white sports car which I imagine we paid for. All we got in return is a bunch of bloody North African kids and a lot more shoplifting.'

'Do you think your Mayor would say the same to my Mayor?' Bruno asked. 'We may have a similar deal in the offing, and from what you say we could do with a warning.'

'My Mayor would shout it from the rooftops if he could. He tried to get our deputy to raise it in the National Assembly but these guys seem to have a lot of political pull. Our lawsuit got nowhere.'

*

Bruno had been a policeman too long to swallow a story, even one as well documented as Lemontin's, without checking the other side. He needed to talk to Foucher and Eugénie, but first he had to find them, and Béatrice's hotel was the place to start. The property was screened from above by a row of poplar trees, which gave way to the beginning of a gravel drive guarded by two tall iron gates mounted on weathered stone pillars. The drive wound down to the terrace where he had found the Baron drinking with Foucher and the Count. In the mostly empty car park he was surprised to see one car he recognized, Fabiola's battered Twingo with its medical centre sticker stuck to a corner of the windscreen. Could this be her mysterious private patient?

The windsock of the helipad sagged emptily as he walked around to the main entrance. He was greeted by an elegant young woman in a black silk suit, cut to emphasize her cleavage. She introduced herself as Cécile. He gave his name and rank and asked for Madame Béatrice. Bruno realized the suit was some kind of uniform when Béatrice arrived, wearing the same elegantly revealing outfit. She gave him a warm smile, offered him a drink and led him to the terrace. Another young woman, clad in the same black suit, arrived within moments with a flute of champagne for her and the glass of mineral water he'd requested.

'How different you look with your clothes on,' Béatrice said, with a teasing glance. 'I hope this is a social call.'

'I'm afraid not. I'm on duty and hoping you can tell me where to find Monsieur Foucher, Lionel Foucher. He was having a drink here the other day. I think he's a business associate of the Count.'

'I believe he lives locally but I don't know exactly where.' Any hint of flirtatiousness had gone. The smile seemed fixed to her face, but it had cooled. 'I can ask the Count but he's not here today. If you wish I'll send him an email. Should I say why you want to see him?'

'You can say it's about a place called Thivion, where I believe Foucher had some business recently.' Her facial expression didn't change but her body language had stiffened.

'It sounds rather official.'

He nodded, his face neutral.

'Very well.' She made as if to rise, although she had not touched her drink. 'Was there anything else?'

'Perhaps you can tell me who owns this place.'

Her eyebrows raised and she studied him a while before replying. 'It's a private company called Antin Investments.'

'Is the Count involved in it?'

'He's one of the directors.'

'But not Foucher?'

'No, not Foucher.' She picked up her glass to take a sip of the champagne, a gesture that allowed her a discreet glance at her Cartier watch. 'If you want to know more I can put you in touch with our company lawyer in Paris. Now if you'll excuse me, we're preparing for a private dinner party this evening and I need to coordinate with my staff.'

'That would be very kind.' Bruno rose, finished his water, replaced his cap and thanked her for her time.

'I can see I've kept you so I'll see myself out,' he said. 'Just one more thing. Do you know a Mademoiselle Eugénie Ballotin? I think she's some kind of business partner with Foucher.'

'I'm not sure that I do,' Béatrice said, looking up the drive to where headlights had suddenly appeared, although the evening was still light. 'I think that will be the first guest so I must go. *Au revoir*, Monsieur Bruno.' She waved and disappeared into the lobby.

Bruno lingered beside one of the folded umbrellas that usually shaded the tables and watched the antique Citroën sail majestically past the car park entrance and turn to park in front of the main steps. For the second time that evening, it was a car that Bruno recognized. And as he walked back to his van in the car park, from which Fabiola's Twingo had disappeared, he wondered what the Baron had in mind beyond the dinner that Béatrice had planned.

14

The evening was setting in when Bruno arrived back at Florence's apartment to collect Balzac, and found children, Florence and his puppy all heaped happily together on the floor. He stayed long enough to help bathe the twins, who insisted that the puppy help put them to bed, and then drove out to Pamela's place to take Hector for his evening ride. Fabiola opened the door of her gîte when she heard his van and came out to the car.

'I know you saw my car at the hotel because I saw yours,' she began. She was already wearing her riding boots and hat. 'And I'm still not going to answer your question about my private patient because it's none of your business.'

Without a word, he handed Balzac to her through the window.

'Oh, thank heaven for that. He's lovely.' She turned the dog upside down to see what sex it might be. 'I wondered when you were going to get another dog and it's about time. Where did you find him?'

'A present from Isabelle,' he said. 'And the Brigadier.'

'She's down again, is she?' Fabiola's tone of voice made it clear that it wasn't a question. She and Pamela were good friends and she was no great fan of Isabelle. 'And now she picks out your new dog.'

'She's here on business, doing a lecture at one of the local training centres.'

'How convenient that it's the end of the week. I assume she'll be staying for the weekend. Not that it's any of my business. What do you plan to do with the dog when we ride?'

'I want him to meet Hector first, but I thought I'd carry him against my chest, get him used to the motion.' He'd thought of it since seeing Rashida's baby tucked against her breast in the shawl.

Fabiola sniffed and went ahead into the stables to saddle Victoria. Bruno followed, tucking Balzac into his jacket, keeping a firm hold on him. Just his head and long ears peeped out. He took one of last year's apples stored beneath the stable bench and approached Hector's stall, talking gently so the horse would know it was him. He held the apple close to his chest so that Hector could see the puppy, and from the sudden squirming against his chest, Balzac was eager to make the acquaintance of this enormous animal before him.

Hector took the apple and chewed it delicately while studying Balzac. Bruno wondered if his horse had any memory of Balzac's predecessor, Gigi. Horse and basset had become good friends, with Gigi sometimes sleeping in Hector's stall and even riding on the horse's back once when they had to ford a river. Hector stepped forward and nuzzled at the puppy, warm air from the horse's nostrils flooding into Bruno's jacket and across his chest. Balzac gave Hector's nose a hesitant lick and then uttered a timid bark. Hector nuzzled him again and then stepped back. Bruno let Balzac down onto the floor of the stall, where he played briefly in the straw, then crept up to rub one of his long ears against Hector's leg.

Moments later, they were walking up the lane to the gate where they turned off and began trotting through the meadow that led to the ridge, Fabiola leading on Victoria with Bess alongside on a loose rein. Squeaks of what he hoped were excitement were coming from Bruno's chest as Hector began to lengthen his stride into the slope. There was still some light in the expanse of sky that unfolded as they topped the ridge, a red glow on the skyline where the sun had just dropped. Bruno slowed to enjoy it and heard the cawing of rooks gathering in the trees for the night. Little Balzac squirmed to get more of his head out, turning it from side to side to see this huge new world of the countryside. Bruno looked too, wondering what Eugénie might say in response to his questions about Thivion. But there was no other rider in sight, just the sound of Victoria's hoofbeats to the rear.

'Have you eaten?' Fabiola asked, coming alongside.

'Not yet.'

'I'm making spaghetti but no promises,' she said as they walked the horses back down the slope, letting them pick their own way in the gathering darkness. 'I got the recipe for the sauce from a book.'

'That's the best place to find one,' Bruno said, grinning at her. He'd long since stopped believing Fabiola's protests that she couldn't cook. 'If you can read, you can cook.'

He attended to the horses first while Balzac explored the stables and rolled happily in the straw. Once they were settled for the night, he stayed in Hector's stall to phone Pamela. She'd probably be at the hospital; she usually was. But when she answered, it sounded as if she were in a restaurant and he heard her say something in English before the background noise dimmed and then he heard her greet him in French.

'This sounds like a bad time to talk,' he said.

'On the contrary, it's a very good time, but I can't stay long. I said you're a potential client to rent a gîte for the summer, but thank heavens you called. I'm having dinner with my ex-husband and he's making an offer he thinks I can't refuse.'

Bruno knew little of Pamela's marriage except that her husband had been a banker who spent most of his time working, had an affair with his secretary and divorced Pamela to marry her. This second marriage had now collapsed.

'He's offering to pay for full-time care for my mother wherever I want, in a nursing home or where I live,' she explained.

'Wherever you live?'

'No, that's the catch. I'd have to go back and live with him, in England. I can have my horses, and my mother.'

'It sounds like a financial transaction,' said Bruno.

'Of course it does, he's a banker.' She laughed. 'It's the only thing he understands. I'd better go. Can we talk tomorrow?'

'Of course, and the horses are fine. I'm about to rub them down while Fabiola cooks.'

'Love to you both.' She rang off, and Bruno picked up his puppy and walked back, frowning, to Fabiola's kitchen, where she was fishing in a bubbling pot for individual strands of spaghetti to see if they were done. He waited until they were seated and served before he recounted the conversation with Pamela.

'I think it's what she has been afraid of,' said Fabiola, grating parmesan over her food. 'The ex-husband must know her quite well, to tempt her this way. He pretends it's about her mother but it's really about using his money to get what he wants.'

'For Pamela, it is about her mother.' He poured out some wine from the bottles he kept at Pamela's house.

'No, he's playing on her sense of guilt over her mother. If there had been children, he'd have used them and their need for a father as well as a mother. As things are, he's made sure that whatever happens, she'll be unhappy. If she stays with him for her mother's sake, she'll be miserable. If she refuses him and comes back here, she'll feel she's letting her mother down.'

'What can we do to help her?' There had to be a way.

Fabiola sat back and looked at him fondly. 'You're a strange person, Bruno. I've never known anyone so sure that there has to be a solution to everything, if we can only find it. As a doctor, let me tell you that for some things there is no cure, that usually the only solution is the lesser of two evils.' She put down her fork and laid her hand on his arm to reinforce her words. 'In this instance, we must do nothing except let Pamela know we'll support her in whatever she decides to do.'

'And now,' she said, with an abrupt shift in mood, 'you can tell all about the latest news of our devil-worshippers.'

'What?' Bruno had been thinking of Pamela, and Fabiola's sudden switch plunged him into a different world. 'What latest news?'

'Didn't you hear the radio? About the cave? About Philippe?'

Bruno shook his head, and felt a flare of anger at Philippe Delaron, but also at himself. He should have made more effort to track down the photographer, rather than just going to the shop.

'Philippe was on that magazine programme they have after the news on Périgord-Bleu, saying there'd been another Satanist thing, in the big cave this time, like a Black Mass with a goat's head. I thought you'd have known.'

'I knew, all right,' he said, wondering whether he should call the newspaper direct and tell them their new devil story was a fraud. No, he owed it to Philippe to tell him first; he might even have an explanation. And there were the boys to consider. 'I even know how he faked it.'

Rather than looking shocked, Fabiola chuckled as she forked up more spaghetti. 'Serves them all right for being so damn gullible.'

15

Bruno had arranged to meet J-J and Isabelle at Fauquet's café for breakfast. First to arrive, he borrowed Fauquet's own copy of *Sud-Ouest*. A photo of the blackened Madonna from inside the cave took up the whole front page. The headline read: *The Devil Rides Again in St Denis*. Inside were two more pages, with pictures of the goat and the candles. The pentagram defacing the image of the church window had been given a page to itself. Father Sentout had been interviewed again, and quotations from some Satanist website advised following one's sexual desires, whatever one's orientation. That seemed little more than an excuse to reprint the photo of the naked woman passing under the bridge.

'Can I buy that copy from you?' a stranger asked, as Bruno folded the paper and pushed it back along the counter. 'In the *Maison de la Presse*, they've sold out. I'll pay double.'

'Not mine, it belongs to the café,' he replied. 'Where are you from?'

'Limoges,' came the reply. 'We heard about it on the radio and came down. Do you think they'll print some more?'

Bruno shrugged and went out to the terrace to wait for the others, noticing for the first time the unusual number of cars with number pates that did not carry the digits 24, which showed they came from the *Département* of the Dordogne.

'Busier than market day, and it's not even eight o'clock,' said Fauquet. He had laid aside his chef's hat and was putting the summer chairs and tables onto the terrace. Usually he didn't do that until well into May. 'Say what you like, Bruno, this Satan stuff is good for business. I've got an extra batch of croissants in the oven already.'

Isabelle arrived first, limping slightly with her cane, and demanding to know what Bruno had done with Balzac. He explained that he'd left the puppy in the stables with his new friend Hector. Then J-J appeared in his big Citroën, looking for somewhere to park. He made two tours of the square before leaving it at the kerb with a big *Police Nationale* card inside the windscreen. They ordered croissants and coffee for Bruno and Isabelle, and the same for J-J plus the full breakfast of *tartine* and jam and orange juice.

'I had further to come,' he explained, after enfolding Isabelle into his bulk and planting smacking kisses on each cheek.

He sat down and studied her, then ordered another croissant for Isabelle, insisting she needed a little more flesh on her bones and a lot more Périgord cooking. J-J was probably one of the few men she'd heed, Bruno thought; it was like watching a father with a favourite daughter. Bruno shifted the empty plates and cups to a neighbouring table that two sets of visitors were squabbling over and spread out the detailed map that ramblers used, a 1:25,000 scale produced by the Institut Géographique National.

'You can see the sites I've marked after the river trip,' he said. There were four left that he thought worth examining from the land side. Two other sites had been checked by Antoine with the local watermen and pronounced clear.

'I'd never realized those bends in the river were so big,' Isabelle said. 'You don't get a sense of that on the roads.'

'The roads can't follow the river line because of the cliffs,' said J-J. 'Remember that case of the kid who drowned up near Montignac, Bruno? Must be seven or eight years ago. We used helicopters as well as boats trying to find him. You couldn't get down from the roads.'

He reached into his briefcase. 'By the way, I've got the final autopsy report.' He put it on the table, turning by habit to the final page where the conclusions were listed.

The woman had been very drunk, with 1.9 grams of alcohol per litre of blood, which was more than three times the legal limit for driving. She'd had the equivalent of more than a bottle of wine, Bruno calculated. He'd have to check how much that meant from the vodka bottle. She had evidently taken temazepam, but less than half a gram. This was not usually fatal even when mixed with alcohol. But she'd also been a habitual cocaine user.

'A busy girl,' said Isabelle, thumbing through the report to the section on the woman's sexual activity. Bruno still got slightly embarrassed discussing such matters with a woman, even a former lover. He noticed that J-J stayed silent. He took the report from Isabelle and looked first for the reference to the object Dr Gelletreau had taken from the woman's vagina. It was listed as 'unidentified flour-based disc, possibly bread'.

He'd have to talk to the pathologist directly. Then he looked for the estimated time of death.

'Time of death before midnight and no evening meal,' Bruno said aloud. 'So the alcohol and drugs would have been more potent.'

He read on, noting that only her prints had been found on the bottle of Smirnoff vodka. She had given birth more than a decade earlier. Her teeth had been capped cosmetically in a resin characteristic of American dentistry; French dentists preferred porcelain. But from the TB vaccination scar on an upper arm, she was almost certainly European by birth; American doctors used a different technique. Her lungs showed she had been a heavy smoker and her liver showed years of alcohol abuse.

'A suicide, not much question about it,' said J-J, his tone of voice suggesting he'd been brought on a wild goose chase.

'I might agree, except for all the other stuff,' said Bruno. 'Did she paint that pentagram on herself? Did she set fire to the boat before taking her last slug of vodka? If so, where's the lighter or the matches? Did she cut the cockerel's head off? If so, where's the knife? Where's the container for the tranquillizers?'

'It's not only that,' Isabelle said, glancing at the nearby tables and keeping her voice down. 'Where did she leave her clothes? Who were the guys she was having sex with? Did they not notice she suddenly left? Why did they not report her missing? And an evening of sex and drugs is not the usual prelude to a suicide.'

She turned to Bruno. 'I'm sure you'll have checked missing

153

persons, but with that dentistry, did you check the American consulate?'

'Any report from them or any other foreign embassy gets on the missing persons list as a matter of course,' said J-J.

'What if she's not formally missing yet, just some questions raised about where she might be?' Isabelle said. 'It's worth a call.'

'She was a striking woman,' said Bruno. 'It's not a face that people would be likely to forget.' He put a photograph on the table. The pathologist had patched up the damage to her eye, cleaned her up and done something deft with cosmetics before taking the picture. She still looked dead, but as if a beautiful woman had died peacefully. Copies would go out to all the *Mairies*, Gendarmeries and municipal police offices in the *Département*, to the fire brigades and medical centres, newspapers and all public offices. Police would be expected to show copies of the photo around the hotels and bars and markets.

The first of Bruno's targets was a small restaurant with a wide terrace overlooking the river and rowing boats for hire. It had been closed when Bruno and Antoine had taken the canoe trip. Now it was open, but the owner had never heard of anyone owning a punt. The second target was a holiday home, still locked and with all the shutters closed. Dead leaves from the previous autumn were still piled up by the double doors of the boathouse. The windows were thick with dust, but Bruno was able to force the doors apart enough to see that the only contents were two rotting canoes. The third was a small manor house with a stream that flowed into the river. There was no boathouse, but Bruno asked the elderly couple inside if he might check the small garage which was close to the stream. It was already open and contained only their Mercedes, with scant room even for that.

'That leaves the Red Château, the one I've been looking forward to,' said Isabelle. She had printed out the reference in *Mérimée*, the historic monuments website of the Ministry of Culture, and read aloud the details. The castle was first mentioned in archives in the eleventh century, and had changed hands several times before being destroyed in the Hundred Years War. It was completely rebuilt at the end of the fifteenth century after the English had been expelled. For fear they might return it had retained the look of a fortress, until softened by some Renaissance windows in the next century. The northern wing, with an open gallery leading into the courtyard and a separate private chapel, dated from the seventeenth century. The whole building had been restored by a local architect in the 1850s.

'Like most of these old places, it's been turned into a company, a *Société Civile Immobilière*, to avoid inheritance taxes,' Bruno said. Taxes to the local commune were paid by the company and the voters' roll for the Commune listed the only full-time residents as two sisters, Hortense and Héloïse.

'Hortense was the famous one, the Red Countess,' said J-J. 'I can't say I ever heard of the other one. She'll be at least eighty by now.'

'There's some confusion over her date of birth,' said Bruno, who had been doing some research by computer. 'She told different people different things, but the citation when she was made a *Compagnon de la Résistance* said she began working as a courier at the age of fifteen, even before the Germans took over the Vichy zone in 1942. So she must have been born between 1925 and 1928.'

'She was a *Compagnon*?' said Isabelle. 'That's impressive. They didn't make many of those.'

'Just over a thousand, and De Gaulle himself had to approve every one,' Bruno said. 'Another sixty-two thousand got the *Médaille de la Résistance*. Not many, in a nation of fifty million. But she earned it. Not just a courier, she organized parachute drops and hid guns and took part in some of the battles after the Liberation.'

'Wasn't there something about an illegitimate child?' J-J asked.

'She gave birth to a daughter in early 1945,' Bruno replied. 'The father had been a Resistance fighter who was killed, and she never identified him. She just called him her own unknown soldier of the Liberation.'

'If this château is the best bet for your mystery woman, we'd better tread carefully,' J-J said. 'Elderly woman, war heroine, aristocrat . . .'

'And don't forget member in good standing of the Communist Party, holder of the Red Partisan medal and Order of the Patriotic War, first class, awarded and pinned onto her proud chest by Stalin himself in the Kremlin,' said Bruno. 'There's a lot about her on the internet.'

'Quite a woman,' said Isabelle, as they turned into the long avenue of poplar trees that led down the gravel drive. 'And quite a château.'

Two round towers of grey-gold stone, only partly softened

by ivy and topped by conical roofs of black slate, guarded an entrance from which the gates had been removed. The towers were magnificent relics, but far too large for the shrunken château that huddled beneath them. The whole structure seemed unbalanced, made to look ungainly by later changes. Off to the southern side stretched a conservatory, and to the north a series of covered arches led the way to the private chapel. What had once been a moat had become a gentle slope of grass and shrubbery.

'It's amazing that buildings like this still belong to the old families,' said Isabelle. 'I thought the revolution was supposed to change all that.'

'Don't forget who owns it,' said J-J. 'I half expect to see a red flag flying over the battlements.'

In the courtyard Bruno saw a familiar white Jaguar parked beside a small Peugeot and a Kango van. As they got out of J-J's car, Bruno donned his official képi. He was climbing the steps when the arched door opened and a maid in a black dress with a starched white apron and a small white cap bobbed a greeting.

'Commissaire Jalipeau, Inspecteur Perreau and Chef de Police Courrèges, to see the Countess on official business,' said J-J. 'But first, have you seen this woman?'

He thrust towards her a copy of the pathologist's photograph and the maid stepped back, startled. She glanced at the picture, blinked and retreated without a word, leading them into a large hall with a chequerboard floor of dark and light-grey flagstones and old tapestries on the walls. She turned and went through a side door, leaving J-J staring crossly after her. It was much colder inside than it had been in the open air. A grand fireplace, as large as a family car, stood empty except for a single fat log left on the firedogs. As he stepped forward to look at the faded battle scenes on the tapestries, Bruno caught a curious, almost medicinal scent in the air. It reminded him of hospitals.

Double doors opened and Lionel Foucher stepped through. He stopped to nod coolly at Bruno and then raised his eyebrows to look at Isabelle with an imperious gaze that raked her from head to foot and back again. Bruno could feel her stiffen at the intrusion of his stare. Foucher half-smiled and opened the doors wide, then moved to one side to allow an elderly woman, dressed in black silk with a high lace collar, to enter the room.

'*Monsieur le Commissaire*, I understand you wish to see my sister. I am afraid she is indisposed. May I be of assistance? I am Héloïse de la Gorce.'

She held out her hand, more as if she expected it to be kissed than to be shaken. It seemed to have a ring on each finger, perhaps to conceal the claw-like twists that arthritis had inflicted. Her iron-grey hair looked as if it had been carved from stone. She wore no make-up, but a large red jewel shone from the lace at her throat.

'Commissaire Jalipeau, Madame,' said J-J, and introduced the others. He looked at Foucher. 'Who's this?'

'Monsieur Foucher helps manage the estate,' she said. Her eyes swept from Bruno to Isabelle and back to J-J.

'When you say your sister is indisposed . . .'

'She is an invalid and has been for some years. How may I be of assistance?' she repeated.

J-J showed the photograph and explained. She took it, glanced at it cursorily and handed it to Foucher with an order that it be circulated among the staff.

'I think the dead deserve a little more respect than that, Madame,' said Isabelle, stepping forward to intercept Foucher. She took the photograph from him and held it up in front of the old woman's face. 'Please look at it more carefully.'

The old woman could hardly avoid doing so.

'Nobody that I know of,' she said. 'That expression, it could be anybody.'

'We have reason to believe that the boat which carried her down the river came from your boathouse, Madame,' Bruno said. 'Please assemble your staff so that we may question them. And perhaps you might explain your sister's illness.'

The old lady studied him coldly and without turning her head told Foucher to call the staff to the entrance hall. She turned back to Bruno and said, 'Follow me.'

She crossed the hall and stood by the double doors on the other side, waiting, Bruno realized, for them to be opened for her. He complied, smiling politely, then narrowed his eyes against the sudden glare of light that came from the next room, the conservatory. The scent of medicine became stronger.

'Here's my sister,' said the old lady, striding to a modern hospital bed which was backed by row upon row of machines that Bruno had hitherto seen only in a hospital. An immobile figure with sparse white hair lay upon the bed. She had tubes up her nostrils and an intravenous drip in her arm. 'I don't think you'll get much out of her. She's had Alzheimer's for years.'

Beyond the bed stood a figure silhouetted against the sunlight streaming in from the conservatory windows. All Bruno could see was a woman dressed in white, her hair tucked into a nurse's cap.

'Isn't that right, nurse?' the old lady asked.

'Indeed, Madame. She's resting now.'

Bruno was sure he knew the voice. As his eyes adjusted from the gloom of the hall to the brightness of this hospital room, he recognized his occasional riding companion, Eugénie.

'*Bonjour*, Monsieur,' she said, giving no sign that she had met him before.

He replied automatically, glancing around the room. There was a handsome desk and chair and a large sofa with a rotating bookcase beside it. An open laptop sat on the desk. A small TV on a stand stood opposite the sofa.

'You spend most of your time in this room, Madame?' he asked.

'I'm the resident nurse, and always on call. Other staff watch her when I'm away, but I spend a lot of my time here. Of course, I walk or ride horses when I can, for the exercise.'

'Does your patient have lucid intervals?'

'Not as long as I've known her, which is some weeks now.'

'My sister hasn't had a rational thought or spoken a comprehensible sentence for years,' said Héloïse.

Bruno's eye was drawn to a large crucifix that hung above the bed and another on the opposite wall, where the invalid could not but see it.

'I thought your sister was a Marxist,' he said. 'Wouldn't that make her an atheist?'

'I believe she takes comfort from familiar things and we were very religious in our childhood. When she seems up to it, we take her to attend Mass in the chapel. We have a wheel-chair.'

'Do you use local priests for the Mass?'

'No, my confessor makes regular visits from Paris. And now perhaps we can return to the hall and get this questioning over with. You too, nurse.'

Without another word, she turned and led the way back. Bruno took a last glance at the woman on the bed. Her eyes had opened and for a moment seemed to be staring delib-erately at him. He looked again but the eyes were blank and the face immobile.

On an impulse he took one of the photographs of the dead woman from the folder beneath his arm, stepped to the side of the bed and held it in front of the Countess's face. 'Do you know this woman?' he asked. The eyes seemed to quiver and on the sheet a wizened hand stirred and gripped at the smoothly ironed cotton. Was that recognition?

'Please,' said Eugénie, coming to his side and gently pushing the photo away. 'Shocks or surprises upset her. We try to keep everything stable.'

Her hand was cool on his own, but then she seemed to squeeze it a little as she turned the photograph so she could see it.

'No, I don't recognize this woman either. Sorry.'

He handed her his card. 'Please call me to arrange a conven-ient time when I can interview you and Monsieur Foucher about another matter. My Mayor has asked me to look into your company's previous development in Thivion.'

16

Bruno directed J-J to turn off from the main road by the river and take a small country lane that wound up the thickly wooded hillside through *la Petite Forêt*. They passed a small lake and then headed down into a valley dominated by the Château de Fleurac, a neo-Gothic pile that could only have been built in the nineteenth century. After passing it, Bruno pointed the way up a gravel track that led up the hillside to an old farmhouse. The shutters on the doors and windows were open and gleaming in a fresh coat of blue paint. It sat snugly in a protected hollow, facing south, with two semi-circular greenhouses behind it, made of thick translucent plastic stretched across metal frames.

Bruno climbed out of the car as the door to the farmhouse opened and a tall, fit-looking man with long white hair in a ponytail and a neat beard emerged, drying his bare chest with a towel. A *porcelaine* followed him, the classic French hunting dog, creamy-white with long ears. It bounded up to greet Bruno.

He turned to make the introductions. 'This is Laurent, not only the best hunter in the valley but also the man who's going to provide our lunch today.'

'*Un petit apéro?*' asked Laurent, shaking hands and eyeing Isabelle with appreciation.

They sat in the sun on a wooden bench before a home-made table while Laurent went back into his house and came out with a tray bearing a large glass jug of a wine so dark it was almost black. With it came a fat sausage, a squat loaf of home-made bread, and four glasses, which Bruno recognized. They had once contained a popular brand of mustard.

As Laurent took the knife from his belt to slice the sausage, Bruno explained that Fleurac had been until the phylloxera outbreak of the nineteenth century one of the best-known wines of France, exported to England and Holland. The De Beauroyre family, who owned the château, had been famous for their wealth but were bankrupted by the vine-killing disease. They sold out and others tried to replant the vines. Unable ever to get an appellation, the new owners cut their losses and took the subsidies in the 1960s that were available for digging up the vines.

'Some of us keep a few rows of vines, just enough for ourselves and friends,' said Laurent, pouring out the rich dark liquid. 'It's a strong wine, perfect after a day of hunting.'

'It's good,' said J-J, smacking his lips. 'Reminds me of a Cahors.'

'It's the same grape, a *côt*, some call it Malbec,' said Laurent. 'My grandfather always claimed it was the wine served at the wedding of Eleanor of Aquitaine to the king of England.'

'No wonder she was such a formidable woman,' said Isabelle. 'Did you make the sausage, too?'

'Me and Bruno together,' Laurent said. 'I shot the deer but he helped me haul it back.'

'Where's Amélie?' asked Bruno. 'Laurent's wife is the real sausage maker. Laurent and I just provide the unskilled labour.'

'She's down at the market in Le Buisson, selling chickens. I'll be heading down there soon to help her pack up. But I've got what you wanted, the first of the crop.'

Laurent led the way to the side of the house and into the first of the plastic-covered tunnels. It was steamy inside, with a smell of jungle overlaid with sweetness. The floor was carpeted with strawberries, still mainly green but some just turning pink. He bent down and looked under a leaf to find a solitary red one, plucked it and handed it to Isabelle.

'*Mon Dieu*,' she said. 'It tastes like perfume.'

'*Marée de bois*, our local speciality,' he said. 'Most people grow Georgettes but we think they're only fit to make jam. Come back in two weeks and you can eat your fill.'

The next greenhouse looked at first as though there were no plants there at all, just rows of small humped cones of soil, with white buds peeking from each top. From a bench at the side of the greenhouse Laurent took a parcel wrapped in newspaper, put it in a plastic bag and handed it to Bruno. As Laurent added an unlabelled bottle of his wine to the bag, Isabelle could restrain her curiosity no longer.

'Show me, Bruno.'

He opened the bag and unwrapped a corner of the newspaper.

'Asparagus, already? I love it and we don't get them in Paris until May.'

'That's what we're having for lunch,' said Bruno, as they

made their thanks and farewells to dog and master. 'There's a micro-climate in this hollow, everything comes just that much earlier than elsewhere.'

As they drove, J-J grumbled that nothing had come from questioning the staff at the château. Bruno told them of his concern about the new holiday village, the involvement of Foucher and Eugénie and Lemontin's findings at Thivion, hoping to spark J-J's interest. But before J-J even looked like rising to the bait, Isabelle asked about Eugénie.

'So you met her before she turned up in nurse's uniform?'

Bruno described meeting her while riding, although he made it sound like a single encounter.

'It sounds odd, making a nurse into a business partner,' Isabelle said. 'You're sure she said she had shares in this investment company? And what's the link to this Count?'

'He's a director of this Luxembourg investment company,' he explained. 'I think he's also involved in this new hotel that's just opened. I've got all the details in a file at home. It's mostly what Lemontin put together, but I'm going to have to do some further interviews to give a decent report to our Mayor.'

'This Count Vexin, the name rings a bell,' she said. 'Do you know anything more about him?'

'Travels by helicopter, good-looking and obviously wealthy. That's all I know so far.'

'Sounds just my type,' Isabelle said. 'How about you, J-J? Any of this sparking your interest?'

'It sounds like a civil matter and I've got enough on my plate with real crimes,' he said curtly. 'We're almost back at St Denis. Where do you want me to go from here?'

They stopped at Pamela's house to greet Hector and to pick up Balzac from where he'd been sleeping in the horse's stall. The puppy seemed delighted at the reunion with Isabelle and nestled on her lap as they drove the back way past the cemetery to Bruno's house.

He left J-J and Isabelle sitting at the table on the terrace in the sunshine, watching Balzac explore his new home. Bruno took from his kitchen a small knife and bowl and went looking for lunch. He could never understand Pamela's obsession with eradicating dandelions from her lawns; he presumed it was some odd British idiosyncrasy like its royal family and its warm beer. Everyone in France understood the pleasure of fresh young dandelion leaves in a salad, but Bruno went further. He looked for the tiny green buds of the future flowers, snipped them off until he had a couple of dozen and then added some leaves of fresh parsley. He went back into the kitchen to peel a few cloves of garlic and wash the white asparagus. Humming to himself with pleasure at entertaining his friends, he cut some slices from the big smoked ham that hung from the main roof beam. He put water on to boil for the asparagus and the tiny new potatoes, cracked a dozen of his own eggs into a bowl and took plates, glasses and cutlery out to the table where Isabelle and J-J were chatting about politics.

He tossed a knob of butter into a large frying pan and turned on the gas, opened a bottle of Bergerac Sec and took it with a baguette of fresh bread and a bottle of Badoit, his favourite mineral water, out to the table. Back in the kitchen, the butter was starting to bubble and he added some crushed garlic and the little *boutons de pissenlit*, the dandelion buds, and began stirring the eggs with a large fork. He seasoned the eggs with salt and pepper and turned back to the *boutons*. When he felt the little buds begin to soften under his spatula, he added the eggs and began to swirl them around the pan. He broke off briefly to stand the fresh asparagus in their special tall cylindrical pan that he'd found in a *brocante*; now they were ready for the boiling water.

'Can I help?' Isabelle asked, coming into the kitchen, Balzac at her heels, raising his nose to sniff the tantalizing new scents of a kitchen. 'It's so good to be back here, watching you cook. It's even better with the sunshine and a dog at our feet. It feels like last summer.'

Bruno threw her a smiling glance before starting to fold the omelette. Last summer had been that first, glorious rapture of their love affair before she had decided to pursue her career in Paris. He could never decide whether he wanted a clean and surgical end to it, or to go on with their thrilling but frustrating reunions on snatched weekends. Just to look at her was to know he could not give her up, although in the back of his mind he knew that her inevitable departure would leave him miserable and guilty at the sense of betraying the distant Pamela.

'You can take this out to the table,' he said, sliding the folded omelette into a large oval dish, and then tearing up the parsley leaves to sprinkle on top. Before she picked up the plates, Isabelle took his arm and turned him to her to kiss him gently on the lips. He felt her tongue tease him briefly before she broke off and picked up the dish.

Bruno watched her go, still limping slightly, and turned back smiling to pour boiling water first into a saucepan for the potatoes and then into the asparagus pan. Congratulating himself that he'd put fresh sheets on the bed, he went out to enjoy his omelette.

'I smell truffles, but I don't see any,' said J-J, fork in one hand and bread in the other. His wine glass was already empty. Bruno refilled it.

'I left a small one in the egg box,' Bruno replied. 'Egg shells are porous so they absorb some of the flavour, not enough to overwhelm the *pissenlit*.'

'It's wonderful. The *boutons* make it taste like springtime,' said Isabelle, and sipped at her wine.

They finished the course in silence, Bruno delighted to see Isabelle follow J-J's example and clean her plate with bread. J-J had been right: she needed feeding up. He went back to the kitchen and sliced butter into the frying pan to melt before he drained the potatoes and asparagus. He put them into new dishes, poured on the melted butter, sprinkled more parsley on the potatoes and rejoined the others. By the time he returned, Balzac was sitting happily on Isabelle's lap and sniffing at her empty plate.

'The asparagus was perfect,' she said. 'But I've always had them with Hollandaise sauce before.'

'You had your eggs in the omelette,' J-J said. 'Bruno's thinking about my diet. I'm supposed to lose ten kilos this year.'

Isabelle glanced at Bruno and raised a quizzical eyebrow as J-J forked a piece of ham and a new potato, dripping with butter, into his mouth.

'Time we got to business,' J-J said. 'Do you think the old woman was lying about not seeing your dead blonde before? That maid who let us in looked very nervous when she saw the photo.'

'I can't say the sister convinced me,' Bruno said. 'I'm pretty sure the punt came from their boathouse, but that doesn't mean she knew about it. The boathouse is a long way from the château. And I've met that nurse while out riding. That's why I asked you to go round to the back of the building when we left. I wanted to see their stables, and there were at least three horses there, yet that nurse claimed not to know where to find a farrier to put a new shoe on her horse.'

'The sister said her name was de la Gorce,' said J-J, looking at his notebook. 'Probably a married name. Ring any bells?'

'I can look it up in the *Almanach*,' said Isabelle. 'From what you say of the Red Countess, *Renseignements Généraux* will have a huge file on her, going all the way back to the 1940s. Watching Communists was their top priority in those days. Still, that château didn't look like the kind of place for a coke-fuelled orgy. But maybe I've led a sheltered life.'

Bruno smiled at her, and turned to J-J. 'The question is whether we've got enough to open a proper investigation.'

'You know the procedure,' said J-J. 'I can draft a report for the *Procureur de la République* but since the pathologist's report suggests suicide, he'll need a lot of convincing to turn this into a full-scale inquiry. Our budget's in enough trouble.'

'All the publicity around this Satanism stuff may help,' said Isabelle. 'But in my experience, he's going to want you to come up with an identity for the corpse before he takes a decision.'

J-J nodded. 'You've checked the missing persons' index and I've sent off a request for a fingerprint search. We haven't gone through the known prostitutes list yet, not even for this *Département*. I doubt that anything will come of it but I'll see that gets done over the weekend. She died Monday evening and it's now Friday. We'll get a new batch of missing persons posted on Monday, but if nothing else comes up, we're stuck.'

Bruno sighed, began gathering the empty plates and asked who wanted coffee.

'No dessert?' asked J-J. 'I don't want you taking my diet too seriously. I get enough of that at home.'

'No dessert,' Bruno said firmly. 'There is another thing that concerns me, based on the story in the paper today about the break-in at the cave.'

He explained about Delaron paying the boys to stage the break-in, but that somebody had been there before them.

'I told them at the cave not to disturb that chapel until I could see whether you'd be prepared to send in a forensic team,' Bruno said.

J-J shook his head. 'Not on what we've got so far.'

'Bruno, perhaps you and I could take another look at the cave?' Isabelle said. 'I'd like to see it anyway and I don't have to be back in Paris until Sunday evening.' She paused, and gave Bruno a roguish glance that reminded him that it was in another cave that he'd first kissed her. 'I have a soft spot for caves, even without prehistoric paintings.'

170

'Just so long as you also have a soft spot for goat's heads, too,' he said, laughing.

He rose and collected the plates. Balzac teetered on the edge of Isabelle's lap, intent on following. She let him down to the ground and he trotted after Bruno, who put the plates in the sink and then gave the puppy the trimmings from the ham. As he made the coffee, Bruno pondered how critical he should be of Marcel, when he saw him at the cave. Since his son was involved, Marcel must have been in on Delaron's hoax. As for Delaron, Bruno suddenly realized he had a perfect opportunity to get the newspaper to investigate the links between the holiday village project and Lemontin's file on Thivion. In the circumstances, Delaron could hardly say no.

Bruno smiled as he poured the boiling water into the cafetière; he liked solutions where everyone seemed to win. He put cups and sugar onto a small tray and carried them outside.

'. . . will be retiring at the end of the year and then I'll want a new chief inspector,' J-J was saying when Bruno put the tray down on the table.

It sounded as if J-J was trying yet again to lure Isabelle back to the *Département*. J-J had already confided to Bruno that she'd be a strong candidate to take over his job when he retired as chief of detectives. Bruno thought the chances of her returning to the Périgord were very slim. Isabelle had the taste of Paris now, with a powerful job on the Minister's staff, international experience after liaising with Scotland Yard and the kudos of having been wounded while leading a successful operation. She could go very far indeed, and she knew it, which was why Bruno cherished what time they had together.

J-J finished his coffee and left, and as his Citroën lurched down the lane Isabelle leant back in her chair, turned her face up to the sun with her eyes closed and said, 'Our puppy has just peed on my lap, so I need a quick shower. But first, why not come here and kiss me?'

17

When he awoke to find Isabelle's head tucked into the hollow between his chest and his shoulder, one of the first things Bruno remembered was that she had called Balzac 'our puppy'. He tried to identify the noise that had woken him, and turned to look down and see a small basset hound worrying at one of the rubber thong sandals he used as slippers. As he shifted, Isabelle woke up and tightened her arm around him.

'What's that noise?'

'Balzac,' he replied, leaned over the side of the bed and picked up puppy and thong together and placed them on his chest. Balzac abandoned the thong and began sniffing his way from Bruno's chest to his neck and then to Isabelle's shoulder.

'What time does the cave close?' she asked.

He checked his watch. 'Usually in about thirty minutes from now, but they may be staying open later. Let me check.' He reached for his mobile, ignoring the long list of messages and missed calls, and called Marcel and then Delaron to arrange to meet them at the cave when it closed.

He kissed Isabelle, climbed into the shower and dressed in uniform. He began answering messages while she showered and changed. He then rang Alphonse, one of the original hippies from 1968 and a respected local figure. The first Green to be elected to the town council, Alphonse also kept goats and made the best goat's cheese in the district. Bruno said he needed Alphonse's advice and asked if he was free to join them at the cave.

Leaving Balzac in the back of his official van with the remnants of Bruno's sandal, they arrived at the ticket office as Marcel was escorting out the last of the tourists. The car park was overflowing, with more cars lined up and down the sides of the road. Delaron, inevitably, was taking photos of the scene.

'Have you spoken to your nephew since he told me what really happened?' Bruno asked.

Delaron nodded nervously.

'And you give me your word that you had nothing to do with the goat's head and painting the Madonna?'

'Nothing, honestly,' he said. 'That's why Marcel wanted to call you in. It got us worried.'

When Marcel joined them, Bruno introduced Isabelle as an inspector from the *Police Nationale*, which was technically correct, and said they wanted to take a further look.

'The chapel is closed off with a rope. People can look in, but not walk in,' Marcel said.

'Has your son told you what he told me?' Bruno asked, his voice cold with disapproval. Marcel nodded, and repeated Delaron's assurances. When Bruno asked if business had been good, Marcel pointed at the car park and said it had been excellent, almost a record.

'So I can be confident you'll be making a generous donation to the school sports fund.' Bruno asked for all the lights to be turned on and for the largest plastic bag they had in the gift shop. He was just heading for the tourist entrance when Alphonse arrived in his truck, the usual hand-rolled cigarette bobbing from his lower lip. Bruno made the introductions and then explained why he needed Alphonse as they entered the cave, took the steps down to the pedal-boats and headed across the lake to the chapel.

'My wife was here all day, making sure nobody went in,' Marcel said, moving to one side the makeshift barrier of two chairs and a rope that kept visitors outside Our Lady's Chapel.

'There's the goat,' Bruno said to Alphonse. 'What can you tell me?'

'It's an Anglo-Nubian, same as the ones I have,' he replied, bending down to look at the severed head. 'A lot of people call them the rabbit goat because of those long floppy ears. It's quite a popular breed, good for cheese because the milk has a high butterfat content, and it's a sturdy animal. That Roman nose is unmistakable.'

'It's not one of yours, is it?'

Alphonse shook his head. 'It's got horns, and like most breeders we de-bud them soon after they're born. I only know one breeder round here who lets the horns grow, and that's Widow Venturin over by Sarlat. She raises males for stud, where people like to see a good set of horns. That flat, gentle curve is distinctive.'

'If it's one of hers, would she recognize it?'

'Probably. I'd recognize all mine. They're very affectionate, the Nubians, and love to have their necks stroked.'

'Could you give her a call, ask if she's sold any recently?'

'I can do better than that. She's coming to pick up some of my cheese because she's running short for the Sarlat market. We often help each other out.'

Bruno saw Isabelle grin at this unexpected insight into the local goat culture. Bruno handed Alphonse the plastic bag and suggested he take the head with him.

'Hang on a moment,' he said. 'Let me just see . . .'

Alphonse began peering intently at the raw flesh where the neck had been severed, and then at the back of the head and the brow. Although the chapel was well lit, he asked for more light. Bruno shone his torch onto the head. Alphonse took it from him to peer more closely at the neck.

'That's nasty,' he said, leaning back on his heels. 'It wasn't killed humanely. There's no sign of a stun-gun being used and there's a deep cut in the neck at the main artery. Without seeing the rest of it I can't be sure, but I'd say this goat was hung up by its heels, bled in the way the Arabs do it before the head was severed. It certainly wasn't killed at an abattoir, like the law says.'

Bruno knew that a fair number of pigs were killed that way by local farmers despite the law, because that was the way it had been done for centuries. Indeed, he'd usually attend at least one such event every year, and collecting the blood was important for making the *boudin noir*.

'Does that mean somebody killed this goat for food?'

Alphonse shook his head. 'It's not like a pig, you don't use the blood, at least I never heard of anyone doing so. This is an old male, which is not good eating, not like a tender kid. There's not much demand around here for goat meat, not that I've heard, but I'll ask the Widow. If it's not one of hers, I wouldn't know where to look.'

Alphonse left with his plastic bag in his hand, the two long horns sticking out of the top. Marcel said he'd see him out and Bruno said he and Isabelle would continue on their own. She had already taken samples of the paint from the Madonna and the side wall and candles and put them into evidence bags. Together they made a careful search of the rest of the chamber, behind the Madonna and around the makeshift altar. Their only finds were a long thread of dark wool and a grubby white tassel. Either one could have come from anywhere and been there for years, but they bagged them anyway.

'So if it wasn't the boys, how did they get in?' she asked.

Bruno explained the limited number of entrances and then told her of the passage the Baron had shown him.

'But I already looked and there were decades' worth of dust there, quite undisturbed.'

She said she'd like to see it anyway, so he led the way back, taking it slowly to favour her wounded leg. They passed Napoleon's Bedchamber and the great organ on their way to the three solid stalagmites that rose like the stumpy teeth of some giant prehistoric beast to protect the entrance to the Baron's secret way. He felt around with his hands until he found the ring and heaved up the trapdoor.

'Follow me down but be careful, the steps are steep and

narrow. Best face forward.' He put his torch between his teeth and gingerly felt his way down. At the bottom, he turned his beam of light down the tunnel and the dust looked undisturbed as before. The light above him dimmed as Isabelle's body filled most of the narrow stairway and he stood ready to help her down.

'I've got you,' he said, his hands on her waist as he lifted her down, surprised at the lightness of her.

'I see what you mean about the dust,' she said. 'But remember your Sherlock Holmes: when all other possibilities have been exhausted, look at the one that remains, however unlikely.'

She played her own torch on the dust on the steps and then at the dust beneath their feet and down the tunnel. She bent to examine it closer and picked up some of the dust. She rolled it between her fingers and brought it closer to examine it more carefully.

'Animal hairs and fluff, probably carpet fluff,' she said. 'That's the kind of dust you'd find when you empty a household vacuum cleaner, not the kind I'd expect in a rocky tunnel.'

She scooped some of the dust near her into an evidence bag and asked Bruno to go further up the tunnel and do the same. He took some from about a metre further along and then some more from a few metres further.

'They're different,' he said. 'The further stuff is all rock and grit. And there are footprints and scuff marks in it, so the path has been used.'

'So somebody thoughtfully covered their tracks in here and

out,' she said. 'Apart from you and the Baron, who'd know about this?'

'Resistance veterans, and whoever they told, I suppose. Now we know, why don't we explore it the whole way?'

'Won't the guys at the cave mouth wonder where we are?'

'You could go out and say I'm still searching. I walk along to the exit and you take my van and meet me at the cemetery in St Philippon. There's a map in the door pocket.'

'It makes more sense the other way round, for me as the specialist to continue searching and you take the van,' she said. 'You're just trying to spare me the tunnel because of my leg. Stop treating me as an invalid.'

He tried to object but she set off down the tunnel, calling over her shoulder, 'You know it makes sense. Go, and I'll see you there.'

'You don't know how long it is,' he called after her.

'I'll find out. Just go.'

Bruno still worried as he climbed back up the steep steps, replaced the trapdoor and covered it with grit again. Checking that he had the evidence bags and they were all labelled, he headed back the length of the cave to the entrance where Delaron and Marcel were waiting. He showed them the evidence bags and said the Inspector was still collecting stuff for forensics.

'I'll keep the key and come back to pick her up later,' he said.

'There's a guy waiting to see you, a journalist, says he knows you from Bosnia,' said Marcel. 'He's waiting in the snack bar.'

'I don't have much time now,' Bruno said. 'And I want a private word with Philippe.'

He took the photographer out to the car park and opened the rear door of his van to see Balzac sitting tangled in the line from Bruno's fishing rod and chewing energetically on one of the training shoes he used for rugby. He found himself grinning and sighing at the same time, and he tried to remember how long it had taken to train Gigi. He gave Balzac a quick pat and pulled Lemontin's file from his briefcase.

'After the trick you pulled with the kids, Philippe, I want to talk with you,' he began, 'and maybe I should include your editor in Bordeaux in the call. What do you say?'

Delaron shrugged. 'It was rather overtaken by events. There was a break-in and it looks like Satanists.'

'That was lucky for you. Do you think your editor will see it that way? Or that people are going to trust you again? Do you think I should trust you in future?'

'From the look of that file in your hand, I'd say you were going to give me a chance.'

'Not quite,' said Bruno. 'I'm giving you a test.' He removed the single page that showed the links between the companies behind the Thivion development and the one planned for St Denis.

'You'll need to do some research. Go to a place called Thivion and take some photos of what was supposed to be a new holiday village just like the one coming here. Their Mayor is pissed off with what happened to them and I don't want it to happen to us.'

'What's this list of names?' Delaron asked, looking at the sheet of paper Bruno had given him.

'The names of companies behind the two developments and their directors. You can see some overlap. I'm not going to spell it out for you.'

'You give me one sheet of paper, but it looks like you've got a big file on this already,' said Delaron.

Bruno simply smiled at the young man, slapped him on the shoulder and said, 'Good hunting.' Then he turned and headed to the snack bar, looking at his watch and wondering how long Isabelle would take to reach the end of the tunnel. He paused outside the door. The figure sitting over a plastic cup looked slightly familiar. Bruno tried to subtract a decade and more from the man's features and a few kilos from the plump waistline. He mentally replaced the neat tweed sports jacket and rollneck sweater with the scruffy denims and down jackets the journalists used to wear in Bosnia. He still couldn't identify him. Then the guy looked up and Bruno realized it was the absence of a beard that confused him.

'Gilles from *Libération*,' Bruno said, pleased at the way his memory had summoned the name. He'd forgotten the surname, but not the slightly hooded eyes. It was Gilles who had written the piece that got *Médecins Sans Frontières* to take over responsibility for the safe house where Bruno and his squad had taken the Bosnian women they'd rescued from the Serb brothel.

'Sergeant Courrèges,' said Gilles, rising. 'You wouldn't recognize Sarajevo these days. There's even a Starbucks.'

'So that's what we were fighting for,' Bruno said. 'I often wondered.'

'I'm with *Paris-Match* these days and you can guess what brings me here.'

Bruno nodded. 'Right now is not a good time. I have a meeting and some forensic stuff to deliver and I'm already late. But here's my card with my mobile number. When's your deadline?'

Gilles grinned. 'No deadlines in these days of instant media. I'll be posting stuff on the website every day.'

'Quite a change, going from Sarajevo to Satanism.'

'At least I'm working, and there aren't too many journalists can say that these days. The Satan thing is a nice detail but that's not what catches my interest. I want to find out who the dead woman was. That's the real story.'

'Would that mean you've got some kind of lead?'

'Maybe, but it's a long shot. As long as I get to keep the scoop for *Paris-Match*, I can guarantee you'll be the first to know. I presume you still haven't identified her.'

Bruno shook his head. 'She doesn't seem to be reported missing anywhere in France, but we're still checking. You've seen the photo we issued?'

'Of course. Is there anything you can tell me that wasn't in the papers? Anything from the autopsy?'

He spoke a little too casually and Bruno's antennae began to twitch. 'Are you just fishing here, Gilles? You know better than that.'

'Not entirely. But perhaps you could tell me if there's anything that suggests she might have been in the States at some point?'

Bruno studied him, remembering that Gilles had been a

good man back in Sarajevo. Serious about his journalism yet casual about the danger, he'd never lost his sense of humour. 'Strictly off the record, the dentistry looks like it was American.'

'Aha,' Gilles said, nodding as if it confirmed something. 'Would that be cosmetic dentistry?'

'It would. And so . . . ?'

'So I could be on the right track. Are you free for dinner later?'

'Sorry, no. Maybe next week or Sunday night, if you're still here.'

'I'll be here,' he said, looking at Bruno's card. He handed Bruno one of his own. 'And I'll call you tomorrow if I get anywhere.'

18

Bruno drove like the wind, thinking of Isabelle doggedly following the tunnel. He cursed himself for agreeing to her demand to explore it alone, despite her lame leg. He had the map unfolded on the steering wheel before him, taking the risk of occasional darting glances as he tried to think how the roads knitted together outside his own commune. The river's twists and the steep rising of the cliffs alongside forced the roads to take strange, illogical routes and confused his sense of direction. As the crow flies, the Gouffre was not much more than a kilometre from St Philippon, but by road it was more like six or seven.

How could he have been so arrogant as not to check the map in advance? Why hadn't he realized that if someone had used the tunnel, they might still be there, or they might have sealed the far end? Maybe he should go back into the cave and follow her through the tunnel. At least the route was known and he'd be certain to find her. No, he had to stick to the original plan. If he got to the ruined chapel and there was no sign of Isabelle and he could not find his way in, that would be the time to retrace his tracks.

He braked hard as he came to a fork in the road. Cursing,

he looked at the map but the light was going. He stepped out to examine it close to his headlamps. He glanced at the setting sun, knowing that was west, and then he used his finger to follow his route from the cave. He found the fork, and saw he was almost there. He roughly folded the map and jumped back into the van, took the right fork and drove more slowly, looking for a turnoff to the left that would take him down to the beginning of the valley that held the ruins of the abandoned village of St Philippon.

He found the turnoff. With his lights on high beam he saw the stark outline of the crumbling cross on the roof of the chapel. He braked, left the engine running and the lights shining into the ruin, calling Isabelle's name as he stumbled forward and almost fell over the shallow hillocks of the graves.

Calm down, Bruno, he told himself. Walk back to the van and get the torch. Check the ground before your feet. If you break an ankle it won't help Isabelle, stuck in the belly of the earth. Remember what the Baron said: the entrance is hidden in the ruins of the chapel. He made himself stop and examine what was left of the structure. About six metres deep and four wide, the roof was formed of *lauze*, the thick slabs of limestone that locked into one another, supporting themselves without wooden beams. About a third of the roof had gone. The gable end had been rotted by the relentless growth of vegetation so that the cross it supported leaned drunkenly, poised to follow the *lauzes* down into the chapel's nave.

The door was just a memory. He shone his torch inside over the confusion of tumbled stone. If there had been a trap-door in the floor, it was long since buried. But somebody had used this tunnel recently; there had to be a way in. He went outside and studied the walls and surrounding ground. He tried to rock at the nearest gravestones but they were solidly fixed. He went back into the chapel and looked again. The only structure that seemed solid was the altar, a long stretch of pale stone. Why would a remote chapel such as this have something so solid and handsome?

Bruno tried vainly to lift the huge slab. He bent down to examine and then knock and probe the front and sides of the altar. At the rear the stone was different; three separate squat flags supported the great weight of the altar. He shone his torch onto the floor and was heartened to see scratch marks on the flags by the central stone. He pushed at the top, at the bottom and then felt just a hint of movement. Finally he pushed at one side and the stone, almost a metre high and nearly as wide, swivelled and opened.

He pointed his torch into the gap and saw steps going down. They looked even steeper and cruder than the ones in the cave. But at least he'd found the entrance. He leaned in and called Isabelle's name, but heard no reply.

He sat back and considered. He'd done quite enough rushing into things this evening. He went back to his van and turned off the lights and the engine. He disentangled Balzac from the fishing line and tucked the puppy into the front of his uniform shirt. In the glove compartment he found spare batteries he'd bought in a rare moment of forethought. He took his small hiking rucksack, put in his first-aid kit, a bottle of water and a stretch of nylon rope. He checked his phone but there was no signal in this remote place, so he pulled out a notepad and scribbled down the numbers of the *Mairie*, J-J and the Baron, saying where he'd gone and at what time, and stuck it under his windscreen wiper. Then he went back into the chapel and squeezed through the hole beneath the altar and down into the darkness.

The light from his torch revealed that he was in some kind of crypt, four rough stone walls probably built at the same time as the chapel above. The floor was made of gravestones, except for one corner where there was a stone-lipped hole with similar steep steps leading down. The steps gave way to a small cave of smooth-walled limestone, too smooth and unbroken to have been made by man.

He was in a kettle, a hollow formed over millennia by underground rivers. The gap he'd come through from the chapel was itself a watercourse. When heavy storms made the underground river surge, the swirling waters must have carved this small cave. He tried to imagine the power of that water, how it had honeycombed these hills and gouged out the caves that prehistoric people had made into showcases for their art. Further down he should find the course of the underground river that led to the Gouffre. Descending carefully, facing the steps, he was now at least a dozen metres below the chapel and the steps still led downward.

He called Isabelle's name, but no response came, the blackness ahead seeming to soak up every sound. At least now he could see some kind of floor when he took his torch from his mouth and shone it downwards. Whoever had come this way with goat's head and paint must have used a rucksack, and must have known the route, too.

The floor and walls of the tunnel were smooth but damp, almost as if he were in a giant pipeline. A small rivulet trickled down the centre. The tunnel was at least two metres high and the same in diameter. Its even floor was disturbed only by small stalagmites growing at irregular intervals, where water dripped from tiny fissures in the rock overhead. He called her name again, upstream and downstream, but got no response.

On an impulse, he took Balzac from his chest and put him on the floor. Young as he was, the dog might pick up her scent. The puppy lapped busily at the tiny stream of water, looked around him and cocked his leg against the wall to leave his mark. Bruno shone the light upstream and with nose to the ground Balzac explored a little that way and then turned back past Bruno and began to lope downstream. Bruno followed, counting his paces to keep a rough sense of the distance he'd covered. He knew from the map that it was no more than a kilometre in a straight line between the Gouffre and the chapel. But this tunnel was turning in dog-leg angles, forced to change direction where the water had hit a harder patch of rock.

At the count of three hundred and sixty, he heard the sound of running water, and after another twenty paces he saw a glow of light. He called out Isabelle's name and with a surge of relief he heard a distant voice, distorted by echoes, but he was sure he caught the last long vowel of his name. He called her name in return and heard what he was sure was an answer.

Although every instinct urged him on, Bruno kept his steady pace and his mental count. By four hundred and fifteen there was a faint glow of light ahead. As he turned a final corner, Balzac darted ahead and they entered a large chamber that was lit by Isabelle's torch, its light strengthened by its reflection from a large pool of still water that lay between him and Isabelle on the far side, perhaps twenty metres away. Balzac barked a greeting as Bruno's torch illuminated her.

'Are you all right?' he called, his heart beating hard as the anxiety flooded out from his system.

'I'm fine,' she called back. 'When I reached this pool I thought I'd wait for you. I don't have a stick to probe it but it's certainly deeper than my arm.'

'There must be a way across,' he called back. 'How else would they have got to the Gouffre?'

He took off his rucksack, shirt and jacket and plunged his arm in. The water was ice-cold but felt as if it were motionless; certainly he could feel neither bottom nor current. He stood up and flashed his torch to each side. The cavern was a large kettle, shaped like a dome. To his right the dome and the lake narrowed into what looked like another tunnel. Isabelle was perched on a thin beach of rock where her tunnel debouched into the cavern.

He walked to the point where it narrowed but it was still too far to jump. There had to be some way across. The sound of running water was coming from within this cavern. Could there be another outflow? Even as the thought formed, he heard Isabelle calling something and looked across to see Balzac scampering towards her on the far side of the lake. How on earth . . . ?

Balzac had been coming from Isabelle's right, so he walked

to his left and the sound of running water was louder. He lay down and put his arm into the lake, close to the cavern wall, and felt the water flowing over his arm. He groped further and touched something like a wall. It must be some kind of dam over which the water of the lake was flowing. The top of the dam was wide, just a centimetre or two below the surface. That was how Balzac had crossed! Bruno went across at a crouch, feeling his way with his fingertips to be sure he did not stumble, and then Isabelle was there with one arm outstretched to embrace him and the other clutching a squirming Balzac.

'That was easy,' she said, laughing.

'Phew! You had me worried,' he replied, holding her tightly. 'There's a vertical tunnel, more like a narrow tube of cave, about four hundred metres back that way, and then it's a steep climb up narrow steps.'

'That's not all we found,' she said. 'Look up.'

Bruno's eyes followed the beam of light from her torch and saw several holes in the walls of the cavern that could be more tunnels.

'The ones I looked at seemed either to go straight up or to plunge down further than my torch could reach,' she said. 'It's as if this chamber were a giant colander with holes everywhere, different ways for the water to escape when the pressure in here built up. And look what I found here.'

She walked to the far point of the lake shore, where it narrowed, and ducked into a hole Bruno had not seen from the other side of the lake. It opened into a sizeable chamber. Isabelle pointed her torch at a rusty green metal box with white markings. Bruno went across.

'W and D with a white arrow and .303 Ball x 500,' he read. Inside were some black candles, smaller than the two he'd found in the punt, and a wrapped package of white candles.

'It's a rifle ammunition box from the British army,' she said. 'It must be left over from Resistance days. Odd to use it to store candles.'

'The Baron said his father told him they'd stored arms here during the war. He never said there was anything left.'

'And then there's this.' She played her torch onto a small cavity where an old-fashioned candleholder stood with another stack of candles and a disposable cigarette lighter. 'I don't think those lighters were invented before 1945, so somebody has been here more recently. Maybe you should ask the Baron if he knows of any other military gear that was stored here. If somebody has got themselves a box of grenades or a few guns, we'd want to know who. But I was glad to find the candles, in case my torch ran out while I was waiting for you.'

'Let's get back. Is your leg OK? There's a lot of climbing up those steps. '

'My leg's fine, but which way are we going? I presume your van is parked at the chapel, so we should go that way, unless you think someone is still waiting for me to emerge at the ticket office.'

'No, they know I have a key. They'll assume I let you out. And besides, there's a new place nearby where we should be able to get a good dinner.'

He picked up Balzac and tucked him back into his chest, and then helped Isabelle over the causeway and up the tunnel towards the chapel.

19

Bruno set off down the unfamiliar road past the cemetery to the handful of lights that signalled the tiny hamlet of St Philippon du Bel-Air, the grand and hopeful title given to their new home by the survivors of the plague-struck village by the cemetery. Almost deserted, it had not prospered. Perhaps the Count's new auberge would restore its fortunes, Bruno thought, as the downhill road through the woods suddenly opened to reveal the lavish lights of the restored château where he hoped to get dinner. As he approached he was aware of two men waving him onwards. Large wrought-iron gates opened electronically. Two helicopters stood by the landing pad and he passed a row of expensive cars before a large bald man in a cheap suit flagged him down.

'Some of those are government cars,' said Isabelle, sounding curious. 'I recognize the plates.'

Bruno stopped and wound down his window to greet the bald man.

'Are you here on police business?' the man asked, polite but his tone was cold. There was a bulge in his armpit. Two more men of similar bulk stood behind him, several paces apart.

'No, we're hoping to get a meal,' Bruno replied.

'In that case, sorry, the hotel is closed for a private party. You can turn here.'

Isabelle leaned across Bruno and looked more closely at the man. 'Is that you, Mascagny?' she asked.

'That's me, but . . . ahh, Mademoiselle Perrault. What on earth are you doing here? This is a Defence Ministry event.'

'As my colleague said, we were just hoping for a meal.' Isabelle introduced Bruno and Balzac, who was clambering eagerly from her lap. 'I had no idea anything was taking place here tonight.'

'It's a bit of a celebration, some procurement contract,' he said, obviously relaxing. He leaned a heavy forearm on Bruno's open window and reached in to shake his hand and then Isabelle's. 'That's a fine-looking pup. You planning to hunt with him?'

'When he's trained,' Bruno said. 'It'll take a while.'

The man nodded. 'Look, if you two are hungry we've got some sandwiches back in the security van. Just the usual ham and cheese, not like the banquet they're getting in there.'

'No, thanks,' she said, laughing. 'A *jambon-beurre* baguette is not my friend's idea of dinner. We'll leave you to it, and see you at the Elysée. *Bonne soirée.*'

As Bruno turned his car around he saw Isabelle scribbling down the registration numbers from the cars and helicopters. Headlights suddenly appeared around a bend, followed by two large Citroën C6 limousines.

'Private cars, chauffeur-driven,' said Isabelle. 'Ever since the president started using a C6 all the big business guys got rid of their Mercedes and BMWs. This is quite an event. I'm surprised I didn't know about it.'

'Mascagny is a security guy?'

'Yes, with the Defence Ministry. I've run into him a few times at Council of Ministers meetings.'

'Why would you know about the various social events that another Ministry organizes?'

'They're usually on the weekly security circular. Mascagny said something about procurement, so maybe it's a foreign sales event. That would explain it.'

'But why would they do that here? I never heard of any defence plants around here, not even in the *Département*.'

'You've got the big Dassault plant at Martignas near Bordeaux and another one down in Biarritz, then there's Airbus at Toulouse and some research centres in Brive,' she said. 'This is less than an hour away by chopper from all of them. I don't know who owns the hotel, but they knew what they were doing when they restored this place. It looks like it's just been finished.'

'It has, opened this year. It's owned by that Count Vexin I told you about. He's the one behind that project I've got to work on.'

'Vexin, Vexin, I know that name from somewhere,' she said. 'Where are you taking me?'

'Les Eyzies. Then you have a choice of restaurants or I can take you back to my place for whatever scratch meal I can put together.'

'Your place and a scratch meal, please,' she replied, slipping one hand onto his thigh while the other caressed Balzac.

194

'Mascagny was right about one thing. Balzac is a special puppy. And talking of animals, what's happening to your horse this evening?'

'I called Fabiola this morning and she'll take him out when she exercises the others. I do the same for her when she's busy.'

Isabelle began punching numbers into her mobile phone, the same secure model that Bruno had been given by her boss, the Brigadier, when they found out Bruno's was being tapped. Bruno barely listened, thinking what was available in his store cupboard and freezer that could be quickly prepared. He had onions and bread and cheese and some good venison stock, so a hearty onion soup would be a good way to start. Isabelle seemed to be reading out the car and helicopter numbers she had noted. He had spaghetti, but he never thought of it as a main course, so he'd make a risotto instead, with some dried cèpe mushrooms and *lardons*. There was still some *mâche* in the garden for a salad.

'Lebanon,' she said at last. He realized her call was over and she was talking to him. 'That was the CD plate. One of the choppers is privately owned by some company, they're checking on that, and the other is a Defence Ministry Gazelle, unmarked.'

'Significant?'

'Not to me, but it might mean more to some colleagues. You seem distracted. What are you thinking about?'

'What to cook for our supper.'

'Don't tell me, I want a surprise. I'll take Balzac for a walk around your property and when it's ready you can stand on the doorstep with a wooden spoon in hand and call us in. There, I've revealed my little family fantasy.'

Her hand squeezed his thigh in reassurance as she said it, stalling the instant retort that family fantasies did not go well with her plan to return to Paris on Sunday.

'I'm trying to figure out what you mean by that,' he said.

'Simple enough. I have this fantasy of staying here with you, marriage, children, family lunches every Sunday. It's what keeps me sane, even though we both know I'll never do it. I think you will, at some point, with some woman, and then my fantasy will have to stop. I'm gambling that by then my career will be so fulfilling that I'll have no regrets.'

Her frankness startled him, not least because she'd said it almost as though the lines were rehearsed, that this was a deeply considered judgement rather than some off-the-cuff remark.

'You don't think you could ever find a way to combine them both, career and family?' he asked.

'Certainly I could, if you moved to Paris and we lived together there. But then you wouldn't be Bruno any more. You'd be miserable away from St Denis. And if I moved down here, I wouldn't be the Isabelle that I hope you'll always be a little bit in love with. I'd lose whatever it is about me that attracts you. So it wouldn't work. That's our fate. But it doesn't stop me imagining you in an apron making Sunday lunch with little Brunos and Isabelles running around your feet and playing with Balzac.'

'And what are you doing in this fantasy of yours?' He couldn't bear not to ask the question.

'I'm not in it,' she said. 'I'm just watching, disembodied, thinking of might-have-beens and knowing they couldn't work. That's one thing you learn: love doesn't always conquer all. It can't, no matter how much we count on it and hope for it and remember those fairy tales that always ended saying they lived happily ever after. Life isn't like that.'

'You timed that perfectly,' Bruno said, turning up the long hill to his cottage. 'We're home.'

Isabelle asked to be let out to walk Balzac back, and kissed Bruno's cheek quickly before climbing out. He drove on, parked, and with an effort turned his thoughts to dinner. It took some determination, even though he'd heard before most of what Isabelle had said. It was a theme they could never let go, like scratching repeatedly at a scab although knowing the wound would reopen. What was new was her fantasy of a family life. But it wasn't going to happen so he thrust the thought aside as he entered his kitchen.

He was just pulling down his glass jar of the short-grain Italian rice that Fabiola insisted he use for risotto when he heard Isabelle's voice praising Balzac and then came a patter of puppy feet down the hall and into the kitchen in search of the source of the tantalizing smells.

'Did you find the wine I brought?' she said from the hall and then bustled in, her cheeks glowing red. She rubbed her hands together and shivered. 'It's cold out there now the sun's gone.'

'Your wine's already decanted and on the table, and there's a fire lit to warm you up but have a sip of this while I finish the soup.' He handed her a glass of the Bergerac Sec and turned on the grill to toast the bread. Once it was done, he ladled the soup into two individual bowls, put the toast and cheese on top and slid the bowls beneath the grill.

'Two more minutes,' he said, walking into the main room where Isabelle now sat, shoes off, her feet toasting before the fire. She had clutched her arms around herself as if trying to hold in the warmth.

'Would you like a blanket round your shoulders?'

'No, thanks, but could I borrow that jacket of yours, just till I warm up?'

He brought it back from his wardrobe, draped it around her shoulders and said, 'I'll do better than that,' and embraced her, rubbing his hands energetically over her back and then down her thighs to warm her. The fire was burning strongly and the house was not cold. Maybe she was coming down with some kind of flu. With a final kiss on the brow, which seemed hot and slightly feverish to his lips, he said, 'We'll forget about the table and have the soup right here by the fire.'

He returned from the kitchen with the soup bowls on a tray, the cheese brown and still bubbling. He had left a kettle of water heating on the stove. Balzac was now settled on Isabelle's lap. She ignored the spoon, cupping her hands around the hot bowl and breathing in the scents of garlic and thyme and venison stock. He brought the glasses and decanter from the table, poured and then put the wine to the side of the fire, away from the direct heat. She sipped at the soup, almost greedily, until most of the liquid had gone, and then she took the spoon to break up the melted cheese and toast.

'I don't feel too good but I'm starving,' she said. 'I'm not sure I'll appreciate the wine.'

'Only one way to find out,' he said, handing her a glass. He sipped at his own and nodded with pleasure. 'Do you want some risotto? It will only take a few minutes.'

She nodded and squeezed his hand. 'Sorry, I'm not good company this evening. I didn't like being in that cave on my own. I knew you were coming but that place made me shiver. It wasn't scary in the usual sense, more disconcerting, almost as if I could sense something . . . maybe alien is the word. I don't know if it was evil but it felt very different, like another form of life altogether.'

He glanced at her curiously as he stoked the fire; this wasn't like Isabelle. He'd never seen her nervous, far less afraid of anything.

'People have usually invested the caves with strange powers,' he said. 'It always seemed to me significant that our prehistoric ancestors did their engravings and paintings in the caves, but they never lived in them.'

'I understand why,' she said, and shivered again.

He felt her brow. 'You've got a fever, and that probably made you feel a bit woozy in there.'

'I feel under the weather,' she said. 'But I still want your risotto. And that book on the table – is that left out because I was coming or do you read it?'

He glanced across at the book of Prévert's poetry that had been her gift.

'That's us, I suppose,' she said, a finger stroking the back of his hand, tracing the line of each of his fingers. 'His poem about parted lovers, and the sea erasing the footprints left in the sand.'

'But we still have to eat,' he said, and took out the soup bowls. In the kitchen he used the almost boiling water to fill a hot-water bottle and put it in the bed on the side where Isabelle always slept. Then he put the shallots and garlic into the frying pan with a little more duck fat and a cup of Arborio rice and began to stir, waiting for the grains to turn translucent and then just slightly brown. He added the mushrooms and a little of the wine, stirring until the rice had absorbed the liquid, and then did the same with the duck stock. He gave it a little more time, tasting until the rice had just the hint of crunch to it. Once satisfied, he served it onto two warmed plates and returned to Isabelle and the fire.

She seemed to be dozing but she stirred as he put another log on the fire, took her plate and began to eat, making purring noises of approval. After a moment, she asked him, 'Can Balzac eat this?' and he nodded and brought her a spoon. She offered a small amount of rice to the puppy, who took it with evident pleasure.

'I made a little extra just for him,' Bruno said. 'Not the mushrooms, just the rice. Let me bring his bowl so he gets used to it.'

He went to his utility room, where he kept his washing machine, his freezer and his shotgun, with the cupboard where he locked his ammunition away. From the top of the cupboard he took down Gigi's old bowls, which he had placed there so mournfully on the day his dog had been killed. It had also been the last time he had seen Isabelle. He washed them quickly in the kitchen sink, filled one with water and the other with the rest of the risotto and took them back to the fire.

'I'm warm now and sleepy,' said Isabelle as they sipped their wine and watched the dog eat. When Balzac was done, Bruno put him in the kitchen with Gigi's old cushion and some newspapers on the floor, and then led Isabelle to bed.

'I only have my very romantic nightgown with me,' she said, as she headed for the bathroom. 'Somehow I don't think I can live up to its promise tonight.'

'Try this.' He handed her one of his rugby shirts, which he used instead of pyjamas on cold nights.

'Perfect,' she said and disappeared. Returning, her face was free of all make-up and she smelled of toothpaste. His rugby shirt hung down below her knees.

'A hot-water bottle, how wonderful,' she said as she slipped between the sheets. Her voice was small and tired. When he joined her, she curled into him and drifted quickly to sleep and he listened to her breathing and wondered at the power of an intimacy that seemed all the stronger for the absence of the erotic surge he usually felt in her presence.

20

Bruno was woken by the sound of an old and asthmatic motorbike coming up the lane. He felt the heat coming from
Isabelle's side of the bed, stretched out a hand and felt the
material of his rugby shirt, soaked with her sweat. He checked
his watch: it was just before seven, about the time he should
rise, since it was a market day in St Denis. He rinsed his
hands and face, slipped on a tracksuit and trainers and went
into the kitchen to put the kettle on to boil. Balzac had
evidently had fun with the newspaper he had put down,
tearing it into shreds, and the puppy gazed proudly up from
the wreckage at his new master. Bruno let him out of the
front door and Balzac went to the nearest tree and urinated
at great length. He seemed to be becoming house-trained
already. Bruno shivered in the morning air. The mist was so
thick that all he could see of the approaching bike was a dim
headlamp growing stronger. He strode down to the corner
where the lane turned into his property to ask the driver to
turn off his engine before it woke Isabelle.

'I've found her,' came a half-familiar voice as the bike drew
to a halt. 'Now you've got to get her back.'

The helmet came off and Bruno recognized Louis Junot,

unshaven and looking as though he'd spent the night in a ditch. He seemed sober and there was no smell of drink on him.

'It's a bit early for a social call, Louis, and I've got to get to the market.'

'It's not a social call, it's about getting Francette back,' Junot insisted. 'I know where she is. It's just up the road, that fancy new hotel at St Philippon, the one with the helicopters.'

'Did you speak to her?'

Junot shook his head. 'It was just something I found in her waste-paper basket, in her room. It was bundled up with wrapping paper from some gift, a card that said "See you in St Philippon." So I went there last night and there she was, all dolled up like a ten-franc rabbit . . .'

'She's eighteen, Louis. She can do as she pleases.'

'I've got to talk to her, Bruno, tell her it's going to be different now. I haven't touched a drop since you came to the farm, honest. Brigitte will tell you the same.'

'Louis, it's market day and I have to get to town. Meet me by the *Mairie* just after noon and we'll go there and see if she's prepared to talk to you. And now I've got to go. You need to get some sleep.'

Junot's mouth worked as if he were holding something back, tears or rage or just plain frustration.

'Go on home, Louis,' Bruno said kindly. 'I'll see you later.'

Bruno watched him go for a moment and then went back inside to make coffee. As it brewed, he peeped into the bedroom where Isabelle was still asleep. He fed and watered his chickens and put out for Balzac some of Gigi's left-over dog food that he'd never had the heart to throw away. He showered and dressed and left a note for Isabelle. He put out a fresh rugby shirt for her and clean sheets and headed into town.

The Saturday market in St Denis was a modest affair, a fraction of the size of the big market on Tuesday. But on this Saturday before Easter it overflowed the arches beneath the *Mairie* and the town square and extended another fifty metres up the main street. The customers weren't buying so much as ordering their lambs and capons and whole fish for the following weekend. The clothing stalls were doing good business as the farmers bought new shirts for the Easter feast. Busiest of all were the stalls selling seedlings of lettuces, courgettes and aubergines. It reminded Bruno that he'd better dig over his *potager* this weekend and get his summer vegetables started. His seedlings had been growing in his greenhouse for the past three weeks and it was time to transplant them.

After his first tour of the market, Bruno went back to Alphonse's stall and asked when he expected the widow who sold goats. About noon, he was told, and Alphonse gestured to a large cool box beneath his stall. Two long horns prevented it from closing fully.

'The head's in there, on as much ice as I could find,' he said. 'The last thing I want is the smell of dead goat turning away my customers.'

Bruno went on to Fauquet's for his usual coffee and croissant and a quick glance at the newspapers. He was relieved to find St Denis relegated to an inside page with a photo-graph of long lines of tourists outside the cave's ticket office and a headline saying *Satan hauls them in at St Denis*.

'Yesterday was my best day since last August and today looks to be even better,' said Fauquet as Bruno shook hands with the men at the bar. 'If it goes on like this, I reckon Satan can sign me up as a believer.'

'It'll calm down next week when the media moves on to something else,' Bruno said.

He took the Baron by the arm and led him outside to the balustrade of the terrace overlooking the river. It was a fine spring day, the sun's warmth softened by some high, thin cloud, and whole columns of new ducklings paddled after their mothers like battle fleets in the age of sail. Despite the early hour, the traffic on the bridge was already building, presumably more tourists for the Gouffre. A new sign caught his eye at the roundabout, a large arrow and the words *To The Devil's Cave*. He sighed. There were rules about road signs. He'd have to pull it down, but maybe he could wait until someone complained.

'You know I talked to the boys about that stunt you pulled with Marcel and Delaron,' Bruno said.

'Yes, and I know somebody else got there before us.'

'Leave that to one side. I hope you haven't made any enemies among the *Procureurs*, because I can just see someone putting together a charge of intent to profit from deception. If that Count Vexin wants to screw you over the sale of the cave you've given him the perfect opportunity.'

The Baron laughed. 'Vexin was in it from the beginning. I

was holding out for more money, saying a go-ahead type like him could push the marketing and bring in a lot more visitors. It was that day when the story about the dead woman was in the paper and he suggested we try to give the story an extra push. It certainly worked – and he agreed to my higher price, so everyone's happy.'

'So we're going to get this Satanist crap regularly from now on, is that what you want?' asked Bruno. 'There comes a point when the Mayor's right, this can easily go too far. How long before we start to get a reputation as the Devil's town?'

'You're exaggerating.'

'Let's hope so. But in the meantime, I need to find out who went into the cave before the kids. Could it have been Vexin?'

'I doubt it,' the Baron scoffed. 'He's from Paris. He wouldn't have the local connections to know about it.'

'Don't be too sure. That other chap you were having lunch with, Foucher, he's living at the Red Countess's château. She told me he's the estate manager, so he could know about it. And I'm told he's some kind of partner in Vexin's scheme.'

'Maybe it was Vexin and his people. But why are you making a fuss?'

'Because they must have come in through your secret tunnel,' said Bruno. 'I've explored it myself and now I know it's a natural watercourse, not man-made, so I'm wondering how many other ways in or out of the Gouffre there could be.'

'How should I know? I explored it all as a kid and there were some side passages, but none of the ones I found led anywhere, at least not to anywhere I could penetrate. But it's a big place. You'd need a professional team to really explore it.'

'There's no shortage of caving clubs round here. Did you ever think about inviting one of them to take a look?'

The Baron shrugged, but looked uncomfortable. 'I remembered what my father said, what I told you back in the cave. It's for us locals. Who knows when we might need it?'

Bruno shook his head firmly. 'That's the problem, Baron. It's not just for us any more, now you're selling the cave to Vexin. He's just the guy to open it all up to maximize his investment. Pay to see the Devil's Cave and then for a little extra fee you can explore the secret tunnel where the Resistance hid their guns. Is that what you want? Or what your father would have wanted?'

'*Putain, tu me casses les couilles*,' the Baron said aggressively. 'Leave him out of this. Why don't you concentrate on finding out who went in before the kids?'

The Baron turned on his heel and strode away. Bruno had never quarrelled with him before. He wondered whether the Baron's interest in Béatrice might explain his cooperation with Vexin. It had been on the tip of his tongue to refer to the Baron's visit to Béatrice's auberge, but now he was glad he hadn't.

'Hey, Bruno,' Julien called from the knot of men leaving the café and heading for the entrance to the *Mairie*. 'The Mayor's called a meeting and Father Sentout's with him. It looks like he's going to give us the OK for the exorcism.'

Back in Fauquet's café, the reporter from *Paris-Match* was still sitting at the same corner table. He'd finished *Le Figaro* and *Le Monde* and was now on the financial stories in *Les Echos*.

'*Bonjour*, Gilles. How goes your inquiry into the dead woman?' Bruno asked, taking a seat opposite the journalist.

'I'm pretty sure I know who she is. I should get confirmation later today.' Gilles looked pleased with himself. 'Hollywood is nine hours behind us, so sometime this evening.'

'Hollywood?' Bruno had not expected that. 'I have a showbiz story for you. I've just come from a meeting with the Mayor and Father Sentout. There'll be a service of exorcism in the cave on Monday morning at ten, and outside those of us who were in the room, you're the first to know.'

'Is it open to the public and will media be there?' Gilles pulled out a computer notebook and started to log on.

'Yes and yes,' Bruno replied. 'How do you get your little scoop out?'

'Twitter first, then the website.'

'And now tell me about Hollywood.'

'Give me a minute here,' Gilles said, tapping away on his tiny keyboard. 'Get yourself some coffee. Are you free for lunch?'

Bruno shook his head and thought of his promise to Junot. 'Duty calls,' he said. Gilles was still tapping at his computer when Bruno got back with his coffee, and at the same time talking into a tiny microphone attached to a stylish earpiece. He made some decisive clicks, closed his notebook, removed the earpiece and beckoned to Bruno to join him.

'Here's the deal,' he said. 'I'll give you the name so you can start your own checks, but on condition that nobody else gets it before I break the story. I'll tell you when that'll be, probably this evening. OK?'

Bruno agreed.

'Then come and sit beside me, watch the screen and put the earpiece in,' Gilles said, shuffling sideways on the bench to make room as he loaded a video program.

'Is this her?' he asked.

An attractive blonde, naked from the waist up, appeared on the screen. Her eyes were closed and she was making grunting noises and rocking up and down. Two male hands came from beneath her and began to massage her breasts. She opened her eyes and stared hungrily into the camera, took one of the hands from her breast and lifted it to her mouth and began to suck on the fingers.

'*Mon Dieu*,' said Bruno. 'It's her, and it's a porn film.'

'Soft porn, 1990s vintage. No pubic hair, no genitals, no penetration. Very tame stuff. Her name on the credits is Athénaïs de Bourbon, which I think we can assume is a stage name. Here she is again.'

He loaded another video. This time Bruno heard American accents speaking fast. On the screen appeared a suburban living room where three expensively dressed women were sitting at a coffee table drinking what looked like martinis. One of them was the woman in the porno film.

'She had a bit part in a soap opera which was pretty big back in its day, using the same stage name. She played a French teacher. I assume that job fell through and she started doing soft porn to pay the bills.'

Gilles brought back the porn film and froze it on a frame where the woman looked relatively normal, her eyes open and her mouth closed. He juggled with the mouse, blacked out the breasts and turned the frame into a close-up showing only the face. Bruno started at her, fascinated.

'I tracked down her agent but the guy who dealt with her is dead. I spoke to a colleague who said none of them had seen her in years. But he's going into his office this morning California time to check his files and try to find the real name that was on her work permit.'

'Whatever they have, a work permit or a resident's green card, it should have a fingerprint. Get them to fax it over to me at this number.' Bruno handed over his card. 'If they have a record of her dentist, we'll need her dental records for full confirmation.'

21

In Bruno's van, Junot could not sit still. He gnawed at his fingernails and asked endless questions, demanding reassurances. Sometimes his feet drummed, or was he pretending to drive, echoing Bruno's moves with clutch and brake? Bruno indulged him, let him ramble on, occasionally tossing in replies as a distracted owner might throw sticks for a dog kept too long indoors. Yes, the auberge seemed a very pleasant place. Certainly there was a good future in hotel work. Indeed, it could be a worthwhile career. And yes, in Bruno's experience they usually came home eventually; blood was thicker than water. But the dreams of a bored, unhappy child, Bruno thought, could be stronger than either.

That was a reply he kept to himself, as he recalled two images from that morning. One was of a woman staring into the camera as she sucked some stranger's fingers. The other was of a different woman, grief-stricken as she stared at the semi-frozen head of a goat and called it Ulysses.

She should never have sold him, Alphonse's friend told Bruno when they met at his market stall. She could have managed without the money. But the Arab Monsieur had been so polite and so embarrassed, explaining that his pregnant wife craved a dish from her Kabyle home, a broth made of ribs of goat. No, she had never seen the Arab Monsieur before; he had come to her in Sarlat market and said he had heard she might have a goat for sale.

His hair was dark and his skin sallow and he might have had a moustache. The one feature she remembered with precision was that he wore beautiful brown brogue shoes, highly polished. He had come to her farm in a large black car with a small trailer. He had paid cash, in new notes.

What day had the Arab Monsieur come to the market, Bruno had asked. On Wednesday, when she was selling her cheeses in the covered market. He had come out to the farm later that same day. The story of the woman in the boat had been in the newspaper that morning. To dream up the hoax in the cave and to arrange the purchase of a goat within hours was impressive, Bruno thought. In other circumstances he might have found it admirable.

'Has Francette been there all this time?' Junot's voice brought Bruno back to the present.

He shrugged. 'I didn't even know she was there until you woke me up to tell me.'

'At least she's not far from home. Even if she stays, she can come back to visit.'

'They have to leave home some day,' Bruno said, and then realized that Junot had never left. He had stayed on the farm he'd inherited and probably expected that some day Francette and her children would take over the property in their turn. But even here in the Périgord where the farming tradition was strong, fewer and fewer people remained on the land.

From what he recalled of Francette, she did not seem likely to take over a failing farm.

'Is this a social call?' Béatrice asked, walking briskly into the reception area after he presented himself to the black-suited Cécile at the reception desk. 'I'm afraid we're still clearing up after a busy evening.' She looked at Junot, still dressed in the grimy poacher's garb he'd been wearing when he turned up at Bruno's cottage that morning.

'No, Madame,' Bruno said. 'Monsieur Junot here, from St Denis, believes his young daughter, Francette, is staying in the hotel and would like to speak with her and assure himself that she's well. I think he's hoping to persuade her to return home, but I've told him that will be her decision.'

She gave Junot a cold look. 'So this is the man who beats his wife and daughter?' Bruno felt rather than saw Junot's fists clench and put a firm hand on the man's arm.

'I think it would be a courtesy to allow Monsieur Junot to see his daughter and satisfy himself that she's well,' Bruno said.

'Might it not have been a courtesy to phone in advance to arrange a convenient time?'

Bruno pulled out his own phone and showed her the log. 'I made two calls to you this morning, Madame, as you can see. It's not my fault if your phone is switched off.'

She dropped her eyes as if trying to look embarrassed. 'I apologize, but it's been a busy morning. Would you mind if I'm present when you see Francette? No? In that case, please come through to my office.'

Pausing to tell Cécile to let Francette know her presence

was required, Béatrice led the way through the reception room to a small but well-appointed bar with a wood-lined alcove beyond that smelt of expensive cigars. A side door led to a large open-plan office where two black-suited young women worked at computers, and a further door gave way to Béatrice's own room, where a modern desk and chair perched on oriental rugs. She offered them the hard-backed chairs that faced her desk, but Bruno said he'd stand.

'Your daughter's ID card says she's over the age of eighteen and is therefore free to live and work where she chooses,' Béatrice said to Junot. He said nothing but chewed his lip and looked at Bruno, who simply nodded.

Francette knocked and entered the room. She ignored the sad little gesture her father made as she walked past him and followed Béatrice's invitation to stand with her behind the desk. She had been transformed from the slightly sluttish girl with too much eye make-up he remembered from the supermarket checkout. Her hair had been professionally styled and her make-up was discreet and flattering. She seemed to stand and walk differently and the suit of black silk that she wore flattered her slim figure. Her eyes looked a little tired, but otherwise Bruno had never seen her look better.

'*Bonjour*, Francette,' said Bruno. 'How are you?'

'I'm good,' she said. 'It's nice to see you again, Bruno.' She smiled and stretched out a hand across the desk for him to shake. Even her voice was different, lower in timbre and she spoke more slowly. She turned to Béatrice, who gestured her to go ahead.

'I've been told that my father wishes to see me. You can see that I'm fine,' Francette said. 'I have a job and I have absolutely no intention of returning home to a drunken father who beats me and my mother. Not now and not ever.' Her eyes were fixed on Bruno. 'He ought to be in prison for what he did to us. And I hope my mother summons the courage to leave as well. Can I go now?'

'I'm sorry,' Junot said nervously, clasping and unclasping his hands. 'But it's different now. Your mother will tell you. I haven't touched a drop in days. I'm sorry for what happened and we miss you at home.'

'I'll make my own arrangements to see Mother, but not you.' There was no anger in her voice, just a chill neutrality.

'At least think it over,' Junot said, his voice cracking. 'Ask your mum when you see her. She'll tell you I've changed.' He paused, his mouth working as if he wanted to say something else, but no words came. He looked to Bruno for inspiration, and blurted, 'We've got the potatoes in.'

Béatrice suppressed a smile and said, addressing Bruno, 'I think there's no more to be said.'

'Thank you both for your time,' Bruno said.

'Please ensure that Monsieur Junot understands he is not welcome on these premises and if he ever returns, I shall call you and expect you to remove him,' Béatrice said.

'I understand,' Bruno said, and turned to Francette. 'It would be nice to see you at the tennis club one of these days. You were pretty good when you were in my classes.' She gave him a quick smile that reminded Bruno of how she looked as a schoolgirl.

215

Junot was trying to say something more, but Bruno guided him to the door and out through the bar. Junot stumbled along beside him, seeming to have lost all will of his own. Bruno led the way to the van, told him to fix his seat belt and drove off.

'There's nothing more that I can do for you, Louis, and nothing more the law can do,' he said. 'Your daughter's an adult and she's made her intentions clear. If I'm called to remove you from these premises in the future, you'll be in very serious trouble. Understood?'

Junot said nothing all the way back to St Denis. He sat hunched, with his hand to his eyes and his head downcast. When he stopped at a junction and looked left and right, Bruno could hardly miss the glistening tears on the man's unshaven cheeks.

Both windows open to rid the van of Junot's pungent smell after dropping him back in St Denis, Bruno drove up the long hill to his home wondering how Isabelle might be feeling. There had been no answer when he called her from the market. He rounded the corner and saw her sitting in the spot by the kitchen window that was a sun trap, Balzac sniffing round her feet and a glass of something on the table before her. She put down a book as she saw his van and waved as Balzac began galloping to investigate this new arrival. Weighed down with a chicken and vegetables, cheese and fresh bread from the last of the market, Bruno bent to kiss her while fending off Balzac's lunges for the bag with the chicken.

'I'm much better,' she said. 'I had the last of the onion soup for breakfast and then spent the morning on my computer. You'll have to be more imaginative with the pass-word for your modem. Gigi and your birthday was too easy. And you'd better put the food in the fridge. I've booked us a table for dinner at the Vieux Logis, my treat. Well, the Ministry's treat. If I add together all my per diem allowances, that should cover it.'

It wouldn't, thought Bruno, making a quick calculation, but kissed her again and smiled his thanks before putting the chicken into his larder. It was cool enough in there, and he was a great believer in hanging meat for a while before eating it.

'And I've done some research for you on your Count Vexin, a very enterprising man. His birth name was de la Gorce. Does that remind you of anything?'

'It's the married name of the sister at the Red Château.'

'He's her grandson. He's also very well connected politically and smart, being an *Enarque*.'

The *Ecole Nationale d'Administration*, its students and gradu-ates known familiarly as *Enarques*, had been founded by de Gaulle in 1945 to train a new French elite to run its civil service. Producing only a hundred graduates a year, the ENA had provided two Presidents of France, half a dozen prime ministers and most of the leaders of France's big corpora-tions. The Count, Isabelle told him, had graduated high enough in his year to join the *Inspection Générale des Finances*, gone from there to Germany to work in EADS, the European Aeronautic Defence and Space Company, and had then started his own private equity company.

'That's where I'd heard of him,' she said. 'He's on our

ministry list of significant figures, not because of the money but because he specializes in defence. He bought into small European defence and electronics companies, cut costs and rationalized them. Then he started merging them, launched them on the stock exchange and made a fortune.'

'So how does he get involved in this provincial property development?'

'That's where it gets interesting,' she said.

In 2006 the Count had started a hedge fund. He'd done very well at first, particularly in property in Paris, London and Brussels. But the timing was against him when the American mortgage market got into trouble the next year. Then had come the crash and the Count lost a lot of money. In recent months he'd returned to private equity deals in the defence industry that he knew best, and had started dabbling again in property.

'This holiday village still seems like pretty small stuff for a guy like him,' said Bruno.

'Don't forget the family, and Granny in the château,' Isabelle replied. This valley was a place the Count knew, she explained, and an opportunity to make some money. The hotel that had turned them away the previous evening was designed to make use of his defence connections, a discreet place to wine and dine clients and celebrate.

'I can see the logic in it,' Isabelle continued. 'And I was going to email you the file I put together. But on second thoughts, maybe I shouldn't, or at least I'd better make a discreet check with my boss. If he's in our files, and he's also on the Defence Ministry's approved list, the Brigadier will want to know why I'm making inquiries.'

'How much of this is in the public domain where anybody can find it on the net?'

'Most of it, starting with this on Google.' She opened another tab and brought up a page of celebrity photos from *Gala* magazine.

'That's our Count and you were right. He is good-looking, and so are those two women with him. But look at the other guy, the one with his arm around him.'

Bruno whistled. 'That's the President's son?' But his eye was drawn to one of the women in the photo. It was Eugénie in a low-cut dress, not named and described as 'a friend'.

'The son by our President's first marriage, and it's a party for the new Airbus, the Count's aviation connections again, and now try this . . .'

'Wait,' he said, and pointed to Eugénie. 'Don't you recognize the nurse at the Red Château?'

'I know. I just wanted to see if you'd say so. OK, you pass the test.' She grinned.

He felt himself blushing. 'What else did you want to show me?'

'Remember the car with Lebanese diplomatic plates? I googled the Count and Lebanon and he's got a house there. And another investment company. And his partner in the company is – tra-la – the son of their Minister of Defence. Here they are together in the Gulf edition of *OK* magazine, this time at a party in Dubai.'

'And you were supposed to be in bed with hot drinks and aspirin,' he said.

'I had to get up. The sheets were soaked, and so was your

rugby shirt so I put them through the washing machine. I think I sweated out the fever. And I drank all your orange juice and a lot of mineral water.'

'How do I find out about his investment company, the one in Luxembourg?' he asked.

'You don't, at least you won't find much on open-source material. And we can't get access to the Luxembourg system unless we have evidence of crime or tax evasion, and then it will be special investigators from the Ministry of Finance. Remember he started as an *inspecteur de finances*. His books will be clean, or at least the ones we can get to see.'

'Is there anything else you can find out without getting into trouble?'

'Criminal records, tax records, the old *Renseignements Généraux* files, but that's mainly political stuff and I think we know he's connected. The juicy stuff will be in Defence Ministry files, and a red flag goes up if I go in there. Still, the Brigadier might think it useful to have a closer look at one of the golden boys of the Hôtel de Brienne.'

Bruno remembered the imposing Defence Ministry building off the Rue St Dominique in Paris, close to Napoleon's tomb at Les Invalides. As a former soldier, he felt a certain loyalty to the place and wasn't sure he wanted to help the Interior Ministry embarrass it.

'I saved the best till last,' she said. 'I was looking for anything on those other names in this development project, the Eugénie woman and Foucher. Look at this.'

She opened another tab, this one from the *New York Times* in November 2007, recording that Lionel Joseph Foucher, a

French citizen, had been fined $400,000, given six months' probation and barred from further employment in a fiduciary capacity after pleading guilty to a charge of insider trading.

'What's that mean?'

'It means he can't work in Wall Street again. What's interesting is that he was working for the New York office of the Count's hedge fund. And now he's a director of one of the Count's companies in Europe. That's loyalty for you. I've emailed our liaison man at the New York consulate asking him to get me the full court documents. That's something to interest the Brigadier.'

'I'm very grateful. I feel you deserve a reward.'

'So do I,' she said. 'I was thinking you could help me bring in the sheets off the line and put them back on the bed and we could test how dry they are. I don't think I'll be needing your rugby shirt.'

22

They had just finished the main course of roast lamb with crispy rice and a blend of red peppers flavoured with olives when Bruno's phone began to vibrate with the call from Gilles. Bruno savoured the last sip of the Grand Millésime of Château de Tiregand, shrugged an apology to Isabelle and left the dining room to avoid disturbing the other diners, or more important, offending the chef. It was not a good moment to leave the table. The roast lamb had been milk-fed, from the celebrated farms of the Grefeuille brothers in Aveyron, where the sheep were carefully chosen for their ancestry. The ewes were of the Lacaune breed, whose milk made the cheese of Roquefort and the rams from the Berrichon, and they produced the white lambs that were becoming essential to the reputation of the finest restaurants of France. Their AAA designation, standing for *l'Agneau Allaiton d'Aveyron*, was as carefully guarded as the appellation of a great vineyard.

'What's the news from Hollywood?' he asked Gilles, a little more testily than he should.

'The bad news is that they have no file on her any more, no documents at all. The good news is that her agent's secretary is still there, and she remembers Athénaïs trying to sell two film ideas, treatments they call them. One was for the Red Countess, who she claimed was her grandmother, and the other was a horror film and love story about Louis XIV and his mistress, Madame de Montespan. Athénaïs claimed to be a direct descendant, and that Athénaïs de Bourbon was one of the several names she was entitled to use.'

'But no films were ever made?'

'The Red Countess had no chance. Hollywood doesn't do commie heroines. "The Royal Mistress", the title she gave to her script, was the project that kept her going financially. It kept getting optioned, but it never went into production because she insisted on the starring role. Apparently Athénaïs was pretty obsessed with her ancestor. She told the secretary that she was the living reincarnation of Montespan so only she could play the role.'

'When will you publish all this?'

'Monday at noon, with the photographs I showed you. It's a great story – suicide of a failed actress, re-enacting the Black Mass of her famous ancestor. I'm sending you a photo to remember her by. See you tomorrow,' Gilles said and rang off.

Bruno made a quick call to J-J to give him the name and background of the dead woman, described his deal with *Paris-Match* and then returned to the table to tell Isabelle that the mystery of the dead woman had been resolved.

'It means that they lied at the Red Château,' he said. 'If she's the granddaughter of the Red Countess, they must have known her from the photo I showed.'

'I should call the Brigadier but I don't want to interrupt

the meal again,' she said. 'I can call him in the morning. Louis XIV, Black Mass, an aristocratic porn star dead in mysterious circumstances . . . he'll love it. And the media will go crazy.'

Bruno was just finishing a superb selection of cheese when his phone vibrated again. It was a message from Gilles with an attachment. He opened it and found himself looking at the cropped photo of Athénaïs, her neck and shoulders bare, her eyes open. He passed the phone to Isabelle. 'That's her, one of the more presentable shots.'

'A strange expression, somehow forced.'

'She's having simulated sex. Perhaps she'd look different if it were the real thing.'

Isabelle closed the phone and handed it back. 'I already chose the dessert,' she said. 'I know it's one of your favourites. Panna cotta with truffles.'

'I'll need to start running marathons to work off meals like this.'

'You and J-J both told me to put some weight on, so I'm just following your advice. Besides, I'll be back in Paris tomorrow night and then it's pizza and pot noodles and frozen dinners for one. I'll miss this and I'll miss your cooking.'

'And I'll miss you,' he said. 'Life always speeds up when you're here.'

'Will you send me regular texts about Balzac and start taking photos and sending them to me? Tell him I expect him to find me lots of truffles so you can make me this panna cotta next time I'm here.'

'What time's your train?'

'Eleven from Le Buisson to Libourne, and then the TGV to Paris. I get in just before four, so I'll have time to do the laundry and clean the apartment before sinking into bed with pot noodles. And then it's back into hospital next week for plastic surgery on my thigh.'

'I've become fond of that scar.'

'I know,' she said, smiling at the memory of the afternoon. 'But it's not a scar, it's a hole I can put my fist into. And then four weeks' paid convalescence leave, since the wound was inflicted in the line of duty.'

'Do you want to come here for it? You'd be very welcome.'

'No, but thank you. It would disrupt your life down here and for me it would feel like moving in, which I don't want.' She leaned across the table and took his hand and gave him her impish smile. 'You're more of an occasional treat, a sort of human panna cotta with truffles. Anyway, I've already booked a cruise around the Greek islands. I'll sit in a deckchair with my bandaged leg, flirt with handsome sailors and read stories about the Trojan wars and ancient Athens. I have it all planned and it's something I've always wanted to do.'

He wanted to ask if she would be going alone, but held back. The waitress arrived with petits fours and chocolate truffles. Reluctantly, he released Isabelle's hand.

'I'll miss the exorcism, or whatever it is the priest is going to perform, but you must let me know how all this works out. And if I find out any more about this cast of characters you've assembled down here, I'll let you know. Who knows, now we've got half of French history involved the Brigadier might take an interest.'

225

'There'll be a burst of publicity and then it will all die away,' he said, and began looking around for the waitress.

'Don't even think of asking,' she said. 'I already paid the bill.'

Balzac in his arms, Bruno waved goodbye as the train pulled out from the station at Le Buisson, heading towards Bordeaux and threading its way through the great vineyards of Pomerol and St Emilion. It had been a sweet morning, waking and taking her a tray with coffee and orange juice and the snuffling of a basset hound to wake her, before some gentle lovemaking. When they rose, they made a tour of the garden and the chicken coop, where she insisted that the hens remembered her as she gathered the eggs. They had taken a slow stroll through the woods with Balzac and then driven down to St Denis for coffee and croissants at Fauquet's, with *France-Dimanche* for her and the Sunday edition of *Sud-Ouest* for him. He bought her a baguette to go with the duck sausage and a jar of his own foie gras and one of Stephane's *tommes* that he had put into a bag along with a bottle of mineral water for the journey. No true Périgourdin thought it safe to travel with anything less, he assured her, as he kissed her goodbye on the station platform.

The Mayor greeted him with a tall glass of his own *vin de noix*, topped up with ice and tonic water, and they sat in the shade of the willow trees by the river as Bruno recounted his researches. The Mayor played with Balzac as he listened to the long tale from Thivion to Wall Street and Lebanon, from hedge funds to insider trading and the political connections that went with being an *Enarque* and a friend of the President's son.

'Could the son be part of this fund that's investing in our holiday village?' the Mayor asked. 'They wouldn't dare try any funny business with us then.'

The shareholdings were a mystery, locked in Luxembourg, Bruno explained. The only safe way to do business with them was with cast-iron legal guarantees, backed up by penalty clauses and good collateral.

'You mean we should insist on holding some shares in his investment company to guarantee us against loss?'

'Yes, but the problem with an investment company is that its assets are the brains of its people, who can leave quickly,' Bruno said. He explained that the Count did possess an asset that St Denis could require as collateral, the hotel at St Philippon. The Count was not going to stop bringing in his defence clients, because he'd want to take the place over again once the holiday village was built and the collateral returned. 'It's the only way I can think of to ensure we don't lose on the deal.'

'What if he refuses to go ahead on that basis? It seems a bit harsh, after they're clearly serious about building us this sports hall. We could lose the whole project.'

'Better that than ending up like Thivion,' Bruno said.

The Mayor was silent, caressing the puppy asleep in his lap. 'I spoke to the Mayor in Thivion. He made it sound even worse than your own account of it. That's not the kind of legacy I want to leave. Mind you, I'm not sure about this Satanist business. Look what came in yesterday's post.'

He handed across an envelope addressed to the Mayor of St Denis-le-Diable. Bruno rolled his eyes.

'It's a joke of course, from one of my colleagues on the *Conseil-Général*, but it's one with a bitter taste.'

'One more thing you should know,' Bruno said, and told him of the tentative identification by *Paris-Match* of the woman in the boat, and his promise to keep it confidential.

'The granddaughter of the Red Countess in a porn film? That'll make a stir.' The Mayor shook his head. 'It's a sad end to what must have been a tragic life.'

Bruno's phone began to vibrate and he saw it was Albert. He was one of the two professionals who ran the town's volunteer fire brigade, which also served as the medical emergency service.

'We've got a bad accident reported on the ridge road to Les Eyzies,' Albert said. 'If you're in town we can go out together while the siren gets my lads in.'

'With you in two minutes,' he replied, and explained to the Mayor. 'Can I leave the dog with you until I get back?'

'I was hoping you would,' the Mayor replied. As Bruno left, the town siren began its eerie, penetrating whine that swooped and fell, a sound that still carried memories of war and dive bombers and even today meant emergency and death. Half-drone, half-shriek, it carried way down the valley. Bruno knew that farmers and shop clerks, accountants and waiters would be heading for the fire station to don their equipment and roll out the big emergency vehicle.

They took Albert's command car, with Lespinasse's son Edouard from the garage as the first-aid volunteer on duty.

Ahmed would bring the emergency vehicle once the full crew of volunteers had assembled. As they roared up to the round-about, Bruno saw Fabiola running from the medical centre and waving them down. Albert braked and she climbed in.

'I just heard the siren,' she said. 'What is it?'

'Accident, could be a death,' Albert said. 'Father Sentout called it in, on his way back from a big Palm Sunday service. There were skid marks and glass on the road and the barrier was broken. He's waiting there to give the last rites.'

As the road hugged the cliff to climb the steep hill they saw the priest's little blue Peugeot first, then Father Sentout himself, a shawl around his neck and a small case in his hand. 'I can't get down, it's too steep, but I can see smoke,' he shouted as they pulled up.

Albert handed Bruno and Edouard a harness each, fixed a rope to the belt buckle and then tied the other end around the towing bracket of his command van. Two of the supports of the protective wooden fence had been uprooted and the sturdy logs splintered and broken. It looked as though a heavy truck had gone through it and over the almost sheer cliff that led down to the river below. Trees and branches were smashed, but over a narrower span than the breach in the barrier. Half sliding, half scrambling and clutching at broken tree stumps, they went down about twenty metres before seeing wisps of smoke rising from the tyres attached to some burned-out machinery.

'It's a motorbike,' Edouard said into the small radio affixed to his yellow jacket. Bruno could not decipher the jumble of static and voice that responded from the road above but

229

he heard the siren as the emergency vehicle arrived. It took another few minutes to find the driver. He had been thrown to one side and lay impaled on a jagged tree branch. The stump poked bloodily from just above his hip. His helmet was still in place but his neck was visibly broken. At least the rider had been spared the fire that had consumed his bike.

'There must be another vehicle down here,' Edouard said, kneeling over the body and checking for any sign of life. 'That gap's much too wide for just a bike.'

There was a scrambling above them and Fabiola appeared with Ahmed beside her. She went straight to the body and after a moment pronounced the rider dead. But Bruno and the other two were staring down at the unbroken woods below them and trying to think where another vehicle might possibly be.

'The damage to the trees stops here, at his bike,' said Ahmed. 'There's no other vehicle down here.'

Bruno and Edouard fixed the harness to the body, eased it off the stump, and Ahmed used his radio to tell the team above to start the winch. Fabiola stepped back from where she'd been working on the body, sealing a small phial she'd taken from her belt-pack that she'd filled with some of the blood that had pooled in the rider's lap.

'Whoever he was, he was as drunk as a lord,' said Edouard. 'You can smell the booze from here. Bloody fool.'

Bruno and Edouard scrambled to keep up as the winch began hauling. It was only when they got to the road and Father Sentout removed the helmet to apply some oil to the forehead that the head rolled towards him and Bruno realized he knew the dead man.

'It's Louis Junot,' he exclaimed, thinking that the scene with his daughter must have destroyed Junot's good intentions and driven him back to the bottle. 'Poor old Louis.'

'Drunk in life, drunk in death,' said Edouard against the sound of the priest's muttered prayers as he knelt beside the body.

Bruno began looking closely at the broken fence and at the skid marks, trying to visualize what had taken place. But he couldn't make the pieces fit. The skid marks might have come from another vehicle that hit and crushed the fence, and Junot had then gone over the edge as he tried to avoid the car. But if that were the case, Junot must have been coming from the other direction. His momentum would have taken him through the fence and to the right. But he and his bike seemed to have gone straight down the hill. And there must have been a second vehicle: the skid marks showed two sets of wheels. Bruno checked the splintered fencing, looking for flecks of paint from whatever vehicle had struck it. What he found instead were threads of what looked like waxed cloth attached to the splinters, perhaps from a tarpaulin.

Once the Gendarmes learned that Junot had been drunk, they weren't going to expend much time or effort trying to work out how it had happened or whether another car had been involved. Bruno called Fabiola over and showed her the threads before he broke off a splinter with a thread attached and put it in an evidence bag.

'Junot wasn't wearing anything like that,' she said.

'What do you make of it, Ahmed?' he asked the veteran fireman, who had climbed back up to the road and was now supervising the winching up of the burnt-out wreck that had been Junot's bike.

Ahmed studied the scene, looked at the broken glass and the shattered fence and shrugged. 'Maybe he comes round the corner, sees the car, swerves but hits it and breaks the headlights, bounces off and over the edge just as the car smashed the fence down.'

'So why didn't the car go over as well? And if he hit the car, he'd be on the road, not going over the cliff with his bike.'

'You could be right; it's a tough one. Can we leave you to notify next-of-kin and arrange for the *Mairie* to get that fence fixed? We'll take the body straight to the funeral home.'

'I can't work it out, either,' said Albert as they drove off. 'There's no way a motorbike could have caused that much damage to the fence. That accident doesn't make sense.'

'In that case, I'm going to ask for an autopsy,' said Fabiola. 'There's something odd about that corpse. If I didn't know the neck was broken I'd have said he died of a massive cerebro-vascular accident, a stroke.'

'An autopsy for a drunk driver?' said Albert. 'They won't like that. Not over a weekend.'

'You don't like the way the accident looked and I don't like the way the corpse smelled and Bruno doesn't like the strange threads where the fence was broken,' Fabiola said firmly. 'That's enough for me. So don't take the body to the funeral home, take it directly to the lab in Bergerac, on my responsibility.'

23

Bruno had to admire Béatrice. Here he was for the third time in as many days, with each visit so far starting with her being friendly and concluding in tension, and she was still smiling at him and saying 'Welcome' as if she meant it.

'Civilian clothes,' she said, her eyes twinkling. 'So at last is this your long-promised social call?'

'I wish it were, Madame. I need to see Francette and to take her away on urgent compassionate grounds. There has been a road accident and her father is dead. I thought she'd want to go and comfort her mother, who has not yet been told.'

'The poor girl, of course she must have some time off to see to her mother,' said Béatrice, looking suddenly maternal. She told the black-suited receptionist to find Francette and bring her down to the office. The girl on duty was not Cécile but might have been; they looked so much alike they were almost interchangeable.

Francette's face was impassive as she heard the news, but her lip and cheek were swollen as if she had fallen badly, or perhaps it was toothache. Her eyes were red and lacked their usual liveliness. Had she somehow heard of his death already?

'Was he drunk?' was her only question when Bruno

described the crash. Hoping to give her some comfort, he said her father had died at once of a broken neck.

'I don't know if he had been drinking. Certainly he was sober when I last saw him,' Bruno said. 'I thought I'd come and tell you myself, and then if you're willing I'll drive you back to the farm. Your mother hasn't yet been told the news and I think she'd want to have you there.'

Francette looked at Béatrice, who nodded and moved to embrace her, but Francette stiffened and said she'd need to pack an overnight bag. She left quickly, her head held determinedly high and her shoulders stiff.

'She seemed down even before I told her the news,' Bruno said to Béatrice.

'One of the guests was rude to her last night, blamed her for tripping and spilling something as she waited on his table. It was his own fault. He pushed his chair back suddenly and she fell. It can become tiresome, having to accept that the customer is always right, even when he isn't. Can I offer you a coffee or a drink while you wait?'

He shook his head and Béatrice excused herself. The car park had been almost empty and he noticed that all the room keys were hanging in their pigeonholes, as if there were no guests. Bruno didn't know much about the corporate entertaining business, but the economics of this auberge seemed odd. Maybe Sunday afternoon was a quiet time, the weekend clients gone and next week's not yet arrived.

Francette had changed into jeans and a sweatshirt, but she still wore stylish shoes. She carried what looked like a fashionable handbag which she put into the back of Bruno's van along with a Louis Vuitton overnight case. She climbed into the front seat amid a cloud of Shalimar, which Bruno recognized because it was one of Pamela's favourite perfumes.

'I know you didn't get on, but he loved you a great deal in his own strange way,' he said.

'I knew that, which is why I never hated him even when I despised him,' she replied. 'You don't need to say anything else, Bruno. I'm not a child any more and you're not trying to get me to follow through on my backhand. I've even worked out that it was you who paid for my tennis shoes when my mum couldn't afford them.'

'There was a special fund we had . . .' he said vaguely, a touch embarrassed.

'And you never asked my parents to pay their share of the petrol money when you drove us to matches with other clubs.'

'Let's get back to the present,' he said. 'You're going to have to make a decision with your mum about staying on in the farm or selling it. At least you seem to have a good job now, and your mum's not far away.'

'Neither of us can drive and we have no car,' she said. 'And my own future is a bit vague.' She lapsed into silence and remained unresponsive to Bruno's attempts at conversation, except when they drove through St Denis and he asked if she wanted to call at the funeral home to see her father's body.

'No, thank you. And since we have no money he'll have to go into a pauper's grave or whatever it is you do for the poor.'

They drove the rest of the way up to the plateau in silence, as Bruno wondered how a girl with a Louis Vuitton bag and wearing Shalimar could have no money. At the farm, she paused only to change from her high heels into a pair of cheap trainers from her bag and left him without a word. Five minutes later, he followed, knocked and let himself into the kitchen where mother and daughter were embracing. Francette was dry-eyed.

'I told her,' Francette said. 'Thanks for bringing me here. We'd like to be alone now.'

'If you want a lift to the funeral home or help with the arrangements, here's my card with all my numbers. There is a death grant available which can cover the funeral expenses and I also have to post the death on the *Mairie* noticeboard, where we usually add the time and date of the funeral service, so let me know,' he said. 'Please accept my condolences, I'm sorry for your loss.'

He'd wanted to ask her how she got the thick lip and how long she was planning to spend at her mother's place and whether they'd like him to make some inquiries among other farmers about renting their grazing land. He'd have to go back at some point and all his questions could wait.

Back in his office, he phoned the Mayor at home to tell him of Junot's death, emailed to himself the photo of Athénaïs that Gilles had sent to his phone and printed several copies, each of which he put into a transparent plastic sleeve. He checked his emails and found a new one from Isabelle, sent from her phone, that said 'Missing you and Balzac already' and replied 'We miss you too.' On an impulse, he added: 'Any information on Béatrice-Amélie Constant, currently managing the auberge at St Philippon for Count Vexin, gratefully received.' He changed into the spare uniform he kept in his cupboard and headed out to his next task.

The same shy maid met him at the doorway of the Red Château where he asked to see Madame de la Gorce. On a long oak table in the entrance hall was a tray with a number of envelopes, two of them addressed to Monsieur le comte de Vexin and two more to Lionel Foucher. One of the letters to the Count was from a firm in Paris named Gallotin, which reminded Bruno of something but he couldn't place it. He was thumbing through his notebook to jog his memory when the maid returned.

'Madame de la Gorce will be with you shortly and suggests you might wait in the library.' She led the way through double doors and into a long room whose tall windows looked out across the fields that ran down to the river. Between the windows and along the length of the other walls were bookshelves, twice as tall as Bruno, and filled with old books covered in leather. There were two large desks at either end of the library, two easy chairs of leather and a reading stand that contained what looked like a large and venerable bible. Bruno crossed the room to examine it. The cover was unusually heavy, made of wood that had been covered with black leather, and the paper felt thick as he turned the pages. The print inside looked ancient and the chapter headings were embellished with ornate drawings of animals that he suspected had been painted by hand. The inside of the front cover was filled with a hand-drawn family tree, so large that a second and third trunk sprawled over onto the next page. In its branches were inscribed names and dates of baptisms and funerals going back to the early eighteenth century, all in beautiful cursive scripts.

Tracing the branches he found the Red Countess, baptized in 1926, and her sister, Héloïse, baptized two years later. But the family tree showed them to have been born to different mothers. The Countess's mother had died soon after her birth and her father had then remarried. Quickly he scribbled the names and dates into his notebook, along with the names of children. Knowing he wouldn't have time to copy down the entire family tree he pulled out his phone and took a series of photos of the large flyleaf with its neat sprawl of names and dates.

In 1945 the two half-sisters had each given birth shortly before the end of the war. The Countess had a daughter, Françoise, who herself had given birth in 1968 to another daughter, Athénaïs. So Gilles was right: the dead woman was indeed the granddaughter of the Countess. The younger sister, Héloïse, had borne a son, Louis-Antoine, and he in turn had a son, César, in 1970. That would be the man Bruno knew as Count Vexin. What Bruno didn't see in the family tree was any reference to the names of the fathers of the children born to the Countess and her half-sister.

He was looking for more information in the end papers when he heard the double doors open and the sister of the Red Countess appeared.

'You wanted to see me?' she said curtly.

'*Bonjour*, Madame. Thank you for receiving me. I was just admiring your wonderful old family bible.'

'Please don't touch. It's very fragile.'

'My apologies. Could you confirm that this woman is your great-niece, please?' He handed her one of the printouts in its sleeve.

She took it to the window and lifted her spectacles, hanging from a gold chain around her neck, held them close to her eyes and then let them drop.

'What a peculiar expression on her face,' she said. 'But yes, that is my great-niece Françoise.'

'Might she be using the name Athénaïs?'

'Françoise-Athénaïs is her first name, so yes. Why do you ask?'

'Is this another picture of her?' He showed her the close-up of the face of the dead woman taken in the pathology lab.

'Yes, I think it is, but it's a very strange picture and why are her eyes closed?'

'Do you not remember me showing you and your staff this photo a couple of days ago when you said you didn't recognize her?'

'My memory isn't what it was. Nor is my eyesight. I can't say I recognized that photo. It's been a long time since I saw her. She lives in America, you know.'

'You have not seen her here at the château or in France in the past month?'

'No, I said so. What is this?'

'I must take a formal statement to that effect, Madame. We have had an inquiry from California asking if your great-niece has returned to France, and to respond I need a brief statement from you. I have the form here . . .'

'I don't have time for this,' she interrupted.

'That's quite all right, Madame,' he said reassuringly, taking out a form and beginning to scribble as he spoke. 'I shall write down very briefly that you recognize your great-niece from the photograph but have not seen her in France for the past month and then show it you for your approval and signature.'

'Are you sure I should not summon my lawyer, or perhaps my grandson, César?' she asked nervously, looking across at the silent maid. Bruno noted to himself the confirmation that the Count was her grandson.

'As you wish, Madame, but it is just a formality.' He read out the curt statement and she signed, albeit reluctantly.

'If your grandson is here I'd like to ask him the same question,' he said.

'He's here this weekend, but not in the house. He's gone out with Foucher and the nurse somewhere. I shall tell them you called.'

'Please do, and say that I shall phone for an appointment to see each of them as soon as possible.'

He put his cap back on, saluted and left. No point in pressing her further, Bruno thought. It was just possible that Athénaïs had come to the château secretly, taken the punt, committed her spectacular suicide and never been seen by the old lady, who seemed sure that Athénaïs was still in California. Possible, but highly unlikely.

He was tempted to stay in the courtyard until the Count, Foucher and Eugénie returned, but he had paperwork to do on Junot's death, Hector to ride and a dinner engagement with Gilles from *Paris-Match*. Back in his office, the first was soon dispatched. Then he began to read the research file on the Count and his business associates that Isabelle had emailed him. When read in conjunction with Lemontin's researches, it looked like a strong case for the presumption of fraud. He opened a new file on his computer, scanned in the key documents from Lemontin's file along with Foucher's insider-trading conviction and then drafted a brisk one-page summary of the key facts and his concerns. He printed it all out for the Mayor and then forwarded it to J-J with a note suggesting that his financial fraud experts might want to start their own inquiry.

The Mayor was in his greenhouse, transplanting seedlings, when Bruno arrived. Little Balzac scampered in from the garden to roll his ears over Bruno's foot. He handed over his report on the holiday village, picked up Balzac and told the Mayor of Francette's claim that she and her mother had no money to bury her father. The Mayor wiped his hands on the seat of his pants to clean off the potting soil and skimmed through the file Bruno had brought. He then turned back to read carefully through Bruno's own summary.

'I have a meeting of the *Conseil-Général* in Périgueux tomorrow afternoon and I'll give a copy of this to one of the legal experts to see what we can do to protect ourselves if this project goes ahead,' the Mayor said. 'That's a very intelligent puppy you have there. He sniffed his way all around the garden and ended up down by the bench, at Bardot's grave. He sat there, looked up at me, threw his head back and gave a little infant howl. It brought tears to my eyes.'

Bardot had been the Mayor's own basset hound, a dog whose hunting skills were a local legend. She had also been the mother of Bruno's dog Gigi, a gift from the Mayor when he had first arrived in St Denis to take up the post of municipal policeman. Bruno had helped dig her grave.

'By the way, the Baron came by earlier with Adrien from the tourist office and Florence from the choir, just to say everything was under way for tomorrow's ceremony at the cave. Florence has been working on the lighting plan and the sound system with Marcel. It sounds like they're planning quite a show. And the announcement of the exorcism has been running on the radio. Périgord-Bleu called me for a quick interview over the phone. They've also had Father Sentout on the air, who announced that he had permission from his bishop to conduct a special ceremony. We aren't short of publicity. I gather the news was first released by *Paris-Match*. Was that something to do with you?'

Bruno confessed that it was and braced himself for a burst of mayoral anger.

'In this case, I approve,' the Mayor said. 'It seems to have caused a lot of interest, but in future perhaps you'd run these bright ideas of yours past me first. Off you go, and I'll see you at the cave in the morning. '

Bruno left with Balzac tucked into the crook of his arm, thinking of the courteous but unmistakable way he'd been rebuked. In the army he'd had officers, supposedly trained leaders of men, without half the natural-born common sense that the Mayor brought to his running of the town and the staff he'd assembled.

Balzac quivered with excitement when Bruno parked his van in Pamela's courtyard. As soon as he opened the door Balzac darted out and trotted straight to the stables. Bruno knew that Fabiola was planning to stay late at the medical centre and it would be his turn to take Victoria and Bess on the evening ride. But first he wanted to call Pamela to see if she knew when she'd be arriving back from Scotland.

'I'm in the stables about to take the evening ride,' he began when she answered.

'I'll be back for Easter,' she replied, adding that the cheapest discount flight she had found was on Good Friday.

She was thinking a lot about money. Her bank had reviewed the likely costs of her mother's care and the almost certain need to sell her mother's house to pay for it. There was a complex legal procedure to be undergone before she could be granted power of attorney over her mother's estate and have the right to sell her mother's house. Even then, she would only be able to use the funds for her mother's care. It was money she'd been counting on to pay off the balance of her French mortgage. Bruno sensed that the real topic on Pamela's mind was the option of going back to her wealthy ex-husband.

He made supportive noises as Pamela spoke. With one part of his mind he understood her dilemma and her sense of duty to her mother. But all his instincts were pushing him to tell her not to tie herself once more into an already failed marriage simply for the financial security it brought.

But what did he know, as an orphan, of the strong ties of love and obligation between a daughter and her mother? He felt further constrained by his own role as her lover, privileged to share her bed often enough, but only at her invitation, and after being told repeatedly that she wanted neither a lasting nor a committed relationship. It still meant that any advice he gave could be construed as self-interest. It left him tongue-tied.

'I dreamed about you last night,' she said, which added a touch of guilt to his thoughts at the memory of Isabelle in his arms. 'It reminded me of how much I miss you, and Fabiola and my house and Victoria and Bess. But it's not long now and I'll see you on Friday. Give the horses a hug from me.'

24

Bruno had not been happy with simply stuffing Balzac into his chest as he rode, worrying that the puppy would squirm free or burrow his way out at the waist. Seeing Pamela's binoculars, inherited from her father, hanging on a hook in the stable gave him an idea. They were an old-fashioned pair with long lenses of the kind he'd seen carried by German U-boat commanders in war movies. He picked up Balzac and inserted him gently inside the leather case. It was so deep the little dog could not see out of the top and gazed pitifully up at him. Bruno extracted him gently, stuffed one of the stable cloths into the bottom and tried again. The fit was perfect, so he hung the case around his neck and tied the long sidestraps to fix it around his chest.

With Victoria and Bess on a leading rein, he took Hector along the lane at a walk before turning off into the field that led up to the woods along the ridge. The case was firm against his chest and Balzac's head was peeking over its rim, his long ears flopping up and down to either side with Hector's stride.

'You look lost in thought,' came a woman's voice, and he looked up to see Bess and Victoria approaching the white mare, on which sat Eugénie with an amused expression on her face. 'We've been watching you as you came up to the ridge. I got the message that you wanted to see me and I thought I'd take the opportunity for another ride. I didn't realize you'd be playing the part of a mother kangaroo.'

She pointed at Balzac in his case and gave a wide grin, the first Bruno had ever seen on her usually controlled face.

'It may look odd, but it works,' he said.

'It looks sweet. You must have a maternal side to your nature,' she replied, her eyes lively with amusement.

Normally he'd enjoy being teased by an attractive woman. But not this one, and not this time.

'I wanted to show you a photograph of the woman in the boat,' he said. 'We may have identified her, but I don't have it with me. I also wanted to talk to you about this development project you're involved in. You're a long way from home.'

'It didn't take me long to get here.' She nudged her mare and they began walking side by side towards the forest ride that would take her back to the Gouffre. 'What do you want to know?'

'It's about the development at Thivion. The Mayor there has told our Mayor that he felt his town had been defrauded, and that what you built fell a long way short of the quality you'd promised.'

'It's true, it did fall short, but that wasn't our fault.'

It was the timing, she explained. When the financial crisis hit the American mortgage market their funding had dried up at the bank. She claimed that she, the Count and Foucher had worked with the Mayor to salvage what they could of the deal, but the Count had lost money in the process. That was the risk that any property development would face, most of all in the worst global recession in seventy years. She launched into a long and complex explanation of the different companies involved in the deal that simply left Bruno confused.

'So this could happen again with St Denis?' he asked.

'No, the funding is secure this time. It's not from a bank.'

'The people of Thivion have some serious allegations against your company. Perhaps I should say companies. There seem to have been several of them involved at various times.'

She dug her heels into her horse's side, rode on a few yards and wheeled the horse to confront him.

'If we'd been trying to defraud Thivion, they could have taken us to court,' she said, rising in the stirrups, her eyes blazing. 'And believe me they tried, but all the lawyers they consulted said they had no case. I know because I had to put my name to sworn statements, spelling out what really happened. We worked night and day trying to make that deal work, and if that damn Mayor of Thivion had guaranteed the loan we'd have had the money to build the place as we planned and the whole project would have worked.'

Her horse was shying at the tension coming from Eugénie and she had to walk it in a circle to calm it, patting her mare's neck and forcing herself to calm down. Hector, aware of some change in the mood, backed slightly away.

'They have no right to make such accusations against us, against me,' she said, calmer now, but her voice still tight. 'There was no fraud, and there's no fraud in what we're trying to do here with St Denis. The Count's grandmother lives here, for heaven's sake. Would he be trying to cheat the town on his family's own doorstep? It's absurd.'

It was plausible. Bruno was aware that the courts were filled with cases of property deals that had been aborted by the recession and most of them were thrown out or settled out of court.

'There's a simple solution,' he said. 'If the funding is secure, then it can be put into escrow so we know it's there.'

'It doesn't work like that. We have written confirmation of the funding but no money will be released until we start work.'

'In that case, my Mayor will almost certainly want some sizeable collateral before he commits town funds for the preliminary work. How about the Auberge St Philippon? That belongs to the Count, I believe?'

'It's a different company,' she said, coldly.

'One of the things that worries us about Thivion is that you seemed to have many companies at your disposal, all doing different things,' he said. 'Their Mayor said every time he dealt with one of your companies another one stepped in.'

'That's common in property deals,' she said. 'One company to do the planning and the finance, one to supervise the construction and another to handle the management.'

'It's not common in Thivion and it's not common round here.'

'You say that as if we're under suspicion! Have you been told about the plans for the sports hall we gave to your Mayor? Doesn't that prove we're genuine? Architectural plans don't come cheap.'

Bruno shrugged.

'Why is the Mayor negotiating through you?' she asked. 'You told me you had no influence in these matters.'

'I'm not negotiating and I have no authority to do so. I'm simply telling you of the town's concerns. I'm very pleased the Count wants to build St Denis an indoor sports centre. It's something I've been trying to raise money for ever since I got here.'

'I'll have to think about all this and discuss it with the others,' she said.

'You're a very unusual nurse.'

'And you're a very unusual policeman,' she replied, turning her horse and riding off.

Bruno looked after her for a while as Hector pawed at the ground and the other two horses looked at him curiously, waiting for the word to follow. He looked down at Balzac on his chest.

'Mother kangaroo,' he said to himself, acknowledging the aptness of her remark, and chuckled as he turned Hector towards the track that led the long way back to Pamela's house.

An hour later Bruno was in his kitchen with the chicken he'd bought, peeling potatoes with a small heap of chopped garlic beside him, when his phone rang. It was Fabiola, calling from the medical centre.

'I exercised the horses,' he told her.

'It's not that. I ran a blood test on Louis Junot. He had so much alcohol in him he couldn't have walked, let alone ride.'

'He was an alcoholic so he'd have had tolerance. How much did he have?'

'Just over three. That means zero point three per cent alcohol in the blood. He'd probably have been unconscious.'

'So you're sure he couldn't have driven?' Bruno knew that this was six times the legal limit in France.

'Yes, and absolutely not with a motorbike, he'd have had no balance.'

'So the crash was faked?'

'I wouldn't go that far but it's certainly suspicious. I'll call the pathologist in Bergerac but you'd better alert J-J and the *Procureur*.'

If she wanted the prosecutor alerted, she must be pretty sure, Bruno thought to himself.

'Will do, but will you call me back when you've talked to Bergerac, because I'll need to say it's their finding. You know how fussy the *Proc*'s office can be.'

Bruno rang J-J's mobile to alert him but had to leave a message. He'd wait for her next call before informing the *Procureur*. He finished the potatoes, peeled some shallots, set the table for two and lit the fire. Back in the kitchen, he opened a can of beer, drank half of it and then used an opener to punch some more holes in the top of the beer can. He took a large chunk of butter and began working it with a knife and mixing in the chopped garlic. He added some fresh rosemary from his garden and then began pushing the buttery mixture under the skin of the chicken as far as he could reach. He used the remainder to coat the inside.

Bruno had already put the giblets on to simmer with some

chopped carrots and celery, an onion, peppercorns and water. He'd skimmed it after ten minutes and left it to reduce naturally. He checked his watch; Gilles would arrive soon. He sealed the neck of the chicken with half a lemon and held it in place with a skewer. He turned on his oven, setting the gas at 180 degrees, and put the half-filled beer can into the centre of the roasting pan. Then he carefully impaled the chicken vertically on the can, tossed some duck fat into the pan along with the sliced potatoes and left it to roast.

He was opening a small jar of his own foie gras when Fabiola called again to report that the pathologist had confirmed her finding on the alcohol level and she was going down to Bergerac to attend the autopsy. This time he called the office of the *Procureur* in Périgueux and left a message with the clerk on duty.

Balzac had been prowling the kitchen and looking for the source of the wondrous smells, so once he'd turned out the foie, Bruno wiped the inside of the jar clean with a piece of bread and handed it to his pup. When Balzac had finished, Bruno took him out to the chicken coop, and with a firm hold on the excited dog he sat with him in the chicken run to get him accustomed to them. The ducks were the first to come up and examine the new arrival, and then came the chickens, pecking at the carrot tops and potato peelings he brought out. Bruno stroked Balzac and spoke to him quietly, restraining him each time he tried to squirm out of Bruno's hand, until he heard a horn sound from the lane and he went out to greet the journalist.

Gilles came with a bottle in each hand, one of Black Label

scotch and the other a bottle of Château Nenin from the Pomerol, a wine well above Bruno's usual price range, even for special treats.

'If we drink all that you won't be driving back,' Bruno said. He had not remembered Gilles being much of a drinker.

'We're not going to drink it all, but think of it as a delayed celebration that we survived Sarajevo. There were times I was so hungry I'd have eaten that little dog of yours,' said the reporter, as Bruno led the way inside. 'But here's my real gift to you.'

He handed across a faxed copy of a dental chart.

'That's the proof of identity you need. Your dead body is Athénaïs de Bourbon.'

'Françoise-Athénaïs, to be exact,' said Bruno. 'A relative identified her from the cropped photo you sent me.'

They ate the first course of Bruno's foie gras and then Bruno insisted that Gilles join him in the kitchen to see his surprise. He opened the oven door, and with great care not to overbalance the chicken on its can of beer, withdrew the roasting pan and set it on top of the stove.

'*Poulet bière au cul*,' he announced in triumph. 'Remember when we got that convoy in? The American radio reporter made this, that guy from Texas. I thought it was great, the way the beer steamed and kept the chicken moist from the inside.'

'*Putain*, I remember that,' said Gilles. 'He kept saying he'd paid ten dollars for the beer on the black market.'

Bruno uncorked the chicken from its beer can, put it on a serving dish with the roast potatoes. He told Gilles to take

252

it to the table and start to carve while he made the gravy.

The chicken was demolished and they were down to the last third of the Pomerol when Gilles's phone went. It was his office on the line, so Bruno cleared the table, brought in the cheese, and began picking out scraps of chicken from the carcass to feed to Balzac. Gilles was still talking and scribbling on a notepad, so Bruno washed up, tidied his kitchen and took some sheets and a towel into the spare room.

'Finished,' Gilles called from the table and poured out the last of the wine to go with the cheese. 'They just wanted to check headlines and captions and play around with the lead. A good story, but a sad one. They want to know what happens next, after the exorcism. Is there going to be a follow-up?'

'What do you think? Won't that put a nice, neat finish on it all?' Bruno asked.

'Not until we know who held the Satanist ceremony in the cave and why Athénaïs made herself a Satanist suicide. Now they want me to get an interview with the Red Countess.'

'It wasn't the Countess who identified her, it was her sister. The Countess has Alzheimer's. She's bedridden.'

'Well, I'll talk to the sister.'

'She didn't strike me as the sort of woman who would have much to do with the press,' Bruno said.

'I'm used to that, and to getting round it. The name *Paris-Match* still works wonders.'

They went back to the fire and to the scotch and Bruno told the story from the beginning: the holiday village in Thivion and the Red Countess in her hospital room at the château, Foucher's conviction for insider trading and the defence industry parties at the Count's auberge. Gilles heard him out, scribbling a few notes, and waited until Bruno finished and had turned to throw another log on the fire.

'The common factor in all this is the Count,' Gilles said. 'What's he got to say for himself?'

'I'm still trying to nail him down for an interview.'

'Would you mind if I had a crack at him, since he's the dead woman's cousin? If Athénaïs was the only descendant then now that she's dead I suppose that makes the Count the heir to the Red Countess.'

Bruno jerked upright in his chair. Why hadn't he thought of that? Then he slumped back. The Count couldn't be the heir.

'Athénaïs had a child at some point, according to the autopsy,' Bruno said. 'Maybe that's your follow-up story; I presume you've got a correspondent in Hollywood. You'd have a better chance of tracking her kid down than I would.'

'More than one,' said Gilles. For this kind of search, the magazine would probably hire a private detective, someone who specialized in tracking people through hospital records, birth registration, school registries and the like. They had already hired one to find Athénaïs's last address from the credit ratings and had found a mine of information. She was flat broke, credit cards cancelled and her car repossessed from the street.

'The dump she was living in didn't even have a garage,' Gilles said. 'That was earlier this year. We've got a sidebar story on her lowlife in Hollywood: porn and bankruptcy.'

'And then she came home,' said Bruno.

'Home to die – that's one of our headlines. Do you want a last drink?'

Bruno shook his head. He'd had more than enough. 'I need to get to bed. I'll have an early start, getting ready for Father Sentout's exorcism. There's a spare bed for you here. If you even touch your car keys, I'll have to arrest you.'

25

The Gouffre looked magnificent. The lighting effects that Bruno had seen in Our Lady's Chapel had been moved to the vast cavern, so that the images of giant rose windows shimmered on each side of the assembled audience. Another rose was beamed onto the concave roof of the cave and its glowing reds, blues and golds were reflected in the stillness of the lake. On the far shore, where orchestras would give concerts, stood the choir of St Denis in their white surplices. Picked out by a spotlight, a long table covered with a white cloth and serving as an altar bore a silver cross, two tall white candles and the accoutrements of the Mass. Behind it stood one of the treasures of St Denis, the great carved crucifix that usually lived behind the altar of the town church.

Solemn organ music played as the last arrivals took their seats. Four TV cameras were focused on the choir. Half the town was there and more people stood in the car park outside listening to the loudspeakers that would carry the words and music out to them. Reporters sat on a row of chairs to one side and photographers crouched and scurried to find the best angles.

The organ music fell silent and, from his vantage point on

the balcony alongside the Mayor, J-J and the Baron, Bruno could almost feel the audience hold its breath when the thunderous notes of Bach's *Toccata and Fugue in D minor* rang out. The beam of the spotlight on the choir swivelled down to the lake itself and crept with slow and steady purpose towards the audience, then back further to the stairs. At their head stood Father Sentout in full priestly regalia. Behind him and carrying a tall silver crucifix was the sacristan in his white robe. Behind them and also in white surplices were Marcel's son Jean-Paul and Philippe Delaron's nephew Luc.

Father Sentout led them down the stairs and across the rocky floor to the strand where a single boat stood waiting. It was not one of the usual jaunty plastic vessels with pedals but the Baron's sturdy wooden fishing boat that could seat six or even eight with ease. Father Sentout climbed in and sat in the bow, the sacristan stood solemn and silent at the stern. The two boys clambered aboard and in unison took the two short oars and put them into the water. Luc loosened the knot that held the boat to the dock and pushed off. The boys began to row the boat slowly across as the *Toccata* died and gave way to the first slow notes of the Kyrie of Mozart's *Mass in C minor*.

As the boat reached the middle of the lake the choir had begun to sing, and by some miracle of timing just as the boat reached the far side and the priest rose to step ashore, Florence began her solo and the high, sweet notes of *Kyrie Eleison*, Lord have mercy, filled the cave.

'They've been practising this half the night and since seven this morning,' whispered the Mayor. Bruno nodded as he glanced at the order of service to identify the music that had been chosen.

'I wouldn't have missed this for the world,' murmured J-J to Bruno. 'But we need to talk later.'

When the Kyrie ended, Father Sentout raised his head, lifted his hands to bless the crowd and began to speak. Bruno could not see the tiny microphone he must be wearing beneath his robes but the words rang out powerfully through the vast space.

'In a famous discourse in the year of Our Lord 1972, the Holy Father Pope Paul VI said that he sensed that "from somewhere or other, the smoke of Satan has entered the temple of God". And here in this majestic cave, surely itself a great work of Our Lord, the smoke of Satan has crept in to pollute and defile the very chamber dedicated to Our Lady.'

He turned and knelt on the small prayer stool placed before the altar as the choir began the triumphant opening notes of the Gloria. When it ended he rose, turned and spoke again. This time his first words were in Latin.

'*Exorcizo te, immundissime spiritus, in nomine Domini nostri Jesu Christi*' – I exorcize you, unclean spirit, in the name of our Lord Jesus Christ.

He paused, the spotlight on him faded and the music swelled, the first almost jaunty notes leading into the glorious affirmation of faith, the Credo, and the choir roared out the words:

Credo in unum Deum, Patrem omnipotentem, factorem cœli et terrae, visibilium omnium et invisibilium. I believe in one God, the Father Almighty, Maker of heaven and earth, and of all things visible and invisible.

The music and the singing rang around the great chamber with such force that Bruno saw tremors appear on the usually still waters of the lake, sending the reflections of the stained-glass windows shimmering.

'The spirit of Almighty God is with us,' roared out the priest.

'Sanctus, Sanctus, Sanctus,' sang the choir in the three great and soaring chords. 'Holy, Holy, Holy, Lord God of Hosts.'

Bruno felt transported. He had never attended any religious ceremony with a fraction of this power and meaning. The sceptic in him was whispering at the back of his mind that the setting of the cave, the skill of the lighting and the magnificent acoustics that enhanced the power of the choir were all working on some childhood memory of church and faith. And the presence of hundreds of his fellow townsfolk, equally rapt and awed by the power of light and music and the newly commanding presence of their own familiar priest, was carrying him on a great communal wave of an experience that was as dramatic as it was unique.

Father Sentout began the sacrament of the Eucharist, raising the chalice of wine and the silver plate of the host to the great crucifix in consecration. And then one by one, still singing *Hosanna in Excelsis*, the members of the choir came down to kneel before the altar and take communion and then return to their places to begin the *Agnus Dei*.

'*Ite, missa est*,' said Father Sentout, and it was over.

At least, Bruno thought it was over. But hardly had the thought formed when a great whirring sound filled the air, followed by a mighty crash, a cloud of dust and a brilliant shaft of daylight coming from the sky.

Then came a chorus of screams followed by the sound of chairs falling as people rose and turned to run. Father Sentout still had his microphone and with great presence of mind he roared: 'A sign, a sign that the Lord our God is with us.'

'Let there be light,' he shouted, pointing at the ray from the sky that pierced the vast space of the cavern. 'And the Lord said let there be light.'

He turned to the choir behind him and like a conductor raised his arms to get them to join him. Amplified by the microphones they chanted in chorus and all that could be heard in the great cavern as the dust began to settle was that single phrase from the Book of Genesis echoing endlessly. The crowd calmed. Many were crossing themselves.

Bruno looked up and saw that the shaft of light came from an evenly shaped circle. He looked at the ground below the hole and saw the crumpled remains of the cradle that could be winched up and down, available to any tourist who was prepared to pay the twenty euros for the ride. The rope that raised and lowered the cradle had come free from the winch and lay in forlorn loops amid the wreckage. Bruno dismissed the idea of any accidental release of the cradle; the timing had been too perfect for that. Some of the crowd were already calling out that it was a miracle.

'And if that doesn't get us onto the TV news tonight, nothing will,' said the Baron, as he slapped the Mayor on the back.

'This way,' said the Mayor as they emerged from the cave's entry tunnel and into the sunlight. 'We're all going to lunch.'

He shepherded Bruno, J-J and the Baron into the minibus

the town used to take its old folk on outings and went back to the cave entrance saying he would fetch Father Sentout, the hero of the hour. J-J climbed back out, signalling Bruno to follow, and apologizing to the Baron. 'Police business,' he said and steered Bruno towards the bushes.

'The Prefect came into my office this morning early, something he's never done before. He told me to think again about pursuing that fraud inquiry into your holiday village project. Then he pointed his finger at the ceiling and left.'

'Pressure from the top?'

'Very high,' came J-J's reply. 'So I made a discreet check with his secretary and he'd had a short call just before he came to see me from the office of the Defence Minister followed by another from the Elysée. Since I have a tender regard for my pension . . .' J-J said, and shrugged.

'I understand,' said Bruno, momentarily distracted by the sight of Foucher coming down the slope towards the ticket office on the path that led up to the staff housing. Bruno caught himself. It also led up to the winch that controlled the basket. 'Thanks for trying,' he added hurriedly to J-J.

'It stinks to me, but there we are. And I think you might want to reconsider your own priorities here. Talking of fraud, I suppose you want me to believe you weren't involved in that little performance in there with the falling cradle?'

He gave Bruno a playful punch on the arm with the false bonhomie of a decent man feeling ashamed of himself. In silence, the two of them walked back to the minibus just as the Mayor extracted Father Sentout and Florence from the knot of reporters and cameras. As Foucher joined them, Bruno made a point of shaking his hand, and saw, as he'd expected, a streak of oil on the man's palm.

'Well done, Father, a wonderful performance,' said the Baron as the priest took his place in the middle row of the bus.

Amid a flurry of congratulations and recollections of this and that event and much courtly praise of Florence, they drove off and to Bruno's surprise they passed through St Denis and headed out on the back road to Les Eyzies. He'd assumed the Mayor had arranged a lunch in the *Mairie* as he did on other civic occasions. Instead, it looked as if they were heading for a restaurant. It was when they turned off on the road to St Philippon that Bruno realized they were heading for the Count's hotel.

Discreetly he opened his phone and looked again at the text from Isabelle that he'd received when he went into the cave some two hours earlier. It was succinct in Isabelle's usual style and he saw it had come from a mobile phone number he'd never known her use before. Perhaps she was taking precautions. It read: 'Béatrice 2 arrests prostitution Paris. No convix. Faxing.'

There were several reasons why an arrest might not lead to a conviction, nor even to a formal charge, particularly with prostitutes who were often dismissed with a warning. Magistrates tended to look askance at a case where the only witness was an undercover *flic* from the morals squad, particularly when the same *flic* appeared in a dozen cases one after another. In some stations a woman could buy herself out of trouble with services rendered, usually sexual but sometimes with information. But Bruno had never heard of such an arrest being made without cause.

A loud horn sounded repeatedly behind them. The driver pulled in and a white Jaguar swept past them, Foucher at the wheel, the Count beside him, and Béatrice and Eugénie waving cheerfully from the rear seat. It was going to be quite a party, thought Bruno, until he saw Father Sentout looking after the disappearing car, his face white and his lips moving as his fingers worked on his rosary beads. Had he been stunned to recognize someone in the car or was he just feeling the reaction from his exertions in the cave?

'We finally manage to get you here for an informal occasion, although you're still in uniform.' Béatrice handed Bruno one glass of Pol Roger and a second to the Baron, who kissed her on both cheeks and called her '*ma belle*'. At a sign from the Mayor, Bruno excused himself and squeezed past J-J's bulky form to join the Mayor and the Count, who were talking business with Foucher. Or rather, the Count was explaining the problems with Thivion in much the same way that Eugénie had outlined the impact of the financial crisis and the attempt to salvage something from the wreck.

'If you want to slog through the paperwork, you're welcome,' the Count concluded. 'You'll find I lost money on the deal.'

'As much as Thivion?' Bruno asked politely. He knew his role when the Mayor summoned him to an encounter such as this. He was to ask the questions the Mayor would have put, except that his Mayor wanted to remain above any controversy so that he could intervene later as the sensible man of compromise and agreement.

'Thivion would not have lost a centime if they'd followed my advice.' The Count remained affable, refusing to rise to Bruno's bait. Suddenly the Mayor excused himself and crossed to join an urgently beckoning Father Sentout, leaving Bruno, the Count and Foucher.

'The Mayor in Thivion is a fool,' said Foucher. 'I spent hours with him, trying to explain that the worst option was to cut back on the quality of the project. But he refused to guarantee the loan we needed, so we had no option. I'm not proud of the way it turned out but we did our best.'

'I suppose you know I've been trying to see you both,' Bruno said. The Count nodded and said he thought he knew why. Bruno put down his glass and took a folded print of Athénaïs's photograph from his breast pocket and showed it to him. 'Your grandmother has identified this woman as her great-niece, your cousin Athénaïs. Do you agree?'

The Count gave the photo a casual glance. 'I believe I do, although I haven't seen her for several years, not since one time when I was in New York on business. She was shopping around a film treatment to some independent producers and we met for a drink. She tried to persuade me to put some money into her film but I declined. We were never close.'

'Did you know she was in France? Or why she'd want to kill herself?'

The Count shook his head. 'We weren't in touch. Not even Christmas cards. I don't know how she knew I was in New York that time, she just rang me out of the blue.'

'How about you?' Bruno asked Foucher. 'You tried pretty hard to stop the boat with her body from drifting under the bridge. Are you going to tell me that was coincidence?'

'I never knew her in life, so there's nothing for me to recognize,' Foucher said dismissively. 'Isn't all this financial stuff a bit above your pay grade?'

'Not when I know someone involved has a conviction for insider trading,' Bruno said, instantly regretting the impulse that made him play an important card for such a petty reason as countering a sneer.

He stared at Foucher until the other man's eyes fell and turned back to the Count, who was watching the exchange with eyebrows raised, an amused look on his face.

'You have been busy,' the Count said. 'Looks like you've been underestimating our local police, Lionel.'

'We'll need somebody to come to the morgue in Bergerac and make a formal identification,' Bruno said. 'I'd rather not impose on your grandmother. Will you do it? It won't take long.'

'I'll do it as a family duty, but I can't say I'm keen to do you any favours. I hear you're the one who's been trying to stop my project.'

'Whoever told you that is misinformed,' said Bruno, with a glance at Foucher. 'I want that sports hall you've kindly promised just as much as you want the project. I just want to be sure that St Denis gets the project it's been promised, unlike Thivion.'

'Fair enough,' said the Count, with a half-smile that seemed genuine. 'That's what I want to build. This place is the nearest

I have to a home, don't forget. I was even baptized in the family chapel. And I'm serious about the sports hall. We even commissioned a design for it from the architects.'

'I took care of that and delivered the plans to the Mayor myself,' intervened Foucher. 'What more do you expect us to do?'

'Tell me about your charming manager,' Bruno said, trying another gambit. 'I'm wondering how you found her. Have you known her long?'

'A few years,' the Count replied vaguely. He was looking across at his other guests where the Baron seemed to have monopolized Béatrice. 'She was working in the corporate hospitality business and we used her company a fair bit when I launched the private equity firm. She impressed me so I hired her.' He handed his glass to Foucher, who went off to fill it again. 'Any more questions or can we join the others? I can't wait to talk to that fascinating singer. I hear she planned all the theatrics. Will you introduce me before we eat?'

'Certainly,' Bruno replied, leading the way. 'But not all the theatrics. I think that last little thunderclap was arranged by you and the Baron and performed by the man who's bringing your next glass of champagne. I'd love to know how you persuaded our priest to go along with it.'

'He loved the idea, once it was properly explained.'

26

A telephone call from Fabiola took Bruno from the table halfway through lunch.

'It's not entirely clear, but from the autopsy I think you may have two cases of murder,' she told him. 'The woman in the boat and Junot both died the same way, of what looked like a heart attack. I'm prepared to bet it was induced circulatory failure. I think they had air bubbles injected into their veins but I can't prove it. What do you know about embolism?'

'Not a lot,' he admitted.

When a pathologist suspected murder, she explained, or when the person had died gasping for breath, it was customary to X-ray the corpse before beginning an autopsy. Air bubbles showed up very clearly on X-rays. There was also a technique to conduct the autopsy underwater, when the air bubbles could be seen to escape, like putting a punctured bicycle tyre in water to locate the leak. But there'd been no reason to do that with the woman in the boat, and Junot's circulation system had been compromised by his injuries.

'We found injection points on the bodies,' she said. There was a small needle mark in the arm of each corpse. Fabiola suspected it had been used to send air to the right atrium of the heart and from there to the lung, where it would block the capillaries and interrupt the circulation system. The person dies gasping, she explained, because the body thinks the problem is a lack of air. Without an X-ray the standard proof was missing.

'In Junot's case, there's bruising that could have been caused by a physical attack, but the injuries sustained in the crash make it very hard to prove. In each case, the injection seemed to be done by someone with medical training and a very large syringe. You'd need about two hundred cc, that's about a cupful. The usual syringe contains twenty cc.'

'So it's your informed opinion that it was murder by air injection? That's enough for the *Procureur* to ask for a full inquiry.'

'But you'll need other evidence,' she insisted. She had indications rather than proof, she explained, and another doctor could disagree. But her pathologist friend was faxing his report to the *Procureur*'s office with a copy for Bruno and another to J-J. As she rang off, Fabiola added that Junot wouldn't have lasted long anyway unless he stopped drinking. His liver was yellow-orange and he had swollen breasts; advanced cirrhosis.

Bruno had been strolling around the car park as he listened and now found himself beside a tall hedge through which he could see more vehicles. One of them was a large pickup truck, rare in France. He squeezed through a gap in the hedge and saw that it was a far-from-new Toyota Hilux, a powerful 3-litre model with crash bars front and rear. He walked around it, wondering if it would have the power to break the logs on a crash barrier. The Toyota's front crash bar, while badly scratched, seemed intact. The rear one was bent but clean. The cargo area was covered by a dirty tarpaulin, torn in places. There was no sign of blood nor of the fresh oil that might have suggested it had recently carried a motorbike. But it could have been used to cover the crash bar while it pushed at the fence on the road where Junot's body had been found. Bruno took a small plastic bag from his pocket, plucked one of the threads from the tarpaulin and bagged it.

He walked back to the terrace, where the lunch party was coming to an end with coffee being served. He went to Béatrice, sitting between J-J and the Baron and charming them both. He apologized for the interruption and asked for a private word with her.

'You can be a very tiresome guest,' she replied. After a final squeeze of the Baron's arm, she led him back to her office. 'Will this take long?'

'I hope not. It's about Francette's father. Did you see him again after he came with me to see Francette?'

'No. What is this, Bruno? You said he died in a road accident.'

'We're just trying to retrace his movements before the crash.'

'Well, I didn't see him here again.'

'Thanks.' He half-turned as if to go. 'By the way, before this job I think you said you were in corporate entertaining. When was that and where? We're doing a review of the beverage licences for all the communes in the *Conseil*.'

'I don't hold the beverage licence. That's the Count.'

'But you're in charge.'

She studied him and then opened a small filing cabinet in the side of her desk. 'Here's a copy of my CV.'

He scanned it, noticing the vague references to 'hospitality industry' and the gaps and asked casually, 'No convictions?' She shook her head. 'No arrest record?'

She sat down at her desk. 'Why not say what it is you want?'

'I'm wondering how you got out of those two arrests without a conviction,' he replied, taking a chair opposite her.

'So even you country coppers can call up police records these days.' She looked not in the least abashed.

'We always could,' he said mildly. 'Why not tell me what happened?'

'You don't look like an innocent to me, Bruno. You can imagine what happened. But do you have any idea what hit the oldest profession when the Eastern Europeans came in? The Russians, the Albanians, the Serbs, the menaces and the threats, the girls terrorized, pimps shot, escort agencies fire-bombed. It was like a war zone in the Nineties. I got out as soon as I could.'

'How did you get started?'

'By being born in Beuvry, up on the Belgian border. The last coal mine there closed just before I was born. No jobs, shit schools, Dad died and Mum was a drunk who kept bringing home men who liked my pretty face – what else was I going to do? When I was fifteen I headed for Paris with my best friend. You can imagine the rest. The friend got into drugs. She's dead now.'

'And the arrests?' Bruno made an effort to his keep his voice dispassionate.

'The first time was working for an escort agency. They rounded up all the girls from the agency records but they couldn't make the charges stick. Maybe they were paid off.'

'And the second?'

'I'd moved on to an exclusive *maison de passe*, not quite Madame Clàude's but close. We were known as Chez Foufounette.'

Her eyes twinkled as she said it. Foufounette was the most affectionate of French slang words for the female genitalia.

'No mistaking the speciality of the house.' He couldn't help grinning.

'You'd be surprised,' Béatrice replied, laughing in return. 'Some of the clients even surprised me. That ended when a deputy from the *Assemblée Nationale* reckoned he'd caught a dose and complained to the Mayor. We were raided but some of the other clients ensured it was hushed up. One of them offered to make me his mistress and set me up in my own apartment. I said I'd be delighted to be his mistress but I'd like a job. He started me in public relations and it went from there.'

'And then you met the Count.'

'And then I met César. He's a very sweet guy, takes good care of his old mistresses. So he knows all about my past. You can't put pressure on me that way.'

'I don't intend to. I really just wanted to ask if Junot had been here. But I also have to ask whether this place has anything to do with your old profession.'

'You mean whether our corporate clients are able to enjoy female company? As I said, you're no innocent. We don't exactly discourage it. The girls can always say no.'

'Is that how Francette got that thick lip?'

'No, it was like I told you.' Her good humour had suddenly gone. 'Francette fell because of a clumsy guest, not exactly sober. At least, that's what she told me. I wasn't in the room.'

'Might Junot have known what his daughter was doing here?'

'Not unless Francette told him. We're very discreet.'

'Yes, I can tell,' he said, rising. 'Thanks for your time. Tell me, is Eugénie also part of your stable?'

'Why? Are you interested?' Her eyes twinkled at him again and he wondered if it was genuine or something she turned on and off at will. 'As it happens, she isn't, but maybe she's spoken for.'

The *déchetterie* of St Denis was run by an old *sous-officier* of the paras, a giant of a man known as Jacquot, who ruled over the municipal rubbish dump as if it were a parade ground. Woe betide any citizen who dared to mix their plastics with their leftovers or their dead batteries with their garden waste, or whose car moved a centimetre outside the painted guidelines that led to each of the huge containers. Bruno parked outside and walked in to shake hands and ask about plastic sheeting or any other kind of wrapping that might have been dumped on Saturday night or Sunday.

'We're closed then,' said Jacquot.

'Yes, but we both know people throw stuff over the fence. They can see which container is which.' Jacquot on occasion hid in his little wooden hut to spy on malefactors and take photos of their crimes. A couple of well-publicized fines had curtailed that practice but not stopped it altogether.

'We'll start with plastic,' said Jacquot, leading the way and placing a stepladder against the container. He had a long pole with a sturdy hook on the end to sift through the rubbish.

'There was a box in the cardboard bin I wanted to take a look at later, hadn't been folded. That always makes me think there's something stuffed inside. They think I don't notice but I'll get them later. See my new box of tricks?' Jacquot pointed to the top of his hut and Bruno saw a small camera.

'Was that working over the weekend?' Bruno asked.

'Of course it was. Why do you think I installed it?'

The sides of the container for cardboard were too high for Bruno to peer in.

'I'll have to get inside,' said Jacquot. 'Bring that other ladder over, the one leaning against my hut.'

He climbed in, pulling a knife from his belt, and Bruno followed him up the rungs to watch as Jacquot began slicing the cardboard with the precision of a master chef. 'This what you want?' he called, displaying a dirty but folded plastic sheet from inside an anonymous and medium-sized box. 'Looks like oil and something else, paint maybe, still sticky.'

'Could it be blood?'

'I'd say so.' Jacquot came out of the container and handed the box to Bruno.

While he waited for the forensic team to come, Bruno called Father Sentout to ask where the baptismal records for St Philippon were kept. At the bishop's office in Périgueux, he was told. And that would include the records for the private chapel at the château? Indeed it would, the priest replied, but why did Bruno want to know?

'Just checking names and dates. The baptismal records have the full names, not just the ones on the birth certificates?'

'Yes, and in old families they often add the names of the godparents,' Father Sentout answered. 'Is there anything in particular I can help you with?'

'Can you find out the names of the various private confessors Madame de la Gorce used? Presumably they'd be the ones who did the baptisms.'

'Usually they would, yes. St Philippon always came under this parish so I have pretty full records. How far back do you want me to go, Bruno?'

'1945, if you can, Father.'

'Goodness, that will mean going through my predecessors' records. Is this urgent?'

'I'm afraid so.' He paused. 'By the way, Father, you seemed to be shocked by something as we were in the minibus this morning. Did you recognize someone at that lunch party?'

'No, no, I was just feeling tired after the service,' the priest replied, rather too quickly.

Bruno rang off, toying with the thought of Father Sentout having known Béatrice in her professional capacity on some discreet visit to Paris. He found it hard to believe. His housekeepers were renowned for their piety and their homely looks and there was no gossip about the priest. Bruno had never understood the Church's rule of chastity, but if anyone kept to it he'd have bet it was Father Sentout.

Resolving to pursue the matter with him in person, he

274

turned to the folder he'd brought from his office with today's mail and the two faxes he'd been expecting from Isabelle. The folder contained printouts of the photos he'd taken with his phone of the family tree inside the bible at the Red Château. Something about the names tickled his memory. Gondrin, Pardaillan, Antin and Mortemart were all family names that recurred in the family tree. When he looked at his notebook he saw that they were also the names of the various companies involved in the Count's project at Thivion.

That reminded him. He called France Télécom's directory inquiries to get the number for the architects in Paris, asking for the office manager. He identified himself and inquired about plans for a sports hall in St Denis.

'I can't find any record of such a commission,' said the woman in Paris, after a long pause in which Bruno had heard the clicking of computer keys.

'It would have been commissioned by César de Vexin and it might come under the holiday village project you designed here.'

'Nothing under that name nor under St Denis.'

'Try St Philippon.'

More clicking. 'Nothing for that, either.'

'It might have been commissioned by Antin Investments.'

'We have a commission on file for a place called Thivion.'

'That's the same company,' he said, and waited again until she came back on the line, her voice suspicious.

'Who did you say you are?'

He explained, gave her the phone number of the *Mairie* and suggested she check his credentials and his mobile number.

'It's not you I'm suspicious of, it's them,' she said. 'We wouldn't do any more work for them. We're in litigation because we haven't been paid yet for the Thivion job. And a sports hall is not something we've ever done.'

'The plans for the sports hall they showed us had your stamp on them.'

'That's fraud,' she said. 'Can you send us a copy of the plans showing that? We'll add it to the lawsuit.'

Bruno called Michel at the public works office to pass on the news, to learn that Michel had done some sleuthing of his own, starting with the *Département*'s own architectural office in Périgueux. They had found the amount of insulation in the plans for the sports hall to be bizarre. They'd put Michel in touch with the school of architecture at Bordeaux University, where he spoke with a young professor who'd done an exchange year at the school of architecture in Quebec.

'It's a Canadian specification,' Michel explained. 'And the guy recognized it, because it was a school project he'd been involved in, designing a sports hall for a town called Jonquière in northern Quebec where it gets as cold as hell. Because it was a public project, the plans were on the internet. It looks like they simply downloaded them, put the Paris firm's name on them and gave them to us. The plans didn't cost them a centime. I was just going to call the Mayor.'

'And tell him what I learned from the Paris architects about the unpaid bill and the lawsuit,' Bruno said.

He turned back to his folders. The faxed copies of Béatrice's arrest records echoed what she had told him in her office but gave him places and dates and the names of the arresting officers. They might be useful. Fabiola's fax was a copy of two autopsy reports with their conclusions and recommendations. Each case was now classified as a suspicious homicide with 'indications of death deliberately induced'. That would do. No discreet little pointing of a finger at J-J's ceiling would derail this inquiry.

Bruno sat back in the seat of his van and pondered how much he should tell Gilles. His story would be published by now, but he hoped that Gilles would follow up the hints he'd dropped about the Red Château. They had parted in the morning as amicably as two hungover men could manage after three cups of Bruno's strongest coffee. Bruno at least had managed a gentle jog through the woods before his shower, but Gilles had not looked markedly better when Bruno had spotted him in the press section of the cave.

'Have you seen the internet?' Gilles asked as soon as he picked up the phone. 'The story's huge, picked up everywhere. Even *Le Monde*'s putting it on page one. We're printing an extra hundred thousand copies. Hold on . . .'

Bruno heard Gilles muttering excuses to colleagues and walking to somewhere more private. 'We're on the track of the daughter and the ex-husband. One of our guys is on his way to their house in Santa Barbara. We thought we'd fly her over for her mother's funeral. Is it scheduled yet? Will it be at the château?'

'I don't know, but there's no funeral in prospect. They're still writing up the autopsy, so the *Procureur* won't clear it for burial for a while.' Bruno didn't say that after the pathologist's report it might be some weeks.

'I've got to do a piece on the Red Countess,' Gilles said. 'We've got a lot of old photos and it's mostly clippings but is there anyone in town who knew her?'

Bruno gave him the names and numbers for Antoine the riverman and Fouton the old schoolmaster. He added Montsouris, as a loyal Communist. 'What did you make of the exorcism?'

'Great for TV, not so much for us and now everybody's trying to prove that the final crash of the basket was faked,' Gilles said. 'Do you know if it was?'

'Not for sure, but you might want to track down a guy called Lionel Foucher. I saw him coming down the path from the winch with grease on his hands. He works for the Count as some kind of estate manager, drives a white Jaguar and lives somewhere in the château grounds.'

'Thanks, and thanks for dinner,' said Gilles. 'It took me a while to recover this morning but once I did I remembered a great evening.'

'We'll talk later. I've got to go,' Bruno said, seeing the familiar forensic van coming round the corner to the *déchetterie*.

Yves was in charge of the team and Bruno had worked with him before. He gave Yves the cardboard box and explained the contents. He then gave Yves the two evidence bags with the threads of waxed cotton, one from the broken crash barrier and the other from the Toyota pickup.

'That's certainly blood on the plastic,' said Yves, and asked him to mark the crash site on a map. 'Have you taken a statement from the guy in charge of this place?' Bruno said no but told him of the video camera.

'Leave it to us. And thanks for that tip about that disc that was found inside the woman in the boat. It was a host, sure enough. I persuaded our local priest to let us have one of his to make a match. Apparently it's just another bit of bread until the service. So what was it doing in her vagina? That's a new one on me.'

27

Father Sentout lived beside the church in a house that was far too large for him. It was too large even with his house-keeper and the priests who visited regularly to help him serve his ever-increasing parish as older curés died and were not replaced. Strangers were startled by the sight of children's toys and tricycles scattered on the path to his house. Bruno wasn't, knowing that the upper two floors were offered to families that the priest in his old-fashioned way called the deserving poor. Father Sentout was in less than welcoming mood when the housekeeper showed Bruno into his study, but Bruno was not to be put off.

'I saw you looking stunned when you recognized someone in that white car this morning and I need to know who and why,' he said. 'I've just had a report from the pathologist that suggests we may be investigating a murder, so please don't prevaricate.'

'Murder? Saints preserve us, I had no idea. But I'm not sure what I can tell you, Bruno.'

'You knew someone from the past. Was it the Count?'

The priest studied him for a moment. Someone who had heard as many confessions as Father Sentout would hardly be innocent of the ways of the world. Something he had read came into his head, that André Malraux had once asked an elderly priest what he had learned of the human race after a lifetime of hearing confessions, and the priest had replied, 'That there are no grown-ups.'

'No, it wasn't the Count, it was Foucher,' Father Sentout said. 'I knew him from the seminary where I was teaching. But he had to leave, he had no true vocation.'

'Why did he have to leave?'

'I wasn't really involved, not directly, but it was quite a scandal, and not long before his scheduled ordination. I believe sex was involved, but that wasn't the most serious thing. It was bearing false witness. I was told unofficially that he tried to fabricate evidence that would have incriminated another youth and one of his teachers. It almost succeeded, except that he boasted of his success to another seminarian with whom he was in an improper relationship.'

'How well did you know him?'

'Hardly at all, he wasn't in my class and I was just a visiting teacher and not resident, but I remember his expulsion. And I certainly knew of him, such a good-looking boy, but what a contrast with the person within.'

'Was that when you were teaching exorcism?'

'Oh no, I was teaching the history of heresies and how to recognize them. Arians to Cathars and everything in between. The students used to joke that I taught heresy from A to C.'

'Do you know anything else about him? Where he came from, where he went?' When the priest shook his head Bruno urged him to find out.

'I haven't done that list of baptisms for you yet,' he said.

'I know, I need that too. What if I bring croissants for breakfast in the morning after I've done my first patrol at the market, say about eight?' The priest sighed but agreed.

Bruno had parked by the *Mairie*. He was walking back along the Rue de Paris from the priest's house when Montsouris slapped him on the back and said he was on his way to meet Bruno's friend from *Paris-Match*. He brushed aside any excuse and insisted Bruno join them for a quick one.

'I've bought every issue of that rag for thirty years and now they want to talk to me about the Red Countess,' Montsouris said as they turned up the Rue Gambetta to Ivan's Café de la Renaissance. 'Think I can maybe get a free subscription out of it?'

Gilles and Antoine were at one of Ivan's metal tables in front of the café, a small digital recorder and glasses of Ricard and an almost empty water jug before them. The ashtray was half-filled with Antoine's yellow Gitanes. Montsouris joined them in a Ricard and Bruno ordered a beer.

'Antoine was telling me about meeting her when he was a boy and his uncle worked at the château as a gardener,' Gilles said. 'How about you?' he asked Montsouris. 'How did you know her?'

'I never met her to talk to but I saw her at one of the great moments of history,' Montsouris said proudly. 'But what's this about? Why the sudden interest in the Red Countess?'

Bruno had forgotten how a lifetime in the Party had left Montsouris suspicious of the capitalist press, even of the *Paris-Match* that he read from cover to cover each week.

'We're preparing an obituary,' Gilles said smoothly. 'You understand that we have to write them in advance, and apparently she's very ill, bedridden up at the Red Château.'

'*Putain*,' said Montsouris, wiping his face with a beefy hand. 'I still think of her as young, but you're right. She'll be in her eighties by now. It'll be a sad day when she goes.'

'So how do you remember her?' Gilles asked.

'It was May 1968, and I was fifteen, looking forward to leaving school and joining my dad on the railways.' Montsouris took a long sip of his Ricard. His father was a militant, he explained, a lifelong member of the Communist Party and on the executive committee of the CGT union. When he went up to help organize the general strike he took his son with him, believing that it was the hour of the revolution come at last.

'My dad and I were together with the students on the Left Bank on the Friday night, helping to build barricades on the Rue St Jacques, when they sent the CRS bastards in with tear gas,' he said. The *Compagnies Républicaines de Sécurité* were the feared and ruthless riot police. He and his father had found a small bulldozer on a building site and used it to shovel heaps of sand and bricks to stiffen the barricades. The general strike was on the Monday and it was later that week when the two of them went to the big Renault plant at Boulogne-Billancourt in the Paris suburbs with its forty thousand workers.

'That was when I saw her. My dad was going to be speaking so I was right up there by the stage and this elegant woman, dressed up to the nines and with her daughter beside her, gave the best speech I ever heard,' he recounted. 'I'll never forget it. Forty thousand people and you could have heard a pin drop.

'She was our heroine,' he said. She had spoken of her time in the Resistance and how it had been the workers and the Party who led it and how they'd been betrayed after 1945. She introduced her daughter, who was a student at the Sorbonne, and said the workers ought to be ashamed to leave the students to face the French riot police alone.

'This was our moment, she said, our 1789, our chance to overthrow a corrupt and rotten system, our chance to storm the Bastille . . .'

Heads were turning in the café and Ivan poked his head around the kitchen door as Montsouris's voice rose and tears shone in his eyes as he recalled a scene four decades in the past.

'That was the only time you saw the Red Countess?' Gilles asked gently.

Montsouris ignored the question. 'I'd have died for her,' he said, rose and stomped away, leaving half a glass of Ricard behind him.

'I never heard that story before,' said Bruno. 'I'm glad I did.' He sank his beer, shook hands and got up to leave, checking his watch. Hector and Balzac were waiting.

'The girl in Santa Barbara,' said Gilles, waving away the coins Bruno was fishing from his pocket. 'Turns out she's in college in Montreal. We're flying a guy in from New York.'

Bruno nodded an acknowledgement as he left. If he had a murder, or even two, he had no obvious motive for either one. He had some proof and plenty of suspects but no chain of logic to bind them together into any kind of coherent explanation for the deaths of Athénaïs and Junot, let alone connect them. If Athénaïs had not committed suicide, had she been a willing participant in some Satanist ceremony that had somehow led to her death? Or had the whole scene in the boat been concocted to cover up her murder?

He stopped in his tracks just before he reached his van. If the scene had been concocted, how had they obtained the candles? He opened his notebook and thumbed back to the notes he'd taken at the supermarket when first looking for Francette when he'd been given the names of the main distributors of candles. Gallotin was the name of the theatrical costumiers and suppliers in Paris, one of the few places that stocked the big black candles that had been in the punt. Then he leafed forward to the pages of notes he had taken from the family bible in the library of the Red Château. When he'd looked at the unopened mail on the table in the great hall he'd scribbled the words '*envelope, count, Gallotin, Paris*'. He recalled the envelope. It had one of those transparent windows that usually signalled a bill.

As he climbed into his van and set off for Pamela's house his phone vibrated. He took it from the pouch to glance at the screen, saw it was Lemontin and pulled over to take the call.

'I managed to dig up something on Antin Investments,' the banker began. He explained that his new bank branch had a very full file because Antin had taken out a mortgage with the Sarlat office to buy and restore the hotel. Antin was owned by an SCI, a property company, which owned a lot of other property in the region. The mortgage application had been signed by two directors of Antin Investments, César and Héloïse de la Gorce, and the monthly payments were up to date.

'It's all a bit complex,' Lemontin said. 'The monthly payments for the Antin mortgage are coming from the parent SCI, in which Héloïse de la Gorce is a very minor shareholder and César is no shareholder at all.'

'What is the parent SCI, do you know?' Bruno asked.

'*Société Civile Immobilière Châteauroux-Vaillant*,' Lemontin replied. 'That's the Red Countess. Châteauroux is the château and Vaillant was the name of her mother.'

'How are the monthly payments made, by cheque?'

'No, by bank transfer on a standing order.'

'Who authorized that and when did the payments start?'

'I'll find out.'

As he drove on Bruno wondered how a woman with Alzheimer's could have authorized such a mortgage, and if she had not, what legal standing her sister and great-nephew would have to do so.

Fabiola opened the door to her house as he pulled into the courtyard. She told him she was just putting on her riding boots and asked him to wait. He didn't really want company as the various questions nagged at him, but he saddled Hector, settled Balzac into the binocular case and waited until Fabiola came into the stables. She left him to lead Bess and set off briskly toward the shallow part of the river and the bridle track that led to Ste Alvère.

They hadn't come this way for some time and he enjoyed it, the long canter over Pamela's fields to the ford, then trotting down the path until the long straight stretch where the horses began to gallop of their own accord. At the fork in the trail, Fabiola stopped.

'Back along the ridge or down the valley and along the stream to the bridge at St Denis?' she asked.

'The ridge.' Bruno wanted the sense of liberty he found amid the big skies and wide views.

'Did you see the Countess yourself?' she asked as the horses began to walk up the slope to the ridge.

'Yes, in her hospital bed in the château, wired up to various machines. She's apparently been out of it for years.'

'Who's her doctor, do you know?'

'No idea. She has a full-time nurse. Why do you ask?'

'I had lunch with the pathologist at the hospital after we finished the autopsy and one of his colleagues joined us, the main specialist in Alzheimer's. He hadn't heard of the Countess's case but he'd certainly heard of her. The thing was, he said he knew all the other Alzheimer's specialists in the area and he was surprised he'd never heard about her. He wanted to know who'd made the diagnosis, so I said I'd ask you.'

'I can probably find out,' Bruno said. 'It may have been someone in Paris and her sister brought her down here for the quiet.'

'How long has she been here?'

'I don't know that either. Nobody seemed to know she was here, not the Mayor or even people in the Party like Montsouris. They kept it very discreet.'

'She must have a doctor locally,' she said as they topped the rise and the plateau spread out beyond with the view down the valley to the old abbey at Paunat. 'I'll ask Gelletreau, he knows all the other *toubibs* from Bordeaux to Toulouse.'

'*Merde*,' she said as her phone jangled. 'I'm on standby tonight.' She listened and turned her horse, mouthing 'Sorry' as she held the phone to her ear. 'I'll be there in thirty minutes,' she said and set off back down the slope.

A familiar white mare was grazing in Bruno's front garden when he pulled into his driveway. Eugénie, dressed in her black riding trousers and sweat shirt, rose from his chair beside the barbecue and greeted him with the words 'Mama kangaroo.' Balzac was still nestled in the binocular case under Bruno's chin.

'Say hello to the baby kangaroo,' he replied, releasing Balzac, who trotted up to greet the visitor. Eugénie's response to the dog was perfunctory.

'I didn't see you riding this evening so I thought I'd come back this way to say hello,' she said. She was tapping her riding crop against her leg, a gesture Bruno had not seen before. In a woman less impassive, he'd have assumed it meant she was nervous.

'I was riding with Fabiola, the doctor you met, and we took the other direction.'

'Avoiding me?' She gave a slow smile.

'No, we had to cut the ride short because she was called out to a patient.'

'Surprised to see me?'

'A little. What can I do for you?' His talk with Father Sentout had made him wary. Could she have come here with some thought of entrapment, ripping her own blouse and calling rape as Foucher leapt out from behind some bush with a camera? Hardly, he told himself. That sweatshirt was not the dress for such a ploy.

'I came because I was curious to see how you lived.' She looked past him at the small cottage that he'd restored from ruin with the help of friends and neighbours.

'Ducks and chickens, a vegetable garden, jars of preserves lined up neatly on the shelves in your barn, it's the real country life.' She suddenly twirled around and gestured with an elegant arm at the view over the long field and the woods that rose to the ridge. 'And a wonderful view,' she said, turning to face him again.

'I'm happy here,' he said quietly, wondering what really had brought her here.

Eugénie went on as if he hadn't spoken. 'I also came because I want to know why you dislike us so much and why you're so opposed to our project.'

'I'm not in the least opposed to it, if it gets built as planned,' he replied, thinking this was not the time to reveal what he knew of the unpaid bills and the faked plans for the sports hall.

'But this latest demand from your Mayor, that the Count signs over his hotel as collateral, that's your plan. Just like all these questions about Thivion, that's also your work.'

'What questions?

'You're trying to tell me you didn't set that reporter from

Sud-Ouest onto us with all those photos of that mean little place we had to build?'

Good for Delaron, Bruno thought. Wait till they also heard from *Paris-Match*.

'I suppose I should be flattered at your faith in my powers, but I don't control the press. You're being ridiculous. Do you want a drink?' He really wanted to take a quick look inside, to see if she'd been in the house.

'So you're saying that my suspicions of you are ridiculous but that yours of me and our project are reasonable,' she said, as if making a joke of it. 'Could you make me a kir, please?'

'Of course. There's something you can help me with. I'd like to talk to the Countess's doctor, ask him whether at some point she might be lucid enough to answer questions about her granddaughter.'

'It's a specialist in Paris, at the Memory Research Centre at the Laboisière hospital. The Count brings him down in the helicopter. But I can tell you that the chances of lucidity are zero.'

'I'm sure you're right, but we'll need a doctor's opinion for my report.' He went inside to prepare the drinks. At a quick glance nothing seemed to have been disturbed. He splashed *crème de cassis* into two glasses, filled them with white wine and was turning to take them when he heard her soft footstep in the hall. She must have taken off her riding boots before she came in.

'Do you mind if I come in? It's getting cool outside.' Without waiting for his answer she went into the living room as if she knew the way, leaving a hint of an unfamiliar perfume in her wake. She sat back on his sofa and flashed him a brilliant smile. It was, he realized, the same smile she had worn in the photo with the Count in *Gala* magazine.

'I do like a real fire,' she said, sipping from her drink and looking at his empty grate. He nodded amiably but said nothing, wondering how she intended this meeting to develop. He found it hard to believe she would try anything so crude as an attempt to seduce him.

'Tell me about Antin Investments. Are you a shareholder?' he asked.

'Haven't we talked enough about business?' she said. 'Why can't we just relax?'

'You face a long ride back and the light's going.'

'It sounds like you're trying to get rid of me.' A pout of reproach was swiftly replaced by that same glossy-magazine smile. 'Have you eaten? I hear you're quite a cook.'

'I'm not hungry, after that lunch.'

It wasn't true. But he was not going to be put into a position where he'd have little option but to invite her to stay for dinner. He looked at her, his face neutral. She raised her arms to her neck, slipped off the band that shaped her pony tail and shook her head to let a cascade of hair tumble over her shoulders. He was tempted to applaud.

'That's better,' she said, tucking her feet beneath her on the sofa but leaving plenty of space for him. He remained in his separate chair, his back straight and his arms folded. 'Don't you agree?'

He gave a polite smile and tried to analyse why he felt so

cold towards her. She was making herself highly agreeable, yet what he felt was a mix of curiosity and suspicion.

'Don't you ever relax?' She put her glass down on the low table, making enough noise that Bruno had to look and notice it was empty. He made no move to refill it.

'Yes, with friends,' he said. He looked across at her and saw a flash of something briefly unpleasant in her eyes, impatience perhaps. This woman had nothing for him and he was getting tired of the shadow play.

'I must get to sleep,' he said, rising. 'It's market day tomorrow so I have to be up very early. Can you find your way back?'

She left without a word, her shoulders as stiff as a member of the *Garde Républicaine* on parade. As he closed the door he heard her stumbling on the path as she tried to put her riding boots back on.

He waited until he heard the sound of her horse going down the drive and then went into his bedroom, sniffing to see if he could sense that perfume of hers. He was sure she'd been in the room. His suspicion growing, he went out to his van for a pair of evidence gloves and then began to search his barn and his home thoroughly. He started with the chicken coop and then he checked the freezer and behind the preserves on the shelves in the barn. In the bathroom he lifted the lid on the cistern, took everything from the airing cupboard and then searched the kitchen. In his bedroom he lifted the mattress, pulled the drawers from his desk and checked their undersides. He went carefully through his wardrobe and cupboards and finally checked his bookshelves before he called Sergeant Jules at home.

'I need a big favour,' he said when his best friend among the Gendarmes answered his phone. 'Could you come up to my place? I think someone may be trying to set me up. And another thing, you know that white Jaguar that's been tooling around town?'

'We've got a bet on for who's going to be first to get it for speeding,' Jules replied.

'Could you make sure the driver is breathalysed, probably a man called Lionel Foucher. The important thing is that you keep the tube when he's done, whatever the alcohol count?'

'You want the DNA of whoever's driving?' Jules asked.

'Any male,' Bruno replied. 'You remember the dead woman in the punt? It's now a suspicious homicide and she had sperm front and rear. Wouldn't it make life simpler if we found a match?'

'I'm on my way.'

28

The priest had been as good as his word. When Bruno arrived with the croissants still hot from Fauquet's oven, the list of château baptisms awaited him, written in Father Sentout's neat script. A steaming coffee pot stood beside it. He had been right about the fashion for adding all the names of godparents: some of the infants had been loaded down with a dozen names. One name appeared twice in the same year, February and March of 1945.

'Who is this McPhee and how on earth do you pronounce it?' Bruno asked. It was the one of the names of the illegitimate child of the Red Countess, and also of her sister's child, born in the same month.

The priest shrugged. 'The name sounds British, perhaps Scottish, possibly American, perhaps some distant relative or friend of the family. It was the year the war ended and France was free. It might have been thought useful to have a connection with our liberators.'

Children born in February and March of 1945 would have been conceived in the May or June of 1944, Bruno reflected, around the time of the D-Day invasion of Normandy or just before it. And the Red Countess had always refused to identify the unknown Resistance soldier who'd fathered her child.

'Excuse me, Father.' He checked the address book on his phone to dial the direct number of the curator of the Centre Jean Moulin in Bordeaux, a man he'd worked with on previous cases. Named after the man de Gaulle sent into France to try to unify the rival Resistance groups until his betrayal, torture and death, the Centre had assembled the best Resistance archives in France. Bruno knew it to be run by dedicated scholars who were usually at their desks long before the attached museum opened its doors.

'Does the name McPhee mean anything to you, around May or June of 1944, here in the Périgord region?' he asked the curator after the usual greetings. He offered to spell out the name but the curator interrupted him.

'Of course,' came the reply. 'He was one of the Jedburghs and I wrote my thesis on them. It may have been the most famous of them all, since one of his colleagues became a president of France. Have you heard of the Jedburgh teams?'

Bruno confessed he had not.

'They were teams of three, one Free French officer, one American and one British,' the curator said. The teams had gone through commando training together, all spoke good French and were parachuted into France in the weeks before D-Day to help train and organize the Resistance and coordinate arms drops. McPhee was an American Captain in the Rangers, an elite unit, and came from an old military family. He had an unusual middle name, Tecumseh, the name of some Indian chief who had fought one of the McPhee ancestors. He'd been dropped into the Périgord region early in 1944 and was reported killed in June, although his body was never found. Major Manners, the British officer on the team, had filed a report that McPhee was seen to be killed in the fighting at Terrasson and his body was probably consumed when the town burned.

'He was well remembered by the young *résistants* he trained,' the curator added. 'They called him their own Red Indian because he shaved his head in an odd way, leaving a strip of hair down the middle of his scalp.'

'Could he have been in touch with the Red Countess?' Bruno asked.

'Very much so,' came the reply. 'She was a courier with the FTP group he worked with and we have a lot of oral interviews on tape, including hers, which recount how McPhee's group got food and sometimes shelter at the Red Château.'

Bruno knew that the FTP, the *Francs-Tireurs et Partisans*, were the Communist wing of the Resistance.

'Do you recall her mentioning McPhee in particular in her interview?'

'Oh, yes, she described him as the bravest man she ever knew, and added he had very progressive views for an American. I think she may have had a bit of a crush on him. She was very young at the time, seventeen or eighteen, I think. What's this about, Bruno?'

'I'm wondering if McPhee could have been the unknown soldier who fathered her child.'

There was a silence on the other end of the line before the curator gave a nervous laugh. 'We'd always rather assumed it was a Frenchman, but I suppose it's possible. Let me know if you get anywhere with this.'

'One more thing,' Bruno said. 'The Countess had a younger sister. Do you have anything about her?'

'She was a half-sister, born after the Countess's father was widowed and then remarried. The Countess was very insistent that they were only half-sisters and that she deliberately tried to keep her away from Resistance activities, saying she was too young. I don't think there was any love lost between the two.'

Bruno closed his phone to see Father Sentout dipping the last of his croissant into his coffee and smiling broadly. 'An American cuckoo in the nest of one of the oldest families in France.' He chuckled. 'War makes for strange bedfellows.'

'So the sister's son Louis was also illegitimate, conceived at the same time, and also given the name of McPhee,' Bruno mused, studying the list of baptisms.

'That was something that never came up in any of the anodyne confessions I was occasionally permitted to hear,' said the priest. But the child was not illegitimate, Father Sentout insisted, since he was later legitimized by her husband, de la Gorce.

'I can imagine the family rows that must have happened when the old Count came home after being released from prisoner-of-war camp to find both his daughters with babies and no husband in sight,' the priest said.

'And now there are grandchildren,' said Bruno, 'including the man we now call the Count. Is that an honorary title?'

'They all are these days, officially. But there are enough

titles knocking around that family to equip them all. They are descended from Louis XIV, after all, even though it was through a mistress.'

The women, Bruno noted, seemed to have stayed true to the genes of their ancestress, the royal mistress. The Red Countess had never bothered to marry and nor had her daughter, the one who had spoken alongside her at the Renault plant in 1968 when the young Montsouris had thought the revolution was at hand. She had been newly pregnant at the time, since Father Sentout's list gave the date of baptism for Athénaïs as January 1969. Had it not been for a change in French law in 1972 that allowed illegitimate children to inherit, neither Athénaïs nor her mother could have assumed the Red Countess's title and property, and Count Vexin would have been the sole legitimate heir. That triggered another thought.

'If we assume that this McPhee impregnated both sisters, who themselves shared a father, what would be the relationship between the two grandchildren, Athénaïs and the Count?'

'Through their mothers, they shared a paternal grandfather, which made them half-cousins, But if McPhee was their common grandfather they would also have been full cousins.' The priest frowned. 'It's an unusual case and rather complicated but I think the family relationship might have been too close for the church to sanction a marriage between them. I'd have to look it up.'

Bruno pondered this. And suddenly an image crossed his mind of the two infant grandchildren, Athénaïs born illegitimate in 1969 and her double cousin, the Count, born the following year as the heir to everything. And then in 1972 the law changed, allowing illegitimate children to inherit, and the Count's claim on the family wealth and titles was suddenly overtaken by Athénaïs. The infant Count would have been too young to care, but his mother Héloïse would have been stunned by the reversal. And from what he had seen of her, Héloïse would have nursed the grudge. Might she have brought up her son to resent his brusque disinheritance? Could that have been a motive for murder?

'How wealthy would the Red Countess be, Father? Would you know?'

'In money, probably not well-off at all. In land and property, extremely rich, but much of the income is doubtless devoured by the cost of maintaining the old buildings. Why, do you think there is an issue of inheritance here? You said the dead woman in the boat was her granddaughter. Who inherits next?'

'She has a daughter of her own in America. Presumably she's the heir, that's why I can't see it as a motive.'

'Make sure she's kept safe. Do you remember your Balzac? I find I read him more and more.'

'Not for years, but I remember what he wrote about every great fortune being founded on a great crime.'

'No, not that, I was thinking of something he wrote in *Le Cousin Pons*, that "to kill a relative of whom you are tired is something. But to inherit his property afterwards, that is genuine pleasure." When I think of the confessions I hear of hatred and malice towards relatives over inheritance, I come close to despair.'

Bruno took his leave and was threading his way through scattered children's toys in the priest's garden when his phone vibrated. It was Fabiola, announcing that she had spent the last forty minutes talking to various doctors at the Memory Research Centre in Paris. They had no record of the Countess being registered as a patient and they had scoffed at the claim that one of them was taken down to the Périgord by helicopter. Nor was she registered on the Alzheimer's support network. Moreover, her colleague Dr Gelletreau could find no other doctor in the region who was treating her.

'What's the law on this?' she asked. 'This is an obviously ill woman with no doctor and those looking after her are lying about her care. We're the medical centre for the region, do we have a legal right to intervene?'

'I have no idea,' he replied. 'It's out of my usual field, but she does have a full-time nurse. Can you call Annette? She's a magistrate and if she doesn't know the relevant laws she can find out. I'll try the *Procureur* but it's an obscure part of the law. And with someone as prominent as the Red Countess, it may get complicated.'

He was trying to phone the duty clerk when he was called to resolve a dispute between two stallholders over the amount of pavement space one was taking, and then another claimed access to her stall was being blocked by the crowd watching the next stallholder demonstrate a new device for chopping vegetables. Usually he enjoyed this routine, joking and jollying the stallholders into seeing reason. But this morning he was brisk and even curt, startling some of them into grumbles and wry jokes about Satan's influence on the market of St Denis.

Feeling harassed and slightly ashamed of himself, and worried that events were accelerating out of control, he ran up the *Mairie* steps to his office and made his call. As he expected, the clerk in the *Procureur*'s office said he'd have to call him back and couldn't it wait? He groaned as he opened his computer to find dozens of accumulated emails waiting. Quickly, he scanned them to see what could not get the clerk's treatment of waiting until Monday. But one address made him pause. It was from someone calling themselves *Prévertlady* on a Hotmail account. It had to be Isabelle. Jacques Prévert was the author of the book of poems she had sent him. The message was a simple mobile phone number, not one she'd ever used before, with the words 'Borrow someone's phone'.

He went down to the market and asked Stéphane, busy serving at his cheese stall, and was handed his phone without question, although his friend gave a pointed look to the phone at Bruno's belt. He called the number and recognized Isabelle's voice saying simply '*Allo*'.

'This is Stéphane's phone,' he said, walking down the steps from the bridge to the privacy of the river bank.

'Mine is a prepaid from FNAC, bought yesterday. You should get one, just in case. Listen, Bruno, this is getting very tricky. The Defence Ministry is trying to find out who's behind these inquiries into the Count, saying there's a big contract with the Lebanese military at risk. We know it's true because we got a routine request to provide security for their defence minister, who's apparently coming in to sign it. The Count's companies have been doing fifty million a year and more in foreign sales and nobody wants to upset that.'

'Have they been on to you?'

'Not yet, but they have been on to the Brigadier and he asked me to find out what you think you're playing at – his words. And he wasn't talking about that charade your priest staged in the cave.'

Bruno explained that this was no longer a possible fraud case, but that the *Procureur* had opened dossiers on two probable murders. Briefly, he described Junot's crash and the injection marks.

'It's out of my hands now,' he said. 'J-J's forensic guys are probably going to require a search of that hotel where we got turned away, so I hope there's no plans for the minister to hold a signing celebration.'

'You should have told me this before.' Her voice was tightening. 'We need to know this.'

'It only began to come together last night.'

'Is there anything that points to the two guys with the Count in those glossy photos I printed out?'

'Not yet,' he said.

'The Ballotin girl in the glossy photos, the one calling herself a nurse, it turns out she isn't. No record of a diploma. And here's some more news. The second time Béatrice was arrested, so was the Ballotin girl. Same time, same place, same profession.'

'I'm not surprised,' he replied. 'But what I can't work out is the motive for all this. It can't be inheritance – Athénaïs has a daughter who'll be the heir.'

'Only if she lives to inherit. Where is she now?' As she spoke, his own phone on his belt began to vibrate.

'At college in Canada, *Paris-Match* tracked her down.' Could Isabelle be serious, that a teenage girl was now at risk?

'The Count's short of money. If this Lebanese deal doesn't come off, he's in real trouble: bankruptcy, lawsuits, he may even be looking at a prison term. The only thing that could save him then would be to borrow more money using the family estate as collateral. We've been on this phone long enough. Get yourself a throwaway and send the number to the email I used to contact you.'

His own phone had stopped ringing but the call had come from J-J. He'd expected this. Yves must have finished the forensic study and J-J would be preparing a search. He called him back.

'Bruno Courrèges?' J-J said, his voice curiously formal, as though someone official were listening in. 'You are required to meet me at the Gendarmerie in thirty minutes. And consider yourself under suspension pending investigation. Your Mayor has been informed.'

He rang off and Bruno was left staring at his phone, momentarily stunned. He checked his watch. Thirty minutes. He could do a lot in thirty minutes. He called Sergeant Jules but an automated voice asked him to leave a message. He considered calling the Mayor, but there was no point. If the Mayor was told his municipal policeman was under investigation he'd have no choice but to agree to the suspension. Bruno climbed the steps back up to the town square, handed the phone back to Stéphane and headed into his office at the *Mairie*.

He pulled out the file with the printouts Isabelle had made, checked the internet address and called up the photo of the Count with the son of the Lebanese minister. He emailed that to his counterpart in Sarlat, a good friend, and followed it with a phone call, asking him to show the photo to the widow who sold goat's cheese in the old church of Ste-Marie to see if she recognized either man. Then he called Fabiola, to tell her that the nurse at the Red Château had no known qualifications. In turn, she told him that she had found Annette at home and she was researching the law. Apparently it depended whether the Red Countess was in *tutelle*, which would mean a court had ruled that she was not fit to conduct her own affairs, and her sister or her nephew might have been named her *tuteur* with legal powers to act for her.

It was time to go. He settled his cap squarely on his head, checked his appearance in the mirror in the men's room and walked briskly down the Rue de Paris towards the Gendarmerie, shaking hands and kissing cheeks as he always did. The thought crossed his mind that this might be the last occasion he would do so. He refused to speculate on the reasons for the investigation, but his inability to contact Sergeant Jules was worrying. Perhaps he should have called the Mayor after all, and he certainly should have called Isabelle.

The Mayor was standing on the steps of the Gendarmerie, a solemn look on his face as Bruno approached. A stately old Bentley limousine from the Fifties was standing in the car park.

'The *Procureur de la République* has come down from Périgueux himself and an accusation of theft has been filed against you,' the Mayor said. 'Sergeant Jules said that was all he knew.'

'Jules is here?' The Mayor nodded. Bruno felt reassured and followed the Mayor inside, where Sergeant Jules greeted him with a wink and a sideways glance at a plastic evidence bag with a book inside. Bruno marched into the familiar office, halted in formal military style, stood to attention and saluted the *Procureur*. After seeing the Bentley outside he was not surprised to see the sister of the Red Countess and Foucher standing by the window. J-J stood to one side of the desk.

'At ease, Courrèges,' said the *Procureur*. Bruno was startled to see him wearing red corduroy slacks, a blue denim shirt and a bright yellow sweater, as if he'd been hauled from a golf course. This was a normal workday.

'One moment, please,' said the Mayor. 'I understand that Chief of Police Courrèges is entitled to legal representation and I would like to say that while ready to provide him what assistance I can, I must protest against the haste in calling this inquiry without summoning a qualified lawyer. I should add that my officer has my complete confidence.'

'Protest noted,' the *Procureur* said and fixed Bruno with a cold stare. 'Madame de la Gorce has filed a formal statement accusing you of stealing from her family library a valuable book, a first edition of Montaigne's essays. She says that you obtained entry to the library with a spurious claim of being on duty and while you were left alone there the book disappeared. She claims that this edition of the book is worth over five thousand euros, but this particular example is priceless, having once belonged to the former royal family. What do you have to say?'

'Not guilty, sir.'

'Were you in the library alone?'

'Yes, sir.'

'Did you see the book in question?'

'Later, sir, I did, but not in the library.'

'I don't understand.'

'Permission to call Sergeant Jules of the Gendarmerie, sir?'

'I hope someone can explain.'

Sergeant Jules entered and saluted, the evidence bag and a slim folder under his arm. He laid the bag on the desk.

'Sir, Chief of Police Courrèges entrusted this book to me yesterday evening at his home. He'd called me to say that he believed this accusation of theft would be launched against him. I have had the book fingerprinted, sir, and his fingerprints are not to be found. However, the fingerprints of a young woman in the employ of the château were found, identified from her previous arrest record. That supports the Chief of Police's statement that the woman in question called at his home and deliberately left the copy of the book in an attempt to incriminate him. Here is the Chief of Police's statement, taken by me last night, and my own statement, sir.'

Jules laid the slim folder on the desk and with a sharp glance at the old lady who was now leaning heavily on Foucher's arm, the *Procureur* began reading the statements.

'What's this about a previous arrest?' Madame de la Gorce interjected. 'They must be in it together.'

'Were you aware that this young woman in your employ, Eugénie Ballotin, had taken this book, Madame?' the *Procureur* asked.

'Absolutely not.'

'Then who is responsible for what seems to be an attempt to incriminate the Chief of Police?'

The old woman looked up in appeal to Foucher, who said smoothly, 'There has evidently been a complete misunderstanding and Madame de la Gorce wishes to withdraw her statement and apologize to the Chief of Police and to you, *Monsieur le Procureur*, and is grateful for the book's safe return.'

'Not good enough,' said the *Procureur*. 'Where is this Mademoiselle Ballotin? I want her brought here now. And for what was she arrested in the past?'

Sergeant Jules coughed discreetly, leaned forward and murmured into his ear.

'*Mon Dieu*,' said the *Procureur*. 'I thought she was supposed to be a nurse.'

'Apparently not,' Bruno interrupted. 'There is no record of her having any nursing qualification, which is a matter of great concern to Dr Stern of our medical centre, who fears that the Red Countess is not receiving any proper medical attention. Dr Stern also tells me that after inquiries in the Paris hospitals Mademoiselle Ballotin's claim that a Parisian doctor was treating the Red Countess for Alzheimer's disease turns out to be untrue. Furthermore, no local doctor can be found who has seen her. Dr Stern wishes to be allowed to see the patient and I filed an inquiry into the relevant legal requirements with your duty clerk this morning, sir.'

The *Procureur* looked startled, and then grave as he thought about the implications of someone as well known as the Red Countess being denied medical care.

'Madame de la Gorce, is your sister in *tutelle*?'

Again, Foucher answered for her. 'No, she is not. We believed from the qualifications Mademoiselle Ballotin presented that we had competent medical attention.'

'Then you will have no objection to my insistence that Dr Stern be allowed to examine the patient and make a recommendation to me.'

'Madame de la Gorce would like to consult her own legal and medical advisers, but of course that medical report would be available to you,' Foucher said.

'Are you a lawyer?' the *Procureur* demanded. Foucher shook his head. 'Then please don't answer for your employer. In fact, I think you'd be most usefully employed getting a chair for Madame de la Gorce.'

She looked frail as she took her seat, but her eyes were bright and they glared at Bruno with malice before she composed herself to turn a polite face to the *Procureur*. Standing behind her, half-screened by the back of the chair, Foucher was looking down and appeared to be doing something with his hands.

'Excuse me, sir,' said Bruno, stepping forward and closing his hand over the mobile phone on which Foucher was tapping out a text message. 'Did you authorize this Monsieur to use his phone?' he asked the *Procureur*.

'Certainly not,' came the reply. 'Take it off him.' The *Procureur* turned to Madame de la Gorce, his voice cold. 'You may bring in whatever other medical expert you choose, but I want Dr Stern to visit the Countess and I want a medical report on my desk by Thursday morning so I can take a decision before the Easter weekend. If there is a diagnosis of Alzheimer's I

308

will apply for your sister to be placed in *tutelle*, with a professional *tuteur*, since I'm not satisfied with the arrangements made by her family. Do you understand?'

'Yes, and my own lawyers will contest that,' she replied, with a glance at Foucher behind her.

'That is your right. However, I give you notice that I shall investigate further this ridiculous allegation against the Chief of Police, who would appear to me to have a substantial case against you, Madame, for defamation. Since you insisted on filing this allegation with my office as a formal and sworn statement, you do not have the right to withdraw it as you please. You may wish to consult your legal adviser on that, and now please wait outside. Sergeant, please see that they don't leave and confiscate their mobile phones. And have this Mademoiselle Ballotin brought here forthwith. I want to see her sworn statement about these events and she is not to consult with her employer in the meantime. Is that clear? Very well, I thank you Sergeant, and well done.'

When just J-J, the Mayor and Bruno were left with him in the room the *Procureur* said to J-J, 'I should have listened to you.' Then he turned to Bruno and said, 'My apologies, J-J told me he suspected a set-up. I should never have listened to the old woman, but she's a social acquaintance of my wife and came to my home first thing this morning with her statement already written out and signed. She insisted I witness it.' He looked down at his colourful clothes. 'It's supposed to be my day off.'

'No harm done, sir,' said Bruno.

'Harm has been done. In tracking down J-J and your Mayor

here, half my office knows that you were being suspended on charges of theft. Word like that spreads fast, which is why you should bring an action against that silly old woman for defamation. I'll be glad to testify on your behalf. It will never go to court, of course, but you should get something in settlement.'

J-J cleared his throat. 'If you're right about these rumours spreading from your office about the Chief of Police, you may want to consider putting out a statement that clears his good name.'

'Good idea. I'll issue a press statement. Now let's all take a seat and Bruno, if I may call you that, tell me what this is really all about and start at the beginning. Why are they trying to shut you up and blacken your name?'

Bruno's phone vibrated. He saw it was his counterpart from the police in Sarlat.

'Excuse me, sir. This call may be relevant.'

He answered, to be told that the widow who sold the goat's cheese had recognized the photo of the Arab who had bought her goat. Bruno thanked his colleague and closed his phone.

'That's a new complication,' he said. 'It looks as if the son of the Lebanese defence minister is involved in this, just as his father is about to come here to sign some multi-million-euro contract with one of the Count's companies.'

29

As soon as the *Procureur* had been briefed, Bruno excused himself, borrowed Sergeant Jules's private phone and went out to the square to tell Isabelle of the Lebanese connection. He had no idea exactly how this would complicate the investigation, but he knew it would. The Bentley was still there, presumably the car that had brought the Countess's sister, which meant Foucher would not be driving his Jaguar and so could not be breathalysed. Bruno wanted Foucher's DNA, even though he knew the lab would take at least a week to produce results. When he returned Jules's phone, he suggested taking Foucher and Madame de la Gorce a glass of water. That should yield an adequate sample.

The market was still in full swing. He stopped at Jolliot's electronics shop and bought a pre-paid phone for fifteen euros as a way to stay in touch with Isabelle. As he passed the church, he felt a hesitant touch on his arm. He turned to see Brigitte Junot, dressed in traditional widow's black. The circles under her eyes were almost as dark. Three days since Junot's death and it looked as if she hadn't slept since. Without a word, she led him into the darkness of the church and to a pew in a side chapel where Francette sat with her head bowed as if in prayer, her features covered by a large black head-scarf. She was dressed as a farm girl, wearing jeans, a shape-less sweater and muddy rubber boots.

'Francette needs your help,' said Brigitte. 'She's scared stiff. Can you take her somewhere safe?'

'You'll have to tell me everything, Francette, if I'm going to be able to help,' he said, taking off his cap and sliding in alongside her.

'It's not a story for church,' she said. Bruno glanced at her mother and raised his eyebrows. She nodded and murmured that Francette had told her everything. Meanwhile Bruno was thinking that his own place was known and so was Pamela's, where he kept his horse. Too many people knew of his friend-ship with Stéphane and his farm was too near to the Junot place. He called Maurice Soulier, an elderly duck farmer who owed Bruno a favour. It was answered by his wife, Sabine, a motherly soul. Their children had long left home and she agreed at once.

'Go down behind the altar to the vestry and wait there. I'll come and fetch you.'

He went back to the Gendarmerie and borrowed the keys to Jules's private car, a well-maintained Renault Laguna. He drove to Father Sentout's house, where he borrowed the key to the vestry from his housekeeper. He loaded the two women into the car and followed the back road past the cemetery, taking country lanes to the Soulier farm. Sabine was waiting for them with a pot of coffee and a plate of her home-made madeleines. Her husband came in from the barn to greet them. When Bruno asked for a place where he and the two guests could speak in private, Maurice showed them to the shaded terrace and left them alone. Humming happily to herself, evidently pleased at the thought of guests, Sabine went upstairs to make up the spare bed and lay out towels.

'I've been a fool,' Francette said dully. 'It's my fault that Dad's dead and now I think Mum's in danger as well as me.'

'Start at the beginning,' Bruno said. 'What made you leave your job at the supermarket?'

'I met this guy, a bit older than me but good-looking, you know?' She described how he'd come to her checkout, chatted a little, and he asked her out. He picked her up after work in his sports car, took her to a dinner in Bergerac and then to a nightclub for dancing before driving her home.

'He was really sweet, just kissed me on the cheek and asked to see me again. Next time he brought me flowers and he took me to a smart restaurant, white tablecloths and everything. He knew all about wines. Then we went to that big disco in Périgueux that the other girls used to talk about, but I'd never been there.'

Bruno nodded sympathetically, suspecting that he knew already how this would turn out. A girl from a poor home who had never been taken out before was suddenly being treated like a princess. The next date had been a day trip to Bordeaux, where he'd taken her to an expensive hairdresser, bought her new clothes and lingerie that he chose for her, and then to a boutique hotel for the afternoon.

'Léo was so kind, so sweet,' she said. Bruno could imagine the contrast between the skilled seduction in the hotel room

313

and the clumsy, insistent fumblings of the boys of her own age from St Denis.

'Was that his real name?' he asked. No, she replied, it was her pet name for him. His real name was Lionel.

Then he had taken her to Paris for the weekend, a hotel on the Quai Voltaire with a room overlooking the river. They had smoked a joint of the strongest dope she'd ever had and then made love until it was time to go to the famous Queen disco on the Champs Elysées.

'There was this long line of people trying to get in, but one look at Léo and they opened the red velvet rope and we went straight in,' she said, her voice wistful, still conveying her pride in that moment. And even in her low mood, Francette had the physical assurance and poise of a woman now aware of her own allure and sexual power. At the disco, she said, she had tried cocaine for the first time.

They slept until late and then more shopping, until Léo took her to an exclusive party where there was more cocaine and endless champagne. Suddenly people were taking off their clothes and Léo was making love with another woman and a man and it seemed the natural thing to join in. She looked up at Bruno defiantly and said that she'd enjoyed it. Then there had been the week at a villa in St Tropez, more cocaine and more sex parties; in hotel suites and even on a yacht. When Léo offered her a job at the hotel, she'd taken it at once.

Bruno felt a cold anger start to build, deep inside him, at hearing of Foucher's cynical seduction of an inexperienced young woman, and one whom Bruno still recalled as a little girl.

314

'I had no illusions about the job.' There was a challenge in her voice, but she wouldn't look at him while she spoke. Her mother sat in silence, listening with her eyes closed, one hand resting on Francette's forearm. 'My eyes were wide open and I'd have taken the job even without the thousand euros in cash he gave me. He called it a signing bonus.'

It was one thing having sex with others when she was high and Léo was taking part, but not nearly as much fun when strangers who spoke no French took her off to their rooms at the hotel. It was even worse when one of them was only able to perform when he hit her. Then there were the dressing-up games: doctors and nurses, cops and prisoners, priests and nuns. Sometimes the clients wanted exhibitions, girls with girls, or nuns with nuns, and pulled out their phones to take videos. There were discipline games, when the girls could be spanked. With all the cocaine available, it didn't seem to matter.

One night, Léo and Béatrice had taken her and some other girls into the Gouffre, dressed them as nuns and filmed them in Our Lady's Chapel. That was the first time since the initial orgy in Paris that she'd met the man they called the Count.

'Did you ever see this woman?' Bruno asked, taking from his breast pocket the photo of Athénaïs.

Francette nodded. 'Tina was with us in the cave.'

'You called her Tina?' Bruno asked, thinking it was probably as close a nickname as she could get to Athénaïs.

'I liked her, she was nice to me after I was hit the first time. Tina really got off on the scene in the cave when Léo dressed up as a priest. But it was the Count that she wanted.

315

Apparently they'd met in New York and they'd had an affair. She told me she was in love with him and he was going to pay for this film project she had about some ancestor who was the mistress of Louis Quatorze. She talked about it all the time, like it was an obsession with her. I remember once she told me she thought was the reincarnation of this Madame de Montespan. She even promised me a part in the movie. But she was going to be the star.'

'Did she ever talk about love potions?' Bruno felt a mounting excitement at the realization that Francette's testimony was breaking open the whole case, along with anger at the way she'd been treated. She was just eighteen. She should be playing doubles at the tennis club, holding hands and locking eyes in a cheap students' restaurant, not dressing up to thrill ageing customers in the defence industry.

'You know about the Black Mass?' she asked, her eyes widening.

He nodded. 'Was Tina trying to make sure the Count fell in love with her?'

'It sounds crazy now, but it all made sense then. She told me it was certain to work, that it worked with Louis XIV.'

'Were you there when she did this?'

'No, Léo organized it. Tina wanted to do the Black Mass in a real church and there was some family chapel over the river he said they could use. He and Richard took her; he's the Lebanese guy but he claimed to have been raised as a Christian.'

'Did you ever see Tina again after that?'

Francette shook her head. 'They said it hadn't worked and

she'd gone back to Paris. It wasn't till I came home that Mum told me about the woman in the boat and I knew it had to be Tina. I was getting scared already but that really freaked me. That's when I said we had to come and see you.'

'You never saw any newspapers or listened to the TV or radio while you were there at the auberge?'

'Some of the clients had TV in their bedrooms but all they wanted to have on was porn.'

'Did you ever see your dad, or did he get in touch with you?'

Francette shook her head, and for the first time she took her mother's hand. Now the story came in fits and starts. With hindsight, she now thought he'd been to the auberge the night after Bruno had brought her father to see her. It had been a doctors and nurses party that night and some of the clients had become frisky over dinner, so the nurses were all topless. There had been some commotion at one of the windows and some shouting. Béatrice had come back and said there'd been an intruder but it was all under control. At the time Francette had thought nothing of it, but looking back that must have been her father.

'That's why I'm responsible,' she said, her voice dull. 'He must have been so worked up after you brought him to see me that he crashed.'

This was not the time to tell her it had been no crash. 'Did you know of any other disturbance on the evening of that day I brought him to the auberge to see you? I'm wondering if your dad might have come back.'

Francette shrugged. 'Not that I heard of. But there was a

big party that night, some guys down from Paris and they had their own security guards outside. We were all ordered to stay indoors.'

The security men from the defence Ministry had been at the entrance to the auberge. But on such a special occasion the Count would not have tolerated any more intrusions from Junot. What if Junot had been caught trying to break in at the rear? Could that have been sufficient motive to kill him? Or to beat him so badly they had to finish him and fake the accident? Lionel, or Léo as Francette knew him, was probably ruthless enough. Bruno had one more question.'Did you ever meet a girl called Eugénie, tall with dark hair?'

'Could she have called herself Gina? She was with the Count at the party in Paris and again with him that night in the cave. She was really beautiful.'

'Have you seen anyone from the hotel since you came back to your mother's place?'

'Léo came yesterday evening to ask when I was coming back. He brought flowers for Mum and was full of sympathy but he said I'd better get back to work soon. It was the way he said it, I got scared. After Mum told me about Tina in the boat, I knew we had to get away. And then this morning Richard came by in the car, just sat there and looked at the house. It was creepy.'

'Richard has been staying at St Philippon?' Bruno asked.

She nodded. 'There and at the Red Château over the river. He's a friend of the Count. I don't like him. He's the one who hit me when he couldn't get it up.'

'How did you get down here from the farm?'

'We walked down through the woods and along the river. There's one more thing, Bruno. You're going to have to be careful, they're really freaked about you. Léo kept asking me if you'd been to see me at home.'

'That's all right, don't worry about me,' he said, and asked her to write down a statement, exactly as she'd told it to him. He gave her the phone he'd just bought and put his own numbers onto speed-dial.

He left mother and daughter sitting silently, holding hands, and went in to explain to Sabine that Francette was being stalked by a violent ex-boyfriend. He asked for some writing paper and took it back to the terrace with his pen. As Francette began writing her statement he went to the duck barn for a word with Maurice.

'I don't think her ex-boyfriend will find her here, but if a white sports car turns up, call me straight away.'

'I've got my shotgun,' Maurice said. Bruno winced. He'd had enough trouble with Maurice's shotgun over another matter when some animal rights activists had tried to liberate his ducks and geese. No guns, he insisted and left to buy another phone from a bemused Jolliot.

As he left the shop, his usual phone buzzed at his belt. It was Lemontin, to say that the signature to authorize the mortgage payments was that of the Red Countess, dated in May of the previous year. But her sister had claimed the Countess hadn't had a lucid moment in years. Not only did this look like fraud; it meant his plan for the hotel to be used as collateral for St Denis's investment in the Count's project couldn't work. The hotel was not the Count's to pledge.

At the Gendarmerie, Sergeant Jules was visibly enjoying himself. Madame de la Gorce had sworn another statement saying Eugénie had been the one who told her that Bruno must have been the thief. In a second room, Foucher was insisting it was all a misunderstanding, while his drinking glass was now ready to be picked up by Yves from the forensic team for DNA analysis. The one problem was that Mademoiselle Ballotin was not at the Red Château and nobody seemed to know where she was.

'If her name's Eugénie, then that last message Foucher sent when you stopped him was to her,' Jules said, holding up one of the phones that lay on the desk before him. 'One word: flee. And here's the bonus,' he went on, holding up a plastic bag that contained a breathalyser unit. 'The driver of a white Jaguar, one Richard Abouard, Lebanese passport, booked for speeding on the Périgueux road, passed his breathalyser test, but here it is. Yves will pick it up with the drinking glass.'

'Excellent,' said Bruno. 'Is the *Procureur* still here? Or J-J?'

'J-J is here taking statements. The *Procureur* has gone to brief the Prefect and the Mayor went with him. That inspector you know from Bergerac is leading the search team at the hotel. The forensic team linked Junot's death to a truck there and J-J said something about the same truck being caught by a camera at the *déchetterie*.'

'Anybody called for a lawyer?'

'Once he'd given his statement Foucher was free to leave, but he's waiting for the old lady. If we can bring Eugénie in, J-J says to hold them both on charges of making false statements.'

'And the old lady's giving a new statement without a lawyer present?' Bruno asked in disbelief.

'First thing he did, J-J got her to sign the release saying she didn't need a lawyer. She said her grandson would take care of everything.'

'So it's all under control,' Bruno said, thinking of the renewed chaos that would follow the delivery of Francette's statement that linked Foucher and the Count directly to the death of Athénaïs.

Then his phone vibrated, and with some premonition that everything was about to go wrong he saw that it was Gilles.

'We missed her,' Gilles said. 'I'm sorry.'

'What happened?'

'It's my fault, I didn't brief our guys in California properly,' the reporter said. His Hollywood correspondent had tracked down the girl's father in Santa Barbara and learned that she was at McGill University in Montreal. But he told the father that Athénaïs was dead, and once the reporter left the father called his daughter to pass on the bad news. By the time the correspondent from New York got to her address in Montreal, she'd already left. Her flatmate said that she'd contacted international directory inquiries to get the number for the Red Château and called there for details about her mother's death. She was already on a plane to Paris by the time the reporter reached Montreal.

'Do you know who she talked to at the Red Château?' Bruno asked.

'The flatmate said she talked to some male relative, an uncle or cousin. Apparently he was really surprised to hear from her because he didn't know her mother had had a child, but he said she should come to France and he'd take care of the ticket. I'm really sorry, Bruno, but we can pick her up when she gets here.'

'Sorry?' Bruno said, the pent-up anger from Francette's story finally exploding. 'You may have signed the girl's death warrant. She's what stands between the Count and inheriting a fortune, and until you blundered in he didn't even know she existed.'

'How was I to know?'

'What flight was she on?' Bruno demanded.

'I don't know, but our guy got there late yesterday so it must have been the evening flight. She'll already have landed in Paris.'

'*Putain de merde*,' Bruno roared, closing the phone, and barging into the interview room where J-J sat opposite Madame de la Gorce.

'Emergency,' he said, and forced himself to remember his manners and the need for discretion. 'Excuse me, Madame, but we need the Commissaire outside.'

Once they were outside the room Bruno explained then slammed his hand against his forehead and called himself an idiot when he realized he'd never asked Gilles for the girl's name. He called Gilles back, apologizing for his temper, and wrote the details down on his notepad.

J-J was already on the line to the security office at Charles de Gaulle airport and repeated the girl's name as Bruno showed his notepad: Marie-Françoise Bourbon Merrilees. It must be her father's surname. Gilles had given Bruno the father's number, the girl's mobile phone and the fact that she had both a French and an American passport. The father might have the passport numbers. Who might speak English well enough to call him?

He tried Gilles but the line was engaged. On an impulse, he rang Pamela in Scotland, briefly explained and asked her to call the father to ask him for the numbers and any other details. And if the father spoke to his daughter, he should tell her to go direct to any police station and stay there while insisting they contacted him or J-J.

'She flew in on Air France and connected with a flight to Bordeaux that should have just landed,' J-J said. He was already calling the security office at Bordeaux's Mérignac airport.

'Check if they've had any incoming helicopters at Mérignac,' Bruno said, reading out the tail number of the Count's helicopter from his notebook. His mind raced as he tried to think of any other useful information he could provide J-J. He almost hopped up and down with frustration as J-J waited, then said who he was, gave his security code and explained what he wanted.

'They're trying to seal off the baggage claim area but it's an internal flight from Paris so there's no customs check,' J-J said as he waited for more information. 'I can hear them calling her on the public address system.'

Bruno's phone vibrated again. It must be Pamela, he thought, snatching it from his pouch, but it was Fabiola.

'I've just had my access authorization to the Red Château faxed from the *Procureur*'s office,' she said. 'You want to join me?'

But of course, Bruno suddenly realized, with the old woman and Foucher at the Gendarmerie, Eugénie disappeared and the Count seeking his long-lost cousin in Bordeaux, the château would be wide open.

'I'd love to,' he replied. 'Pick me up at the Gendarmerie whenever you want.'

J-J closed his phone. 'They missed her. Apparently she had no checked baggage and there's no helicopter flight plan into Mérignac. They'll check other airports nearby and call me back. Meanwhile I'll have to call the Chief of Police at Bordeaux and I'd better brief the *Procureur*. Who's planning to pick you up?'

'Dr Stern, Fabiola. We're going to see the Red Countess at the château. But you also need to know about what looks like financial fraud, using the Countess's signature to pay for bank loans when she's supposed to be comatose.'

'It's the girl who's the priority now. Let's get going, I can phone from the car. I'll go with Sergeant Jules and you wait for the doctor.'

'You'd better warn Inspector Jofflin, who's running the search at the auberge, just in case the chopper lands there,' Bruno said.

30

Fabiola's old car was wheezing as it tackled the long hill leading to the ridge that overlooked the Red Château. Isabelle had been briefed, which meant the Interior Ministry could now deal with the Defence Ministry. Bruno kept his eyes on the western horizon in case a helicopter came into view.

'I've worked out the identity of your private patient, or patients,' he said.

'I thought you might,' Fabiola replied. 'I'm just surprised it took you so long. And even more surprised that you thought I'd be practising medicine for money.'

'Béatrice didn't pay you for doing check-ups on the girls at the hotel?'

'No, she made a donation to the abused women's shelter in Bergerac, a very generous donation. I suppose that's going to end now.'

Bruno shrugged. He imagined that some other defence company would soon be dispensing corporate hospitality somewhere else. They might even use Béatrice, so long as she wasn't linked directly to the death of Athénaïs.

Fabiola parked beside the Gendarmerie van. The main door to the château was already open and Sergeant Jules was standing on the steps waiting for them, a nervous maid wringing her hands at his side.

'*Bonjour*, Mademoiselle, who else is here?' Bruno asked her.

'*Bonjour*, Monsieur, the groom is in the stables and the other maid is with the Countess,' she said. 'Everyone else has gone.'

'When did the Count leave?'

'Just over an hour ago. He'd been waiting for Madame's return and asked me to tell her he couldn't wait any longer.'

'Did he leave a message for her?'

'Not with me, Monsieur.'

Bruno showed Fabiola the way to the hospital room where J-J was skimming through a file on the nurse's table.

'This non-qualified nurse kept decent records, I'll give her that,' he said, looking up as they entered. 'What's a proper dose for temazepam?'

'It depends. I'd use no more than fifteen milligrams for insomnia,' said Fabiola. 'How many is she on?'

'It says she's on thirty in these notes.'

'That's a lot. I'll need to see what else she's on.' Fabiola cast an expert eye over the array of machines against the wall as she took the Countess's pulse. 'It has too many side effects for my liking and it can become addictive quite quickly. I've seen it used in suicides. Can you see if there are any prescription bottles around? They should have the prescribing doctor's name on the label.'

She pulled back the sheets and took out a stethoscope to listen to the Countess's heart and then began to palpate her limbs. Bruno heard Fabiola muttering to herself about muscular atrophy, when J-J's phone rang.

'Where? Which airport?' J-J said. 'We're near Les Eyzies. What's the flying time to here? '

When he rang off he looked at Bruno. 'It seems there's a small private airport called Souge, a few kilometres west of the main Bordeaux airport. That's where he landed and he took off again about thirty minutes ago. He could be here in ten or fifteen minutes.'

'His usual heliport is at the hotel,' Bruno said. 'But there are police all over it. If he decides to land here, do you think he'll do so with a Gendarmerie van in the courtyard?'

'See if you can move it under cover. Do you think he's likely to be armed?' J-J pulled his Manurhin revolver from a hip holster and checked the rounds. 'What about you and Sergeant Jules?'

'Jules has his standard PAMAS handgun. I'm unarmed.'

J-J raised his eyebrows and shrugged. 'The last thing we want is a hostage situation.'

'I'll move the van.' On the way out to the van Bruno asked Jules to look around for an envelope or message that the Count might have left for his grandmother or for Foucher. The keys of the van were in the ignition and he drove it out of the courtyard and round to the stables, where he found a barn half full of hay that was big enough to take it. He looked around the stables but could not see the white mare Eugénie had ridden, nor any sign of a groom. In a cupboard in the tack room he found a large syringe, too big for his standard evidence bag. He used two bags and took it to show Fabiola.

Back in the hospital room J-J was taking notes as he listened on his phone, and Fabiola was poring over the logbook on the nurse's table. He put the syringe on the desk beside her and her eyes widened. J-J beckoned him across and asked whoever was on the phone to wait.

'I've got Inspector Jofflin on the line,' J-J said, beaming satisfaction. 'The search at the hotel has got a result. They've identified microscopic drops of Junot's blood in the back of that truck you found. They've also found Junot's blood spots on some shoes in the room of Richard Abouard, so we're putting out an arrest warrant for murder. Computer enhancement on the video from the *déchetterie* shows that Abouard was one of the two men there. And as a nice bonus, they found over a hundred grams of coke in Abouard's room, along with his Lebanese diplomatic passport.'

'My bet is that Foucher was the other man at the *déchetterie*. We'll need that forensic team to come here and search Foucher's rooms once they're finished at the hotel,' said Bruno, taking out his new phone to call Isabelle.

'Jofflin is asking why this Lebanese guy would be involved.'

'He's a partner in the Count's investment company,' Bruno said as Isabelle answered her phone. Quickly he told her of the results of the search at the hotel and the arrest warrant and the expected arrival of the Count's helicopter. A thought struck him and he asked her to hold on. He turned to J-J. 'Did he refuel at the little airport?'

'I don't know, why?' asked J-J.

'It's nearly three hundred kilometres there and back. If he didn't refuel at Bordeaux he might have no choice but to put down here.'

J-J started dialling Bordeaux airport again and Bruno returned to the conversation with Isabelle. 'Did you hear all that?'

'Yes, got it. The Brigadier wants to know if the evidence on Abouard for the murder is really certain.'

'It's forensic, blood on his shoes and a video of him dumping the plastic sheet the body was wrapped in.'

'That should do. Get copies of the forensic report and the video to me as soon as you can. Good luck and let me know if there's anything we can do from Paris.'

'J-J already called up reinforcements from Périgueux, some of the lads from *la Jaune*,' Bruno said, using the nickname for the *Gendarmes Mobiles*.

'Right, wait one moment.' Bruno heard another voice speaking in the background and then she came back on the line. 'The Brigadier says he's alerted a military chopper from the base at Bordeaux to follow him and keep track. I'll let you know when they have him on radar.' She rang off.

Bruno went to the window, opened it the better to hear, and scanned the sky. J-J closed his phone. 'He didn't refuel,' he said. 'He boarded his chopper from an airport cab and a young woman was with him.'

'So we know he's got her but we don't know how much he knows about what's happening here, unless Foucher managed to reach him,' said Bruno.

'Foucher's being kept at the Gendarmerie with the others and no phones allowed,' said J-J.

Bruno shook his head. 'De la Gorce was there but Foucher was allowed to leave. He could easily buy another phone.'

'*Merde*, so he could have briefed the Count about the failure to entrap you.'

'Problem is, the Count might simply say he was picking up his long-lost cousin and looking after her until the funeral,' Bruno said. 'All we've got on him is circumstantial evidence and a lot of suspicion.'

'You've got a bit more than that,' said Fabiola from the nurse's table. 'This old woman may or may not have Alzheimer's but she's been very heavily sedated for months, according to these notes. But they only date back to last year and the notebook is marked as number three, so I want to find numbers one and two. They've had her on chlorpromazine as well as the sedatives. That's not treatment, it's criminal abuse. I can find nothing physically wrong with her except for a bad case of bedsores, but she's had no exercise and I imagine she'll now be dependent on these drugs for the rest of her life.'

'But it's not murder,' said J-J. All three of them turned to the window as the first clattering beat of a helicopter could be heard.

'They tell me he flies a Eurocopter Colibri. It has a range of seven hundred kilometres, so he wouldn't have needed to refuel.'

'There are no facilities to refuel here or at the auberge, so he wouldn't have started with a full tank,' said Bruno, and then he saw it coming up the valley from the west at about a thousand metres but losing height as he watched. He couldn't tell at first if the machine was heading straight for the château or not. Then the angle changed and it was heading for the far side of the river.

J-J was calling Inspector Jofflin to warn him to keep out of sight as the chopper began circling lower over the auberge, apparently preparing to land. Perhaps he was just showing the place off, because after a final circle the engine note rose and it began heading across the river towards them.

'He's going to land here,' Bruno said, the noise of the rotors getting louder as it passed overhead, not much more than a hundred metres above them and circled around the château. All three of them raced across the room and into the long hall to try to keep it in sight, and then J-J groaned aloud.

'*Putain*,' he said, at the sight of Sergeant Jules, holding his képi onto his head, standing in plain sight and in full uniform in the centre of the courtyard.

'It's my fault, I should have told him to stay out of sight,' said Bruno, as the engine note changed again and the chopper began to rise and soar away back towards the river.

'What's he telling the girl?' Fabiola asked. 'Is he just showing her the sights or what?'

'How much of a warning has Foucher given him, that's the question,' said Bruno.

He tried to put himself in the Count's place and think through the various options. If the fuel gauge on the chopper was nearing empty, what could the Count do? The chopper was above the hotel now but it wasn't losing height. It was rising, following the road up to the plateau with the abandoned village and ruined chapel of St Philippon.

'I think he's going to try the secret tunnel and come out at the cave. Foucher could meet him with a car,' Bruno said, thinking aloud but suddenly aware that J-J and Fabiola were staring blankly at him. Quickly, he explained the route of the secret tunnel.

'Can you get the *Gendarmes Mobiles* to head for the Gouffre and block the entrances, including the basket from the roof if it's been repaired? I can take the Gendarmerie van across the river and up to the cemetery, it's got four-wheel drive. Then I'll follow him through the tunnel so we seal both ends. You'd better call the Gouffre and tell them to evacuate the public.'

'Look, I think he's landing,' said Fabiola, staring through the window.

'That's where the ruined chapel gives access to the tunnel,' said Bruno.

'You aren't armed,' said J-J. 'I'll come with you and we'll bring Sergeant Jules.'

'I have to stay with the patient,' said Fabiola.

'If any of them make it back here, you could be in trouble,' J-J objected.

'We can get reinforcements of our own,' said Bruno, pulling out his phone and calling Montsouris to ask him to get to the Red Château to help protect the Countess as soon as he could, and to bring along some burly friends.

Collecting Jules on the way, Bruno and J-J jogged to the stables and took the van down the track to the ford across the river. J-J sat in the back, phoning in turn the *Mobiles*, the Gouffre, Inspector Jofflin and finally the *Procureur*. Bruno drove and tried to explain to Sergeant Jules along the way. They reached the ford, where the water looked to be both fast and high.

'She'll make it,' said Jules, with a confidence that Bruno didn't feel as he engaged four-wheel drive.

'You want to get some speed up,' said J-J from the back.

'We don't want a bow wave,' Bruno replied, remembering a long-ago driving course in the military. He went into the water slowly, telling Jules to open his door so water could come in and its weight help hold them down onto the river bed. He kept the revs high and slipped the clutch to keep the exhaust clear, using his brake to hold the speed down as they went through the deepest part of the ford, water splashing over the door sill but not quite high enough to flood in. The four-wheel drive gripped and they lurched through and up onto the far bank. They picked up Inspector Jofflin in his standard police Renault as they accelerated past the hotel and up the winding road to the chapel.

'Call Isabelle and make sure that military chopper hovers up here and keeps watch on both ends of the tunnel,' Bruno said, fighting the heavy vehicle around the corners. 'If Foucher gets hold of a car we want to be able to follow it.'

They saw the empty helicopter as they topped the rise, leaning slightly to one side on the sloping ground by the cemetery, its rotor blades drooping. Bruno braked hard and stopped at the ruined chapel, waiting impatiently as Jofflin came out of his car with a uniformed policeman beside him, apologizing that they had found nowhere to hide the police cars when the Count's chopper had first appeared.

'It doesn't matter now,' said J-J, telling him to stay at the tunnel entrance and coordinate from that end. He gave Jofflin his own phone, saying all the numbers he'd need were in the memory. He checked that Jofflin had a firearm and then ordered the uniformed policeman to give his own PAMAS semi-automatic to Bruno and to hand over the torch from his car.

Bruno had already taken the torch from the Gendarmerie van and now he worked the action of the gun, remembering the manual de-cocking lever, the same as the military model he'd carried for years. He removed the magazine, squinted down the barrel with his thumbnail at the end to reflect some light in. The barrel was clean, the action smooth and there was a thin film of oil. He gave an approving nod of thanks to the cop from Bergerac. Then he remembered to warn Jofflin that he might have trouble getting a phone connection up here on the plateau, but if he went down the road he should pick up the signal that served the hotel.

'Mine's dead but the Commissaire's phone has a single bar,' Jofflin replied, looking down at the two mobiles. 'I'll manage.'

Bruno turned to J-J. 'I don't think you should come in. You'd be more useful—'

'Don't even try to stop me,' snapped J-J. 'You know the way so you lead. I'll go second, then Jules.'

'Just a moment, sir,' Jules said. 'If Inspector Jofflin calls the Gendarmerie at Les Eyzies, they might be able to get some armed men to the Gouffre entrance before the *Mobiles* can get there.'

'Good idea,' said J-J. 'Do it. And make sure you've got para-medics on standby at both ends, here and at the Gouffre.'

Even as Jules made the suggestion, Bruno borrowed one of Jofflin's phones to call Albert at the St Denis fire station to ask if he had a big fire engine free.

'You do? Could you bring it up to the entrance to the Gouffre as soon as you possibly can? We're in pursuit of a bad guy who's probably armed and he may have a female hostage. Can you blast a high-pressure water jet at anyone who comes out who isn't me or Sergeant Jules or J-J? You'll also need your full paramedic team.'

Then Bruno led the way into the far end of the chapel and saw that the stone beneath the altar had been closed again. Could the Count be fooling them, pretending to be using the tunnel when he was really looking for cover on the plateau? He dismissed the thought. The Count had no reason to think anyone else would know of this route. Keeping his body to one side in case he was met by gunfire, Bruno pushed at the central stone until it swivelled and opened the way into the dark silence of the crypt.

31

By shining each torch from the side, they were able to check that the crypt was clear before Bruno handed J-J his light. With one hand on the pistol he eased himself inside and down the stairs. He stood guard by the hole he remembered that led down to the cave. J-J and Sergeant Jules were large enough to need to struggle through the gap in the altar to join him. He shone his light down the next set of steps. It seemed clear. This time he descended with his back to the stairs, letting his rump slide from step to step as he kept the pistol at the ready. With his other hand, he held his torch as far to his side as he could, reckoning that anyone with a gun would aim for it.

Once the others had followed him down, Bruno thought it was time for silence. He took off his boots, tied the laces together and hung them round his neck, advising the others to do the same. J-J wore slip-on shoes without laces, so he stuck them into his ample belt.

'Watch out for stalagmites in the floor,' Bruno whispered, feeling grit beneath his stockinged feet. Behind him, J-J was breathing loud enough to make Bruno want to shush him. J-J's shadow, thrown by Sergeant Jules's torch, loomed huge on the stone above Bruno's head.

This is folly, came a whispering at the back of Bruno's mind. What could be more dangerous than going down a dark tunnel with an armed adversary waiting somewhere ahead? Bruno squashed the thought, telling himself that the Count probably had no gun. With the innocent girl at risk, there was no choice. Had the Count been alone, they could have pumped in tear gas from both ends until he crawled out, blinded and coughing and fighting for breath. They still could do that, came the insidious voice in his head. Tear gas wasn't lethal. The girl was young, she'd recover fast enough. Nonsense, he told himself; the tunnels were so vast that the gas would dissipate.

They were now in the long, smooth tunnel he thought of as the pipeline, where there would be no escape and a single bullet could go through one man and hit a second. Even a missed shot could ricochet and do damage. He turned off his torch and told J-J and Jules to do the same.

Whispering to J-J to stay where he was, Bruno crept along the pipeline, every sense alert for any sound or glimmer of light from ahead. Crouching, he peered down its length. Even as he did so, the skin began to crawl on his scalp as he remembered that the pipeline ran both ways from here. He'd gone downhill to find Isabelle, but hadn't bothered to explore uphill. There could be another exit, or it would make a fine spot for an ambush. He turned his head to look the other way but saw nothing. He'd have to leave Jules at this point, just in case he'd been wrong and the Count wasn't heading for the Gouffre at all, but the other way. With Jules there, at least the one certain exit would be blocked.

He crept down into the pipeline, waited and listened, then covered the lens of his torch with his hand so that only a faint glow emerged pinkly through his fingers. He whispered to J-J to follow him down. When Jules joined them, Bruno explained that the pipeline ran in both directions and Jules should wait at this junction. The old Gendarme at once handed J-J his torch.

'If I'm staying still, I won't need it,' Jules said. 'Anything that comes down from the right, I'll shoot it. Anything that comes up from the left, I'll challenge once and if it's not you I'll fire.'

'If you go back up the steps a little and wait, you won't have to challenge anybody. Just hit them on the head as they go by, but make sure it's not me,' said J-J.

Reminding J-J to watch for stalagmites, Bruno set off in darkness, remembering his previous count of just over four hundred paces before he'd reached the lake where Isabelle was waiting. When he reached the first of the several dog-leg corners, he waited for J-J and breathed into his ear, 'Wait here while I get to the next bend. I'll make a little click with my mouth when it's safe to follow, and then we'll do it again at the next corner.'

Bruno felt a little tug of nostalgia for the troops he'd led in Bosnia. He'd trained them so hard they didn't need this kind of briefing at every turn. He'd warned J-J how many steps they'd have to go, but every time the big detective joined him his breathing was ragged. Even so he never once faltered. It took guts to do this for the first time in the dark. Whatever they pay us, thought Bruno, it isn't enough, and he set off silently again down to the next bend in the pipeline.

He had counted three hundred and five when his foot felt something strange and sharp as he was about to put his weight on it. He stepped back and knelt down, feeling with his hand. It was a small ring, attached to a tiny bar that felt like metal. An earring. Perhaps the girl had dropped it as a signal, or the Count had left it as a trap, something he'd hear if it was kicked aside. He slipped it into his pocket, paused to listen and then moved on.

He heard the sound of water a few paces sooner than he'd expected. He dropped into a crouch, put the gun into the belt at his back and moved cautiously forward on feet and fingertips, keeping low in case a shot came, and trusting that the noise of water would cover any sounds of his movement. He could smell the water now, a freshness in the air. He waited at the final bend until J-J caught up.

'We're at the lake,' Bruno whispered into J-J's ear. 'I'll go in low and then light my torch. I'll have my eyes closed and if he's there it should blind him but he'll probably fire anyway. You then come round this bend and if you see him, shoot. I'll have rolled to a new position and I'll be shooting, too. Ready?'

Bruno felt him nod. He squeezed J-J's shoulder and dropped down again to creep forward. His elbow just brushed the wall so that he'd know when the pipeline opened out onto the rocky beach beside the lake. When he reached it, he stopped, crept back a few metres and put his boots back on, tying double knots. He'd need firm footing. Then he went through the army drill that he'd done so often it was second nature.

ROWAS was the acronym: Rules of engagement, Objective, Weapons, Ammo, Support. The rule was fire if fired upon. The objective was to save the girl and arrest the Count. He was carrying a PAMAS G1, which meant no safety catch but a double-action trigger on the first round. He had fifteen shots in the magazine. Support was J-J with Sergeant Jules as back-up, and be aware of possible friendlies coming from the other end.

Then he rehearsed in his mind how it would be. He'd be full-length on the floor, his left arm stretched out high and to one side, holding the torch, the gun in the other. His eyes would be squeezed shut. He'd turn on the light, take a count of two and lay the torch on the floor. Then he'd roll to his right and open his eyes and be ready to shoot. He'd take three points of aim: one, straight ahead, to the tunnel that led to the Gouffre; two, hard left, to the little causeway beside the waterfall; and three, hard right.

He felt in his pockets for one of the paper tissues he usually carried, tore off half, soaked it in his mouth and put it into one ear. Then he repeated the process for the other ear. Gunshots in an enclosed space like this from the nine-millimetre he was carrying could rupture eardrums.

He took three deep breaths, stretched out, closed his eyes, raised his arm and turned the torch on, feeling the sudden flare even through his closed eyelids.

'Police,' he shouted. 'Drop your weapons.'

He laid the torch down and rolled, his eyes opening and his gun straight ahead. He heard the crack and saw the flare of a gunshot from his left, the direction of the causeway, and he was already switching aim. His first shot came at the same instant as the second shot from the causeway.

Tap-tap, high-low, he fired two shots and rolled. Another shot came, this time from straight across the small lake. There was a second shooter. He fired two more shots, low-high, and rolled again. No more shots from the causeway and a splash as something fell into the lake.

Then silence. The shadows on the walls and the reflections from the lake were swinging crazily as his torch rolled on the ground. He felt J-J emerge behind him, the damn fool.

'Get back,' he urged him. 'Second shooter.'

'Halt, police,' he shouted and rolled again. There was something stretched out at the mouth of the far tunnel. He took aim. 'Stay where you are. This is the police.'

'Hello?' came a plaintive voice, female, not French.

'Marie-Françoise, is it you?' he called, in his bad English. 'I am police.' Could she hear him with her eardrums blasted?

'*Oui, oui, Marie-Françoise,*' she called back. '*Non tirez*, don't shoot.'

'Is it you only?' he called, his gun pointing at the shape in the tunnel across the lake that was waving an arm. His eyes swept left and right, scanning the lump in the lake for movement. It splashed, feebly.

'*Oui, oui*, alone,' came the girl's voice. It sounded strained and he heard a cry. She spoke again, '*Je suis seule.*'

'Not move,' he shouted, not knowing whether to believe her. *Merde*, but that other shot had sounded different and the flare of it had felt different, as if it came from a different place.

There was only one way to find out if there was a second shooter. He rose fast to his full height, turned on his torch and then dived hard to his left, landing on the torch to smother the light as a shot came. Then a second.

He turned the light off as the girl screamed and two more shots came from behind him, J-J's revolver. *Putain*. Bruno rolled back and swept his legs like a scythe, sweeping J-J's feet from under him. 'Stay down,' he shouted over J-J's curses and rolled back.

He closed his eyes and thought it through. He had two options. He could get J-J to blast fire across at the tunnel while he sprinted over the causeway, dropped and fired from the side, catching the shooter in a crossfire. That would work but it would probably kill the girl. Or he could creep into the water and try to use the floating body for cover. But he didn't know how deep it was. If he had to swim one-handed he'd splash and be an easy target. And he'd still have to try not to shoot the girl.

The third option was to wait, to send J-J back up the tunnel to the chapel and then get the *Mobiles* to come in from the other end. J-J could come back down the tunnel with a couple of gas masks and they could throw in the tear gas. That should work but it would take an hour or two. And whoever it was in the lake would die of hypothermia even if they hadn't bled to death. There were no good choices.

He heard the sound of scuffling from across the lake followed by a muffled shout from the girl and then two fast shots. In the flashes he saw two figures struggling. That made five shots fired by the second shooter, he told himself as one of the figures jumped or fell into the lake. There was another shot, that made six, and Bruno heard another scream, muffled by splashing and then footsteps running away.

He fired twice into the tunnel across the lake, shouted to J-J to stay back, turned on his torch and ran at a crouch across the causeway, firing two more shots into the tunnel. That made eight shots he'd fired, seven left. Now he was spread-eagled at the mouth of the tunnel that led to the Gouffre, shining the beam of light down its emptiness. He called back to J-J to get the girl out of the lake and see how badly she was shot.

Bruno stayed on watch, telling J-J how to cross the narrow causeway. Then he heard Sergeant Jules calling his name.

'This is Bruno, I'm fine and it's clear to advance,' he shouted back, thinking how Jules must have groped his way in darkness along the length of the pipeline when he heard the gunshots, not knowing what he'd find.

'Help Jules over the causeway and he can replace me on guard,' he said to J-J, who was knee-deep in the lake and reaching for the girl.

'I've got her.' J-J hauled her ashore. She was spluttering and choking but at least she was alive.

'Pull her out of the line of fire,' Bruno said. 'Over there to my right. Then guide Jules across.'

Jules came along the causeway, dragging a floating body. The current must have taken it to the rim. Once Jules replaced him at the tunnel entrance, Bruno flashed the torch onto the face. It was the Count. Bruno checked the neck for a pulse. It was feeble, but it was there.

'How's the girl?' he asked J-J.

'I can't see and she won't tell me.' The girl was sobbing and gulping, close to hysterics.

'Wait,' said Bruno, and went to the small cave that Isabelle had shown him and came back with the candleholder and the lighter. Once he had the first candle alight he brought more and soon the cavern was bright.

'Get the wet clothes off them or they'll get hypothermia,' he said, starting to strip the Count. He had one wound in his knee and a second high on his chest. There was a big exit wound at the back but the icy lake had slowed the bleeding. Bruno stuffed the hole with the Count's shirt, wrung out his wet trousers and used them to hold the dressing in place. The Count's belt had to do for a tourniquet on the knee. He took off his jacket to drape it over the Count, whose face was deathly white.

The girl was too gone in shock to resist as they stripped her. With her wet clothes off Bruno could find only a graze wound on her side, just below the ribs. He asked where she was hurt but got no reply, so he tried making reassuring noises in his broken English and repeating that he was from the police. In the candlelight he could see that her face had been badly beaten. One eye was closed, blood still seeped from her nose and she'd lost some teeth. They rubbed her dry with J-J's sweater, then dressed her in Jules's jacket and his oversized trousers.

'What now?' J-J asked.

'You stay with the wounded. Jules goes back for the para-medics and I go forward,' Bruno said, not knowing quite why he said it but feeling that he had to finish this. 'I fired eight shots so I'll need to reload from Jules's magazine.'

He was reloading when there came a distant flurry of shots from the tunnel to the Gouffre, one of them a burst of automatic fire and another the boom of a shotgun. That had to be the *Mobiles*.

Then came shouting and the sound of running feet and a call of 'Police, throw down your weapons.'

'Police here and clear,' Bruno called back. 'Weapons down.' He stood up, his gun on the ground beside him, raised his hands in the air and told the other two to follow suit. In the light of a dozen candles, it was clear they were unarmed, although they hardly looked like police with his and Jules's uniforms now draped on the wounded.

'Identify yourselves,' came a voice from the tunnel, very close.

'Commissaire Jalipeau, *Police Nationale*.'

'Jules Ranquin, Sergeant, *Gendarmerie Nationale*.'

'Bruno Courrèges, *Police Municipale*, St Denis, plus two wounded who need urgent attention. One hostage, one gunman. Our weapons are down and our hands up. We are standing in clear view.'

The characteristic shape of a FAMAS assault rifle poked into view at knee level and then a double-barrelled shotgun at shoulder height. Two black-clad *Gendarmes Mobiles* with helmets and body armour stepped into the cave. A third followed them, a FAMAS slung by his side. He looked around the cave once and shouted back 'Medics'. Then he turned to face them and introduced himself as they lowered their hands.

'Capitaine Moravin, *les Jaunes*.' He saluted J-J, and said, '*Monsieur le Commissaire*, we have one dead gunman in the main cave. He came out of the tunnel shooting and ignored my order to drop his weapon. We also have one secured prisoner who was arrested outside the cave, name of Abouard, Lebanese. He's claiming diplomatic immunity.'

'Ignore it until you hear otherwise from me or the *Procureur*,' J-J said.

Two black-clad Gendarme medics came in, followed by Ahmed from the St Denis fire brigade.

'The girl's wounds are superficial, but she's in shock and she doesn't speak much French,' Bruno said. 'The Count's a lot worse, two gunshots, knee and upper chest.'

The medics attended to the Count and Ahmed opened his shoulder case and began cleaning up the girl's face.

'Have you identified the dead gunman?' J-J asked.

'The ID card in his wallet says he's called Foucher, but the shotgun blew his face away,' said Moravin. 'We'll have to wait for fingerprints.' He turned to the medics. 'Have you got a stretcher coming?'

'On its way, *chef*.'

The stretchers came with Albert the fire chief close behind, puffing a little from the trot up the tunnel. He shook hands all round, visibly relieved that none of those shot were people he knew.

'Sorry you didn't get to use the water hose,' Bruno said as the first stretcher took the girl up the tunnel. Ahmed and one of the medics carried her as Moravin and his two *Mobiles* led the way back to the Gouffre. Another medic was still working on the Count. He had a mobile drip plugged into the Count's arm and an oxygen mask on his face.

'It might have saved a lot of trouble,' Albert replied, taking off his helmet and wiping his brow. 'The Mayor's out in the main cave with the Baron and Father Sentout. Half the town's waiting outside the Gouffre. Florence is there with her kids and your new puppy.'

Bruno grinned at the thought. 'Has anybody relieved Fabiola at the Red Château?'

'The Countess is on her way to hospital in Périgueux with Fabiola. Montsouris insisted on going along,' Albert said. 'Someone from the Minister of the Interior's office has been on the phone with the Mayor, insisting on speaking to you as soon as you're near a phone. And there's a guy outside from *Paris-Match*, claims to be a friend of yours from Sarajevo.'

'Right, we'd better go, if the Count is stabilized enough to move him,' said Bruno. 'How's it going?' he asked the medic.

'Give me another few minutes,' said the medic. 'They'll send a couple of guys back to help with the stretcher. Then we can go.'

Bruno nodded and turned back to gaze across the black stillness of the lake and at the dark mouth of the far tunnel. It had been four days since he'd first seen it but he knew he'd want to return, perhaps join one of the exploring clubs and see what other secrets these honeycombed hills contained.

'Can't be soon enough for me,' said J-J. 'It gives me the creeps, being underground like this and thinking of all that weight above us.'

Bruno turned back from the lake to J-J and Sergeant Jules. 'After this, I think we all deserve a very large drink.'

As he spoke the last word, the sharp cracking sound of a distant explosion came from the far side of the lake followed by a long, swelling rumble. A rush of dust and air blasted from the tunnel that led back to the ruined chapel to send a surge of lake water over their feet. It extinguished most of the candles they had lit.

32

'*Mon Dieu*,' said J-J, looking at Sergeant Jules. 'They've booby-trapped the tunnel where we came in, where you were waiting. Thank God you came and joined us.'

'That might not be the only bomb,' said Bruno. 'Follow me, quickly.' He helped the medic to drag the Count, drenched from the wave of lake water, around the corner into the smaller cave where the candles had been stored.

'Maybe that's why Foucher took the chance to run, if he knew there was another bomb timed to blow and seal him in,' said Bruno.

'So it could seal us in, too,' said Jules, gathering more candles from the old ammunition box and lighting them one by one. 'How long do we have to wait before we know?'

Bruno tried to work out how long the timer would have been on the bomb. Most timers were set for five, fifteen or thirty minutes, but they weren't always that accurate. He wondered if Ahmed and the girl had managed to get out of the tunnel before the blast. It would have taken time to get that stretcher up the stairs and across the three big stalagmites that guarded the entrance to the tunnel.

'They probably set that timer as they came through the tunnel with the girl. They can't have been much more than ten or fifteen minutes ahead of us, but then more time passed when the *Mobiles* joined us. So it was probably set for thirty minutes. But if there is a second bomb, I've no idea when they might have set it. If we stay here for an hour, we should be OK.'

'If we don't get this guy to hospital before then, he's not going to make it,' said the medic.

'Tough,' said J-J. 'I'm not risking my skin for a bastard like that.'

'I'm going back into the cave by the lake,' said Albert, tapping at his walkie-talkie. 'I can't get a connection in here.'

'Don't go out just yet,' said Bruno. 'Just put the radio round the corner and see if you get anything.'

Albert did so, and a crackling of garbled voice and static came from the small speaker. He thumbed the button to speak and identified himself but there was no answer.

'It's no good, I'll have to go out if they're going to hear me,' he said and began to rise to his feet. At that moment, a second, much closer blast slammed into the cave, knocking Albert to the ground, deafening them all and blowing out every candle but one.

'Jesus, we're sealed in,' said the medic.

'They know we're in here,' said Albert, picking himself up and trying to rub dust from his eyes. 'They'll get equipment in and dig us out. We've got water. We can last for days.'

'This guy doesn't have an hour. His blood pressure's collapsed,' said the medic.

'Let's see how bad the blockage is,' said Bruno. Lighting more candles, he led the way around the rocky corner onto the beach where they'd been standing when the first blast came. He looked into the tunnel that led to the Gouffre. The first few metres were clear and then rubble began to pile higher and higher until it reached the ceiling.

'Try the radio from here,' he said to Albert, but there wasn't even the sound of static.

'There must be at least fifty metres of tunnel before the Gouffre,' said Albert. 'If it's all like this, we're in for a long wait, and who knows what damage the blast did to people inside the Gouffre.'

Bruno thought of the Dragon's Teeth, the three giant stalagmites that guarded the way to the tunnel, each of them many tons in weight. They'd need to get cranes and bulldozers and mechanical diggers into the Gouffre to clear them.

'If we've nothing better to do, we might see if there are other ways out, maybe through some of those holes up by the roof,' he suggested. 'I'll go and check the other tunnel to see how blocked that is.'

He crossed back over the causeway, holding a candle high. With Sergeant Jules following him into the place that had so nearly been Jules's grave, he advanced into the tunnel. Counting his steps, he managed just over a hundred metres before the rubble became impassable and they turned back. Now that the dust had settled, he sniffed, catching the faint scent of something that might have been glue, something he'd smelt often enough in his army days.

'*Plastrite*, French military issue' he said to Jules. 'So when we're out of here, the first job will be to find out where the hell they got hold of our own plastic explosive.'

Back at the other tunnel, Albert and J-J were lifting stones from the rock pile one by one and tossing them down. Was that the best they could do, Bruno wondered. They were four grown men, plus the medic. They were alive, healthy, and they had light, water and whatever assets they carried.

'Can we make an inventory of what possessions we have?' he asked them. He began emptying his own pockets, laying down gun and wallet, handkerchief, folding knife, torch and mobile phone, notebook, pen and the rubber gloves and plastic evidence bags he always carried.

Sergeant Jules and J-J had little more, but Albert had a 25-metre coil of rope, an axe, torch and helmet and his breathing apparatus strapped to his back. The medic had a commando knife and his rucksack of medical equipment. There were twenty-two candles in the ammunition box, each lasting about an hour. Bruno went round and collected the ones already lit, blew them all out but one. He then picked up those drenched in the wave from the lake and set them aside to dry.

'From now on, we'd better ration the candles, but the rope will be useful,' said Bruno. 'How much air in that breathing equipment, Albert?'

'Fifteen, twenty minutes, depending on your exertion rate.'

'I might need that for the patient,' said the medic. J-J snorted and Jules rolled his eyes.

'Is your torch waterproof?' Bruno asked Albert, thinking of the jets of water firemen used.

'Supposed to be, but it's probably more like water-resistant, depending on the pressure.'

'So if we took it underwater, best wrap it in plastic,' Bruno mused. He sealed the torch into two plastic bags and pointed to the lake.

'At the end of the lake there's a causeway where J-J and Jules and I crossed. It acts as a kind of dam but water falls over it and then drops. When I was last here, I used a stone and rope to measure the drop and it was twelve metres. That water has to go somewhere and my guess is it flows into the lake in the Gouffre. With the breathing equipment and the torch, we might be able to get out that way.'

'This patient couldn't make it,' said the medic.

'From what you say about getting him to hospital within the hour, he's not likely to make it anyway,' said Bruno. 'This could be his only chance.'

'What if you get stuck?' Albert asked. 'Isn't it better to wait here until they can clear the tunnel and get us out? If we carry on moving stones out of the way I might get through on the radio.'

'There's a lot of tunnel to clear, and I smelt military-grade plastic explosive back there. That stuff's powerful and it will have brought down a lot of roof. Rather than just sit back and wait to see if we get rescued, I think this is worth a try. And if I get stuck, I'll have the rope tied round my waist and you can pull me out.'

'Wait,' said the medic, and unhooked his Kevlar helmet from his belt and tossed it to Bruno. 'You might need this.'

'Thanks.' Bruno put it on, fixing the familiar chinstrap. Rather than let any discussion drag on he picked up the rope and the sealed torch, asked Albert to bring the breathing equipment and headed for the causeway. He tied one end of the rope around his crotch and shoulders, and the other to Albert, then lay down, bracing against the shock of the cold water as it flowed over the stone and down into the depth below. He turned on the torch through the plastic, put his head over the rim and looked down. If there was a bottom at twelve metres, he couldn't see it. It might just have been an outcrop of rock his stone had landed on before. He'd soon find out.

'I'm going to climb over the lip here and then you let me down with the rope,' he said to Albert, slipping off his boots. 'When I reach somewhere I can stand, give the rope to J-J and then you come down with the breathing equipment. I'll need you down there to pull me out if required.'

He rolled over the lip, holding on with one hand, the torch in the other, and he told Albert to let him down slowly.

'You're mad,' said Albert, but with Jules and J-J helping him hold the rope, the fire chief began letting Bruno down, a few centimetres at a time.

Bruno turned his head to one side to avoid the rush of water, but told himself it wasn't much stronger than the powerful showers at the rugby club. He felt the water filling his clothes and adding to his weight. Under his stockinged feet the rock felt very smooth. There would be no handholds to help him climb back up.

'Twelve metres,' shouted Albert from above, his voice almost drowned out by the waterfall.

'Keep going,' Bruno shouted back. 'There's another couple of metres of rope wrapped around me.'

354

Suddenly his foot touched something flat. He tested it and it took his weight. He explored with his other foot and found he was on a flat ledge, maybe a metre wide, with a smoothly rounded lip that had been worn away by countless centuries of water. But he could stand and turn and the light showed him the froth of the waterfall at his feet, falling into a pool perhaps ten metres wide and not much more than two metres across. To his left the wall of rock was smooth and unbroken. To his right, in the direction of the Gouffre, was a tunnel though which he could see the water flow. He put his hand in; the current was insistent, rather than strong. He could probably swim against it on the return journey. With Albert pulling him, he was sure he could.

He looked up and pointed his torch, and through the mist rising from the falling water he saw Albert's bullet-shaped head poking over the rim.

'It's fine, there's a ledge. Come on down,' he shouted, and beckoned Albert to join him. He steadied the rope as the burly fire chief let himself down hand over hand.

'*Putain*, that plastic rope gets slippery when it's wet,' said Albert as he let go of the rope and studied his raw palms. 'I had to take my gloves off, I had no grip.'

Bruno helped him off with the breathing apparatus and strapped it onto his back. Albert took off his goggles, unhooked the breathing mask from where it hung around his neck and checked the connections before handing them to Bruno.

'Let me check something first,' said Bruno. 'I'm going to turn off the torch because people in the Gouffre should have the lights on and we may be able to see a glow.'

'The bomb could have killed the lights,' said Albert.

'Let's try it anyway.' Bruno switched off the light.

The blackness was not quite total. A faint glow came from above them, over the lip of the waterfall where a single candle barely illuminated the cave. He saw the silhouettes of the heads of J-J and Jules as they looked down at them. Bruno could not be sure, but he thought he felt as much as saw a glimmering deep in the water.

'What's happened?' shouted J-J, dimmed by the water.

'It's OK,' Bruno called. 'Just checking the light.' And he turned it back on. 'Let go of the rope so we can use it down here.'

It snaked down and Bruno tied the loose end of the rope around Albert's crotch and shoulders and showed him how to lie on the ledge, his feet braced on the wall beside the tunnel. It might be a problem to throw the rope back up to Jules and J-J but he'd cross that bridge if he came to it.

'That gives me twenty metres of rope to explore that tunnel, and if there's light in the Gouffre, I should see it by then,' he said. 'If I jerk the rope three times, that means pull me out, OK?'

'Good luck,' said Albert, and they shook hands. Bruno sat on the ledge, fixed his face mask, tasted the sharpness of the oxygen and let himself slip into the water. Head first, or rather helmet first, he tucked the torch tight against his chest. With the other arm ahead of him to feel for obstacles, he let the current take him through the dark mouth of the tunnel and into the underground river.

Once past the mouth of the tunnel where the turbulence

meant that all he could see were air bubbles, he began to make out the loom of walls and roof through the murky water. He lowered his feet but could feel no bottom. To account for such depth, there must be more water coming into this river than just the flow from the waterfall. He raised his hand and was sure he felt air above the surface. He turned onto his back and knew he was floating and could see the smooth stone of the tunnel roof passing above him at something like walking pace. It meant he might even be able to navigate this passage without the breathing equipment. That might give the Count a fighting chance of survival, him with the face mask and Bruno alongside. He could breathe the air in the space above.

Suddenly he felt the speed of the flow increase and his feet touched bottom. The tunnel was narrowing as it shallowed but its floor was too smooth for him to get any grip with his feet. The tunnel seemed to turn in a dog-leg bend and he felt himself thud against something, a kind of projection that gave him just enough purchase to stretch out his legs and brace his feet against the far wall as the current washed over him.

There was no pocket of air above him now but there was still some slack in the rope, and he wondered if Albert could haul him back against this current and around the dog-leg turn. That was a big risk. Before he took it, he turned off his torch to see if there was any sign of a glow ahead.

There was more than a glow. It was as if his torch was beaming into a mirror in front of him, a strong ray of light shining at his face and a second light behind it. Suddenly he was not alone. Human shapes were almost upon him, heads in goggles and face masks, arms clutching at bars that seemed to be braced against the tunnel walls. A hand came slowly towards his face, a thumb up in the universal sign that it was going to be all right.

The hand then pointed at Bruno and signed that he should follow back towards the Gouffre. Bruno shook his head and pointed to the rope tied around him. Then he pointed back the way that he had come. He nodded his head vigorously to insist that this should be done his way and gave three sharp tugs on the rope.

Bruno felt his body lurch as Albert hauled with all his strength and he tried to swim to help the burly fire chief. Now there were supporting hands on his shoulders to push him along, and those strange metal bars that seemed to appear ahead of him and give purchase on the smooth walls of the tunnel.

Faster than he had come, he was hauled back to see Albert straining at the rope. His face was tight with effort and coils of rope lay festooned across his body. Albert's eyes widened in surprise as one, two and then three strange heads appeared above the water in a blaze of spotlights, pushing Bruno up onto the ledge. He took off his breathing mask and hugged Albert in gratitude, then helped the first of the strangers onto the ledge.

'Périgord cave rescue team, I'm Miko,' said the stranger. 'Miko Moreau from Les Eyzies. We're very glad to see you. Where are the others and how's the patient? We've got a doctor with us.'

'Very good to see you too, and thanks,' said Bruno, hearing

his voice high and squeaky from the oxygen. He was shivering from the cold but surging with adrenalin. 'The others are fine and there's a medic from the *Gendarmes Mobiles* with the patient. They're all in the cave above the waterfall here.'

'It's a good job you came down it then, we'd probably never have looked up there. We could have missed you altogether,' said Moreau. 'This is Fernand, our team leader, and this is Pierre, our doctor.'

'What are those metal rods you used to pull against the current?' Bruno had to ask.

'Telescopic poles, like the ones hikers use, only they're spring-loaded so we can brace against smooth walls. How tall is that waterfall?'

'Twelve metres.' Bruno looked up and saw J-J's face beaming in the spotlights.

'That's OK, we've got an expandable ladder,' said Miko. 'It's attached to this rope around my ankle. You know you were almost at the Gouffre when we found you? There's quite a reception committee and we've got a rope running all the way through the river, so just keep a tight hold and you'll all be fine.'

'Was anybody hurt in the explosion? What about the girl?'

'A militia captain got concussed and one of his men has a broken leg. But they're all going to be OK. The girl should be in hospital already.'

'Just look at me a moment,' the doctor said, waving a finger before Bruno's eyes and checking his pulse. 'You need warming up and a good rest. Get yourself checked by your own doc in the morning.'

Within minutes, the ladder was in place. Miko and the doctor had climbed into the cave and Fernand had put a breathing mask onto Albert and was leading him into the underground river. Sergeant Jules was the first down the ladder, and once Fernand returned, he led Jules down the river and into the Gouffre.

'Your turn now,' said Fernand when he came back.

Bruno shook his head. 'There's an overweight and rather older Commissaire of Police up there. I'd like to make sure he gets out safely. Then I think you might need help with the stretcher.'

It was another hour before Bruno hauled himself out of the lake and into the vast and well-lit space of the Gouffre. Some of the light came from TV cameras, and some from the flashes of Philippe Delaron's camera. The warmth was in the welcome that awaited: the Baron hugging him careless of the soaking water, and then Father Sentout and the Mayor, beaming at him with Balzac squirming in his arms.

The Baron handed him one of the stone beakers from the cave, filled to the brim with cognac. Bruno took a deep draught, and then stripped off as the Baron handed him an enormous towel and led him to a heat-blower someone had erected. Albert and J-J were standing before it as if they never wanted to leave, the folds of their heavy towels blowing back with the force of the hot air. Sergeant Jules was sitting to one side, still enjoying the heated air, but even happier to have his wife beside him.

'*Putain*, you had me worried for a while back there,' said

the Baron, gathering underwear and T-shirt and tracksuits and waiting to help Bruno dress.

Bruno just grinned, feeling the warmth of the towel and the heater and the glow of the cognac. The Baron had been in the army; he knew the unwritten rules. It was good to see him again and to know that none of their recent arguments meant a damn thing.

'I never doubted that you'd make it out of there,' said the Mayor, 'even after they told us it would take weeks to clear the tunnel.'

More members of the rescue team, all in wetsuits, were plunging into the lake to help bring out the stretcher bearing the Count. They pushed Bruno and the others away from the hot-air blower and stood the stretcher before it while the doctor checked the Count again and attached another mobile drip.

'He's still with us, just, but I don't think he's going to make it. Is the helicopter ready?' the doctor asked, stripping off his wetsuit. Another member of the rescue team confirmed that it was standing by, rotors turning.

'Right, get those hot towels around him and we'll run him out to the chopper.' Within moments, they had gone. Bruno, J-J and Albert gathered back around the hot air, stone beakers in hand.

'There'll have to be an inquiry,' J-J said. 'One shot dead and another wounded, maybe dying. You know the procedure. It'll be a formality but they'll need all our written statements before Friday.'

'Whoever runs the inquiry can go back into that cave themselves to look for my gun and the guns of the bastards who tried to kill us,' said Bruno. 'I don't fancy making that swim again anytime soon. And I don't think there'll be much of an inquiry with no weapons evidence.'

'Then they'll adjourn the inquiry until they can retrieve the weapons,' said J-J thoughtfully. 'We could be suspended on full pay for months.'

'Your new *Procureur* seemed the type to find a way round that.'

'If he doesn't my wife will probably shoot him first and then me,' J-J said, in that mournful way that usually meant he was joking.

Bruno looked around the cave. There was little damage from the blast except for the Dragon's Teeth that had guarded the entrance to the tunnel. One of the great pillars had been tossed onto its side, crushing a rack of jugs that were slowly being transformed into stone. Beside it lay Foucher's body under a blanket, on the spot where the blast of a Gendarme's shotgun had felled him. Another pillar had rolled half into the lake, crushing a pedal-boat, and the third still stood, a fat, phallic sentinel above a secret underworld that Bruno knew he wanted to start exploring. He'd have to talk to Miko about joining a cave exploration club.

But right now he wanted to go home, to feed his chickens and ride his horse and walk his dog and then to have a bowl of soup and sleep the clock round. He put down the towel and dressed in the garments the Baron had brought. As if it were a signal, the Mayor came forward and steered him to one of the TV cameras where he submitted to a brief interview on the dramas of the day.

'Home?' asked the Baron. Balzac was tucked into the crook of his arm and he handed the puppy to Bruno. 'Dinner's on me if you want it, but you look like you need some sleep. You'll find quite a welcome outside.'

'Home,' Bruno agreed, relishing the soft rasp of Balzac's tongue on his ear. He braced himself for whatever awaited in the open air. At first, he just stood and looked at the sky, amazed that it was still light, even more amazed at how blue it was. The evening sunlight looked unbelievably fresh and perfect after his hours underground. Then he saw the beaming faces and heard the welcoming shouts of his friends and neighbours. He shook hands and kissed cheeks all the way back to the Baron's car. He paused to kneel down and kiss Florence's twins, and then their mother, accepting an invitation to dinner the following evening.

He'd just got his hand on the door of the Baron's lovely old Citroën DS when he heard Ahmed calling his name and hurrying his way through the crowd.

'We've got a call-out and it sounds like your place,' he said, his mouth to Bruno's ear and his voice low. 'Maybe you'd better not go back until I get confirmation. I've got an engine on its way, should be there by now.'

'You mean a fire? At my place?' Bruno asked, seeing the answer in Ahmed's eyes. He jumped into the car and told the Baron to drive like the wind, wondering how and why but already suspecting he knew the answer. He held Balzac tightly to him as he heard the sound of the siren behind him. Ahmed was following in the little command car. He turned to face forward, thinking of the house he'd built with his own hands, of his ducks and chickens and the garden he'd made, of the wine in the cellar and his books on the shelves.

There were two fire engines at work when he arrived but only one was still jetting water onto the roof of the house. There were black scorch marks around the broken windows of the living room and kitchen and the entrance door had gone. His ducks and chickens were all right. The barn and his bedrooms had been spared.

'It could be a lot worse. We were lucky somebody saw smoke from the road and called it in,' said Ahmed, coming to stand at his shoulder. Raymond was with him, the crew captain of the second fire engine. 'It was just the curtains in the kitchen. All the real damage is in the living room.'

'How did it happen?' Bruno asked.

Raymond led him forward to the smashed window of the sitting room, the walls charred black and the furniture in smoking ruins.

'That glass on the floor is not just from your window,' said Raymond. 'It's a bottle, and you can smell the petrol as well as I can. Somebody threw a Molotov cocktail inside.'

'Jesus,' said the Baron. 'What sort of sick bastard would do this?'

'They tried the same in the kitchen but just hit the outside of the window frame,' Raymond said.

Raymond led Bruno round to the back and pointed to the petrol cap hanging loose from the side of Bruno's elderly Land-Rover. He then gestured at the bottle tree where Bruno stored his empty wine bottles until it was time to fill them again from the annual hogshead he shared with the Baron.

'It looks like they used your bottles, your petrol,' Raymond said. 'I'm sorry.'

'It wasn't a They,' said Bruno. 'It was a she. And I don't think she's finished yet.' He turned to the Baron. 'How fast can you get me to Pamela's place? I think she'll go for my horse next.'

The Citroën DS was the car that had been fast enough, rugged enough and had the endurance to save Charles de Gaulle's life twice from successive assassination attempts, as the Baron never tired of saying. But his car was now fifty years old and its legendary suspension groaned as the Baron hurled it down the lane from Bruno's home. They hit the road into town with the speedometer touching eighty and still accelerating as they went past the Gendarmerie. The Baron had to slow for the roundabout but accelerated hard onto the old stone bridge across the river, the imperious klaxon blaring as other cars scattered and scurried to the side of the road.

As they entered the long lane that led to Pamela's house. Bruno scanned the horizon for a sign of smoke but saw none so far. And when they crested the rise, still accelerating so they briefly left the ground, he saw no sign of horse nor rider in the grounds around the old farmhouse. Above all, there was no flare of flame in the stables.

He looked up towards the ridge and there was nothing. But then from the long forest ride he saw the flash of white as the mare came down through the trees at a gallop, the rider tall in the saddle, one arm held out and holding something that glinted in the sun.

'That's her,' Bruno said.

'*Putain*, it's going to be close,' the Baron said, ignoring the steam that was coming from the long bonnet of his car and the flaring red lights on his dashboard. 'When I tell you, hit the handbrake as hard as you can.'

Urged on by its rider, the white mare found a new burst of pace as it reached the level field that led to Pamela's courtyard and the stables beyond. But the Baron held his speed as the DS hit the bump where the gravel drive began. He threw the car into the bend, ignoring the loud scrape that came from the wing brushing the gatepost. Understanding what his friend intended to do, Bruno released both seat belts. He tucked Balzac firmly into his shirt, buttoning him in.

The white mare was in the courtyard, suddenly slowing as the rider released the reins. She held a lighter to the petrol-soaked rag in the mouth of the bottle and was reaching back her arm to throw.

'Now,' shouted the Baron, stabbing at his brakes.

He threw the car into a four-wheel drift as Bruno hauled on the handbrake and the Baron hit the throttle a final time. The white mare was rearing on its hind legs. The bottle caught the light and Bruno could see the flame. With the shriek of an avenging fury Eugénie hurled it onto the car that was sliding into her path, blocking her way to her chosen target of Hector's stable.

Bruno grabbed the Baron's arm and opened his door. Bracing a foot against the steering-wheel column he hauled his friend bodily out of the car. They fell and rolled together onto the sharp gravel of the courtyard as the car exploded behind them and they heard the piercing scream of an animal in mortal pain. Horse or woman, they could not tell which.

It might have been both, from the great surge of fire that roared up from the stricken car to embrace and devour the mare and rider together. Erupting anew, the flames caught the white mane of the horse and the flaring darkness of Eugénie's hair as both crumpled into the burning wreckage of the car.

Epilogue

Ironic, thought Bruno as the tiny bell tolled, that Athénaïs should be buried beside the Red Château's family chapel where she'd gone through the Black Mass that had been the prelude to her death. Even more ironic that she would rest at arm's length from her cousin, the Count, whose own grave had been dug alongside. At least Athénaïs had a respectable gathering of mourners. They were led by her grandmother in her wheelchair and by her teenage daughter from America, Marie-Françoise. The Red Countess looked desperately frail, but her eyes were dry and her grip on Marie-Françoise's hand was firm. She kept her gaze fixed on Father Sentout as he spoke the Latin phrases she had requested for the funeral service.

Her sister Héloïse sat hunched and muttering to one side, casting the occasional venomous glance at Bruno and J-J, each now formally absolved of fault by the *Procureur*'s inquiry into the shooting. It had established that Bruno's shot had hit the Count in the knee and J-J's had been the fatal bullet in the chest. Marie-Françoise had testified that the Count had fired first, after Bruno's shout of 'Police – drop your weapons.' It had helped when the Gendarme medic told the inquiry that Bruno had insisted on trying the underground river once it was clear that the Count would certainly die unless he reached a hospital within the hour.

It was Bruno's second funeral in three days. There had been a smaller turnout for Louis Junot at the crematorium outside Périgueux; just his widow and Francette, and Bruno who had driven them there. At the last minute, the white Jaguar had driven up the gravel road and Béatrice stepped out to join them, stylish in black. She and Francette had exchanged a cool air kiss, and then Béatrice had stood apart and alone. She had left before Bruno could exchange a word.

With the Count, Foucher and Eugénie all dead, the interrogation of Béatrice had been of critical importance as the *Procureur*, J-J and Bruno all tried to unravel the events and motives that had led to their deaths and those of Junot and Athénaïs. Béatrice had been accompanied by an expensive and protective Parisian lawyer, who seemed to have more than a professional relationship with his client, which came as no great surprise to Bruno. She had admitted taking part in the first Black Mass in the cave, with Athénaïs, Francette and Eugénie. It had been just an elaborate sexual game, she insisted, of the kind she'd known in her previous life in Paris. Foucher had played the role of the priest. Abouard the Lebanese and the Count had taken part, along with a couple of the Count's business clients.

Béatrice claimed no knowledge of the second Black Mass in the family chapel at the Red Château at which Athénaïs had died. But she knew that Athénaïs had been obsessed with her ancestor, the royal mistress, and equally obsessed with the Count. Bruno had asked if Béatrice could confirm that

Athénaïs had believed she could win the Count's affections with a love potion from the Black Mass, just as her ancestress had done.

'Absolutely,' Béatrice had replied. 'She spoke about it all the time. It used to drive Eugénie crazy because as far as Eugénie was concerned, the Count was hers.'

'Crazy enough to want to kill Athénaïs?' the Procureur had asked.

Béatrice had nodded decisively. She insisted she had not been present when Athénaïs had died, but she knew there had been a panic at the Red Château. She had seen the fire in the lagoon across the water and watched it flicker and die as the boat drifted out into the main stream and down the river. But she knew better than to ask questions of Foucher or the Count. It was only when she saw the newspaper that she realized the boat had carried the body of Athénaïs.

'But even if the Count wanted Athénaïs dead, he also needed her body,' the Procureur had objected. 'Without it, he could not have inherited.'

'The Count wasn't there. He was with me that night. Foucher called him, panicking, and we got up and looked out of the window and saw the fire. The Count left in his car but then he had to drive to the bridge to cross the river. I dressed and went down to the river and saw the boat drifting away but the Count must have still been on the road. I know he was furious when I saw him the next day.'

Bruno knew they might never be sure of the full truth. But the conclusion was that Eugénie had killed Athénaïs and then she and Foucher had put her body in the boat to dispose of it by fire. And then Foucher had tried to sink it or to recover the body when it floated to the bridge at St Denis.

'Remember,' Béatrice had concluded, 'Athénaïs, Foucher and Eugénie were all stuffing themselves with coke.'

'That's speculation,' the lawyer had said, and ended the interrogation. The Procureur was still deciding whether to charge her with withholding evidence and obstruction of justice.

At this second funeral, Béatrice was dressed in the same black silk and veil and standing close beside the Baron. Had the Baron's broken arm not been in a sling, Bruno suspected she'd have had her hand resting possessively on it. But they had not arrived here together. Bruno was aware Béatrice had suggested the Baron buy the Auberge St Philippon from the Red Countess. But the Baron knew as well as Bruno that there would be no more Defence Ministry events to boost the revenues. Maybe some professional hotelier could make a success of it, once the scandal had died down.

Béatrice was a survivor, Bruno thought. If she couldn't attach herself to the Baron, she'd find someone else. She seemed to have acquired the white Jaguar and her lawyer was already demanding what Béatrice insisted was her share of the Auberge. She'd even talked to the Baron about reviving the project for the holiday village, but without the Count's ability to raise money that idea seemed dead. All that was left were his debts, his hollow property companies and the profitable group of defence companies. Various bureaucrats and businessmen in Paris were arguing over their fate, now that the Lebanese arms deals had collapsed and Richard

Abouard had taken advantage of his diplomatic immunity to return to Beirut. According to Isabelle, Abouard had stood to take a fat commission from steering the Lebanese contract to the Count.

The disposal of the estate would be up to the Red Countess, or more likely, up to Marie-Françoise. The bruises on her face were fading. The girl had been transformed from a Californian teenager to heiress of one of the grand families of France and the lands and châteaux that went with it. She seemed to have forged a close friendship with Fabiola in the days when her grandmother was being nursed out of the tranquillized fog in which she'd been kept. Fabiola had arranged for the girl to have intensive tuition in French. She'd also driven her to Bordeaux to arrange for Marie-Françoise's transfer to the university there, and to persuade the best dentist in the city to shift his schedule and start repairing the damage Fouchet's gun butt had done to the girl's mouth.

The girl was a keen horsewoman, so Fabiola had brought her along on the evening rides. She had shyly avoiding looking at Bruno the first time, as if she remembered his stripping her in the cave to rub her dry and dress her in Sergeant Jules's voluminous uniform. Balzac had overcome her hesitation, and the first time Bruno had seen her laugh was when she saw him tuck his puppy inside the binocular case as he mounted Hector. She now seemed fine, and had insisted Fabiola drive her to see Bruno's burned house, where the builders were already at work to repair the damage. The insurance payment had been agreed in record time; the Mayor had made sure of that.

Bruno wondered what role her American father would play in the inheritance. He looked a decent man, standing behind his daughter and looking solemnly at the coffin of his estranged wife. He was a few years older than Bruno, and seemed to have forged a friendship with Gilles, with whom at least he could speak English. Bruno knew from Gilles that the man was a moderately successful scriptwriter, and he was already talking of reviving Athénaïs's film project on her ancestor, the Royal Mistress. Somehow, Bruno could not think Marie-Françoise would want her mother to be commemorated that way.

'*Requiem æternam dona eis Domine; et lux perpetua luceat eis. Requiescant in pace*,' intoned Father Sentout, and made the sign of the cross over the two coffins as they were lowered into the adjoining graves. One was covered in wreaths, but the Count's bore just two: one from his grandmother and the other from Béatrice. '*Amen.*'

Marie-Françoise helped her great-grandmother to the edge of Athénaïs's grave and gave her a small handful of soil to toss down before pushing the wheelchair away. She and the Red Countess ignored the second gap in the earth where only Héloïse stayed to mourn. Pamela squeezed his good arm, the one without the bandages from the scraping of the gravel, and they joined the line following the wheelchair into the courtyard of the Red Château to pay their respects to the Countess.

'You do seem to get into extra trouble when I'm not here to keep an eye on you,' Pamela said.

'That seems like an excellent reason why you should stay.'

Author's Note

This is a work of fiction and all characters and places and events are inventions. The Devil's Cave does not exist, although some may recognize different features of the Gouffre de Proumeyssac and the Gouffre de Padirac, two magnificent caves in the region. The kindly folk at my local Crédit Agricole would never behave so badly to one of their employees and none of the fine local mayors of the Périgord would induce them to do so. The idea that businessmen in the French defence industry or hedge-fund financiers would ever resort to the exploitation of loose women in pursuit of profit is, of course, as ludicrous as it is outrageous. And the journalists for the splendid regional newspaper *Sud-Ouest* would never behave as Philippe Delaron does in this novel. My imagination must have run away with me.

Madame de Montespan did indeed take part in a Black Mass in 1666 to win the affections of King Louis XIV, according to witnesses testifying before the special heresy court, the *Chambre Ardente*, whose records are preserved in the *Archives de la Bastille*. The King decided to close down the court soon afterwards. According to Gabriel Nicolas de la Reynie, then Lieutenant General of the Paris Police, the royal mistress got away with it because 'the enormity of the crime proved her safeguard'. The text of exorcism that I use is taken from the 1614 Ritual, and Pope Paul VI did indeed say in 1972, 'from somewhere or other, the smoke of Satan has entered the temple of God.' Otherwise, the service in the cave is my own invention.

This novel is dedicated to two very dear friends who first brought our family to the Périgord and have taken loving care of us ever since. Their kindness has been characteristic of the welcome we have received in the Périgord, whose traditions and cuisine, countryside and characters are the real heroes of the Bruno novels. I just hope the welcome stays as warm now that the novels are being published in French.

As always, I owe particular thanks to my wife, Julia Watson, who checks all my fictional meals and recipes. Readers of her articles in *Gourmet* magazine and of her food blog eatwashington.com will recognize her expertise. Our elder daughter Kate runs the brunochiefofpolice.com website with great verve and dedication. Our younger daughter, Fanny, who is an eminent poet back in Scotland, brings a supportive but discriminating eye to my first drafts. Along with the much-mourned Bothwell and his successor Benson, our basset hounds, they have shared in the Bruno enterprise from the beginning. Finally, great thanks are owed to the magical editing gifts of Jane and Caroline Wood in Britain, Jonathan Segal in New York, and to my German-speaking family at the Diogenes publishing house. Daniel Keel, the legendary founder of Diogenes, sadly passed away just as I finished this book. One of the great literary figures of Europe, he also enjoyed a good *Krimi* and I will always be grateful for his kindness to me and his early support for the Bruno series. The books and authors, readers and friends that Daniel leaves behind him are as close as any of us human beings can come to immortality.

Read on for a taste of Bruno's next investigation,
a mystery whose roots lie buried in World War 2

THE
RESISTANCE
MAN

Prologue

It was shortly after dawn on a day in late spring that carried all the promise of summer to come. The fresh green leaves were so bright they startled the eye, dew was already steaming from the grass under the first rays of the sun and the woods around the cottage were clamorous with birdsong. Benoît Courrèges, *Chef de Police* in the small French town of St Denis and known to everyone as Bruno, could identify the different notes of warblers and hoopoes, woodlarks and woodpeckers. But he knew these were just a fraction of the birdlife of the sweet valley of the river Vézère where he made his home.

Bruno wore his old army tracksuit in which he had just taken his morning run through the woods. His eyes were fixed on Napoléon and Joséphine, his two geese. These monarchs of his chicken run paced forward with slow dignity to study the quivering puppy held firmly in Bruno's grip. Behind the geese, twitching his head from side to side, came Blanco the cockerel, named after a French rugby hero. Blanco was followed by his hens and the two pheasants Bruno had added to his flock because he liked their smaller eggs and the careful way the hen pheasant would hide them in the undergrowth.

Raising a basset hound to be a hunting dog was slow work, but Bruno was becoming convinced that Balzac was the most intelligent dog he had ever known. Already house-trained, Balzac would even abandon an alluring new scent to obey his master's summons. Now he was learning that the birds in Bruno's chicken run were to be treated with courtesy as members of the extended family, and to be protected against all comers. Balzac was eager to bounce forward to play and send the chickens squawking and jumping into the air. So Bruno held him down with one hand and stroked him with the other, speaking in a low and reassuring voice as the two geese advanced to see what new creature Bruno had brought onto their territory this time.

Bruno had already familiarized Balzac with the deep and sensual scent of truffles and shown him the white oaks in the woods where they were usually to be found. He took the dog on his morning jogs and his dawn and dusk checks of the security of the chicken coop, and thought the time was approaching when Balzac would be able to run alongside when he exercised the horses. Bruno suspected he'd miss the now-familiar feel of the large binoculars case strapped to his chest, where the puppy was currently stowed when his master went riding.

Napoléon and Joséphine, who had grown familiar with Bruno's previous basset hound, Gigi, came closer. Blanco flapped his wings and squawked out his morning *cocorico*, as if to assert that however large the two geese, he was really in charge here. The puppy, accustomed to sleeping in the stables beside Bruno's horse Hector, was not in the least awed by the size of the geese. He cocked his head to one side to gaze up at them and made an amiable squeak of greeting. The geese cruised on past Bruno and his dog, leaving Blanco to stand on tiptoe and fluff out his feathers to enlarge his size and grandeur. Balzac looked suitably impressed.

Watching his birds and stroking his hound, Bruno knew he could not imagine a life without animals and birdsong and his garden. He delighted in eating apples plucked straight from his own trees, tomatoes still warm from the sun and salads that had still been growing moments before he dressed them with oil and vinegar. At the back of his mind lurked the question of whether there would one day be a wife and children to share this idyll and enjoy the stately progress of the seasons.

He turned his head to glance at his cottage, restored from ruin by his own hands and the help of his friends and neighbours in St Denis. Repaired now from the fire damage inflicted by a vengeful criminal, the house had grown. Bruno had used the insurance money and much of his savings to install windows in the roof, lay floorboards and create two new bedrooms in the disused loft. The plan had long been in his mind but the decision to carry it out felt like making a bet on his own future, that in time there would be a family to fill the space.

On the desk in his study lay the estimate for installing solar panels on the roof, along with the tax rebates he would receive and the terms of the bank loan he had been promised. Bruno had done his sums and knew it would take him almost ten years to earn back his investment, but he supposed it was a gesture to the environment that he ought to make. Now, gazing at the honey-coloured stone of his house topped with the traditional red tiles of the Périgord, he worried what the panels might do to the look of the place.

His reverie was interrupted by the vibration of the phone in his pocket. As he extracted it, Balzac squirmed free and began creeping towards the grazing chickens. Bruno reached out to haul him back, missed, dropped his phone and a furious squawking erupted as the puppy bounded forward and the hens half-flew and half-scurried back to the protection of their hut.

'Sorry, Father,' Bruno said as he recovered the phone, having seen that his caller was the local priest, Father Sentout. He picked up Balzac with one hand and headed back to the house.

'Sorry to disturb you so early, Bruno, but there's been a death. Old Murcoing passed away and there's something here that I think you ought to see. I'm at his place now, waiting for his daughter to get here.'

'I'll shower and come straight there,' Bruno said. 'How did you learn of his death?'

'I called in to see him yesterday evening and he was fading then, so I sat with him through the night. He died just as the dawn broke.'

Bruno thanked the priest, filled Balzac's food and water bowls and headed for the shower, wondering how many towns were fortunate enough to have a priest who took his parochial duties so seriously that he'd sit up all night with a dying man. Murcoing had been one of the group of four or five old cronies who would gather at the cheaper of the town's cafés. It had a TV for the horse races and off-track betting on the *Pari Mutuel* and the old men would nurse a *petit blanc* all morning and tell each other that France and St Denis were going to the dogs. Without knowing the details, Bruno recalled that Murcoing was one of the town's few remaining Resistance veterans, which could mean a special funeral. If so, he'd be busy. The decision about the solar panels would have to wait.

1

As if determined to make it his last sight on earth, the dead man clutched what at first appeared to be a small painting on canvas or parchment. Bruno moved closer and saw that it was no painting, but a large and beautiful banknote, nearly twice the size of the undistinguished but familiar euro notes in his wallet.

Impeccably engraved in pastel hues stood Mercury with his winged heels before a port teeming with sailing vessels and steamships. Facing him was a bare-chested Vulcan with his forge against a backdrop of a modern factory with tall chimneys belching smoke. It was a Banque de France note for one thousand francs of a kind that Bruno had never seen before. On the quilted counterpane that was tucked up tightly to the corpse's grizzled chin lay another banknote, of the same style and value. Picking it up, Bruno was startled by its texture, still thick and crinkly as if made more of linen than paper. It was the reverse side of the note the dead man held. Against a cornucopia of fruits and flowers, a proud cockerel and sheaves of wheat, two medallions contained the profiles of a Greek god and goddess. They stared impassively at one another against the engraved signatures of some long-dead bank officials, and above them was printed the date of issue: December 1940.

His eyebrows rose. For any Frenchman 1940 was a solemn year. It marked the third German invasion in seventy years, and the second French defeat. But it was the first time Paris had fallen to German arms. In 1870, the capital had withstood months of siege before French troops, under the watchful eye of the Kaiser's armies, stormed the capital to defeat and slaughter the revolutionaries of the Paris Commune. After the invasion of 1914, the Germans had been held and eventually defeated. But in 1940, France had surrendered and signed a humiliating armistice. German soldiers had marched through the Arc de Triomphe and down the Champs-Elysées and launched an occupation that would last for over four years. France under Marshal Pétain's Vichy regime had retained some shred of sovereignty over a truncated half of the country while the Germans took over Paris, the north and the whole Atlantic coastline. So this was a Vichy banknote, Bruno mused, wondering how long after the war's end it had remained legal tender.

There were more notes, all French and for varying amounts, inside a black wooden box that lay open at the dead man's side. Alongside them were some old photographs. The one on top showed a group of young men and boys, carrying weapons from shotguns and revolvers to elderly submachine guns. They were squatting on the running boards or leaning against a black Citroën *traction-avant*, one of the most handsome cars France ever made. A French *tricolore* flag was draped across the bonnet.

Bruno picked up the photo and turned it over to see the scrawled words *Groupe Valmy, le 3 juillet, 1944*. Mainly dressed like farmers, some wore berets and two had the old steel helmets from the 1914–1918 war. An older man sported a French officer's uniform with leather straps across his chest and ammunition pouches. He held up a grenade in each hand. Each of the men had an armband with the letters FFI. Bruno knew it stood for *Forces Françaises de l'Intérieur*, the name De Gaulle had chosen for the Resistance fighters. The next photo showed the same car and an ancient truck parked beside a train. The doors of a goods wagon were open and men in a human chain were passing sacks from the train to the truck. On the back were the words *Neuvic, 26 juillet, 1944*.

'I've never been allowed to see inside his box before,' said the woman. She eyed the photos but made no move to touch them or the banknotes. Her hands, work-worn and gnarled, remained clenched in her lap. She looked to be in her sixties. Father Sentout had introduced her as Joséphine, one of the dead man's three daughters. The priest was packing away the breviary and holy oils he had used to give the last rites. A spot of oil gleamed on the dead man's forehead where the priest had made the last sign of the cross and another on the eyelids.

'Eighty-six,' the priest said. 'A good age, a long life and he served France. Your father is with our father in heaven now.' He put his hand gently on the woman's arm. She shook it off.

'We could have done with that money when I was growing up,' she said, staring dry-eyed at the banknotes. 'They were hard times.'

'It was the banknotes that made me call you,' said Father Sentout, turning to Bruno. 'I don't know what the law says about them, being out of date.'

'They're part of his estate so they'll go to his heirs,' said Bruno. 'But those photos mean I'll probably have to plan for a special funeral.' He turned to Joséphine. 'Do you know if he had the Resistance medal?'

She gestured with her head to a small picture frame on the wall above the bed, below the crucifix. Bruno leaned across the bed to look closer. The curtains were open and the sun was shining but only a modest light came from the tiny courtyard. He saw the stone wall of a neighbour's house barely two metres away. A single light bulb hanging from the ceiling in a dingy parchment lampshade did little to help, but he could make out the small brass circle with its engraved Cross of Lorraine hanging from a black and crimson ribbon. Beneath it in the frame was a faded FFI armband and a photograph of a young Murcoing wearing it and holding a rifle.

'I'll have to check the official list but it looks like he qualifies for a Resistance funeral with a guard of honour and a flag for the coffin,' Bruno said. 'If that's what you want, I'll make the arrangements. The state pays for it all. You can either have him buried at the big Resistance cemetery at Chasseneuil or here in St Denis.'

'I was wondering if he'd left enough to pay for cremation,' she said, looking around the small bedroom with its faded floral wallpaper and a cheap wardrobe that had seen better days. 'He was waiting for a place in the retirement home so the *Mairie* stuck him in here.'

The old man had lived alone in the small apartment formed from the ground floor of a narrow three-storey house in one of the back streets of St Denis. Bruno remembered when the

Mairie had bought the building and converted it for social housing. Four families were stuffed into the upstairs apartments and another from the waiting list would be moved into this place as soon as the old man was buried. The recession had been hard on St Denis.

'Paul should be here by now,' she said, looking at her watch. 'His grandson, my sister's boy. I called him as soon as I called the priest. He's the only one my dad ever had much time for, the only other man in the family.' She looked sourly at the corpse in the bed. 'Three daughters weren't enough for him.'

'I'll need your phone number to let you know about the funeral,' Bruno said, taking out his notebook. 'Do you know where he kept his papers, if there's a will?'

She shrugged and gave her number. 'Nothing much to leave.' She looked at her watch again. 'I have to go. I'll take whatever food he's left.' Through the open door they heard her rummaging in the small fridge and the food cupboard before she stomped down the narrow passage beside the garage that led to the street.

'Not much sign of grief there,' said Bruno, taking out his phone to call the medical centre. A doctor would have to certify death before Murcoing could be removed to the funeral parlour.

'He didn't have many visits from his family, except for Paul,' the priest said. 'All the sisters live down in Bergerac. Joséphine told me she works as a night nurse, so she probably sees more than enough of the old and sick.'

'How sick was he? I haven't seen him in the café for a while.'

'He knew he was dying and he didn't seem to mind,' Father Sentout replied. 'He had pneumonia but refused to go to hospital. That was the sickness we used to call the old man's friend. It's a peaceful passing, they just slip away.'

'I remember seeing him coming out of church. Was he a regular?'

'His wife dragged him along. After she died he didn't come so often at first, but this place is close to the church so he'd come along for Mass; for the company as much as anything.'

'Did he ever talk about the money?' Bruno gestured at the open box on the bed and the banknote still held tightly in Murcoing's dead hands.

The priest paused, as if weighing his words in a way that made Bruno wonder whether there was some secret of the confessional that was being kept back.

'Not directly, but he'd rail against the fat cats and the rich and complained of being cheated. It was just ramblings. I was never clear whether he reckoned his daughters had cheated him out of the money from the farm or it was something else.'

'Is there something you can't tell me?'

Father Sentout shrugged. 'Nothing directly linked to the money. I presume it's from the Neuvic train. Don't you know about it? The great train robbery by the Resistance?'

Bruno shook his head, reminding the priest that he'd only been in St Denis for a little over a decade. He'd heard of it but not the details. These days, the priest explained, the story was more legend than anything else. A vast sum of money, said to be hundreds of millions, had been stolen from a train taking reserves from the Banque de France to the German naval garrison in Bordeaux. Despite various official inquiries, large amounts had never been accounted for, and local tradition had it that several Resistance leaders had after the war bought grand homes, started businesses and financed political careers.

'If that was his share, he didn't get much,' the priest concluded, nodding at the banknotes on the bed. After the war there had been so many devaluations. Then in 1960 came De Gaulle's currency reform; a new franc was launched, each worth a hundred of the old ones. 'In reality, that thousand-franc banknote is today probably worth less than a euro, if it's worth anything at all.'

Bruno bent down to prise the note from the cold fingers. As he put it inside the box with the photographs, he heard footsteps in the corridor and Fabiola the doctor bustled into the small room. She was wearing a white medical coat of freshly pressed cotton and her dark hair was piled loosely atop her head. An intriguing scent came with her, a curious blend of antiseptic and perfume, overwhelming the stale air of the room. She kissed Bruno and shook hands with the priest, pulling out her stethoscope to examine the body.

'He obviously didn't take his medicine. Sometimes I wonder why we bother,' she said, sorting through the small array of plastic jars from the pharmacy that stood by the bed. 'He's dead and there's nothing suspicious. I'll leave the certificate at the front desk of the clinic so you can pick it up. Meanwhile we'd better get him to the funeral home.'

She stopped at the door and faced Bruno. 'Is this going to stop you getting to the airport? I'll be free by five so I can do it.'

'It should be OK. If there's a problem, I'll call you,' he replied. Pamela, the Englishwoman Bruno had been seeing since the previous autumn, was to land at the local airport of Bergerac just before six that evening and he was to meet her and drive her back to St Denis. Pamela, who kept horses along with the *gîtes* she rented out to tourists, had been pleased to find in Fabiola a year-round tenant for one of the *gîtes* and the two women had become friends.

Bruno began making calls as soon as Fabiola and the priest left. He started with the veterans' department at the Ministry of Defence to confirm a Resistance ceremony and then called the funeral parlour. Next he rang Florence, the science teacher at the local *collège* who was now running the town choir, to ask if she could arrange for the *Chant des Partisans*, the anthem of the Resistance, to be sung at the funeral. He rang the Centre Jean Moulin in Bordeaux, the Resistance museum and archive, for their help in preparing a summary of Murcoing's war record. The last call was to the social security office, to stop the dead man's pension payments. As he waited to be put through to the right department, he began to look around.

In the sitting room an old TV squatted on a chest of drawers. In the top one, Bruno found a large envelope marked 'Banque' and others that contained various utility bills and a copy of the deed of sale for Murcoing's farm in the hills above Limeuil. It had been sold three years earlier, when prices were already tumbling, for 85,000 euros. The buyer had a name that sounded Dutch and the *notaire* was local. Bruno remembered the place, a ramshackle farmhouse with a roof that needed fixing and an old tobacco barn where goats were kept. The farm had been too small to be viable, even if the land had been good. Murcoing's last bank statement said he had six thousand euros in a *Livret*, a tax-free account set up by the state to encourage saving, and just over eight hundred in his current account. He'd been getting a pension of four hundred euros a month. There was no phone to be seen and no address book. A dusty shotgun hung on the wall and a well-used fishing rod stood in the corner. The house key hung on a hook beside the door. Left alone with the corpse until the hearse came, Bruno thought old Murcoing did not have much to show for a life of hard work and patriotism.

He wrote out a receipt for the gun, the box and its contents and left it in the drawer. Beside the TV set he saw a well used wallet. Inside were a *carte d'identité* and the *carte vitale* that gave access to the health service, but no credit cards and no cash. Joséphine would have seen to that. There were three small photos, one a portrait of a handsome young man and two more with the same young man with an arm around the shoulders of the elderly Murcoing at what looked like a family gathering. That must be Paul, the favourite grandson, who was supposed to arrive. Bruno left a note for him on the table, along with his business card and mobile number, asking Paul to get in touch about the funeral and saying he'd taken the gun, the box and banknotes to his office in the *Mairie* for safe keeping.

As the hearse was arriving, Bruno's mobile phone rang and a sultry voice said: 'I have something for you.' The Mayor's secretary was incapable of saying even *Bonjour* without some hint of coquetry. 'It's a message from some foreigner's cleaning woman on the road out to Rouffignac. She thinks there's been a burglary.'